Also by THOMAS TRUMP
Crime Fiction

Inspector Chris Hardie, Murder with a Scottish Connection

Inspector Noal, Sarah Angel or Devil

Inspector Noal, Nightmare

Inspector Chris Hardie, Murder with a Spy Connection

Inspector Chris Hardie, No Peace for Mrs Brown

Inspector Chris Hardie, The Smell of Talcum Powder

Inspector Chris Hardie, The Postman Called

Inspector Chris Hardie, Murder with Brothel Connection

Inspector Chris Hardie, Marriage

I dedicate this book
to my beloved parents,
Olive May Trump and Thomas Trump

I also dedicate this book
to my wife SEVIL TRUMP,
the love of my life.

Introduction

*D*uring the early 1900s, Detective Inspector Chris Hardie and his team Detective Sergeant George House and Detective Constable Cam Streeter of Winchester Criminal Investigation Department (CID), investigated the murders, which seem to have no motives or reasons, the cases were complicated, but after many twists and turns, they were able to solve the cases.

Winchester, Ancient Capital of England is a city and the county town of Hampshire, lies in the valley of the River Itchen, surrounded by magnificent green countryside.

The early 1900s, Winchester was a small compact city of about twenty thousand people, dominated by the Cathedral with many communal packed streets, all within easy reach of the main high street. The high street was long, and upwards, but most of the shops with their bow fronted windows or open fronted was situated at the bottom end, around the Guildhall, the street lights ran on gas and were lit by teams of lamplighters. Roads leading both ways from the high street, was also full of shops, pubs, barbers, rag and bone merchants, butchers and even a stable for horses all made up the bustle of the Winchester High Street.

It was a friendly town, in which most everybody knew each other. Murders and violent crimes were relatively rare, however murders, rapes, violent crimes occurred, most of the crimes were young boys scrumping apples from someone's garden, children on their way to school trying to pinch a sweet from the many sweet shops in the town, very few crimes were committed that warranted the birch, or imprisonment.

Detective Inspector Chris Hardie and his team Detective Sergeant George House and Detective Constable Cam Streeter, investigated the murders, investigations were not always straightforward, range from the very simple straightforward to the very complex and complicated, the detectives were taking a meticulous approach to gathering the information needed.

BOOK ONE

INSPECTOR CHRIS HARDIE

HATRED

AND

GREED

Chapter One

Chris smiled to himself as he stood outside the Police Station, his wife Elizabeth was fussing with his top coat.

"There you are darling, can't have you going down with a cold, especially on our anniversary," she smiled happily.

"But I'm just going inside where I shall take the overcoat off," Chris explained.

"Now if you are not outside at six, I will carry on home darling," Elizabeth said, planting a kiss on his cheek. "Your sandwich is in your pocket."

Chris smiled his thanks, he had never before been fussed over like he was now, he pretended to be annoyed sometimes, but knew in his heart that he loved it. "What's this about an anniversary?" Chris asked in a surprised tone.

"Silly," Elizabeth giggled as she looked up at Chris, her eyes sparkling. "We have been married a month today."

Chris watched as Elizabeth walked away towards her bank, he wondered what he had done to deserve such a woman. Chris waved to her as she turned to look at him, then entered the station a smile on his face.

"I must have done something good," he thought to himself.

Sergeant Dawkins looked at the clock as Chris entered. "The early bird," he remarked seeing that it was ten minutes to nine.

"A pleasant good morning to you Sergeant," Chris greeted him taking no notice of his comment. "Anyone in?" he asked.

"All," replied the sergeant as Chris took off his overcoat.

"Well we are the ones that catches the worms," Chris spoke with a smile on his face as he entered his office.

George and Cam, who were both at their desks, looked up and smiled as Chris entered.

"Weather is improving," Chris remarked as he hung his overcoat and trilby.

"How would you know?" George replied. "You are still on your honeymoon."

"You are as bad as Elizabeth, she told me a moment ago that today was our anniversary, I asked how come, and she told me we had been married a month today, I have no idea that anniversaries came every month."

"You will have to remember all these little things," George advised.

"Never miss a birthday or anniversary, otherwise they will think you have another woman, or that you don't love them anymore, no one, not even the doctors know a woman's mind," George laughed loudly at the idea.

"Better get a diary," Cam suggested as a knock came on the door and sergeant Dawkins entered.

Chris smiled inwardly, he saw the smirk on the sergeant's face, and wondered just what was coming.

"Two bodies have been found Sir," sergeant Dawkins said politely.

"Really!" Chris answered. "Am I to know where?"

"The park, under the bandstand," sergeant Dawkins replied. "I have done the normal."

"Such as?" Chris enquired.

"Sergeant Bloom is on his way there now, he will get a beat bobby en-rout and take him with him," sergeant Dawkins replied. "I have left message for Bob Harvey the Police Surgeon."

"Good man," Chris replied with a slight smile.

Chris looked at Cam. "Cam, this might be your first serious crime with us, so you had better come with George and myself, you might get some experience, bring your murder bag."

"Great," Cam smiled, already getting his detective bag that laid under his desk.

Chris smiled at his keenness. "You better go out the back of the station, we want three bicycles."

Cam wasted no time, snatched up his hat and left the room.

"Two bodies, might be a suicide pact," George said getting his coat from the coat stand.

"Whatever, Bob won't be pleased," Chris answered putting on his coat and trilby.

Cam had three bicycles outside in the Broadway by the time Chris and George left the police station. The bicycle ride was not too long, leaving their bicycles along side of the small stone bridge just inside the park entrance, they walked across the playing field to the bandstand. Sergeant Bloom and a constable was there with the park keeper.

When Sergeant Bloom saw them he came hurriedly to meet them.

"Good morning Sir," he said politely, nodding at George and Chris. "It's not a pretty sight Sir, whoever shot them like this must have been full of hate."

"Really!" Chris replied. "Well we better get it over then, lead the way sergeant."

The three detectives stared down at the two bodies, both were naked, even to their shoes. Their faces were just blob of flesh and blood, no one could have recognised them. Chris and George turned away for a second their eyes squeezed. Returning their gaze to the bodies, they found Cam was kneeling at the heads.

"Shot with a double barrel 12 bore I would guess," he stated. "One barrel in each face, whoever fired it was only a foot away," Cam remarked with absolute certainty.

"Really!" Chris murmured for a moment amazed, he looked at George who also had an amazed look on his face.

"How do you know it's a 12 bore?" Chris asked, surprised.

"Well Sir," Cam rose to standing. "I am familiar with these guns, my father was a game keeper at one time, I spent many hours with him."

"Really!" Chris replied. "But how can you tell it was a 12 bore?"

"The pellets Sir," Cam answered. "I have often filled the cartridges myself, I believe bore guns are sized from eight to thirty three, the higher the bore the less pellets, had this gun been fired at a bird at this distance, the bird would have been completely destroyed."

George studied the bodies. "What do you think happened here then?" he asked Cam.

Cam fingered his chin. "Well it looks like they were ready to make a bit of love making," he answered. "They are both naked."

"Only their clothes were taken," Chris stated having heard the question and answer.

Cam looked at the bodies again before speaking with a slight blush. "I see what you mean Sir," he sighed nodding his head in agreement.

"The woman would never have permitted a man intercourse while like that," George remarked. "I doubt if any man would want too."

"Why did they take off their clothes then?" Cam asked bewildered.

"They didn't," George answered. "They were stripped by whoever shot them, can you see any clothes around?"

"No Sergeant," Cam replied looking around. "But why strip them after killing them?" he asked with confused voice.

"There may be other reasons Cam," George replied. "But seeing their faces destroyed and their clothes gone leads me to believe someone did not want them to be identified."

"There is blood on the grass each side of their faces, which means that the bodies had been rolled over, possibly to take off their clothes," Chris remarked who had been looking around and studying the bodies. "George, better look under the bandstand while I go and speak to the park keeper."

"Get your torch Cam," George said looking in his bag for the torch. "We will check underneath the bandstand, one of the side panels comes away I should think."

Chris crossed to where Sergeant Bloom had remained talking to the park keeper.

"This is Mr Jarvis Inspector," sergeant Bloom introduced him. "He found the bodies."

"Good Morning," Chris said to Mr Jarvis. "I am Detective Inspector Hardie, finding the bodies must have given you a shock?"

"Made me vomit," replied Mr Jarvis. "Never seen anything like it."

"Nor me Mr Jarvis," Chris replied. "Will you run me through just how you found them?"

7

"I usually take a stroll around the park during the mornings, we do get couples sneaking in at nights, anyway I walked over here to the bandstand, we keep chairs and music stands under it, then I saw them, I saw their faces, and that's as far as I went, I felt sick. I phoned straight away to police station, that's all I'm afraid," Mr Jarvis shrugged his shoulders.

"It is obvious two shots were fired Mr Jarvis," Chris said. "Very loud shots, have you heard nothing during the evening?"

"I lock up at seven, I stroll around for a bit before closing up, I often have to drive youngsters out, last night about seven thirty I went to the Foresters for a drink, I live just over there," Mr Jarvis pointed towards a path way leading to Gordon Road.

"I don't get paid for twenty four hours a day you know."

Chris smiled. "I'm sure you don't Mr Jarvis, tell me are there many places where people can get into the park after closing time?"

"They can get in from the back," Mr Jarvis replied. "They would have to come from the Worthy Road area, there are a couple of small gates, that one might get over, and there is also a path running down the side of my house, but that means getting by me, I sit in the room facing the path."

"When you are in Mr Jarvis," Chris corrected, with a slight teasing smile.

Mr Jarvis shrugged his shoulders. "I don't go out much."

The sound of an engine made Chris and those with him turn towards the small stone bridge, Bob Harvey the Police Surgeon had arrived.

Excusing himself to sergeant Bloom and the park keeper, Chris took a few steps towards Bob who was hurrying across the playing field towards him carrying his bag.

"Sorry I was out when your call came through Chris," Bob explained in an apologetic tone. "What have you got for me?" Bob Harvey asked.

"I got two dead bodies," Chris replied. "Not pretty, both with their faces missing."

Bob followed Chris to where the bodies lie, he looked at the bodies. "Not pretty at all," he commented. "Naked as well."

"Not going to be easy identifying them," Chris answered.

Bob knelt down and studied their faces, as George and Cam came out from under the bandstand. "Nothing under there apart from chairs and music stands," George informed.

Bob rose and smiled at George. "Hello George," he greeted him.

"Hello Bob," George greeted him back. "A bit gruesome."

"Agreed," Bob remarked bending over the bodies. "They got bashed in the face, shot by a shotgun I would say."

"You meet the new member of our team Bob," Chris said as rolled his eyes at Cam. "Yes Bob, this is Detective Constable Cam Streeter," Chris introduced.

Bob offered his hand. "As a member of this team, you will soon get to know me," Bob said with a smile as they shook hands.

"It's nice to meet you Sir, I have heard about you," Cam replied.

"Enough of the Sir, my name is Bob, and everyone calls me by it," he said with a straight face.

Cam smiled his thanks.

"Now what can you tell me about the gun used Cam?" Bob asked.

"Well Sir, sorry Bob," Cam corrected himself. "I'm sure it was a 12 bore, double barrel."

"I know that the bore is a popular sporting gun, I have to say however I get very little to do with them, not many would be used for murder, as I am told that they only effected in killing a bird less than fifty feet," Bob commented. "However," Bob continued looking at the faces. "These faces must have been very near the end of the barrel, wouldn't you say Cam?"

"About a foot, I would say," Cam replied.

"Well I will soon find out," Bob continued examining the bodies. "I would say they died any time around eight last night, but before ten, that's the best I can do," Bob said standing up again.

"Thanks Bob," Chris replied, he looked at Cam. "There is a row of houses to the right over there Cam," Chris indicated with his hand towards Gordon Road. "Give the doors a knock see if anyone heard a noise around say eight last night?"

"On my own Sir?" Cam asked with a smile.

Chris nodded his head. "A third man on my team is no good, if he needs someone with him all the time, it defeats the purpose."

"Very good Sir," Cam said taking his leave hurriedly.

"Will he make it?" Bob asked curiously.

"He seems alright, this will be his first murder investigation, George takes him under his wings, but he will have to trusted to be able to act on his own, still once this case is over, we'll know," Chris expressed.

"He seems keen enough," Bob granted him. "Still this case seems to be difficult for you both, no face, no clothes, and no cartridges I take it?"

"Right on all accounts," George agreed. "We need a starting point."

"I think they are both within their thirties the woman's body seems firm, tells us that she probably have not reached her forties, the man's body also gives us that impression of being youngish, his body is also firm, seems strong as well," Bob spoke.

"No birth marks or such?" Chris asked.

"Not on the front Chris," Bob replied looking towards the stone bridge and seeing two men walking towards him carrying a stretcher and a red blanket. "Here comes my men Chris, I'll examine their backs when they lift them."

"One stretcher," Chris murmured looking at the two approaching men both dress in blue uniform.

"We were not told it was two bodies," Bob answered.

Getting a few instructions from Bob, the morgue men lifted the woman first so that Bob could take a look at her back.

"Well this woman will be easy to be identified, especially if she is married," Bob said with confidence. "She has a birth mark on her right cheek, shape like a banana I think, what your opinion Chris?" Bob asked standing back and allowing Chris to see.

Chris looked at the birth mark. "Yes near enough," he agreed.

While the morgue attendances carried the woman's body to the meat wagon, standing just outside the park gates, Chris turned to George.

"If we take it that the crime was carried out between eight and ten," Chris muttered looking at George."

George looked around. "Gordon Road is screened by those trees," he said. "Behind this grandstand, it would have been a job to notice anything, unless you were actually looking, the rest of the park is wide open, but was closed, and there are quite a few trees blocking parts of the view to this bandstand."

Chris nodded in agreement. "Pity the park keeper picked last night to go out and have a drink," he remarked. "Had he not he would surely have heard the shots," Chris looked to where sergeant Bloom was still talking to the park keeper.

"Just a moment," Chris excused himself from George and Bob, then going over to them.

"Mr Jarvis," Chris smiled. "Sorry but can you tell me, do you usually go out on a Sunday night?"

"Not as a rule you know," Mr Jarvis replied. "But last night I had a date."

"Are you not married?" Chris asked.

"No Sir," Mr Jarvis replied laughing. "Single I am, and single I'll stay."

"Forgive my questions Mr Jarvis, but did your date turn up?" Chris asked.

"No," Mr Jarvis replied with a shrug of his shoulders. "You win a few and lose a few you know."

"Mr Jarvis," Chris asked as he saw the two morgue men coming back, would you mind coming to the station this afternoon, just to get what you saw down on paper."

"I don't mind, but I wonder about the council?" he replied,looking worried.

"Any trouble there Mr Jarvis, I will sort out," Chris assured him.

"Any time?" Mr Jarvis questioned.

"Three or around would be fine," Chris answered. "Now you will have to forgive me, I'm needed at the scene."

Chris joined George and Bob, and watched as the morgue men lifted the man's body so that Bob could examine his back.

"Nothing here," Bob said, giving the men instruction to move the body. "I might be able to tell you more when I have examined them on the table at the morgue."

"Thanks Bob," Chris thanked him as he watched Bob follow behind the morgue men.

"I have asked the park keeper to call at the station this afternoon George," Chris said. "He told me he had a date last night, which I want to know more about, I would rather question him at the station, "Chris spoke. "I wonder how Cam is getting along?"

"Do you want me to see?" George asked.

"No, it would be better if you were there, but we have to give him leeway on his own, he has to learn," Chris replied.

"We'll go back to the station, I'll ask Sergeant Bloom to wait for him."

Chapter Two

Chris and George entered the Police Station, although the weather was not too cold, they felt the warmth as they entered the station.

Sergeant Dawkins smiled at them as they both discarded their top clothing. "Thought you may be interested Inspector, we have had a missing person reported since you've been out," sergeant Dawkins informed.

"Really!" Chris remarked taking off his trilby. "What's the details?"

"Mr Cole Crompton, living at 27 Colebrook Street reported that his wife did not arrive home last night," he answered. "Knowing that he might be of interest to you Sir?" sergeant Dawkins grinned. "I asked him if he would not mind waiting for your return, he agreed, and at this moment is enjoying a cup of my tea in the back room."

"That was good thinking Sergeant," Chris looked at George who had a grin on his face, Chris sighed. "Perhaps you will be good enough to bring him to my office, and tea for George and myself," Chris added.

A knock on the door made them look up, Sergeant Dawkins appeared at the door.

"Mr Crompton Sir," he said respectfully. "Would you like your tea now or later?" he asked.

"After Mr Crompton leaves," Chris replied standing and offering his hand to Mr Crompton. "I am Detective Inspector

Hardie, my colleague Detective Sergeant House, please take a seat," Chris indicated with the palm of his hand to the interview chair.

Mr Crompton smiled at George with a nod as he seated himself.

Chris looked at Mr Crompton, he was well groomed, with collar and tie, wearing a brown single breasted suit with waistcoat, he was average height with well combed hair, Chris thought him to be about middle thirties.

"Mr Crompton," Chris began. "I have been told that your wife did not arrive home last night?" he asked as he raised his eyebrows.

"Correct," replied Mr Crompton.

"I take it that this was not in your wife's character?" Chris asked.

"Never happened before Inspector, we have been married nine years," Mr Crompton replied.

"Would you know of any reason why she would not arrive home, I mean were there words between you?" Chris asked curiously.

Mr Crompton shook his head. "No nothing like that, as far as I know we were happily married, perhaps the odd disagreement, but nothing else, I cannot explain any reason."

"We will need to ask you some questions, Mr Crompton," Chris went on. "Perhaps we can have your full name and address?"

"Mr Cole Crompton, I live at 27, Colebrook Street," he stated, then added. "I am a teacher at St Thomas Boys School in Romsey Road."

"Your wife's name?" Chris asked.

"Mrs Pauline Crompton, of the same address, works as a chambermaid at the Suffolk Hotel," Mr Crompton answered.

Chris looked at George hoping that he was able to keep up with his writing.

"What age would your wife be?" Chris asked.

"My wife 34, I am 36," Mr Crompton replied.

Chris clasped his hand on the desk in front of him, he looked at Mr Crompton. "Mr Crompton, I must now ask you a couple personal questions, I am sorry, but need to know, would your wife have any distinguish marks, such as birth marks etc?"

Mr Crompton shifted in his chair, and did not answer immediately.

"Well Inspector, obviously you need answers to your questions, she has a birth mark on the cheek of her bottom," he replied showing no emotion.

"Can you say, what the birth mark looked like, I mean was it round, long, that sort of thing?"

"I saw very little of it Inspector, but I would say it looked like a half moon."

"Similar shape to a banana?" Chris offered.

"Similar," Mr Crompton agreed.

Chris looked at George, both knowing that there was the possibility that the dead woman had been identified.

"Mr Crompton," Chris went on. "I have to ask this question, I am sorry, but were there any trouble or thoughts in your marriage, that another man might have been involved?"

"I take offence at that question Inspector, my wife was not that kind of person, my wife's idea of marriage was, her love would last until death and beyond in the grave," Mr Crompton exploded turning red in the face. "What has this got to do with her missing for one night?"

"I am sorry to upset you Mr Crompton," Chris replied quickly. "You must realise that these things do happen, would you have a picture of your wife?"

Without answering Mr Crompton took a photo from his inside pocket of his coat, and handed it to Chris. Chris took the photo, and looked at it, he saw a slender woman standing in a long dress holding a spray of flowers. Chris did not recognise the woman, nor had he expected to, he only saw a naked woman with no face. "Your wife is very attractive Mr Crompton," Chris remarked. "Would you mind if we keep this photo?"

"No, you can loan it," Mr Crompton replied. "But I would like it back."

"Of course Mr Crompton," Chris assured him handing the brown and white photo to George.

"Why did your wife go out last night?" Chris asked.

"My wife went to church of course," Mr Crompton replied. "She left about six thirty for the seven o'clock service at Holy Trinity."

"Obviously you did not go with her," Chris remarked.

"No, I'm not a church goer," Mr Crompton responded. "I had a lesson to prepare," he added. "Then about seven thirty, I went to the Standard Public House for a pint, and was home again at around eight waiting for my wife to return, but she never arrived."

"What do you teach Mr Crompton?" Chris asked, with a slight smile.

"I teach history Inspector," Mr Crompton replied.

"Just one last question Mr Crompton," Chris said. "What was your wife wearing when she went out last night?"

Mr Crompton scratched his head. "To be honest I can't say, I was doing some marking when she called and said she was going, I just said OK without looking up, but she would have worn a top coat over her dress."

Chris stood up. "Thank you for what you have told us Mr Crompton," he said seeing Mr Crompton rise. "We do have a routine that has been proven many times that we put into action on a missing person, can we able to get in touch with you if we need more information?" Chris asked, his voice was calm and authoritative.

"I have taken time off, I shall be home all day every day for a while," Mr Crompton confirmed. "You will keep me informed of the progress?" he asked wondering.

"Certainly Mr Crompton, also you inform us should your wife turn up."

After shaking hands, Chris watched as Mr Crompton left the office before sitting at his desk.

"I thought you might have told him about our naked woman," George remarked. "It seems that the woman is his wife."

"I nearly did before I saw the photo George," Chris replied. "I noticed his wife was wearing glasses, and thought Bob might find glass pieces buried in her eyes, with no face it's better to be sure on two counts than one."

"She might have taken them off," George argued.

"If it is Mrs Crompton, George," Chris explained. "Wearing glasses while having a photo taken, makes me believe that she wore them all the time, if you are saying the shooter took them off before shooting into her face, did not leave the frames behind."

"I take your point Chris," George agreed as the door opened and sergeant Dawkins entered carrying two cups.

"DC Cam Streeter is here," he remarked, emphasising the DC. "I told him to have a cuppa in the back room while you were seeing Mr Crompton."

"Very wise Sergeant," Chris answered as he accepted the cup of tea.

Cam entered the office while both Chris and George was enjoying their tea, and going straight to his desk, and opening his notebook.

George looked at Chris and smiled before turning to Cam.

"Did you get any lucky Cam?" George asked curiously.

"I think so George," Cam replied looking at his notes.

"The first house was out so no luck there, the occupants of three houses were at church last night, and did not arrive home until after eight thirty, they heard nothing, however Mrs and Mr Grant at number seven told me that they were in, listening to the radio, around eight fifteen they told me they heard two bangs in quick succession, took no notice of it. The man in number eight told me that just after eight he heard two sort of cracks, he looked out his window, but saw nothing and forgot about it."

"How do you think that information has help us then Cam?" George asked.

Well Cam hesitated not quite sure of himself. "The way I see it, it tells us the time that the gun was fired, two residence said around eight thirty pm they heard something," Cam replied.

"That's good Cam," George praised, and Cam smiled.

"Yes very good Cam," Chris agreed. "So we can at least say that victims were shot between eight and eight thirty."

George then told Cam what had happened since their return.

"Looks like we have got the identity of the woman," Cam remarked.

"Looks like it I agree," Chris answered. "Let's hope that finding the identity of the man will be as easy, however we will play with what we have."

"That is?" George asked.

"We know where Mrs Crompton worked," Chris answered.

"You want me to interview the hotel manager?" Cam asked a little excited.

Chris looked at George, they both smiled at his keenest.

"You can go with George, Cam, but please try not to overtake, you have a lot of learning to do, watch George, and you will gradually understand the technique of interviews," Chris said in a very convincing voice.

Cam went silent, his feelings a little hurt.

Chris took out his watch. "It's now just eleven thirty, I suggest George that you take Cam with you and go to Suffolk Hotel and see the hotel manager, you know what we want, before coming back have a lunch break," Chris gave his opinion.

"Going to join us in the break?" George asked.

"No, not today," Chris said with a shake of his head. "I do have this report to write."

"What about food?" George asked.

Chris smiled looking at his overcoat. "Elizabeth has put sandwiches in my overcoat pocket, I better eat them."

Chapter Three

George and Cam entered the Suffolk Hotel on the corner of Middle Brook Street.

"It's the first time I've been in here," Cam remarked.

"Me too," George replied. "Seems a bit expensive," he added crossing the low dimly gas lit lobby to the reception desk.

"Good morning Sir," the well groomed slender receptionist greeted them. "How might I help you?"

George introduced himself. "I would like to see your manager please."

The receptionist looked at George and Cam just for a moment.

"Just a moment Sir," the receptionist said before leaving behind the counter and knocking on a door to the right, he entered the room, reappearing within seconds.

"The manager Mr Wood will see you gentlemen," the receptionist said holding the door open for them.

George and Cam entered the manager's office, it was a oak panel office, clean and tidy, and the chairs looked comfortable. George compared it with his own office back at the station, there was no comparison.

Mr Wood was standing behind a large polished desk with a smile on his face. George saw that he had grey hair, grey eyebrows and a large grey moustache that covered his upper lip, the face was however pleasant.

"I understand you are from the police," he said politely.

"I am Detective Sergeant House, and my colleague Detective Constable Streeter," George introduced themselves.

"Well grab a seat," Mr Wood replied indicating the chairs with a wave of his hand. "Tell me how I can help you?" he asked with a surprised tone.

Both George and Cam chose a chair near to the desk.

"We are making enquiries regarding a Mrs Pauline Crompton," George informed him. "We understand that Mrs Crompton works here as a chambermaid."

"She do," Mr Wood replied quickly. "A very capable woman, polite and cheerful, a bit of a looker as well," Mr Wood grinned. "But I'm afraid if you want to see her, you are out of luck, she did not turn in this morning," Mr Wood lost his grin. "Nothing wrong is there Sergeant?" he asked with confusion and concern in his voice.

"At the moment Mr Wood, all we know is that her husband reported her missing this morning, she did not arrive home last night from church," George replied.

"Dear, o dear," Mr Wood murmured, looking confused. "I know she goes to church a lot, what could have happened do you think?"

George made no comment on that question. "One guess is as good as another at the moment Mr Wood, we are hoping that you might be able to help us?"

"I don't see how Sergeant, we have a friendly team here, but as manager I do not socialise with the staff a lot," Mr Wood replied. "I can tell you she is competent in her work, always smart and friendly."

"Is she a good time keeper?" George asked.

"She has been with us about three years Sergeant," she always turns up for work normally a few moment before time."

"What are her working times?" George asked.

"She is employed as a chambermaid, which means she cleans the rooms and makes the beds every morning, however she cannot start until nine, some guest like to lie in," Mr Wood explained.

"She works with two other chambermaids, and between them they have forty five rooms to attend to, when they are done, they go home, on a weekly rota," Mr Wood continued. "One chambermaid comes in nightly around eight to turn the sheets down for the guest."

"Last night was it Mrs Crompton's turn to turn down the sheets?" George asked.

"I can't tell you that Sergeant, should I be working late I sometimes sleep here in a spare room, last night was not one of those nights."

"Would it be possible for us to have a quick word with your other chambermaids Mr Wood?" George asked in a calm voice. "One never knows what they might know?"

"Be my guest Sergeant," Mr Wood agreed hastily. "Anything to help sort this problem out."

George looked at Cam who had sat quietly listening, Cam knew George's look was the go ahead for any questions if he had.

Cam cleared his throat before he started to speak. "About your guests Sir," he began. "Were any missing last night, I mean were they all accounted for this morning?"

Mr Wood looked at Cam for a moment before answering. "I have no idea Constable," he answered. "What do you have in mind?"

Cam hesitated. "It's just that I thought she might have met one of your guests outside the hotel, shall we say?"

Mr Wood looked at George. "The chambermaids obviously sometimes meet the guests in their rooms or outside the hotel, I can't believe it of Mrs Crompton, but can the possibility be ignored?"

"I don't think so Mr Wood," George agreed. "Can you check while we are speaking to your other chambermaids?"

"I'll get on to it straight away," Mr Wood assured him. "Now if you will follow me, I will get the linen mistress to take you to the chambermaids, call in when you are finished.

George and Cam, stopped at the Guildhall Tavern and had a pint and a sandwich before entering the police station, in the office they found Chris busy writing.

Chris watched as George and Cam hung their overcoats before going to their desks, but made no comment.

George placed his notebook before him.

"We saw Mr Wood the manager, he was very friendly and helpful, but not in the way we were hoping for. He gave a glowing report on Mrs Crompton. As far as he was concerned she was a good woman, a church goer, and a good time keeper. He allowed us to ask questions to other three chambermaids, and they were of the same opinion. Cam asked Mr Wood if any of his guest were missing last night, it was a good question, which Mr Wood felt could not be ignored. However he checked the breakfast list, and all guest were accounted for."

George smiled as he continued. "I did speak to the receptionist and a barmaid, the hotel has a small but well stocked bar," George grinned.

The barmaid did not like Mrs Crompton. "A stuck up bitch who thinks she is holier than holy, why would she want to empty peoples piss pots, her husband being a teacher," that was the her words.

"That was a good question, Cam," Chris spoke for the first time ignoring for the moment what the barmaid had said. "It needed asking, you took it that she was friendly perhaps with a hotel guest?"

"Well we know she was with a man, we have her naked body," Cam replied. "It could have been someone from the hotel?"

"I agree with you Cam," Chris assured him. "But although we have the man's body, we are only guessing at the moment that Mrs Crompton was having an affair with him, there will be another reasons why they were both in the park after it was closed, it might turn out that they were having an affair, but at the moment all we know that she was a good woman, that is apart from this barmaid George questioned," Chris commented.

George sensed that Chris wanted to know more about the barmaid.

"Her name is Mrs Sharon Wedge lives at 32, Cromwell Road Stanmore, she has worked at the hotel for some four years as a barmaid, which she took after her divorce, she described her ex husband as good riddance to bad rubbish," George smiled. "She is attractive, black hair, with a slim figure, about thirty five I would say."

"Do we know where her ex husband lives George?" Chris asked.

"She has no idea," George replied. "Her description of him could fit most men, apart from the fact, that he was only called a man because he was male."

"It's not a good attitude to have someone behind the bar of an expensive hotel is it?" Chris asked, rather confusedly.

"She seems to make up for it by being on top of her job," George replied.

"The receptionist told me that she was always helpful to the customers, she knows all their drinks without asking, all they had to do was raise their glass, she knows what was wanted, in fact the guests like her."

Chapter Four

*I*t was mid afternoon when Sergeant Dawkins ushered Mr Jarvis the park keeper into the office. Chris stood and offered his hand, then indicated him the interview chair.

"You know my colleagues Mr Jarvis?" Chris asked.

Smiling at both George and Cam, Mr Jarvis nodded his head. "Yes they were with you in the park this morning."

"Now Mr Jarvis," Chris continued. "I am sorry to drag you here, but I do want to know more about the date you had on Sunday?"

"The one who did not turn up?" Mr Jarvis replied with a grin.

Chris smiled. "Can you describe her?"

Mr Jarvis shifted in his chair, he shrugged his shoulders. "Well I thought she was attractive, a lot younger than me, in fact it did my ego good, I am nearly fifty," he said forcing a smile.

"Really!" Chris flattered. "You keep your age well."

Happy with the comment Mr Jarvis continued. "She was smallish around five-foot, one-inch I would say, long blonde hair almost touching her shoulders, every time I saw her she was wearing glasses, you know glasses that people wear in the summer."

"Sun glasses?" Chris coaxed gently.

"That's right sun glasses," Mr Jarvis agreed. "I thought that's unusual, it's not really hot at the moment is it?"

"Tell me how you came to have a date with her?" Chris asked curiously.

"I always walk around the park every morning, I count the benches, it's not often but a bench do sometimes disappear during the night you know."

"No, I did not know," Chris replied with a surprised tone. "I will look into it, please carry on."

"About three weeks ago, I was walking around, and I saw this woman sitting on a bench, as I passed I looked at her and said good morning, to my surprise she was there almost every day after, and after a few days, we were talking," Mr Jarvis explained.

"About what?" Chris asked interested.

"We spoke a lot about my job, she asked a lot of questions, really interested she seemed, she told me her name was Susan, and she was not married, and asked me if I was married, which I am not," Mr Jarvis paused for just a second.

"Anyway," Mr Jarvis continued, turned his head looking at George and Cam smiling. They were listening intently.

"I thought I had a chance so I asked her if she would like to have a drink with me, to my surprise she said she would, but would let me know later what night it could be, I gladly accepted this. It was Friday last, that she told me she was free on the Sunday night, she told me that she would be going to church but would meet me wherever, around eight, but not to be surprised if she was a little late, as sometimes when leaving church she chats to people she knows. I told her I would wait for her at the Foresters Pub in the North Walls, she kissed me on the cheek before going, telling me not to forget to wait should she be late, and there you have it," Mr Jarvis ended hitting his knees with the palms of his hands.

"Thank you very much Mr Jarvis," Chris replied.

"This woman Mr Jarvis," George spoke softly. "Would you be able to recognise her again?"

"I shall hardly forget her," replied Mr Jarvis.

"Was there anything distinguish about her, I mean in jewellery she might have been wearing, any birth or beauty marks?" George asked.

Mr Jarvis thought for a moment before answering. "None that I am aware of, her hair covered her ears, so I did not see any earrings, she had no blemish on her face, and she dressed smartly, one thing though, she did not wear a hat most women do."

"When she left Mr Jarvis," Cam interrupted. "Which way did she leave the park?"

"She walked towards Monks Road entrance, but I did not see if she used it," Mr Jarvis replied.

With no more questions coming, Chris stood up offering his hand.

"Thank you again for coming," Chris said as they shook hands. "I hope your next date will turn out better than this one, should you see her again, please let us know, we would like to speak to her, just one thing before you go Mr Jarvis, when you checked the grounds on Sunday before closing up, did you check under the bandstand?"

"I did not check under the bandstand," replied Mr Jarvis. "As far as another date, I'm now a bit wary you know, it takes a lot for a man at my age to ask a younger woman out, still you lose some and win some," he smiled at George and Cam as he left the office.

With Mr Jarvis exit, both Chris and George looked at Cam.

"What?" Cam asked seeing their stare.

"Your question Cam," George said.

Cam felt uncomfortable. "Well, what Mr Jarvis told us, makes me to consider that possibility that this woman he met was a decoy in getting him away from his bungalow on Sunday night, to enter into the park after closing time. You see, all possible escape routs after closing time are to the right of the park, to the left only the main entrance is a possible way out, but the entrance has two very high iron gates. I wanted to know which way the woman left, had she left by the main entrance, I would have said she lives at the bottom of the town, but leaving as she did, I believe the woman we are looking for comes from the top half of the town."

"Very Good Cam," Chris praised him. "There are flaws, but I get your overall point, and many times these small points fits the jigsaw of a case when eventually solved. However, why would an intentional murderer employ a decoy, is it possible for the decoy to be the murderer?"

"What we saw this morning," Cam replied. "I cannot bring myself to believe a woman shot them?" Cam said with confidence.

"Stranger things happen," George butted in. "Women are capable, have you never heard of a woman's scorn?"

"I still can't believe it," Cam argued. "And while we are on about how the murderer left the park, how did the victims get into the park, Mr Jarvis checks the park before locking up, and why if Mrs Crompton and this man were not having an affair would they both be in the park at that time, I mean it's a funny place to meet if only for a talk?"

"Cam," Chris interrupted. "As far as your question goes it was good and needed asking, but you must forget the sexes, only suspecting men will lead you very often to the wrong conclusion, because you would be excluding half of the possible suspects, every one must be a suspect until you are sure, don't make that mistake," Chris said.

"Now regarding the victims getting into the park, you have given several problems there, the victims being in the park after closing time, well they could have hidden under the bandstand, which Mr Jarvis did say he had not checked under, the park is a large area, there must be many places one can hide, I did not say they were not having an affair, I simply said there could be other reasons, but why in the park after closing time I have no idea, only that they must have been familiar with the park?" Chris commented.

Bob Harvey the police surgeon poked his head in the door. "Can I come in," Bob asked with a smile.

"Anytime Bob," Chris answered pleasantly. "Take a seat," he offered as Bob said hello to George and Cam.

"I have not done the autopsy yet," Bob said taking the interview chair.

"But I have looked at their faces, I am afraid I won't be able to save them, both are just pulp, I think Cam was right, both these faces had a barrel each, completely destroyed the faces, however with the woman, her eye sockets were littered with glass fragments, she must have been wearing glasses."

"Thank you Bob," Chris smiled, and asked George for the photo, which in turn Chris handed to Bob.

"We believe this is the woman, this is her photo, her husband who reported her missing told us of the birthmark she had, he thought it to be a half moon, we were just waiting on you about her wearing glasses."

"Well she was, so I take it you know her name?" Bob asked.

"Mrs Pauline Crompton, lives at Colebrook Street, did not arrive home last night from church," Chris explained everything to Bob.

"I suppose he will want to identify his wife?" Bob stated.

"Well it has to be done," Chris agreed. "We can't say for sure until it's done."

"He won't be able to identify the face Chris," Bob informed. "Let's hope he can recognise her body in some way, but leave it until Wednesday, let me do the best I can first," Bob shifted in his chair. "Now about the man, any progress?"

"Not a thing Bob," Chris replied with a disappointed look on his face.

"Well perhaps I can at least help you with the man, a half of his small finger is missing on his left hand," Bob said in a serious voice.

"Bob you're a treasure" Chris replied in a loud voice. "Anything more?"

"How he lost half his finger I don't know, but it was medically healed I can tell you that," Bob stood up from his chair.

"Chris, George, Cam, I have to rush I have two post-mortems to carry out, it will take me the rest of today and all day tomorrow, I'll try to get you details by Wednesday," Bob said goodbye with a smile.

"Well," Chris said after Bob had gone. "That was helpful, perhaps we can now get on."

"What now then Chris?" George asked.

"I have a job for Cam," Chris replied looking at Cam. "This is your first murder case, and not very straight forward, so I'm going to give you a job on your own."

"Thanks Chris," Cam replied all smiles.

"I want you to go to every doctor in Winchester, if our male victim is from Winchester, his missing half finger should be on file somewhere, we might be able to put a name to the missing face, you know his build, Sergeant Dawkins will help you with the list of doctors," Chris said.

"Thank you Chris, I'll get straight on to it," Cam replied getting his coat. "It might take some time."

"Don't come back until you have seen the lot," Chris smiled as Cam was about to leave the office.

Chris was smiling as he turned to George. "I believe he will become a good detective, don't you think?"

"I'm sure he will, he certainly has a different way of looking at things, which I would say is a very good thing," George replied. "What now?" he asked.

"How about an hours overtime tonight George?" Chris asked smiling.

"No worries," George replied. "Be glad to get out of my bedsit for a while."

"Good man, I want you to go to the Foresters Pub, and the Standard Public House, just verify Mr Crompton and Mr Jarvis alibis for Sunday night."

George smiled. "Getting paid for having a night out, seems fair to me."

"If you are late in tomorrow morning, I'll understand," Chris replied with a grin.

"But now George, we have Mr Crompton to see," Chris added.

Chapter Five

Chris and George walked back from Colebrook Street to the Police Station.

"I hate this part George," Chris remarked.

"One expects a woman to show grief and that's bad enough, but a man when he breaks down there is something about it," Chris shrugged his shoulders. "I don't know, I just didn't like witnessing it."

"I know what you mean Chris, the feeling one gets is unexplainable," George replied. "He certainly broke down, with a woman you can ask, but with a man you can't ask if there is anyone you can get to stay with him, I only hope he can control himself on Wednesday when he goes to identify his wife."

Chris nodded his head in agreement as they reached the corner of Colebrook Street.

"I'll leave you here then Chris," George remarked. "Elizabeth will be waiting for you, the clock has struck six."

"Alright George," Chris replied with a sigh. "Take it easy on the alcohol tonight," he said as George crossed the high street making for Cross Keys Passage.

Elizabeth smiled as she saw Chris approach.

"Hello darling," she said planting a kiss on his cheek. "You've been out," she continued fussing with his overcoat, which Chris had not bothered to button up. "I keep telling you," she scolded. "To keep your overcoat buttoned up."

"It's not that cold," Chris replied still with Mr Crompton in his mind. "I have just had a very unpleasant duty to perform," he added.

Elizabeth looked at Chris. "You do look sad darling," she replied grabbing his arm. "You don't have to go into the station now do you?"

"No, we'll go home," Chris replied.

Elizabeth grabbed his arm as they walked towards home.

"Do you want to talk about it darling?" she asked. "You can you know I am your wife."

"When we are home and alone," he replied. "Let's have tea first."

"When we are tucked up in bed together," Elizabeth giggled. "I wonder what mum is cooking for tonight, I'm starving," she changed the subject.

"We will soon find out," Chris replied.

Olive served up pork chops and vegetable, with spotted dick pudding and custard for afters.

"Olive, I must say you are a good cook," Chris flattered her on her cooking pushing his empty pudding dish away from him. "I can't move for the moment."

"Service is the best thing that ever happen for a woman," Ron interrupted.

"My Olive here," Ron continued reaching for his wife's hand. "Did her time in service, she is a good housekeeper, and good cook, and knows how to look after her husband," Ron said proudly, his face expressed emotion of caring and love.

"You can stop your flattery," Olive scolded him. "Service do not teach one how to look after a husband, husbands should be taught how to treat their wives, you are lucky, having made me your skivvy."

"She loves me you know Chris," Ron grinned.

"I know that Ron," Chris replied looking at Olive who was blushing.

"Women have a way of pretending their feelings I might add," Olive said with a wink at Elizabeth as she rose from the table. "Come Elizabeth let's clear the things away before your father makes more of a fool of himself."

Elizabeth rose with a smile on her face. "Don't take them seriously Chris, they have been like this all my life, anyway they like a little banter."

Chris smiled. "I know that," he agreed.

While Elizabeth and her mother was in the scullery washing up the tea things, Chris followed Ron, and made himself comfortable in an armchair, he felt uncomfortably full.

"Heard anything regarding your last case Chris?" Ron asked.

"The court case is pencilled in for next month I believe, at Portsmouth, I'll have to go."

"Well if you are away for a couple days, don't worry over Elizabeth, she will stay here."

"I know, thank you Ron, I haven't said anything to Elizabeth yet," Chris replied.

"Let's hope you get it quiet until then," Ron remarked.

Chris grinned. "Not possible Ron, I started a new one this morning, I am unable to talk about it yet but I have two victims."

"Winchester is such a small city, yet we seem to get our share of murders," Ron remarked.

"My Chief Constable told me that during my last case, London it seems do not get many more than us," Chris answered. "Crime cost the country a lot of money, and we do seem to be getting value for money."

Ron laughed. "That's true yet funny," he said. "But we have you Chris, London do not," Ron praised him.

Chris smiled. "Any news on the war front?" he asked changing the subject.

"Not much coming through, some sort of battle broke out at the end of April, while you were on your honeymoon, but I don't know where, the war has been on now for two years, can't see any end to it, what I do know is that we are losing a lot of men," Ron replied.

It was almost nine pm when Chris and Elizabeth said goodnight to Ron and Olive, and made the short journey to their own home, and within a short time were cuddling up to each other in bed.

"You can tell me about your day now darling," Elizabeth said, as she laid on his arm.

Chris staring at the ceiling, told her all that had happened.

"How horrible darling," she said, easing herself up so that she was looking down into his face. "I can understand how you felt when you had to break the news to Mr Crompton, poor Pauline what a way to die."

Chris turned his head towards her. "Did you know her?" he asked in a surprised tone.

"Only as a customer, I know Mr Crompton as well," she said.

"Know anything about Mrs Crompton?" Chris asked curiously.

"Only that she was a smart sensible woman," Elizabeth answered. "I did get the impression that her husband bullied her, but perhaps I should not say that, I did not know them socially."

"No, go on," Chris encouraged.

"I've only seen her a couple of times since they opened their account, I don't think I have seen her since, but I do remember when they came in and opened an account, Pauline wanted a joint account, but Mr Crompton said no, it would be in his name, and that was the end of it, no argument from Pauline," Elizabeth answered.

"Did she seem the flighty type to you?" Chris asked.

"If you mean the type that go with other men, I would say no, for one thing she did not seem that kind of woman, but how would one know?"

Chris was quiet for a few seconds, then he spoke. "He was pretty broke up when I told him about his wife being dead," Chris remarked.

"Really!" Elizabeth murmured turning her head towards him. "But it was a horrible death darling, he may have been the forceful partner of the marriage, but that don't mean he did not love his wife," Elizabeth remarked.

Chris stared at the ceiling, his mind going over what Elizabeth had been saying.

Chapter Six

*C*hris entered the police station the next morning, he was smiling and shaking his head, after having his instructions from Elizabeth.

"If you go out, wrap up, your sandwich is in your pocket," with "I love you," and his usual kiss on the cheek, she had walked away with a smile towards to her bank.

George was already at his desk. "Good morning George," Chris greeted him hanging his overcoat and trilby.

Crossing to his desk Chris smiled. "No headache then George?" he asked him jokingly, with a grin on his face.

"Didn't really drink a lot, just two or three, but it was a night out something to do," George shrugged his shoulders. "I called at the Foresters first, the landlord was friendly enough. Mr Jarvis was in there about seven thirty Sunday night, it seems Mr Jarvis usually stand at the bar and chats, but now on Sundays he had the habit of sitting at a table facing out on North Walls, then about eight forty five he gets up and leaves," George studied his notebook.

"That's in the plural George," Chris remarked.

"Yes it seems that for several weeks now he has done the same," George replied.

"The landlord did think it was strange as Mr Jarvis never sits at a table on Sundays."

Chris raised his eyebrows and looked at George. "That covers Mr Jarvis's alibi, for Sunday night," Chris remarked. "But he has not told us the complete truth, still he seems clear for Sunday, I just wonder why he lied about his usual routine?"

George grinned at the thought. "I then went to the Standard Public House, I could not ask any questions, Mr Crompton was in there."

"Really!" Chris murmured softly, he was surprised. "Did he see you?"

"No I used the saloon bar, I saw him through the partition," George replied.

Chris thought for a while. "How did he seem?" Chris eventually asked.

"He seemed alright," George answered. "Can't be sure, I was in the other bar."

"Of course George," Chris agreed. "It seems strange to me that a couple hours after we saw him completely destroyed one might say, that he was in a pub drinking," Chris said in a bewildered tone.

"People have their own way of dealing with grief," George replied. "Perhaps he thought he could not bear to be alone in the house last night and decided to have a pint."

"Perhaps George," Chris agreed. "However we still need to check his alibi."

"I'll pop around tonight Chris," George offered. "It's only a few minutes walk."

"Good man," Chris thanked him. "Elizabeth knew Mr and Mrs Crompton," Chris added.

George looked at Chris but made no comment.

"Only as customers, however, it seems they opened an account with the bank when they came to Winchester, Elizabeth thought him a bully," Chris carried on.

40

"Elizabeth is a strong minded and sensible woman," George commented. "She would not have made that state-ment just as gossip."

"You are right George, she would have honestly believed it," Chris answered. "Still keep it in mind, now I wonder how our Cam is getting on?"

It was about eleven o'clock in the morning when Cam finally entered the office, his smiling face assured Chris and George that he had got a result. After morning greetings Cam went to his desk, he was not wearing a top coat, Chris and George kept quiet and waited.

"I called at several Surgeries before I hit the right one," Cam smiled as he opened his notebook.

"Finally I tracked the doctor down at St Cross Road, a Dr Green," Cam said with a smile.

"The doctor had a large envelope file on a Mr Patrick Wedge, the doctor told me that when he was a young lad, young Wedge had gone into a butcher shop with his parents, behind their back, the young boy had turned the handle of the bacon cutter, perhaps seeing the circular cutter coming towards him, and not knowing that circular cutter move-ments were back and forward, he put his hand up, to try to stop it, he lost half his little finger that way," Cam swallowed and gave himself a little shiver at the thought, he looked at Chris and George, getting no comments he carried on.

"Dr Green said he was the family doctor, he treated his parents who are now dead, and Patrick the only child carried on as his patient. Mr Wedge got married and lived at 32, Cromwell Road, Stanmore, he was not his wife's doctor, however he understood that a divorce happened, and Mr Wedge now lives at 40, Western Road, he has not seen him for several months," Cam concluded by closing his notebook.

Chris smiled at George before answering.

"Good job Cam," Chris praised him bringing a smile to his face. "It seems that although there may be others with a finger missing, seems you have hit on the right one."

"How can you be sure?" Cam asked.

"Because I do not believe in coincidence," Chris replied. "You should remember that George and yourself already met Mrs Sharon Wedge at the Suffolk Hotel where she and Mrs Crompton was working."

"Of course," Cam replied. "I remember."

"I wonder why he was not reported missing?" George queried. "It's now Tuesday, he should have been missed?"

"Not if he was living alone George," Chris answered. "I doubt he was working, otherwise more likely his work would have reported him so."

"What's your thoughts then Chris?" George asked impatiently.

"Let's get Cam's thoughts first," Chris replied. "I would like to know them."

Cam felt a little nervous, he hesitated a few seconds before answering. "Well my thoughts are that there has got to be a connection between Mr Wedge and Mrs Crompton."

"What would your first steps be now that you know this Cam?" Chris asked.

"Go and see Mrs Wedge at the hotel," Cam commented.

Chris gave this some thought before answering. "Not yet Cam," he replied.

"First we must double check on what you have found out, I feel you have got the right man, but first, you must go to number 40 Western Road and find out, if the man is missing or haven't been seen since Sunday, ask questions," Chris advised.

"You want me to go?" Cam asked not expecting to be asked.

"Of course," Chris smiled. "Finding out about Mr Wedge is your job."

"Thank you," Cam replied getting up to leave the office.

"Get yourself some dinner before you come back," Chris advised as Cam left.

"It's now past twelve, I want to make a couple of calls then we can have a liquid lunch, you can share my sandwiches that Elizabeth always puts in my pocket," Chris suggested.

"You're spoiled," George replied with a grin. "Where are we calling?"

"First to the rag-and-bone merchant Middle Brook Street," Chris replied. "I have been thinking about the bag of clothing that the killer took, I have asked the council to tell their dustmen to keep a look out, also the beat bobbies have been told, the rag-and-bone merchant has only just come to mind."

"I pass it every morning," George replied. "I could have called in tomorrow morning?"

"As I said George it's only just come to mind," Chris answered.

"Then where?" George asked.

"I thought we would have our lunch at the Standard Public House, it will save you going tonight and kill two birds at once," Chris said, laughing.

"Fair enough," George stood up from his chair.

Chris and George entered the wide open frontage of the rag-and-bone merchant, after waiting a moment a tall slender man in a brown trilby and wearing odd clothing came towards them, a smile appeared on his face.

"Sergeant," he said trying hard to say the surname, Chris was about to tell him.

"No, hang on, I have a good memory, I know it's a Scots name, oh yes," he said fingering his chin. "Sergeant Hardie, how are you?"

"I'm very well thank you," Chris replied shaking the man's hand. "I am Inspector now, and this is Sergeant House," Chris introduced.

The man smiled and nodded at George, who returned the smile.

"Your inspector is a bit of a hero here," the man said to George. "Rescued a man on a motorbike accident who smashed into a large pile of jam jars, he could have been cut to pieces."

Chris smiled. "It wasn't that difficult," Chris replied a little embarrassed. "Anyway I need some information, since Sunday, or shall we say Monday morning, have anyone brought in a bag of clothing that would contain the outer and underwear of a man, and same for a woman, there might also be shoes as well?"

The man scratched his head. "No nothing like that," he replied shaking his head.

"I see," Chris replied a little disappointed. "Well should you get such a bag, would you let me know?"

"You can be sure of it Inspector," the man answered in a reassuring voice.

They crossed the high street, and entered Colebrook Street, they came to the Standard Public House, that had a full view of the Cathedral Grounds.

"Let's go into the saloon bar," Chris suggested. "Should Mr Crompton be in, then it's likely to be in the public bar."

The saloon bar was empty of people, and they found the landlord polishing the counter, he smiled.

"Gentlemen how can I help you?" he looked at Chris.

"I'm Inspector Hardie and this is Sergeant House," he introduced themselves.

"I saw this gentleman last night," the landlord replied looking at George.

"I'm here today to ask you about Mr Crompton, who lives in Colebrook Street, he lost his wife on Sunday Night," Chris informed the landlord.

"Yes, I heard," the landlord replied. "What a terrible way to die," he added. "Anyway take a seat and let me get you both a drink, then I will come around and talk to you, we don't get many in dinner times, hardly worth opening," he smiled.

"Well," Chris replied. "We are on a dinner break, we'll have a pint of bitter, do you mind us eating a sandwich?" he asked.

"Be my guest," the landlord replied with a smile as he disappeared.

Chris took the wrapped sandwiches from his pocket and opened the package inviting George to take one.

The landlord put two pints on the counter, lifting the counter flap, he took the two pints and took them to the table where he sat by Chris and George."

"On the house," he smiled. "Now how can I help?"

"Mr Crompton?" Chris asked. "What can you tell us about him?"

"I don't like talking to the police about my customers Inspector," the landlord replied. "We can lose a lot of trade if it was known, but I feel the criminal should be locked away for good, Mr Crompton is a regular here, so this conversation never happened," the landlord said with a worrying look on his face.

"What conversation?" Chris smiled at him understandingly and nodded his head in agreement.

"Mr Crompton is a school teacher, and a heavy drinker most every night, I often wonder how he teaches the next morning, but truth will out, he can hold his drink," the landlord added in a low voice.

"Would you say he was a ladies man?" Chris asked.

"Beautiful women were made to be looked at Inspector," the landlord replied with a grin on his face. "Mr Crompton was no different to any other man, you might ask did he ever go out of the pub with any of them, I don't know, but you must remember, very few women come in unescorted."

Chris looked at George as he took a drink.

"Sunday night was Mr Crompton in here?" George asked.

"As I said most every night, however Sunday, he left early, I remember being surprised, he usually stays longer, he came in about seven just as we opened, and was gone by eight, I may not be sure of the time, but it was no later," the landlord answered.

"Would you say he is a bully, aggressive, in any way?" George asked curiously.

"He can be a bit aggressive after he has had a few, however he has never been any trouble in here, but I have heard that he is capable, when you look at him, he seems strong enough," the landlord smiled.

"Thank you very much landlord," Chris said seeing George had finished his questioning, he pushed his empty glass towards the landlord.

"We will have another for the road, landlord, and this time one for yourself."

Back at the police station, Cam had returned, and was sitting at his desk when Chris and George entered, he looked at them with a smile.

"I think Mr Wedge is our man," Cam stated as he watched Chris and George hang their overcoats and make for their own desks.

"Mr Wedge lodges with a Mr and Mrs Simpson, old friends of his parents, they are both getting on," Cam continued. "They told me that Mr Wedge never got over his divorce, fell into depression, he was a good lodger, no trouble, and paid his rent regular on time, Mr Wedge left the house after tea Sunday night around six and he hasn't been back since," Cam paused for a moment. "I asked them why they had not reported him missing, they told me, it was early days, Mr Wedge was a single man, if he wanted to stay out at nights, it was his business, we only give him lodgings, we don't control him they told me."

"Sounds reasonable," George replied. "Did you ask about his wife?"

"No, I didn't," Cam replied looking worried. "Should I have done?"

"Well it's always worth asking Cam," Chris said. "They may have confirmed that his ex wife works in a hotel, also you knew we had a Mrs Wedge working at the Suffolk, a divorcee with the same name."

"I made a slip, I'm sorry," Cam replied blushing a little.

"No need Cam, you will remember these questions to ask in future," Chris said. "Did you ask what Mr Wedge was wearing when he left that night?" Chris asked.

"I did," replied Cam. "They could not remember, but the man thought he was wearing a brown suit."

"We will have to go and see this Mrs Wedge, she can confirm her ex husband had a half of his small finger missing, and we will have to break the news of his death to her," Chris said looking at George.

"Do I come with you?" Cam asked hoping.

"No you have a report to write out," Chris replied dampening his enthusiasm.

"Three of us cannot walk into a manager's office, too many."

Chapter Seven

Chris and George was shown straight into Mr Wood's office at the Suffolk Hotel. He was already standing and shook hands with both of them.

"I am Detective Inspector Hardie," Chris introduced himself. "You have met my colleague Sergeant House."

"I have had that pleasure," Mr Wood replied smiling at George.

"Sit please," he offered as he sat behind his desk. "How can I help, I take it it's about Mrs Crompton?"

Both Chris and George chose a chair, Chris rested his trilby on his lap. "Mr Wood," Chris began. "What I am going to tell you, must be in confidence for a while."

"Be sure," replied Mr Wood all ears.

"Sunday night we discovered two bodies, one we are sure is that of Mrs Crompton, although not a hundred percent sure, we have discovered that the other body found with Mrs Crompton could be that of a Mr Wedge."

"You mean our Mrs Wedge's husband, or ex husband?" Mr Wood asked unable to stop himself interrupting.

"As I said Mr Wood, we are not sure, however I need to question Mrs Wedge to make sure," Chris replied.

"Of course Inspector," Mr Wood replied. "She is in, shall I get her for you?"

"Is there some room where we can question her in private?" George asked.

"This office should suit you?" Mr Wood replied. "I was about to take my stroll around the hotel when you came in, I have to keep the staff on their toes you know," he smiled. "I'll bring her to you," he said standing and about to leave the office.

"Thank you very much for your cooperation Mr Wood," Chris added.

"Think nothing of it," Mr Wood said as he closed the door behind him.

"Nice office," Chris remarked as he sat looking around the room. "Twice the size of ours."

"With all these chairs, he probably hold meetings in here," Chris managed to say as a knock came on the door, and Mrs Wedge entered.

"You wanted to see me," she asked, she smiled as she recognised George. "Nice to see you again," she said to him, her eyes showing her pleasure.

Chris rested his trilby on the edge of the desk as he stood and offered his hand which she took. "I am Detective Inspector Hardie, you have already met Sergeant House."

"I have," she said with a giggle, as George placed a chair for her.

"Is this about Chamber Pot?" she gave a little giggle.

"Chambermaid," George corrected smiling to himself.

"Whatever," she said seating herself.

"You do not like Mrs Crompton?" Chris asked as he leaned forward in his seat.

"No, but she is now dead, let her rest in peace," Mrs Wedge replied.

"Really Mrs Wedge, just how do you know she is dead?" Chris asked, there was a surprised, puzzled look on his face. "Even we are not sure," Chris added.

"It's the talk of the hotel," Mrs Wedge answered.

Chris looked at her, she was as George had described, dark, attractive, with an attractive figure. "Can you tell us why you dislike her?" Chris spoke with eagerness in his voice. "All the reports we have are favourable to her."

"Well they would be wouldn't they?" Mrs Wedge replied fidgeting in her chair. "She was a silent one that one."

"Can you be more specific Mrs Wedge?" Chris asked.

"Sharon please," she snapped, scowling. "I don't like being called Mrs Wedge, anyway, Mrs Crompton was always pleasant and helpful, was no better than me, although she put on graces, I caught her in a bedroom with one of the hotel guest," she spoke sternly.

"Really!" Chris replied taken back and rather shocked. "How come you were around the guests rooms?"

"I sometimes have to take drinks to their rooms," Sharon replied. "I was taking drinks to one of our guest, it was around two in the afternoon, passing one door that was ajar, I heard a commotion coming from it, moans of delight you might say," Sharon giggled looking at George. "Anyway, I looked through the slit in the door, I am a bit nosy, and I saw Mrs Crompton running around the bed naked, the man guest caught her, and they ended up on the bed."

"You saw all that through a slit in the door?" George asked bewildered.

"Reflection," Sharon replied. "I saw their reflection in the large full length mirror, all rooms have one, and I saw what was happening in the room."

"I see," Chris remarked. "So you think she was carrying on with a hotel guest?"

"Think what you like?" Sharon answered. "I am telling you what my eyes saw."

"Did she know you saw her?" Chris asked.

"She should have guessed, I made several remarks, yes I think she realised that I knew about her," Sharon replied.

"Do you get asked to go to guest rooms?" George asked.

Sharon giggled. "All the time, I could go to every guest room, most are dreaming of me, but their dreams don't stand a chance, but I suppose dreaming of me offers them some satisfaction."

"Can you tell me where were you on Sunday night?" Chris asked her. "It's just a routine question we ask everyone known to Mrs Crompton."

"Sunday," Sharon replied. "I was at home, I put my boys to bed at six, they have to be up for school Monday morning."

"You never went out after?" George asked.

"I would never leave my children in a house on their own," Sharon responded quickly.

"How old are your boys?" Chris asked.

"Eleven and twelve," Sharon replied. "They both go to Stanmore school, I see them there, and I am there when school is finished."

"I hear you are divorced Sharon?" Chris remarked.

"Yes," Sharon giggled. "I had wasted ten years of my life on a loser, I did not intend wasting any more of it."

"Do you know where your ex husband lives at the moment?" Chris asked.

"Someplace the other side of town, I believe he lodges somewhere, don't know where, don't care," she giggled again.

"Did your husband have, how can I say," Chris asked thoughtfully. "Any deformity?"

Sharon giggled again. "Plenty, but I suppose you are referring to his small finger he had cut off."

"Your husband's Christian name, was it Patrick?" Chris asked.

Sharon nodded. "A bit of Irish in the family perhaps," she replied.

Chris looked at George, both were now sure that the unidentified corpse was Mrs Wedge's ex husband.

Chris spoke as gently as he could. "Mrs Wedge, when we found Mrs Crompton, we also found a man, both naked and unable to be identified. We identified Mrs Crompton because of her husband who reported her missing, the man we could not, he had not been reported missing, however the man had only a half of a little finger, and our investigation led us to 40 Western Road, where we found a man had been missing since Sunday, he was living in lodgings, his name was Patrick Wedge about forty," Chris explained everything thoroughly.

Sharon had been listening, her eyes had opened wider and her mouth half open as she heard what Chris was saying. "Are you telling me it was my ex husband that was found by the Chamber Pot?" she asked her breath coming in quick gasps.

"We believe he is," Chris replied. "Would you be able to recognise him, he was shot with a shotgun at close range, he is not a pretty sight."

Sharon looked at Chris and then George, she saw their faces were serious, she giggled having got over her first shock.

"So Chamber Pot had my ex husband, perhaps she wanted to get revenge because of what I know about her, would you believe it, do I really have to identify him?" she asked.

"He must be identified Sharon," George replied. "Otherwise we can't be sure who he is?"

"What about his ring?" Sharon asked.

"No, it was taken with his clothes and his shoes, nothing we could go on was left, what was the ring like, we know that Mrs Crompton was wearing a wedding band," Chris added.

"He had a large signet ring, it was a large blue stone, he would not have given it away, it was his father's," Sharon replied.

"I see," Chris nodded. "However he must be identified," he said, his voice was firm and his words were loud and clear.

"Oh very well, I will do my best, tell me when?" Sharon agreed reluctantly.

"Thank you," Chris said in the kindness voice. "We will let you know, I am sure Mr Wood will cooperate, just before we go, do you know the park keeper Mr Jarvis?"

Sharon thought for a while. "I have seen him in his peaked cap, but I don't know him, should I?" she asked, in a bewildered tone.

Chris smiled as he got up. "Just wondering Sharon," he said. "No reason."

Chris and George left the hotel after first thanking Mr Wood the manager.

"That was some interview," Chris said with a smile. "She certainly matched your description."

"No grief over her husband, she must have hated him," George commented.

"I suppose her alibi for Sunday evening will hold up," Chris remarked.

"Are you considering Sharon a suspect?" George asked a little bewildered.

"Everyone in the frame is a suspect until proved otherwise George," Chris explained. "Remember what I told Cam, you cannot disqualify woman from any investigation."

"I know Chris, I know she vain and seem to have no feeling for her ex husband, but she is obviously a good mother," George responded.

"It's what she told us about Mrs Crompton that shocked me, it goes against all we know about her," Chris shook his head in disbelief.

George did not reply as they reached the police station and Elizabeth was waiting outside the station."

"Hello George," Elizabeth greeted as she was about to give Chris a kiss on the cheek.

"Hello Elizabeth," George replied with a smile. "You spoil that man."

"That is my intention," Elizabeth smiled. "I think it's about time you have a young woman to spoil you," she giggled.

"That's enough of that," Chris replied, quickly buttoning his overcoat that he left undone. "George will find one, one of these days."

"Well if he don't I may be able to help him," Elizabeth giggled again. "I do know a lot of nice single girls."

"No match making now," Chris remarked, then speaking to George. "I'll see you in the morning George."

Chapter Eight

*W*ednesday morning, was quite warm, and for once Chris was able to leave his overcoat at home without a fuss from Elizabeth, having said his usual goodbye to Elizabeth outside the police station, he had entered his office and found George and Cam already there.

"You two been here all night?" he spoke jokingly as he hung up his trilby. "It's only ten to nine now."

"We are both single," George answered with a teasing smile on his face.

"Do that make a difference?" Chris asked as he sat behind his desk.

Cam laughed loudly, leaning forward in his seat.

Chris smiled to himself, he knew what they meant, he looked at his desk. "No report from Bob yet?" he asked.

"He'll drop it in some time today I expect," George answered. "He did say by Wednesday."

Chris leaned back in his chair. "Let's go over what we have," he said to George and Cam, both who was watching him.

"We now know that our unidentified bodies belong to Mrs Crompton and Mr Wedge," Chris began. "The good character of Mrs Crompton, has been stained by Mrs Sharon Wedge, who says she caught Mrs Crompton committing adultery, Mrs Wedge also ran down her husband, as being a loser and no good as a husband, so both our victims are given bad characters by the same person," Chris commented.

"We don't know much about Mr Wedge," George remarked. "Only what Mrs Wedge told us, he could be quite a decent man, he seems well liked at his lodgings, perhaps we are dealing with a woman's scorn here?" George added.

"Perhaps," Chris replied as he leaned forward.

"Why don't we ask those we interviewed whether or not they have a shotgun?" Cam unable to stop himself interrupting.

Chris looked at Cam, and smiled inwardly. "Good question Cam, as far as I know there is no restrictions on anyone owning a shotgun, you do not have to have a permit, those in the frame at the moment hardly seem to be people having a shotgun, but even if they did, would they admit it, as we will be seeing them all again, we can ask that question."

"Who do we have in the frame Chris?" George asked. "All alibis seem to be holding up."

"They do seem to George," Chris agreed. "We seem to be at a dead end, we have to find another opening, we can only work with what we have, until we get another break."

"Cam," Chris said looking at him. "I want you to go and check out Mr Wedge's room, you're good at that, get any trouble with his landlord, explain to them that this is a murder investigation."

Cam smiled. "I'll get straight on to it, I take it I will only know what I am looking for when I find it."

"That's right Cam," Chris praised him as he watched Cam leave.

"Any ideas George?" Chris asked after Cam's departure. "I seem to be a bit stumped at the moment."

"I would like to know who this mystery woman Susan is that Mr Jarvis told us about?" George gave his opinion.

"I been thinking about Mr Jarvis," Chris replied.

"His alibi seems full proof, we know he was in the Foresters until almost nine, and his alibi seems solid, the mystery woman Susan could be a ploy to get him out of the park," Chris said with a disappointed look on his face." If that is so, then the murders were planned, I can't see Mr Jarvis himself being involved, what the hell would be his motive?"

George shrugged. "Where do we go from here?" he asked. "What about Mrs Wedge?" George asked. "She put her boys to bed at six, they could have been fast asleep by eight and she could have pop out?"

"Agreed George, but it's a long way from Stanmore to the park," Chris argued.

"By bike?" George offered.

"That means she would have had to cycle away with a sack full of clothes unseen all the way to Stanmore, you could say she dumped the sack somewhere, but where, it has not been found, but I agree she could have left the house after the boys were asleep."

"What about Mr Crompton," George remarked. "He left the Standard Public House about eight o'clock Sunday night."

"How long would it take to walk to the park from Standard Public House?" Chris expressed his opinion. "At least fifteen minutes I would say, time do not add up unless he knew straight away where to find his wife, even then it would be too tight in my opinion. Don't forget who ever committed the murders must have carried the shotgun, Mr Crompton did not have the gun with him in the pub, but did he go home after leaving the Standard to get the gun?" Chris said.

Bob Harvey the police surgeon poked his head around the door. "Can I come in?" he said with a smile.

"Always welcome Bob," Chris replied. "We were expecting you, come and have a seat."

Bob made his way over to the interview chair, winking at George as he did so. "I have not completed my report yet Chris," he said as he sat. "But I thought I had better come and see you, how is the case going?" Bob asked curiously.

"Waiting for a break," Chris said with a smile. "We have of course managed to put a name to the bodies."

"Who's the man?" Bob asked. "I know the woman is a Mrs Crompton."

"Mr Wedge, his wife worked with Mrs Crompton at the Suffolk Hotel, it was the missing finger that found him."

"I should not have missed that at the park," Bob admitted. "Still it was just one of those things," he shrugged. "When will the bodies be identified?"

"Mr Crompton has agreed to identify today, Mrs Wedge is waiting on us," Chris answered.

"This afternoon will be fine Chris," Bob answered. "I shall be in the morgue all afternoon, but I have a little something to tell you, Mrs Crompton was about eight weeks pregnant."

"Really!" Chris said with a surprised tone.

Bob continued with a smile. "The father is not Mr Wedge," he confirmed.

Chris looked at George who was listening with interest.

"You're absolutely sure?" George asked wondering if it could be her husband.

Bob nodded. "I have done a blood test on both, I always do that regardless, I can assure you Mr Wedge is not the father, probably her husband's child."

"That helps us even less Bob," Chris remarked. "Had the father been Mr Wedge we could have had a motive."

"Have you found the weapon yet?" Bob asked.

Chris shook his head. "With no where to go, that would have been our next step, but first, I think Mr Crompton will have some more questions to answer."

"Well," Bob said getting up. "I am a busy man, as I said I will be available all afternoon if you can arrange the identify the bodies."

"Thanks Bob," Chris replied. "I'll get on to it."

"That's a turn up for the book," Chris said to George after Bob had departed. "I never thought of that side."

"Me neither," George agreed. "I hope it is her husband's, if not Mrs Wedge could be right about her."

"When you checked under the bandstand, was it a good search George?" Chris asked."

"Hardly Chris, I was looking for a sack or a pile of clothes and the gun, and that's what I told Cam to do, however we only had our torches, not a good light, there is quite a big space under there, filled with folding chairs, and sheet music holders, and other rubbish," George replied. "But in all honesty it was not a good search, why, do you think the gun could be under there?" George asked looking at him.

"It's possible George, I'm going to have a couple uniforms to clear the lot out from under, so that we can search it properly, now George you can either take charge of that, or go and see Mr Crompton?" Chris remarked.

George smiled. "I know you have your own questions for Mr Crompton, I'll take the bandstand."

"I'll grab myself a bike," George said with a smile, as he took his trilby from the hat stand.

Chris knocked on the door of 27, Colebrook Street, the door opened and Mr Crompton stood there with a whisky glass in his hand.

"Inspector," he said. "Come in," he offered standing to one side. "Go through to the kitchen," he said closing the front door. "It's warmer there, make yourself at home."

Chris did as he was told and sat at the table, there was a whisky bottle on the table. "How are you copping Mr Crompton?" Chris asked as he watched him sit opposite thinking that he looked a bit drawn.

Mr Crompton shrugged. "Would you like a drink Inspector?" he offered ignoring the question.

"No, thank you," Chris replied. "It's a bit early for me, and I'm on duty."

Mr Crompton took a sip from his glass. "Is this call about Pauline?"

"I would like you to identify your wife this afternoon, I will send a constable to take you," Chris replied.

"That's OK, I'll be here," Mr Crompton said, biting his bottom lip. "I have been wondering whether there could be a mistake of some kind, so I will be pleased in a way to know for sure."

"I take it that you have no children?" Chris asked.

Mr Crompton stared into his whisky glass and shook his head, Chris thought he saw his eyes watering. Mr Crompton did not reply immediately, and silence remained for a while. "When we married, we decided not to have a child straight away, I had a good job, and Pauline wanted to work, we decided to get our own house first."

"You own this house?" Chris asked.

Mr Crompton nodded. "The Lock Stock & Barrel Home, it took us several years however."

"Still well worth it Mr Crompton," Chris replied, trying to cheer him up a little.

Mr Crompton stared at Chris, his eyes were watery. "Was it?" he said with sadness in his voice. "When we decided to have a child, I found myself impotent, sex was the last thing I wanted, I could not give my wife a child, I felt guilty as a husband, my wife was a young healthy woman, she had her needs the same as I did, being impotent I was unable to give her needs," his face flaming with embarrassment.

"I'm sorry to hear that Mr Crompton," Chris replied softly. "It must have been very distressful for you and your wife?"

"Pauline seemed to overcome it by going to church, I saw very little of her, she was always at church, I took to drink, I drank far too much, I laid beside my wife in bed, unable to be romantic towards her, I have always had a guilty conscience, but I am not responsible for my condition, it just happened and I still suffer, drink allows me to fall off to sleep, even if it's just for a couple hours."

Chris shook his head, he felt sorry for Mr Crompton.

Mr Crompton took another sip of his whisky. "Anyway Inspector, you did not come here to listen to my woes, was there anything else?"

"Just a couple of questions to clear up Mr Crompton, but I can come another time?" Chris replied. "They are only routine."

"No, now that you are here," Mr Crompton insisted. "Let's have them."

"Just to sure of what you told us before," Chris stated. "You left the Standard at around eight on Sunday night, then came back to wait for your wife?"

"That's correct," Mr Crompton replied.

"Do you have a shotgun?" Chris asked.

Mr Crompton finished the last of his whisky. "I have never considered shooting wildlife as sport, I play cricket, never own a gun," he answered.

Chris stood up. "I am sorry that I had to trouble you Mr Crompton, but thank you for your frankness, the constable will call this afternoon."

"I'll be here Inspector," Mr Crompton replied about to pour himself another whisky.

Chapter Nine

*C*hris took his trilby off as he entered the police station. Sergeant Dawkins looked up from his desk. "I have sent two constables with Sergeant Bloom to the park," he said with a smile.

"Thank you Sergeant," Chris replied. "I knew I could leave it in your hands, Sergeant House should be there as well," Chris added as he entered his office.

Cam who had been sitting in Chris's chair stood up as Chris entered. Chris wondered as he saw a young woman sitting in the interview chair.

"This is Miss Melanie Roberts, an old friend of mine," Cam introduced her as Chris hung his trilby. "She works as a cleaner in the Suffolk Hotel."

"Really!" Chris replied offering his hand interested. "I am pleased to meet you, I am Detective Inspector Hardie," he introduced himself.

"Likewise," replied Melanie as Chris went and sat at his desk waiting for Cam's explanation.

"I met Mel, I mean Miss Roberts outside the Suffolk Hotel, she told me a story, which I thought you should hear first hand, so I persuaded her to come in," Cam explained.

Chris smiled at Melanie, he was interested and wondered. "It's kind of you Miss Roberts, would you like a cup of tea before you start?"

"No thank you," Mel replied. "I had one before I left work."

"Then I shall be pleased to hear your story," Chris said with a smile.

"I met Cam as I was leaving," Mel began. "I knew he was a policeman, I thought he had a day off he not being in uniform," she smiled. "When he told me he was a detective, I asked him about Mrs Crompton who was found dead, Cam asked me if I knew Mrs Crompton and I told him what had happened a couple weeks ago," Mel looked at Cam who winked at her.

"What did happen a couple weeks ago?" Chris urged gently.

"Well I am not one for telling tales," Mel continued. "But a couple of weeks ago there was an almighty row in one of the bedrooms, it seems that Sharon, that's the barmaid who thinks she is in charge of everyone, was delivering drinks to a guest when she saw Mrs Crompton entering another guest room, as it turned out it was the room of Sharon's latest, being mid afternoon Miss almighty stood at the door for a while, wondering what Mrs Crompton was doing in the man's room, then opened it and found Mrs Crompton in bed with her latest boyfriend," Mel stopped and looked at Cam with a broad smile on her face.

"It was all the talk in the hotel staff room," Mel went on getting excited. "Until the under manager put a stop to it, he told us to keep it quiet, the staff was a team, and should that kind of talk get heard outside, the hotel would get a bad name, and if Mr Wood the manager found out, he would sack the culprits," she continued.

Chris thought of what he just been told. "Let me recap Miss Roberts," he said. "Mrs Wedge or Sharon as you called her, found Mrs Crompton having an affair with a guest, now this guest was also going out with Mrs Wedge?"

"Simply put and true," Mel replied.

Chris smiled inwardly. "Tell me Miss Roberts, do you know the name of this guest?"

"I'm afraid not, I am only a cleaner, we don't go into rooms, we clean all around the hotel accept the rooms which the chambermaids do," Mel answered. "The under manager would know," Mel added. "All I know he was a traveller, visits pharmacy and often stays at the hotel when he is this way."

"Is he there now?" Chris asked.

"No as far as I know he left the hotel the next day, two or three weeks ago," Mel replied. "I don't know if he has come back."

"Do you know if there was any violence between Mrs Wedge and Mrs Crompton?" Chris asked curiously.

"Not in the hotel," Mel replied. "But it must have hurt her ladyship's feeling."

"You are not a fan of Mrs Wedge?" Chris voiced his opinion.

Mel laughed. "You're joking aren't you?"

"Well our reports show that she is popular in the bar," Chris replied.

"Amongst the males," Mel answered.

"How long have you been working at the hotel?" Chris asked.

"Several years now," Mel replied.

Chris smiled at Mel. "Thank you for this information, you have done us a great service, would you like Constable Streeter to walk home with you?"

"I wouldn't mind," Mel laughed. "But I do have shopping to do."

With Mel gone, Chris smiled at Cam. "Good work Cam, it might be useful, how did you find my chair?" he asked with a hint of accusation in his voice.

"Sorry Chris, I only sat there, otherwise I would have been looking at Mel's back with her sitting in the interview chair," Cam explained in an apologetic tone.

"You could have turned the chair," Chris replied. "Anyway what did you find in Mr Wedge's room?"

"Clean as a whistle," Cam replied.

"Very neat and tidy, apart from photos of his wife and sons, no letters or albums, in fact apart from his clothes and tools, the room had just the normal furniture you would expect, I checked all drawers and cupboards without success."

"Well not to worry, what were the tools for?" Chris asked.

"Carpentry as far as I know," Cam replied.

"I have two jobs for you this afternoon, I want you to take Mrs Wedge from the hotel to the morgue, then bring her back here, then take Mr Crompton from Colebrook Street to the morgue, no need to bring him back here, I have just seen him," Chris spoke. "Take Mrs Wedge first, Mr Crompton expects you when you call, I would advice you to take a lunch break now and carry on afterwards."

Chris checked his pocket watch, then decided to call on under manager of the Suffolk Hotel, he crossed the room, and took his trilby from the hat stand before leaving the office.

"I'll be at the Suffolk Hotel Sergeant," he said to sergeant Dawkins, before he left the station.

As it happened, the under manager was talking to the receptionist when Chris entered the hotel.

"Roger Webb Sir," the under manager introduced himself with a smile. "How can I help you?"

"I am Detective Inspector Hardie," Chris replied. "The manager Mr Wood has given me a free hand to question the staff regarding Mrs Crompton, I would like to ask you a couple questions Mr Webb."

Mr Webb a tall, slender man with a clean face, and wearing spectacles, Chris thought him to be about thirty. "Only to happy to be of service Sir," Mr Webb replied. "I do have a small office, we can go there" he said pointing the way with his hand.

Chris followed Roger into a small barely furnished office. "Please Inspector," Roger invited as he sat behind his desk. "Take the chair, I'm sorry but being under manager I have only one chair in my office, should I ever become manager, I will have a carpet on the floor and a hat stand."

"Really!" Chris smiled to himself as he sat, thinking of his own office with a single chair and no carpet."

"Yes," Roger spoke with a smile, the higher you go, the better your office is furnished. "Now how can I help you Sir?"

"What are you able to tell me about Mrs Crompton?" Chris asked holding his trilby in his lap.

Roger rested his arms on his desk. "She was a good worker, employed as a chambermaid, not a lot I can say accept that she was satisfactory," Roger replied.

"Morally, how was she?" Chris asked the straight question.

The smile left Roger's face, he looked uneasy. "I'm not sure what you mean Inspector?" he murmured.

"I mean was she known to have affairs with any of your guest?" Chris replied.

Roger still looking uneasy, shrugged his shoulders. "I'm not aware that she was."

Chris realised that he was uneasy because if Melanie Roberts was telling the truth, he was trying to hide the fact from the manager Mr Wood.

"Mr Webb I am in charge of finding a murderer, should you not tell me the truth, I can assure you I will eventually find out, and then you will be charged as an accessory. I know that a couple weeks ago something happened between two of your employees and a guest, and I want you to tell me," Chris said his voice now full of authority.

Roger was taken back, he hesitated. "Can you tell me who brought this to your notice?"

Chris gave a weak smile. "Mr Webb, what anyone tells me is always in confidence, what you tell me today will never go out of this room," he said to him with a very reassuring voice.

Roger lifted his arms from the desk, then allowed them to fall back. "Very well Inspector, but if Mr Wood gets to hear it, a few of us will get the chop."

"I can assure you, Mr Wood will not hear it from me," Chris replied.

Roger cleared his throat. "It happened a couple weeks ago, it seems that our guest was having an affair with two of our staff, which I might add, is strictly forbidden, however I have a great team here, of course there are squabbles, but that's only human nature, when this disregards for our rules came to my notice, I saw the staff concerned, and gave them a severe warning, I thought it had all been forgotten."

"It would have probably, had Mrs Crompton not been murdered," Chris replied gently. "I admire your concern regarding your staff, I only hope that covering this event up from Mr Wood will not come to haunt you."

"So you think it will," Roger asked feeling dejected.

"Not from me Mr Webb," Chris assured him again. "Now this guest, when did he leave the hotel?"

"The next day actually," Roger spoke from memory.

"He was booked in for two days longer, you see he calls here when he is this way, calling on all his outlets in the area, he was told about the trouble he had caused or he thought the row in his room would soon be known about and decided to just get out of the way, I can only guess this was the reason he left early."

"So he left and have not been back say fifteen days ago, long before Mrs Crompton was murdered?" Chris asked.

"That is true," Roger agreed.

"I shall want his name and address," Chris said sternly.

"I can get that for you," Roger replied without hesitation. "I think he lives at Bournemouth."

"You don't get much time off do you?" Chris asked changing tactics. "Do you live in?"

"Yes I have a single room here, Mr Wood do not however, so I'm on call all the time," Roger replied. "Still I like what I do, who knows in a few years I could be a manager."

"I'm sure you will make a fine one Mr Webb, but have you any hobbies?"

"Cricket, I'm not in a team, no time but I like watching it, when I get a break on the weekend, I go to the park and watch local teams play."

"Was there a match on this weekend?" Chris asked.

"There was," Roger smiled. "Sunday evening, it was very enjoyable."

"What time did it finish?" Chris asked.

"Around six, I had the evening off, Mr Wood was sleeping in the hotel that night, he don't as a rule, but when he do, I get the evening off without any worry."

70

"What did you do with the rest of the evening?" Chris asked a smile on his face.

"Had a couple of pints, and tried to forget about work," Roger smiled back.

"Where was this match played at the front or back of the park?" Chris asked.

"At the back of the park the Salvation Army Band was playing in the bandstand when I left, the match was played at the back of the park."

"Really!" Chris said surprised. "Was chairs set out around the bandstand?"

"There seem to be plenty yes," Roger replied.

"What about guns?" Chris asked. "Do you like them or have any?" he asked as he raised his eyebrows.

"No," Roger shook his head. "I know why you are asking Inspector, no I have never owned a gun."

"Thank you for your frankness Mr Webb," Chris smiled as he rose and offered Roger his hand. "If you will get me that name and address I'll leave you in peace."

Roger left the office and returned with the hotel register, he turned back a few pages. "Mr Wright was here several times during April, but at the end of April he booked in for a week, but as you know he left early."

Chris wrote the address, and the other details down, and left the hotel, his mind full of what Mr Webb had told him. He looked at his watch, it told him he had a couple hours before Cam would be in the office with Mrs Wedge, Mr Wood already knew she would be collected. He decided to go and see how George was getting on hoping that Mr Jarvis would be around.

Chris crossed the playing field, he could already see chairs and other items piled up around the bandstand, and saw the figure of Mr Jarvis.

George was coming out from under the bandstand as Chris stopped and spoke to Mr Jarvis.

"Oh hello Inspector," Mr Jarvis greeted him. "Been watching your men."

"Don't worry Mr Jarvis, there will be no damage to your chairs," Chris said with a meaningful grin on his face.

"It's not that Inspector, I only hope that they put them all back, underneath is low, and my back aches when I do it you know," Mr Jarvis explained in an apologetic tone.

"Don't worry Mr Jarvis, they will all be put back," Chris assured him. "When did you last have to do it?"

"Sunday night," came the reply. "I had a date that night as you know, and there was a band playing, which did not end until between five and five thirty, so I was in a bit of a rush, lucky however a few kids that were playing around gave me a hand."

"Really!" Chris replied. "What about adults, did any of those help you?"

"Some folded their chairs and bring them to the entrance," Mr Jarvis replied. "But not many."

"So the chairs were packed away by six?" Chris asked.

"Before that I would say," Mr Jarvis replied.

"Nothing here Chris, searched the interior, the ground is just dirt, I'm afraid nothing is hidden here," George said.

"It was something we had to do George," Chris said disappointedly. "I now know that a band was playing here Sunday up to about five thirty, I was thinking that a gun as large as a twelve bore, might have been hidden here before the shooting and perhaps are hidden after, that seems unlikely now, anyway, you better complete your search, I'll see you back at the office."

Chapter Ten

*C*hris was at his desk when Cam entered with Mrs Sharon Wedge, Chris stood and shook her hand offering her the interview chair, while Cam took his leave, he had Mr Crompton to take to the morgue.

"Not a pleasant event Mrs Wedge having to identify a dead body," Chris said as a knock came on the office door and Sergeant Dawkins entered with two cups of tea.

"Thank you Sergeant," Chris said as he watched the sergeant place a cup before Mrs Wedge and himself.

"I was making one," the sergeant replied.

"Very thoughtful," Chris replied as sergeant Dawkins left the room. "I'm sure you can do with one Mrs Wedge?" Chris said with a smile.

"Thank you," Sharon giggled taking the cup with both hands and taking a drink. "But please call me Sharon, the name of Wedge annoys me."

Chris took a drink from his cup, then waited until Mrs Wedge had put her cup down.

"As I said, it's not a pleasant event," Chris remarked.

"I went in with my back to the corpse," Sharon replied. "I did not look at his face that was all messed up, just his hand, it was easy to recognise, Patrick has short stumpy hand and fingers, not long slender fingers like a pianist have, it was Patrick alright."

"Well that's one thing over," Chris replied. "Now while you are here, I would just like to go over the story you told us about seeing Mrs Crompton in a guest room, it seems that many of the staff knew about it, but none of them matches what you told us."

"Well, I was there, others whoever they were are speaking about rumours what they heard," Sharon hesitated a bit.

Chris thought for a while, what Sharon said could be true. "You told us that you saw what was happening in the room owing to the reflection in a full length mirror, you did not go into the room?"

"I would have told you had I?" Sharon replied taking another sip of her tea.

"I am also told that you were having an affair with the same guest in that room," Chris continued.

Sharon giggled as she put her cup down. "If he said that, it was only in his dreams, I knew the man, but he was married, he was always trying it on with me when the bar was open, I don't know his name apart from him being called Peter."

Chris decided to change the subject. "It must have been very hard for you with two children to divorce your husband," Chris remarked.

Sharon leaned back in her chair. "Yes it was, but I had enough, the only thing good about him, he was a master cabinet maker you know."

"Really!" Chris replied.

"Yes," Sharon answered. "He earned good money, but I am very careful with money, however it was hard after the divorce, many women are like me, they can get no help at all, they stick with their husbands."

"What about the parish, won't they help?" Chris asked.

74

"Who would want to go to the parish," Sharon giggled. "You have to answer a load of questions, and before they give you a couple of bob, they come to your home and tell you what you should sell, it's called a means test, I wont be beholding to people like that."

"Just how did you manage then?" Chris asked.

"As I said I have always been careful with money, I had a few pounds saved, another good thing was I had two boys, you can pass the oldest boy's clothes for the next the youngest one, had I had a son and a daughter things may have been harder, you cannot pass clothes of a daughter to a son. Anyway I got lucky, this job was going and I got it, I can just manage now," Sharon continued.

"What about your boys?" Chris asked. "Do they know their father is dead?"

"He has never once got in contact with them since our divorce, and they do not mention him much, I shall tell them at the right time," she replied.

"You must have some feelings for your husband when you married him," Chris remarked interested.

Sharon giggled. "You have no idea have you Inspector, girls marry today not for love, but to get out of service, or a girl in a large family will do so to get out of poverty, but the dream is soon shattered, you marry, have children, and you find yourself back into poverty, and I might add, a slave to the man, who keeps you short of money and at times beats you."

"Really!" Chris replied shaking his head. "Surely many marry for love?"

"Perhaps," Sharon replied. "But poverty and children, will soon ruin any love match."

"Well Sharon, you certainly paint a terrible picture of life," Chris commented.

"Only for the poor Inspector," Sharon replied.

"Getting back to what we were saying, you did not have an affair with Mr Wright?" Chris asked.

"Only in his dreams," Sharon giggled.

"I must thank you for coming in Sharon, I have spoken to Mr Wood your manager, you will not lose any money by doing so," Chris said in a reassuring voice.

After Mrs Wedge left, Chris went over in his mind all what was said, he picked up his phone and dialled.

"Poole Police Headquarters," came a voice.

"Good afternoon," Chris answered onto the receiver. "I am Detective Inspector Hardie of Winchester, would Detective Inspector Willett be available?"

"I'll make enquirers Sir," came the reply.

Chris shuffled a few papers around on his desk, while he waited.

"Chris," a voice boomed over the phone. "How did your honeymoon go, as if I can't imagine?"

"Hello Fred," Chris answered. "It went well, how are you and your wife?"

"I'm well Chris, the wife is about the same moaning all the time, we both enjoyed the wedding."

"Thank you Fred, I'm glad," Chris answered. "Are you busy?"

"Not too busy to help you Chris, what can I do for you?"

"I'm up to my neck in a double murder Fred," Chris replied, hearing a laugh at the other end. "You could save my Sergeant a trip to Bournemouth."

"You certainly get your share Chris, I am quiet at the moment, I could do with some practice," Fred replied with a laugh. "Anyway, how can I help?"

"The name of a traveller in medicine has come up in the investigation, he is not a suspect, I believe he left Winchester at least two weeks before the murders, but I would like to meet him, he lives in Bournemouth."

"Tell me his name and address, and what you want, I'll get on to it."

"His name is Mr Peter Wright, he lives at 2, Ocean Drive Bournemouth."

"Got that Chris," Fred replied over the phone. "Anything else?"

"It seems that he was having an affair at the Suffolk Hotel in Winchester where he was staying, with a Mrs Crompton, who is one of our victims, I want his version, he is married I believe," Chris explained.

"Leave it with me I'll do my best," Fred replied.

"Thanks Fred," Chris replied. "My regards to the wife."

Chris was putting back the receiver when George entered, followed by Cam.

"Every thing alright Cam?" Chris asked.

"Mr Crompton broke down when he identified his wife, I got him back home, asked if he wanted tea, but he went on the whisky, I left him sitting in his armchair getting drunk," Cam replied.

"Did you watch him Cam?" Chris asked. "I would like to know whether he looked at her face or not at the morgue?"

"He did," Cam replied. "Even kissed the top of her head."

"What about you George?"

"Found nothing," George replied. "I had a word with Mr Jarvis, he has a double barrel shotgun, he showed it to me, told me it had not been fired in years, I can have it brought in should you want it?"

"Perhaps if we should find the cartridges George," Chris replied after a thought. "Still it's good to know," Chris looked at George.

"I have spoken to Mrs Wedge again" Chris remarked and continued to tell George and Cam about the interview. "There is a tea cup here George that Mrs Wedge drunk from, test it for fingerprints will you?"

George got up taking the cup from the Chris's desk by the handle carried it to his desk.

"Have you ever done fingerprint dusting Cam?" Chris asked as George placed his detective bag on his desk.

"No," Cam shook his head.

"Then you better watch George," Chris advised.

Cam watched as George gently dusted the cup with powder, he blew the powder gently.

"There is several good ones here," George remarked. "See them Cam?"

"Amazing," Cam said as he studied the prints that clearly showed on the cup. "But what do we do now?"

"We will photograph the prints, should we find the gun used, we try to match these prints or the others we have, with any that might be on the gun," George explained.

"I do know that everyone is supposed to have different fingerprints, I never thought that they were much good in crime," Cam murmured.

The phone rang, Chris lifted the receiver.

"Inspector Hardie," he said into the receiver. "Fred, didn't expect to hear from you so quick," he spoke in a loud voice.

"I got in touch with a friend," Fred explained. "I don't know whether it will help you, but Mr Wright of that address was reported missing a week ago by his wife, checks this end put him in Basingstoke about a week ago, when his firm received his last order."

"Really!" Chris replied.

"Can I help you in any other way?" Fred asked.

"Should you hear he has been found, I would appreciate a call," Chris replied.

"You can be sure Chris, regards to your wife," Inspector Fred added pleasantly.

Chris replaced the receiver and looked at George. "That was Inspector Willett, you met him at my wedding."

"Your last Sergeant," George replied a smile on his face.

"Before I saw you at the park, I called at the Suffolk Hotel and saw the under manager, he was quite helpful and eventually gave me the name and address of the man who we are told having an affair with both with Mrs Crompton and Mrs Wedge. His name is Mr Peter Wright from Bournemouth, he has been reported missing by his wife, last known address was Basingstoke," Chris explained.

Chapter Eleven

Chris checked his watch, it told him it was five past six, Cam had left the office earlier, he was following up a break in at a local tobacconist.

"Anything on tonight George?" Chris asked as he cleared his desk.

George shook his head. "Only the usual, lying on the bed in my room."

"Well it is Elizabeth's half day, she will be home now, fancy a pint at the Rising Sun?" Chris suggested.

George grinned. "Best offer I've had all day."

The Rising Sun felt warm as they entered, it was just twenty past six, and they found only two men in the bar playing push halfpenny. Alfie the landlord greeted them with his usual smile. "Chris, George," he welcomed picking up two glasses. "What will it be today?"

"I fancy a boiler today Alfie," Chris replied. "What about you George?" Chris asked as George was making for their usual seat by the window. "Same as you Chris," he replied.

"One for yourself, Alfie," Chris said as he watched Alfie pouring a brown ale in each glass before filling the glasses with beer.

"I'll have a brown ale," Alfie said with a smile taking the sixpence that Chris had put on the counter. "That lovely wife of yours is letting you off the leash tonight is she?"

"Something like that," Chris replied with a smile taking the glasses to where George was sitting. "How is Liz, well I hope?" Chris enquired as he sat.

"So, so," Alfie replied turning the palm of his hand over and backwards. "You can never tell about a woman, they are always suffering from something that men can't understand, suffers a lot with headaches," Alfie said, winking at George.

Chris smiled knowing what Alfie meant. "You have to respect them Alfie," he replied. "Women's body is much different to a man when they give birth, their body must take a beating, and for that reason they are different and should be respected."

"My wife is always telling me I don't respect her, but I do, it's just that I cannot say it in words," Alfie replied, a wide grin spread on his face.

"Then you should find a way Alfie, you would be lost without your Liz," Chris answered, meaning it.

Alfie took up a glass and washed it without comment, Chris turned to George.

"We are at a dead end with this case George, it's a pity we can't find that gun and their clothes," Chris said, annoyance in his voice.

"What would your Inspector Noal do?" George asked.

"I've told you before George, when Noal got stuck, he always started from the beginning, we did on our last case, and broke through."

"You don't like hanging do you Chris?" George asked.

"Not really, so many murders are done on the spur of the moment, not intentionally, but there are others that is so evil, like the case we are on at the moment, the murderer deserves to be hung," Chris replied before taking a drink.

"I agree with what Sergeant Bloom said when we first saw the victims," Chris said as he replaced his glass on the table. "Who ever did this must have been full of hate."

"If I solve a case, and the killer was hung, only later to be proved innocent, I would give up this work that's why I am always so careful. Mind you I do believe that life should mean life, accident or not a life was taken, no one should be allowed out of prison early to enjoy life after taking one," Chris commented.

George stood and collected Chris's glass. "Same again?" he asked and smiled at Chris who nodded.

George returned and put the two full pints on the table. "So we start again from the beginning," George queried.

Chris took a drink before answering. "Those houses in Gordon Road that Cam knocked, you go over them again George, Cam might have missed something?"

"Something on your mind?" George asked.

"Several things George," Chris said with a smile. "Was Mrs Crompton and Mr Wedge having an affair, if not why were they together at the park, where is that sack of clothing, that might also be with the gun and cartridges, and of course it would be helpful if we could find this Susan who made a date with Mr Jarvis. I also wonder Mr Crompton, he left the Standard pub around eight, where did he go, did he go home as he said he did?"

"Questions, questions, If we knew all that?" George said after taking a drink. "I'll do Gordon Road before I come in tomorrow, and hopefully find the tenants in."

"I'm sure that their clothes must be nearby where they were murdered," Chris remarked.

"Those clothes put in a sack could not be carried under the arm, it would be risky for anyone carrying the sack, the clothes must be nearby where they were murdered, I shall get Cam and a couple of constables to search the park from top to bottom, I should have done it earlier," Chris spoke with an annoyed and disappointed expression on his face.

"We have only had the case for three days Chris," George remarked after taking another drink. "Three days is not a lot, the victims were not supposed to have been recognised, but we did it, and if the murderer knows this, they might be getting scared," George tried to cheer him up.

"We can hope, I am sure the victims were shot in that way so that it would take time for us to identify them," Chris replied.

Chris drained his glass and he rose from his chair. "But we got lucky, I must get home now George, my dinner will be getting cold, you stop if you want I'll see you tomorrow."

Chris arrived at his mother-in-law's house at seven fifteen, Elizabeth was waiting for him with the door open, she kissed him. "Had a long day darling?" she smiled.

"In a way," Chris replied. "George and I had things to go over, so we popped into the Rising Sun for one."

"You deserve one darling," Elizabeth replied helping him off with his overcoat.

Chris put his trilby on the wall hanger and holding Elizabeth around the waist walked into the front room, where Olive had his dinner on the table and Ron was sitting in his armchair. Chris apologised for being late as he kissed Olive on the cheek.

"Had a pint have you?" Ron remarked with a wink. "You could have told me?"

Chris smiled as Olive scolded Ron. "He deserves a drink, he works all day long, what do you do, sit there reading your paper, now let Chris eat his dinner in peace."

"I would have made the effort had I known?" Ron teased muttering, smiling at Elizabeth.

Olive laughed. "I'm sure you would to go to the pub, but you can't make an effort to do the jobs that need doing around the house."

"You only have to ask me my precious," Ron replied as Chris sat at the table.

"Spotted dick for dessert," Elizabeth remarked as she sat near to Chris. "Your favourite."

"I'm getting no where with this case, I had to talk it over with George, it's better to do it outside the office, you are more relaxed," Chris excused himself for being late.

"You can go for a drink whenever you want," Elizabeth replied. "I know you work hard, you need some relaxation."

"When is your day off Chris?" Ron asked.

"Saturday Ron," Chris replied.

"Perhaps we can walk down to the pub together and have a pint," Ron queried.

"Perhaps not," Olive interrupted him. "Chris and Elizabeth might have other plans."

"I have to work on Saturday morning." "I have no objections mum," Elizabeth answered.

"Perhaps Chris want to take you out in the afternoon?" Olive argued.

"It's only Wednesday today mum, who knows what we may do Saturday?" Elizabeth said with a smile.

Chris finished his dinner and pushed the plate away from him. "As usual Olive, that was a meal worth eating."

Olive smiled. "Thank you Chris, at least you appreciate what we women do," she said looking at Ron. "Now sit back in the armchair and enjoy your pipe while Elizabeth and I wash up."

While Elizabeth and Olive was in the scullery, Chris sat in the armchair to one side of Ron, filled his pipe, and drew on it contentedly.

"Difficult case Chris?" Ron asked.

"It seems that way," Chris replied. "Tell me Ron, if you had a sack full of clothing, too risky to be seen carrying it, what would you do?"

Ron thought for a while. "We are talking about being in the park, and still light?" Ron asked.

Chris nodded.

"Then I suppose I would hide the sack in bushes or behind a wall if one was close by, and collect the stuff when it was darker," Ron commented.

"I'm not sure about that Ron," Chris replied. "After all two brutal murders had been committed, would whoever it was want to even go near the park again to collect it later if it was hidden in the park, whoever it was would take the risk of being spotted by the park keeper?"

"The killing should have taken place later when it was dark," Ron remarked.

"The risk still remains Ron," Chris replied. "Greater in fact the park keeper would have heard the shots."

Ron shrugged his shoulders, fell silent for a moment before speaking again. "Are you sure that this sack had to be carried through town?" he asked.

Chris pondered the question. It was a good question, one that Chris had pondered and thought of, he was still pondering when Elizabeth and Olive appeared.

Chapter Twelve

Only Cam was in the office the next morning when Chris entered, it was a warm day, and Chris was without his overcoat, he hung his trilby and crossed to his desk. "How is that case of yours going Cam?" he asked.

"Solved," Cam replied with a smile. "A couple boys from St Thomas's School stole a carton of cigarettes from a shop, I spoke to them in the head master's office, then one confessed, it seems that they offered them all around to the boys at playtime, I'm doing the report now."

"Good man," Chris praised. "After you have finished your report I might had a job for you."

"While I was in the head master's office waiting for the boys to be brought in, I asked the head master if he knew a Mr Crompton, he told me that Mr Crompton was a competent master, and he would be sorry to lose him as he was leaving at the end of the term," Cam remarked.

"Really!" Chris replied as he stood up full of interest. "Did he say why he was leaving or where he was going?"

"No," Cam replied. "It was at that moment when the boys were brought in."

"Pity," Chris murmured reaching the door of the office. "But well done Cam, always remember that an odd remark will often furnish you with information you did not know."

Cam smiled as Chris left the room, by the time he re-appeared, Cam had finished his report.

"Sergeant Dawkins is arranging for you to have three constables Cam," Chris spoke. "I want you to search the park, from the back to the front, it will take you time, perhaps wasted time but it has to be done, divide the park in sections, search everywhere, leave no stone unturned as they say," Chris said in a serious voice.

"I can do that Chris," Cam replied excitedly, leaving the office.

Chris smiled still pondering over Ron's question. "Are you sure that this sack had to be carried through town?" it was the words Ron had asked.

It was a half way through the morning when George showed up. "What time did you leave last night?" Chris asked.

"I had another pint of bitter before I left," George replied. "I had nothing to do, I got fish and chips on the way home."

"You have been knocking doors I take it?" Chris asked.

"I have, number one the first house was out, I questioned the neighbour next door, he told me that new neighbours moved in about ten days ago, last Sunday night it seems that people were coming and going, making a bit of noise, but since they have not been seen," George spoke in a calm voice.

"Could he recognise anyone?" Chris asked.

"No, it seems that number one, has a side entrance, sep-arated from the park by a wall, which people calling can use without entering by the front door. They are terraced houses, but only number one, has a side entrance. The neighbour was an old soldier, I asked him if he heard a gunshot, he said he might have done, but with the noise next door, could not swear to it."

"That's interesting," Chris remarked. "Do we know who owns the number one, or it is a rented?"

"It is rented," George replied. "But not council, rented through an agent, it's called Collins and Collins estates agents. I have already made an appointment to see the manager at twelve."

Sergeant Dawkins knocked and entered. "I have a farmer at the desk, he is reporting the disappearance of his son."

"Really!" Chris replied looking at George. "Thank you Sergeant, perhaps we had better see him."

"I'll bring him in," replied the sergeant leaving the room.

The farmer entered, he was an elderly person perhaps around sixty five, he wore working clothes, with a oldish brown trilby covering his hairless head.

Chris stood up, introduced himself and George, then offered the interview chair.

"I understand you are reporting your son missing?" Chris asked.

"That's right," replied the farmer. "It might be a waste of time, but it is unusual for my son not to keep in touch."

"I see," Chris replied. "Perhaps I can have your name?"

"My name is Robert Morris, my son is Ronald Morris."

"I understand that you are a farmer?" Chris remarked.

"That's right, not a large farm but enough to run, my farm runs alongside the Worthy Road, and stretches down towards the back of the park."

"Really!" Chris replied looking at George and visualising in his mind the area. "How long has your son been missing?"

"He left home early Sunday morning to go to a shooting, Owslebury way, we have not seen him since, enquiries tell us

he was at the shooting, left at the end, so where is he?"
Mr Morris shook his head in confusion.

"This behaviour is unusual for him?" Chris asked.

"Certainly," replied the farmer. "He might stop out
the odd nights, but we run the farm between us, farming is
not easy with the two of us, let alone just me."

"I'm sure it isn't Mr Morris," Chris replied. "Tell me,
does he have his own gun?"

"Yes he has his own gun, a double barrel twelve bore
shotgun, but what would a gun have anything to do with
him not returning home?" Mr Morris asked, surprised.

"We like to know all the background Mr Morris," Chris
replied in a gentle tone. "Did he have a girl friend?"

"Plenty, he is the son of a farmer, good looking, age
thirty five, normal build, you don't put much weight on in
farming, he is strong and stands at about five feet, ten
inches."

Chris smiled inwardly. "We have to take the view that he
could be staying with a girlfriend?"

Farmer Morris shifted in his seat. "He goes with quite a
few, I don't know of any that he is serious with?"

"Do you know of any names or places of works of these
girls, he might have mentioned about them at sometime?"
Chris asked trying to get him to remember.

"He just tells me he is going out, it's normally late, farm
work has a lot of hours, come to think of it, he did tell me
he was meeting a girl who works in the Suffolk Hotel, but
that was several weeks ago," he replied.

"Any name?" Chris asked impatiently.

"Funny I remembered this one, her name was Melanie,"
replied the farmer.

"Really!" Chris replied trying not to show his excitement. "Any others?"

Farmer Morris shook his head. "I am always too busy to take in what Ronald is saying, half the time goes in one ear and out the other, he has probably told me plenty."

"Your farm is on the Worthy Road, where do you live?" Chris asked.

"Farm House, Worthy Road, it's a little way off the main road."

"Are you on the phone?" Chris asked.

"I am," the farmer replied.

Chris pushed a sheet of paper and a pencil towards the farmer. "Please write it down, we might have to get in touch with you urgently."

The farmer took up the pencil and started to write. "I hope you are not thinking the worse?" he asked as he raised his eyebrows.

"It is now Thursday Mr Morris, your son has been missing since Sunday, almost four days, why did you wait before reporting it?" Chris asked knowing the usual answer.

"When he did not turn up Sunday night, we thought he had gone off with a couple of friends, he is entitled to, he works hard, each morning we expected him to walk in, but today my wife told me to report him missing, or she would do it," he said.

"The evening newspaper reported two unidentified bodies found in Winchester," this report made us worried.

Chris smiled as he stood up and offered his hand. "Tell your wife that we have identified the bodies, neither is your son, we get many missing persons Mr Morris most of them turns up."

Mr Morris murmured his thanks, took Chris's hand and nodded to George left the office. Chris leaned back in his chair, took his pipe and sucked on it. "Could be interesting George?" he remarked.

"His farm reaches to the rear of the park, a way out without being seen," George replied.

"But what do a farmer's son and Melanie I take it from the Suffolk Hotel have to do with Mrs Crompton and Mr Wedge's murder?" Chris took a puff on his pipe.

"Beats me," George replied. "Anyway if you are going to see Melanie, you will be on your own, I have an appointment in half an hour with the estate agent."

"I've got Cam searching the park at the moment, Cam knows Melanie from way back, I am wondering if it would be best for him to have a word with her?" Chris remarked. "He may get more out of her, I can't see at the moment how these two connects with our case?"

George entered the office's of Collins and Collins estate agent, and straight away was ushered into the manager's office, where he shook hands with Mr Dodd.

"Thank you for seeing me Sir," George said politely. "I am interested in number one in Gordon Road, who I am told is rented through your office."

Mr Dodd smiled. "It is indeed Sergeant along with the nine others in the Road, but I am sorry if you wanted to rent, number one was taken about ten days ago I can however put you on the waiting list," he said politely.

George smiled. "No sir, I am interested only as part of a police enquiry, I am interested in who rented it?"

"I see," replied Mr Dodd. "Can I know why you are interested?"

"Last Sunday Sir, there was a double murder in the park, both shot, we need to know everyone who may have heard the shots, number one is the only tenant that we have been unable to see," George informed him.

"I did hear about that Sergeant, terrible crime," Mr Dodd remarked with a serious face, he opened a large ledger in front of him.

"Now let's see," he said turning over a couple of leafs. "Yes here we are, a Mr Light, Alfred Light, rented the house on the Monday 12th of May, paid a month's rent in advance."

"Is he a local man?" George asked.

Mr Dodd checked the ledger. "No, he came from Dorset, a place called Beaminster."

"Married I suppose?" George asked.

"So it says here, married with two children," Mr Dodd replied looking at the ledger. "Now any more questions?"

"Do you check those who wish to be tenants?" George asked.

"Used to, but not so much nowadays, people are coming into Winchester from all over the country to find work, in the same way people are leaving Winchester looking for work in the war factories, we rely on identification now, receipts, old rent books that kind of things," Mr Dodd added.

"I understand Sir," George replied. "Mr Light was able to prove who he was by producing receipts in his name at an address in Beaminster?"

"That is correct Sergeant," Mr Dodd agreed.

"You would not know his work I suppose?" George asked.

"Traveller of some kind I believe," Mr Dodd replied. "Might be the reason why you are unable to catch him?"

"You are probably right Sir," George agreed standing up and offering his hand. "Thank you for seeing me."

Chris had returned to the police station having spoken to
Cam at the park. A short man wearing a blue pin stripe suit,
wearing a bowler hat and carrying a briefcase was talking to
Sergeant Dawkins.

Sergeant Dawkins looked up as Chris entered. "Inspector,
this gentleman is enquiring about a Mr Wedge?"

"Really!" Chris replied wondering. "Perhaps Sergeant I
better see him, would you please come into my office Mr..?"

"Morgan," the man replied, taking off his bowler hat.
"Thank you."

Chris sat at his desk after offering Mr Morgan the interview chair. "Now Mr Morgan how can I help you?"

Mr Morgan was an elderly man, wearing glasses, and
wearing a well groomed moustache, he rested his brief case
on his lap, and put his bowler hat on top. "I am from
Morgan and White," Mr Morgan explained. "A firm of
solicitors with office in St Peters Street."

"I know the street," Chris remarked. "Tell me why do
you want to find Mr Wedge, do you have a Christian name?"

"Yes Patrick, Patrick Wedge," Mr Morgan replied. "I
have seen his ex wife in Stanmore, she had no idea where he
was, but told me she would try to find out, that was almost
three weeks ago, but I have not heard from her, which
prompted me to call here. Mr Wedge had an uncle Mr John
Newman on his mother's side who emigrated to Australia
several years ago, he became a farmer, and very rich, but
sadly he has died. He had no relations over there, his wife
had died, it was a childless marriage. Checks have been
made, and it has been found that Mr Patrick Wedge is his
only surviving blood relation, which means his money will
go to Mr Wedge."

"Really!" Chris murmured. "If you can't find him or you
have proof of his death, who gets the money?"

Mr Morgan shifted in his chair. "His ex-wife cannot make a claim if Mr Wedge is dead they have been divorced several years, but should Mr Wedge be dead, the money would go to his sons, which I believe there are two, however the ex Mrs Wedge would be their guardian, and control the sum until the son's became of age. If however we cannot find him without knowing whether he is dead or alive, after say seven years, the sons would get the money."

"I see," Chris replied not at all sure whether to tell Mr Morgan of Mr Wedge's death at the moment, and wondering why Mrs Wedge who knew of her ex-husband's death had not notified to Mr Morgan. Chris decided not to say anything for the moment.

"Do you have a picture of Mr Wedge?" Chris asked.

"Unfortunately not," Mr Morgan replied. "Just a description, which fits a thousand men, Mrs Wedge did not have one, telling me she tore them all up."

Chris smiled at the thought. "Like finding a needle in a haystack."

"Most certainly Inspector," Mr Morgan agreed.

"Would you give me a few days on this Mr Morgan, I will phone you some time next week, I may know of a lead I can follow."

"I have no where to go Inspector," Mr Morgan replied. "I would be most grateful to you, should I hear from Mr Wedge or Mrs Wedge in the meantime I will let you know."

"Before you go Mr Morgan can you tell me the value of the inheritance?"

"I don't see why not," Mr Morgan replied. "The farm included some twenty thousand acres, the cattle and the house, worth I'm told about fifty thousand, until the heir is found, Mr Newman's solicitor will keep it running."

"That's quite a sum," Chris remarked standing, offering his hand, which Mr Morgan accepted warmly.

With the office empty, Chris settled down and wrote his notes, when a knock came on the door and Bob Harvey the Police Surgeon poked his head around the door.

"Busy Chris?" he asked, a smile on his face.

"Not for you Bob, come and take a seat, want a cup of tea?"

"No thanks Chris, makes me run too much, I was on my way to the morgue, thought I would pop in."

"Glad you did Bob, I wanted to ask you a question about the case?"

"How's it going, complicated?" Bob asked.

"Getting too much information, confuses the mind not knowing what bit fits and what bits don't," Chris smiled.

"You have often told me that a case is like a jigsaw puzzle, it will all come together, too much information is better than none I imagine," Bob commented.

"You are right of course Bob," Chris agreed. "I do have the start of a picture, anyway what I wanted to ask so far there is no reason why Mrs Crompton and Mr Wedge should have been in the park after closing time, I have no knowledge that they even knew each other, I wonder, could they have been killed somewhere else, then brought to where they were found?"

Bob shook his head. "No, too much blood about for that, they were alive when they were shot."

"Sure Bob?" Chris asked, confusion plain in his voice.

"Yes I am, but they could have been unconscious," Bob replied.

Chris's mind went over the idea. "That would mean Mrs Crompton and Mr Wedge were carried to the spot where they have been found?"

"The time of death Chris, it's not accurate, you can give a half or an hour to what I told you, I'm sure they were killed around eight thirty, but I cannot bring it down to the exact time," Bob gave his opinion.

"Well earlier not worth considering, but later, I wonder?" Chris replied. "You have given me something to think about, as for being unconscious, there is a lot of ifs and buts to consider."

Bob shrugged. "There are tablets you can take that will make you unconscious, unaware of what is happening."

"It's getting hold of them though, these tablets not easy to get," Chris remarked.

"They would not be sold over the counter," Bob smiled. "If these corpses were drugged, it would mean knowing someone who would supply them, however, I have not checked for drugs, no doubt about what killed them no one would survive being shot in the face at close range with a twelve bore, but I will check for drugs before I make my report."

"Thank you Bob," Chris replied.

"When the bodies were identified, that Mr Crompton seemed to go over board with grief, Cam had an awful job with him," Bob remarked.

"Yes I heard," Chris replied. "Being a school master, you would have expected a little composure, anyway according to Cam, he was having whisky when he left."

Bob smiled. "That Mrs Wedge was opposite, she did not look at her ex husband, just his finger, then she was gone, it was a horrible sight, but you would have expected her to want to look."

"Did you tell her his face was just a pulp and unrecognisable?" Chris asked.

"No, I say nothing, I always believe that the person identifying has been told by the police, and then Mrs Wedge must have known anyway," he said, rising from his chair.

Chris was replacing the phone receiver when George entered the office. "I have just been on to Inspector Willett, asking if he can get a photo of Mr Wright, he will do his best."

"Might come in handy?" George replied, then told Chris of his meeting with Mr Dodd the manager of estate agent.

"Where is Beaminster George?" Chris asked as George finished.

"Situated in the West Dorset I believe, same county as Mr Wright," George replied. "I am still in the dark Chris," George murmured. "Can't get a grip on this case?"

"That's what I told Bob when he called, too much information, much do not fit into a picture, however, he brought up about drugs," Chris leaned back in his chair and took his pipe out of his pockets which he sucked on. "He was sure that the victims were unconscious when they were shot, he is going to check for drugs."

Chris filled his pipe and lit it, puffing out a cloud of smoke. "However George, I also had a meeting with a Mr Morgan, solicitor from St Peters Street, he was here when I returned from seeing Cam in the park."

"What did he want?" George asked taking an interest.

"It seems an uncle of Mr Wedge has died in Australia, and left him a vast estate."

"Well he won't inherit now," George voiced his opinion.

"No, but his sons may," Chris replied.

"Do Mrs Wedge know?" George asked.

"According to Mr Morgan, he met Mrs Wedge several weeks ago, she knows, I just wonder why she did not tell us?"

"Have we got a motive Chris?" George asked curiously.

Chris shrugged. "Could be, but I can't see Mrs Wedge killing on her own, I don't think she could have done it on her own, two killings then stripping them too much in my opinion for a woman to do on her own."

"You are suggesting that she had a partner in crime?" George asked.

"I'll tell you that George when you tell me how Mrs Crompton and Mr Wedge were together in the park," Chris looked over the top of his nose, with a meaningful grin.

Chapter Thirteen

*P*hone rang a few times before Chris picked up the receiver. Chris picked up the receiver. "Inspector Hardie," he spoke onto the receiver.

"Chris, this is Cam, I'm phoning from a box in Nuns Road, I think you better get up here, we have a male body."

"Settle down Cam," Chris replied noting the excitement in Cam's voice. "Where about in the park?"

"Left hand side, way at the back," Cam replied.

"Well get back there Cam, don't let the constables with you walk all over the area, I'll be there as soon as possible."

"Will do," Cam replied.

Chris replaced the receiver and looked at George who was listening. "We need two bikes George, Cam has found a male body back of the park, I'll get the sergeant to phone Bob, he is not going to like it."

"Might be the farmer's son?" George replied getting up to fetch the bikes. "I'll meet you outside station."

Chris after giving instructions to Sergeant Dawkins, he left the station where he found George waiting for him.

Cam met them by the narrow bridge that separated the park from Monks Road.

"Leave your bikes here," Cam remarked. "At the back," Cam pointed with his hand. "It's overgrown and wild underfoot, and quite dense with bushes etc."

Chris and George did as they were told.

"Lead the way then Cam," Chris remarked smiling inwardly.

They left the path that went around the back of the park, and entered an unkept part, that was covered in undergrowth and bushes.

"This probably separates the park from the Worthy Road farm," Chris remarked. "Having trouble Sergeant?" he asked.

"Blasted brambles," George moaned. "How did the body get through this stuff?"

Chris and George having caught up with Cam, looked down on a body that was lying on its back in long grass, between several bushes.

"Anything been touched Cam?" George asked without looking from the body.

"No one has been more than a yard to it," Cam answered.

Chris looked away from the body, towards the constables standing a few yards away. "This spot is isolated," Chris spoke to Cam. "Have one of your men go to the bridge to meet Mr Harvey when he comes," he suggested.

Cam did not answer as he moved to one of the constables who moved off after being given instructions.

"He looks as if he has been here a few days," George remarked looking at the body.

"I agree George," Chris replied. "He also fits the farmer's son description."

"At least he is fully dressed," George remarked as he bent looking at the face. "No obvious signs of how he died?"

"Get your men to search around Cam, I'm looking for a shotgun, if it is the farmer's son, he should have a shotgun, we were told he went to a shooting Sunday morning taking his gun, but never returned home," Chris commented. Chris walked around the body. "No signs of a struggle, but if he was killed on Sunday, the pressed grass around him would have returned to normal by now, he had to be killed, if not where is his gun?"

"Someone walking could have come across him, noticed the gun which are expensive, took it and kept quite about the body," George argued.

"Possible," Chris agreed. "I don't as a rule believe in coincidences, we know if this is the farmer's son, and I believe he is, that when he left home he had his shotgun with him, a twelve bore double barrel gun, we also know that our faceless victims was shot with a similar shotgun, which so far we have not found, however should the gun turn up around here, then with might be, that this is not related to our case."

"All personal belongings have been taken," George said after he finished searching the body.

The sound of voices made Chris and George to look towards the sound. Bob Harvey stood and looked at Chris and George before speaking.

"Cam found it," Chris said. "He was doing a routine search of the area for the clothing and shotgun from the Sunday victims."

"He found this one instead," Bob replied bending towards the corpse. "I suppose it's too much to expect that you know who it is?"

"I believe he is Mr Ronald Morris, his father reported him missing a few hours ago," Chris answered. "He is a farmer's son, their farm stretches along Worthy Road, all the way down to the back of this park."

Bob studied the face and the body. "Nothing this side," he remarked. "Let's turn him over."

George knelt, and with Bob rolled the body over onto his face.

"Ah there it is," Bob almost shouted as he pointed to a large red mark on the back of the neck. "That obviously killed him, he must have had a wallop," Bob remarked as he examined the neck and back of the head.

"What with Bob?" George asked impatiently.

"A part of a tree branch perhaps, something hard and firm," Bob answered.

Chris looked around, he could not see any parts of tree branches, there were no trees around only bushes.

"When do you think he died Bob?" he asked.

"Hard to tell Chris," Bob said standing up. "By the state of him, I would say a few days ago, but that's only a guess."

"What about a cricket bat?" Chris asked.

"Bob knelt and looked at the neck again, the side of a cricket bat perhaps," Bob replied. "There is a sort of a V indenture, what made you think of that?"

"There was a cricket match here on Sunday," Chris answered.

Bob stood and rubbed his chin. "I can't say for sure Chris, when I have him on the table at the morgue I will try and match of what it could have been, but one thing is sure, he could not have done it himself."

"Another murder then?" George replied.

Bob shrugged. "The meat cart should be here anytime Chris, can they take him?"

"I can't do anything here Bob," Chris replied. "I need to get him identified."

"He just needs cleaning up a bit, unclothed he might have a birth mark, I'll know that within the next hour, however I will not be able to touch him until Friday, I'll phone you Chris."

"Then I will wait Bob, before I see Mr Morris," Chris replied.

"We might as well get back to the police station George," Chris suggested. "I'm sure if there are anything to be found, Cam will find it."

Back at the station, Chris began to puff at his pipe, no doubt arranging his opinion in his mind. He decided to phone Mr Wood at the Suffolk Hotel. "Mr Wood, Detective Inspector Hardie here, how are you?"

"I'm fine thank you, yourself?" Mr wood answered pleasantly.

"Well, but confused," Chris replied. "We have found another body."

"Dear oh dear Inspector," came the reply.

"I have no idea at the moment whether or not it is connected to the case I'm already investigating, we have an idea who it might be and if that is proven true, one of your staff has been mentioned who would know him. I am wondering, would you be so kind as to send her across when she arrives tomorrow morning?" Chris asked in the kindness voice.

"Certainly Inspector, oh dear oh dear, I hope all this is not going to give the hotel a bad name, am I allowed to know who you believe this new body belongs to?"

"At the moment Sir, what I am saying to you is strictly in confidence, the new body has not been officially identified, so I cannot say who we believe he is," Chris commented.

"Is it another murder?" Mr Wood asked with a tone of disbelief in his voice.

"I'm afraid it is, that is why I need to speak to your staff member."

"What's the name Inspector?"

"Miss Melanie Roberts," Chris replied.

"Very well I'll have her over about nine thirty tomorrow morning, should that be to your liking?"

"I am in your debt Sir," Chris replied as he put the phone down.

Chris smiled at George. "I was going to leave it to Cam, but now Mr Morris have been found murdered, I must see her myself, at first I thought it might have been Mr Wright from Bournemouth."

"I can't see any connection with our case," George remarked.

"The shotgun would George," Chris replied.

George gave a small laugh. "There are plenty shotguns around, are you saying that someone would murder to get a shotgun, to commit other murders?"

Chris thought for a while before answering. "It do seem strange George I agree, but let's take our double murder, had it not been for the birth mark on Mrs Crompton and the missing finger of Mr Wedge, how long do you think it would have taken us before we could start an investigation not knowing who they were."

George shrugged. "There is the dentist," he murmured.

"I agree but both had a full and good set of teeth, it could have taken us ages to find out who they were, Mr Crompton reported his wife missing, had it not been for her birth mark, he would never had been sure that it was his wife, Mrs Wedge only identified her ex husband because of his missing finger, their faces were destroyed for a reason, even their clothes were taken to delay identification," Chris continued.

"There was nothing done to prevent Mr Morris's identification," George replied.

"No need George, there is no connection between our double murder and Mr Morris, it was just a case of another murder."

"Who ever killed Mr Morris must have known that he would be reported missing," George argued. "Looks as though we are up the creek."

"Well planned murders are never perfect George," Chris remarked. "Always a little thing will catch, look at our double murder, they had obviously forgot about the small details of a birth mark and a missing finger."

"Perhaps the murderer did not know about these things?" George argued.

"That's what I am saying George, these small things, not known or forgotten, or the unexpected happenings are often the downfall of a perfect murder," Chris replied.

The phone went, and Chris answered.

"Hello Bob," Chris said onto the receiver.

"Your man has a light scar running down the side of his left leg Chris, looks as though it was ripped open at sometime ago, apart from that his body is clean."

"Thank you Bob," Chris replied.

Chris replaced the receiver and told George about the scar. "It should help," Chris spoke in a calm voice.

"When do we tell the Mr Robert Morris?" George asked.

"As soon as we get a report from Cam, you never know, he might find the gun?" Chris smiled.

"Yeah, and pigs might fly," George replied with a grin on his face.

Chapter Fourteen

*C*hris laid on his back looking up at the ceiling, he felt the warmth of Elizabeth who was on her side close to him, her right arm flung across his chest.

"You are not happy with the way your case is going Chris?" she remarked concern evident in her voice.

"You can tell?" he asked a smile on his face.

"I know you darling," Elizabeth replied resting her head on her other arm and looking at him. "You don't talk, you are thinking all the time, I know."

Chris turned his head to her side and looked at her. "You know darling, it is said that marrying a beautiful woman, which you are, with a sharp and clever mind, which you have, can only lead to disaster."

"You are joking," Elizabeth scolded slapping his chest. "I just want to be a part of you in everything, if you have thoughts share them with me, whatever you think or do, I want to be a part of it," she smiled. "I mean when you are at home don't shut yourself away from me, they say a problem shared is a problem halved."

"I only wish that was true," Chris remarked once again looking at the ceiling. "But I am sorry darling if I seem to cut you out, it's not intentionally but police work is difficult to discuss."

Elizabeth did not comment and remained silent. Chris on the other hand felt guilty, he did realise that at night he would stare for hours at the ceiling, his mind going over every word that had been said during interviews and debates of a case he was working on.

"Another body was found today, at the back of the park," Chris said in a serious voice.

Elizabeth raised her head and looked at Chris, she kissed his cheek. "I'm sorry darling, you have all this worry, and I'm being selfish."

Chris smiled. "You are a distraction, but then it's not your fault that I adore you."

"You do say the nicest things darling," Elizabeth replied with a giggle. "I have to say that I like being your distraction."

Chris turned on his side and faced Elizabeth. "I like you being a distraction as well," he smiled.

"Do you know who the body belong to?" Elizabeth asked touching his face.

"As far as we are aware, his name is a Mr Morris he was killed by a blow to the head."

"I know of a Morris, but they are farmers, along Worthy Road, if my memory serves me," Elizabeth said. "Oh Chris," Elizabeth spoke in a soft voice. "Rosemary will be so sad, she loved her parents and especially her brother, she dots on him, was it her dad?"

Chris stared at Elizabeth. "No, her brother, Ronald Morris."

"Oh dear," Elizabeth sobbed. "Surely it can't be."

"You must not upset yourself darling," Chris said raising his head so that he looked down on her. "It's one reason why I do not discuss cases with you, like your mother you get upset."

"I'm sorry," Elizabeth replied wiping her eyes with the back of her hand. "It's just that I know Rosemary."

"Do you know them personally, or through the bank?" Chris asked.

"Through the bank mostly of late, but I did go to school with her, I have met Rosemary a few times, had a cup of tea together now and again, I know she idolizes her brother, she is a beautiful girl Chris, I was thinking of her this week when speaking to George."

"You mean match making?" Chris scolded her with smile.

"Well she's beautiful, and single about twenty six years old, brought up on a farm, she would make a good wife," she said and gave him a slight smile.

Chris smiled back at Elizabeth. "Apart from being brought up on a farm you described yourself."

"Oh Chris," Elizabeth muttered. "I do love you."

Chris put his arm under the neck of Elizabeth, and for a while they laid close together in silence.

"Do the family know?" Elizabeth asked breaking the silence.

"I had every intention of going to tell them, but I have Cam searching the park, I am waiting on his report, he never came back to the station tonight, and I knew you were waiting, so I will do it tomorrow."

"It won't be pleasant for Rosemary, or his mother," Elizabeth replied. "They both adore him, it will be a great loss to them, you must catch who ever is responsible Chris."

"I will do my best," Chris assured her.

Chris and Elizabeth laid like that for a while, Chris smiled as he heard the gentle snore of Elizabeth, realising she was asleep, he gently took his arm from under her neck turned back on his back, his thoughts went straight to his case.

Chapter Fifteen

Chris entered the police station after waving goodbye to Elizabeth, he had been given his instructions on wrapping up should he go out, and also to eat his lunch she had put in his pocket, with the usual kiss on the cheek, he had watched his wife as she walked away.

"Morning Sergeant," he said seeing sergeant Dawkins at the desk.

"Morning Inspector," he replied. "Last one in," he smirked.

Chris checked his watch as he made for his office. "Ten minutes to go yet sergeant, I'll have time for a nice cup of tea before I start work."

Chris entered his office and found George and Cam at their desk.

"Dawkins have just told me I'm last in," Chris said as he hung his overcoat and trilby before crossing to his desk.

"I was in first," Cam replied. "He asked me if I had been kicked out of home?"

"He's never short of a remark," George commented with a laugh.

"I told him I had time for a cup of his tea, I did not hear his reply," Chris said with a smile sitting behind his desk. "Now Cam, I expected you last night, how did you get on with the search in the park?"

"Time just went," Cam replied. "It was Mr Jarvis telling us he was closing the park gates that made us stop. A good search was made, we completed the whole area, but found nothing, I did call in here around seven fifteen."

"You want overtime then?" George queried.

Cam smiled. "No not really, but I did keep the constables a couple hours over their time, without thinking I might add."

"I'll see to it Cam," Chris replied. "They deserve a little reward."

Sergeant Dawkins entered with a cup of tea he put before Chris. "I saw your Mr Crompton last night, you know the man who came in reporting his wife missing," sergeant Dawkins remarked. "In Colebrook Street."

"That's where he lives," George remarked.

"He was on a bicycle," replied the sergeant.

"I wonder where he had been?" Chris muttered.

"Not been," sergeant Dawkins answered with a grin. "Going, he was heading towards town."

"Really!" Chris responded with a tone of disbelief in his voice, looking at the sergeant. "What time was this?"

"Around nine, I was having a sneaky pint in the Guildhall Tavern before going home."

"Did he see you?" Chris asked as he picked up his tea cup.

"Doubt it, it was dark, and I left the pub following a couple other chaps," the sergeant replied.

"Thank you Sergeant," Chris praised with a smile after taking a drink. "Thank you for keeping your eyes open."

"Uniform is trained to keep their eyes open, as well as their ears," sergeant Dawkins remarked with a grin as he left the office.

Chris returned the grin. "What he told us was interesting, we are told Mr Crompton drinks heavy at nights, and here he is on a bike at nine o'clock riding up town, where could he be going?"

"For now time is passing," Chris turned to George.

"We can't keep the Mr Morris in suspense any longer, they must be told, I am expecting Melanie Roberts any minute now, would you take Cam with you and inform them about their son?"

"No problem," George replied, wondering, Chris had always been present before when having to give bad news. He looked at Cam. "We better get going then, we will walk."

A few moments after George and Cam left the office, Sergeant Dawkins was ushering Melanie Roberts in the office. Chris stood, offered his hand, and while offering her the interview chair thanked her for coming.

"That's alright, Mr Wood our manager has told me I would lose no money," Mel spoke as she sat.

Chris smiled at her. "Yes he seems an ideal manager to have, the reason I wanted to see you Miss Roberts, was because we have found a body, indications points to the body being that of Mr Ronald Morris a farmer's son at Worthy Road, your name has been mentioned as one of his girlfriends."

Mel's face saddened, looked down at her lap. "I'm sorry to hear that Inspector, he was a nice pleasant fella, yes I have been out with him a couple times."

"You were not steady then?" Chris asked.

"We could have been, he had a lot of girls after him, I did not mind that, because he always came back to me, and each time we grew a little closer."

"Really!" Chris replied. "So when was the last time you went out with him?"

Mel thought for a while before she answered. "Seven or eight days ago."

"What happened after that?" Chris asked.

"About eight days ago he came to see me at the hotel, we were going out that night, he was carrying his shotgun, he had been invited out on a shoot, he wanted to tell me that he might not be able to make the date."

"I see," Chris murmured. "He carried his shotgun into the hotel?" Chris asked with a surprised tone.

"It had a cloth cover," Mel replied. "But you could tell it was a gun, the same as when one is carrying their violin in a case, you can tell."

"I'm sure," Chris replied. "Then what happened?"

Mel shifted in the chair. "After he told me, I had to carry on cleaning, the hotel do not like you to have callers while working, anyway I was passing the bar twenty minutes later, and saw that Ronald was still there talking to Gods gift to men."

"Are you talking about Mrs Sharon Wedge?" Chris asked.

"Who else?" Mel said.

"What happened next?" Chris asked very interested.

"I waited until he left the hotel, then went outside and spoke to him, I was lucky no one was around, I told him not to go out with her, otherwise we were finished."

"His reply?" Chris asked as he raised his eyebrows.

"Not very encouraging," Mel replied. "Anyway," Mel continued, one word led to another, which led to me saying I did not want to see him anymore, I regretted saying that later that day."

"Are you saying Mrs Wedge is a loose woman?" Chris asked.

Mel laughed. "She has been married, has two sons, she can be as loose as she likes, whoever married her now would not expect her to be a virgin," Mel blushed.

"I understand that you do not like her Miss Roberts," Chris said. "You were not surprised then at what happened in the hotel room a couple weeks ago?"

"I don't think anyone was," Mel replied with a titter.

"Did you know Mr Crompton?" Chris suddenly asked.

"Only by sight," Mel replied. "I did warn Mrs Crompton about allowing her husband to speak to Sharon."

"Really!" Chris answered. "Why was that?"

"I caught them in the Cathedral Close sitting on a bench laughing and joking."

"Really!" Chris replied getting very interested. "How long ago?"

"Couple months ago now," Mel replied.

"Did she know you saw her?" Chris asked.

"No I don't think so, I turned back and retraced my steps, I did not want to pass them."

"Have you ever handled a shotgun Miss Roberts, did Mr Morris ever let you hold his gun?"

"I have held it, but never fired it, it's too long and heavy for me," Mel replied. "But then I am not particularly interested."

"Well thank you again Miss Roberts you have been very generous with your answers," Chris said standing. "I better not keep you longer, I don't want Mr Wood thinking I am taking an advantage."

Mel smiled. "He's alright," she replied as Chris opened the office door for her.

George and Cam walked the small gravel path to the front of the house. George knocked, then stood waiting for it to be answered.

"You had better let me do the talking Cam," George advised. "This is not a pleasant task, prepare yourself to witness grief."

Cam gave a weak smile as the door opened.

George could not speak for a moment as the young lady answering his knock, took his breath away, she was slender standing at about five-feet, three-inches, wearing a long floral dress. George thought her beautiful, she has small face with rosy cheeks, and curly blonde hair hanging to her shoulders.

"Can I help you?" she asked pleasantly.

Seconds passed before George was able to reply. "Excuse us please, we are here to see Mr Morris or his wife," he said in an apologetic tone.

The young lady smiled, and George knew he loved her in that instant.

"Father is in one of the fields at the moment, and mother is in town shopping, I am their daughter Rosemary, can I help?"

George cursed Chris at that moment, not wanting to be the bearer of bad news to this young lady. He took a deep breath. "I am Detective Sergeant House, and this is my colleague Detective Constable Streeter, we need to speak to your parents."

"It's about Ronald isn't it?" Rosemary asked directly, her face showing worry.

"I'm afraid so," George replied feeling bitter about it.

"Is it bad?" Rosemary asked.

"I have to ask a couple question first before I can answer that with any authority," George replied gently.

Rosemary fell backwards to the door, and George grabbed hold of her to stop her falling, George looked around, and saw a bench seat a few yards away on a grass patch to the side of the gravel path.

"Please," George remarked gently. "Let's sit on the bench, you need air," without any protest, Rosemary allowed George to convey her to the bench, where she sat.

"Thank you," Rosemary said with a trembling in her voice. "Have you found my brother?" she asked, her eyes widened.

"We have found a body, I am sorry, but until I have asked a couple of questions I can't be sure who it is, he had no identification on him," George replied as gently as possible.

"Perhaps I can help you," Rosemary replied with a deep sigh and wiping her eyes with her hand.

"Would you not rather wait for your parents to be here?" George asked softly.

Rosemary shook her head and sniffed. "It will kill my parents," she replied. "if I am able I would like to answer your questions, I can then comfort my parents from a complete shock."

A slight breeze was blowing, and George looked at Rosemary's face, bits of her curly hair was stuck to her face, George felt he wanted to clear her face, but knew he would have been out of order.

"Are you younger than your brother?" George asked.

Rosemary nodded with a sniff. "Some seven years."

George looked towards the road, he saw a woman approaching, she was wearing a bowler shaped hat and a long blue top coat, and she was carrying two wicker shopping bags. Seeing her daughter looking in distress, she dropped her baskets and ran to her.

"What is wrong Rosemary?" she asked as she sat and put her arm around her. "Why are you upset?" she looked at

George who was sitting the other side of Rosemary. "What have you been saying to my daughter?" she demanded.

"It's alright mother," Rosemary said with a sniff. "They are from the police."

Rosemary's mother looked at George, and then at Cam who was standing to one side of George, her face looked worried. "It's my son?" she choked on her words.

"I'm sorry Mrs Morris, I called to tell your husband that we have found the body of a man who matches your son's description, only your daughter was here, before I can confirm, I need to ask a couple of questions."

"Then get on with it," Mrs Morris replied her face frightened but serious, as she pulled Rosemary nearer to her.

"The body we found had no identification on him, our only hope is for someone to identify him, however it's not a pleasant task, we cannot invite people to identify a body, unless we are one hundred percent sure," George tried to explain.

"I understand," Mrs Morris nodded. "Please what do you want to know?"

"Did your son at some time during his youth cut his left leg, for which he received hospital treatment?" George asked in a kindly voice.

Mrs Morris stared at George, George thought she was trying to hide her tears, then her face flooded with tears. "Oh no," she groaned in a pitiful cry.

George looked at Cam bewildered, unsure what to do, it was obvious that the body was of her son. George did not interfere with their grief, which he thought was heart breaking, he again cursed Chris for sending him on this task.

It was several minutes before Mrs Morris broke away from Rosemary, she took a hanky from her coat pocket and dried her eyes and face, there was still a sob in her voice when she spoke. "I do not know your name?" she said, her voice trembling.

George introduced himself and Cam.

"My son Sergeant, was climbing trees, he was twelve years old, somehow he had an accident, and split his leg open, it was so bad we rushed him to the hospital, where he had fourteen stitches, it has left a whitish scar," Mrs Morris stated. "It seems likely that your body is my son," again her face flooded with tears which she wiped away with her hanky.

"Come Rosemary, I think we should go inside now," she said pulling Rosemary to her feet. "We must get hold of your father."

While Cam went to pick up the shopping baskets that Mrs Morris had dropped, George followed Mrs Morris and Rosemary who were both weeping and helping each other into the flag stone floor kitchen of the farm house.

Mrs Morris sat on a dining chair, then looked at the clock. "My husband usually comes in about this time for a break."

"Please have a seat, I should not think he will be long, I'll put the kettle on, I expect you can do with one?" she said with a sob and wiping her eyes.

"Please don't bother yourself for us," George replied sincerely.

Rosemary rose from her chair, her eyes was red. "Mother I'll do that," she said. Rosemary went to the range, the kettle was already boiling, her whole body shaking managed to put the tealeaf into the teapot and pour the water into it.

"Where was my brother found?" she asked with a sob as she brought the teapot to the table.

"Constable Streeter here, found him while on a routine search at the back of the park, on land adjoining to yours," George replied.

Mrs Morris let out a groan. "How was he killed?" she choked out the words without looking up.

Cam looked at George, this was the first time he had been the bearer of bad news, and did not like it. "We believe he was struck on the back of the neck," Cam replied his voice shaking. "I don't think he suffered."

Rosemary rushed to the kitchen door. "Father's here," she shouted, dabbing the tears from her eyes.

Mr Morris entered the kitchen, he saw his wife and daughter in distress. He looked at George and Cam.

"What's going on?" he asked, his face stern and angry as he hurried over to his wife. Mrs Morris looked up to him with her tear stained eyes, she grabbed his hand. "They have found Ronald," she sobbed.

For a moment Mr Morris did not speak, then still holding his wife's hand he sat in the vacant chair next to her. Rosemary came and sat next to him.

"Oh dad," she sobbed, as she held her father's other hand. "Ronny is dead," she said,her voice trembling uncontrollably.

George could see that Mr Morris was fighting against his emotions, his eyes were already watery. George introduced himself and Cam.

"Constable Streeter was doing a routing search at the back of the park yesterday, he found a body fully clothed but without any identification, the description fitted that which you gave to our Inspector."

"You have waited until now to inform us?" Mr Morris asked in a whisper.

"We have to be sure before we upset people who have missing relatives," George replied. "Descriptions are one thing, but in many cases, we need other things to enable us to be sure, like a birth mark, or in your case, a scar on his left leg," George explained with a very professional manner.

"How long had he been dead?" Mr Morris asked in an acceptance voice.

"We believe since Sunday," George replied.

Mr Morris nodded his head. "The night he fail to return home, you said he had no identification on him, no wallet?"

"I'm afraid not Sir," George replied respectfully. "No watch, no ring, not even a key, everything was taken from his body."

Mr Morris nodded his head. "Why were you searching the park, did you have some idea?"

George shook his head. "No sir, it was being searched for another reason."

"So my son could have laid there for several more days or weeks even had it not been for this other reason," Mr Morris remarked with anger in his voice.

George shrugged, his eyes fell on Rosemary, he saw the tears in her eyes sparkling like the stars. "If we can do anything for you?" George remarked before stopping with Mr Morris interruption.

"When can we see him?" he asked.

"I would say tomorrow, he is with the police surgeon at the moment, a constable or myself will take you Sir, your son must be identified formally before his body can be released," he said in a very convincing voice.

"We shall be here waiting Sergeant," Mr Morris said getting up. "Thank you for calling, but now we would like to be on our own."

"Certainly Sir," George replied getting up. "I am so sorry to be the bearer of your bad news."

"Is it always like that?" Cam asked George as they walked back to the station.

"Losing a love one, is bound to bring grief Cam," George replied. "Unfortunately it's a part of the job, we have to do it."

"Worse part," Cam replied.

Chris was at his desk when George and Cam entered, he could see that they were not happy. "Bad time?" he asked as they went to their desks.

"I rather give up this job than do that again," George replied unsmiling.

"No, you won't George," Chris replied. "You are a policeman, sometimes, especially in our branch, we have to do unpleasant things, but you're a policeman because you want to catch the people responsible for peoples grief, sometimes you are the bearer of bad news, sometimes you can also deliver good news, even to the people you have given bad news to."

"They took it badly anyway," George replied.

"Did you see their daughter Rosemary?" Chris asked.

George looked at Chris. "Did you know there was a daughter?" he asked wondering.

"Only last night, she was a school friend of Elizabeth," Chris replied. "Elizabeth thought her to be beautiful."

"She is certainly," Cam spoke up. "Don't find many like her, at least I don't."

George controlled the little jealousy he felt with Cam's remarked, and wondered why he should feel so. "She is certainly beautiful, I have told them they can identify the body tomorrow, if there is no objection, I would like to take them," George spoke in a quiet, calm manner.

Chris thought for a while, he knew he was on his day off tomorrow, he lifted his receiver and spoke into the mouthpiece. "Sergeant get me Mr Bob Harvey if you can," he said replacing the receiver.

"Will they all be going?" Chris asked to George.

"Don't know, but they seem to be a very close family, perhaps they might all want to go," George replied.

The phone rang, and Chris took the receiver. "Hello Bob, are you busy?" Chris said into the mouthpiece.

"Don't tell me another body?" Bob replied.

Chris laughed. "No Bob, tomorrow is Saturday, Mr Morris want to see his son tomorrow, I'm just wondering, will this be possible?"

"I won't be there," Bob replied, but there will be someone there until midday."

"Thank you Bob, just wanted to make sure," Chris replied.

"I'm glad you phoned Chris," Bob continued before Chris put the phone down. "I have checked the bodies for drugs as you wanted, I found they had a barbiturate in their blood."

Chris quickly picked up a pencil. "What do they do?" Chris asked.

"It is used in operations," Bob replied. "Used wrongly they can put you into a coma, even lead to death."

"Really!" Chris replied as he scribbled the details on a sheet of paper.

"I have no idea what barbiturate was used, but I would say that they were both unconscious when shot," Bob spoke.

"That could be why they were together?" Chris aired his thoughts.

"Another thing Chris, your theory regarding a cricket bat could be right in the case of Mr Morris, I would utter a guess that he could have been struck with the edge of a cricket bat."

"Thank you Bob," Chris replied.

"Well that's settled then," Chris remarked replacing the receiver. "I had to check George, tomorrow is Saturday, I was not sure," Chris explained.

"I completely forgot," George remarked. "It's your day off as well."

"You will have to get Morris family down the morgue before midday," Chris answered.

George nodded his head. "What's this about drugs?" he asked.

"It has been on my mind, wondering how two people who we believe do not know each other came together in the park and both shot," Chris thought for a moment before answering. "The thought crossed my mind that they might both had been drugged and were carried there, so I asked Bob to check, he found barbiturates in their blood."

"What are barbiturates?" Cam asked.

"They can put people to sleep," Chris replied not really knowing about them.

"If they were carried to the park wouldn't they wake up?" Cam asked curiously.

"Bob told me that barbiturates are used when a person is operated, they can also put you into a coma, that could lead to death," Chris replied.

"Even so," George joined the conversation. "Carrying two bodies into the park would have been risky and very difficult?"

"That's the flaw in my thinking George," Chris replied. "But however it was done, I am sure they were both carried there, Bob also told me that Mr Morris was probably killed by being hit with the edge of a cricket bat."

"How did your interview with Miss Roberts go?" George asked.

"Useful, she did give one more lead to our case, she told me she caught Mr Crompton and Mrs Wedge together several weeks ago in the Cathedral Close. She managed to get away without being seen by them, she told me they were laughing and joking."

"That could be useful," George replied.

"She did go out with Ronald Morris for a while, but gave him up when Mrs Wedge made a play for him, and if I understood her rightly, Mrs Wedge did go out with him," Chris spoke.

"Mrs Wedge seems to go out with every man," Cam remarked seriously.

Chris made no comment to that.

"What's our next step then Chris, it's a job to keep up with everything, all that seems to lead nowhere," George asked.

Chris smiled. "I'm not so sure about that George, a picture is beginning to form."

"I wish you would tell me then," George replied with a grin, knowing until sure, Chris would not air his thoughts.

"Me also," Cam remarked. "I have no idea where we are, I am following you two."

"I am always asking myself in a case like this, how was it done, where was it done, and why, once I know that all the information then we will have who done it," Chris replied with a grin. "However, I am now going to see Mr Morgan the solicitor in St Peters Street, I feel I should inform him about Mr Wedge."

"Anything for us to do?" George asked.

"Well it's coming to midday," Chris replied. "I would take a break, but remember Mr Crompton's name is cropping up more and more, thoughts on how we can get more information on him would be useful?"

"Do you think, Chris do know who the murderer is George?" Cam asked after Chris had left.

"I'm not accepting that two bodies were carried into the park and shot," George answered. "But to your question the answer is yes, he has some idea."

"Have you?" Cam asked.

George nodded his head. "I have thoughts who it could be, Chris sees things that most do not, perhaps as he said, he wonders how it was done, rather than who done it, and that gives him a better insight."

"Why don't he tell who he thinks it is?" Cam asked.

"As a team we know everything that is said and going on," George replied.

"We all have the same information, we are three minds, and Chris wants each of us to use them, should Chris tell us who he believes may be the killer without really knowing, he believes that our minds might concentrate on his thoughts only, and that's not good, he always admits that he could be wrong."

Chapter Sixteen

C hris entered the office of Morgan and White Solicitors in St Peters Street, and was shown straight into Mr Morgan's office.

"I was about to phone you Inspector," Mr Morgan remarked after he offered Chris a chair. "Mrs Wedge phoned, she told me her ex husband had been found dead."

"I do owe you an apology Mr Morgan," Chris replied. "His body had been found and identified by Mrs Wedge by the time you had called on us, it was I'm afraid my detective mind that stopped me from telling you, you see I could not understand why she had not told you of his death, she knew five days ago you visited us, also why she had not told us about your visit?"

"I see," Mr Morgan replied. "Do you understand her delay now?"

Chris shook his head. "The reason escapes me at the moment."

"Was he murdered?" Mr Morgan asked.

"Definitely," Chris replied. "Will it make a difference to her sons?"

Mr Morgan cleared his throat as he shuffled a few papers in front of him. "It will hold things up for a while, but as long as the sons are not involved in their father's murder, it should be straightforward."

"I would doubt that very much Mr Morgan," Chris replied. "The oldest son is only twelve."

"Nevertheless, I will have to follow the case until it is solved, any idea how long it will take?"

Chris shook his head. "Sorry no way of telling."

"Can you keep me informed?" Mr Morgan asked.

"Certainly Mr Morgan," Chris replied getting up. "Once again I must apologise."

"No harm done I suppose Inspector, I await your outcome of the case, I shall need his death certificate," Mr Morgan said offering his hand.

Chris left the solicitor's office, it was just a few yards from North Walls, turning right and crossing the road as he did so, he entered into the park. He felt his pocket, and smiled as he felt the sandwiches that Elizabeth had put there, he saw a bench seat on the verge of the playing pitch facing to Gordon Road, and decided he would eat his sandwiches there.

As he ate, Chris stared at the side wall of number one, while he was there, Chris decided he would knock on number one. There was no answer to his knock, Chris looked into the window, through a slit in the drawn blinds, the room seemed bare, he only saw a table and chairs, but that was all, on the table there were glasses and bottles. Chris decided to try the side gate, after all he was on police business but was disappointed to find it locked.

"You won't find anyone at home," a voice said, making Chris look at the next door neighbour that was standing on the pavement outside number two. He was an oldish man, with grey hair. He wore a collarless shirt, trousers and waistcoat, with only slippers on his feet. Chris who was wearing his overcoat wondered if he felt the cold.

"I'm looking for Mr Alfred Light," Chris replied.

"That's his name is it?" the man replied with a smile. "They are new tenants, moved in I believe last Sunday, though for a week before there was noises in the house during the evenings."

"You have seen them?" Chris asked.

"Not that I would be able to recognise them," the man replied. "They seem to come after dark, it could be that they are working during the day."

Chris walked towards the man. "I am Detective Inspector Hardie," Chris introduced himself. "You are..?"

"Bill Taylor RSM, Regimental Sergeant Major, retired Sir," replied the man proudly.

"Army man," Chris remarked.

"Thirty years, I served Queen and Country," he replied proudly "And a couple for King and Country."

"Congratulations Mr Taylor," Chris replied a smile on his face. "I did wonder how you dealt with the cold, standing outside without a top coat, you want my wife, she would tell you off."

"My misses is the same God Bless Her," Bill laughed. "But we are tough, had to be with the places I've been, must have cold blood, don't fill the cold a lot like other people."

"You should however keep warm," Chris insisted. "Remember you are not as young now."

"I've just made a pot of tea, come in and have one, you never know your friend might turn up a little later, the wife God Bless Her is in town shopping, I'm on my own."

Chris smiled, but did not refuse, he welcomed the thought. "Thank you Mr Taylor," Chris replied removing his trilby, as he followed inside.

Chris was shown into the room with the bay window that looked out onto Gordon Road, it was clean and neatly furnished.

"Have you lived here long?" Chris asked taking a seat at the table.

"Ever since I retired, eleven years now," Bill replied. "The wife God Bless Her likes it here, it's quiet and peaceful."

"I'm sure it is," Chris agreed as Bill put a cup of tea in front of him.

"A Sergeant House was here," Bill remarked as he was about to take a drink of his tea. "I remembered his name because I live in one," he laughed loudly at the idea.

"Easy name to remember," Chris laughed, he saw the funny side of his remark. "You did not hear any noise that sounded like a gun going off last Sunday night?" Chris asked.

"I've heard thousands of guns going off," Bill smiled. "But for the life of me I can't honestly say I did, I have been thinking since the Sergeant called, I can only think that if there was a gunshot I was in the toilet or somewhere that would block the noise out."

"That could be Mr Taylor, what about your wife?"

"My wife God Bless Her was in this room all evening listening to the radio, there was a band playing, that could be the reason," Bill replied.

Chris took a drink of his tea. "You said there was a lot of noise coming and going that night at number one," Chris questioned as he put his cup down on the table. "Were there many people?"

"A couple women and two or three men," Bill replied. "I went to the window to watch for a while, but the wife God Bless Her, told me to come away it was none of our business, I saw a man and woman come to the house about quarter to eight, but not together. About half past eight or around that time I took another look and saw a man and a woman carrying something going into the house."

"Really!" Chris replied now very interested. "Would you be able to recognise them?"

Bill gave a little grin. "Not at that time Inspector, you can see the outline only, no lights around here, but the first man and woman, although not together were both young I would say in their thirties."

Chris got up and looked out of the bay window. "Mr Taylor, say around eight to half past can you see the park keeper's bungalow?"

"Not half past eight," Bill replied. "Just the glow from park keeper's window, as I told you we have no lighting around here, the park has no lighting, it's just a solid mass of darkness apart from the glow from the bungalow."

"I take it there is no way you can get into the park from here after the park is closed, apart from the path way pass the bungalow?" Chris asked.

"The gate for horse and carts is over there, you can see it from where you are, but that is kept locked, at this side of the park," Bill added. "Plenty of ways at the top end."

Chris turned away from the window. "In your opinion Mr Taylor, what would be the risk of being seen entering the park, say eight or after at night without being seen?"

Bill thought for a while. "As I said with no lights in the road or park, it's very dark, only the park keeper's bungalow lights penetrate the darkness, the park keeper keeping his eyes open would be able to see all that used the path, and Sunday was no exception."

"Really!" Chris remarked.

"It was park keeper's lights that enabled me to see the shadowy figures approaching number one," Bill remarked.

Chris took his trilby from the table. "Thank you Mr Taylor, you have been very helpful, and thank you for the tea, but I must get along now," Chris added.

Chris fumbled in his waistcoat pocket and brought out a card. "I would be most grateful should you find number one is occupied, if you could ask him ring the station any time day or night the number is on the card."

"You can rely on me Inspector, and please call any time," Mr Taylor replied showing Chris the door. "It's a pleasure for me to have a chat with a man for a change, the wife God Bless Her do not like men's talk."

Chris went over in his mind what Mr Taylor had told him as he made his way to the police station, where he found just Cam at his desk.

"George on a mission?" he asked Cam as he took off his top coat and trilby and hung them.

"I took the first lunch break," Cam informed him. "George is having his."

Chris crossed to his desk. "How are you getting on with this case in your own mind Cam?" Chris asked, not wanting to tell of his morning activities until George was back.

"I have no idea Chris," Cam answered. "Somehow I can't see a woman shooting two people in the face stripping them and disappearing, however I have come to the conclusion that, there is more than one involved in these murders, perhaps three, I don't see it's possible for just one person. However, we only have Mr Crompton and Mrs Wedge as possible suspect at the moment, and neither of them seems capable, especially Mr Crompton who seemed genuinely upset with his wife's murder, if I am right about three being involved, I only have Mr Jarvis, and that missing guest, Mr Wright to consider, and Mr Jarvis is really out of it, he do have an alibi."

"Apart from Mr Morris our latest victim, you have named most of the people who could be involved Cam," Chris reminded him. "You have not mentioned the Morris."

"You don't really suspect any of those do you?" Cam asked seriously.

"I suspect everyone that could possibly be connected," Chris replied. "What you have to consider now is the reason or motive for the killings, and which of those names you mentioned had the reason or motive, and the opportunity. The motive should be your first line of thought, once you have that, you have the murderer, you do have all the information that we have," Chris added.

George entered the office. "Had a pint and a sandwich," he said crossing to his desk.

"Didn't really enjoy it, this case always on my mind, I am however sure that the motive for this crime is to do with Mr Wedge's inheritance, but if Mrs Wedge committed the crime, and I don't know how she did it, what would she gain?"

"She would have the opportunity of digging into that money, also she would be able to run her son's farm for several years without interference," Chris replied.

George did not comment. "How did you get on with Mr Morgan?" he asked.

Chris told them of his visit.

"He did say that as Mr Wedge was murdered, nothing could be finalised until after the case is solved, so we do have breathing space."

George shook his head, he was quiet for a few seconds, then he asked. "After all, if she is going to Australia, she will have to book a ships passage?"

"Good thinking George," Chris replied. "Don't forget however, she might have booked through an advert in the papers, not all crossings are at the travel agency."

"I'll bring a couple newspapers in tomorrow," George replied.

"Don't forget you are going to the morgue tomorrow morning George, that might take time," Chris reminded him.

"Cam can go to the travel agents, only one in Winchester I think," George suggested.

"My mum always have the daily paper, I'll look through them tonight," Cam offered.

"Good, now we are moving again," Chris replied, and told them about his meeting with Mr Bill Taylor number 2 at Gordon Road.

Chapter Seventeen

*E*lizabeth was waiting for Chris as he left the police station, she gave him a kiss on the cheek and smiled as she did up the buttons on his top coat, that he had no chance of doing before leaving the station.

"It's colder at night," she scolded, as they started to walk home and she clung to his arm. "You're not happy with this case are you darling?" she asked.

Chris smiled and patted her arm. "Actually I think I know who done it but not how it was done, I am lacking one piece of information before I can complete the picture."

"It's an important piece?" Elizabeth asked.

"Without it I have no case," Chris replied.

"It will come darling," Elizabeth reassured him. "Are you hungry?"

"I can eat, but I do feel a little tired," he replied. "Those sandwiches came in handy today, I enjoyed them."

Elizabeth smiled, and squeezed his arm. "Mum will have a meal ready for us, we won't stay long, we will have an early night, I'll cuddle you and give you my warmth, you will soon fall asleep."

Chris smiled to himself, Elizabeth was like a piece of toast in bed, and feeling her warmth had several times drove him to sleep while thinking of the case. True to her word, Elizabeth made excuses to Ron and Olive after their meal and after a short time of chit chat, Chris found himself in bed before nine, which was unusual for him, and he fell straight to sleep.

Chris woke feeling fresh, he gently lifted Elizabeth's arm which was over his chest, and slid out of bed, his bedside table clock told him it was seven thirty. Making as little noise as possible, Chris dressed and left the bedroom, going to the scullery, he washed and shaved, then prepared the breakfast of bacon and eggs. He knew that Elizabeth had to work during the morning.

It was past eight when Elizabeth came downstairs, she was dressed, but her hair was all over her face.

"Why didn't you wake me darling?" she said as she kissed him good morning.

"You looked very peaceful," Chris replied. "There is hot water for you to wash, and I have your breakfast ready."

"Smells good," Elizabeth replied as she took the kettle from the gas stove and poured the water into a bowl lying in the sink. "What time did you get up?"

"Only half an hour ago," Chris replied as he transferred the bacon and eggs from the frying pan to the plates. "Tea is ready on the table," he said as he took the plates into the front room.

"You are sweet darling," Elizabeth said as they sat face each other at the dining table. "You should be having a lay in bed, it's your day off."

"I slept well," Chris replied. "I feel like a new man."

"You should have woke me up," Elizabeth giggled as she poured out two cups of tea. "I'm here to obey."

Chris smiled as he ate his bacon and eggs. "I might go and have a pint with Ron dinner time," he said.

"Dad will like that," Elizabeth replied as the newly install telephone rang. "That's our first call," she added.

"Yes but I'm dreading on who it can be?" Chris replied as he got up and went to the sideboard where the phone stood. "Good morning," Chris said into the receiver.

"Sergeant Williams here Sir," came the reply. "I have just had a call from a Mr Light of number one at Gordon Road, he has heard that you wanted to see him, and that he will call at the station after nine this morning."

"No definite time Sergeant?" Chris asked.

"No Sir," came the reply.

Chris thought for a while, he knew that George was taking the Morris family to the morgue that morning. "Very well sergeant, tell Sergeant House when he comes, I'll pop in around nine."

"Very good Sir," came the reply and the phone going dead.

"From the station," Chris said to Elizabeth as he returned to the table.

"Oh dear darling," Elizabeth replied. "Eat your breakfast before it gets cold."

"I'm not called in," Chris remarked as he ate. "It's just that a man who we need to interview will call at the station after nine, George has an appointment this morning, I'm worried that the two meetings might overlap."

Elizabeth filled up Chris's empty tea cup without comment.

"I'll walk you to work love," Chris offered. "I'll call in the station on my way home."

The Guildhall clock struck nine, as Chris got his kiss on the cheek outside Elizabeth's bank. Chris dug his hands into his trouser pockets as he made his way back to the station, it was a warm morning he wore no top coat.

Both George and Cam greeted Chris as he entered the office.

135

"I had a call this morning from Sergeant Williams, did you get the message George?" Chris asked.

"He left the message with Sergeant Dawkins when he came on duty," George replied.

"You are going to the morgue this morning, and with no definite time for Mr Light to come, I am wondering what do you intend to do?" Chris asked as he sat at his desk.

George felt annoyed, not at Chris who he knew was not interfering, but at himself, he wanted to see Rosemary again, he also knew that the interview with Mr Light was a must. He knew also that Chris would expect him to send Cam to escort the Morris family to the morgue.

"I thought I would wait until ten or ten thirty, if Mr Light had not turned up I would send Cam to escort the Morris family," George replied.

"Good man," Chris replied getting the answer he expected from George.

"Well I leave you both, I'll have a pint in the pub with my father-in-law at twelve," he smiled getting up. "I'll be home until then George if you need me."

"Let's hope not Chris," George replied. "You need a day off, clears the mind," he smiled.

"Well if I don't see you both before I'll see you both Monday," Chris replied as he left the office, but really wanting to stay.

Chris left the station, he could have stayed and took charge, but he did not want to undermined George, who he knew was perfectly capable of taking the interview with Mr Light, but still his mind was uneasy. Halfway home he changed his mind and decided to pop into his in-law's house, where both Ron and Olive welcomed him with a cup of tea.

Ron who was sitting in his armchair reading the paper, looked at Chris over the top of his glasses. "Want to talk about it Chris?" he asked. "You have something on your mind."

Chris smiled. "This case, it all seems too far fetched to be true, yet it's got to be, or I am well off the track."

While Olive was busy elsewhere in the house, Chris told Ron of his thoughts and his belief about who done it.

"I don't know much about detective work Chris," Ron admitted. "But it do seem you have all the suspects all neatly tied up, you have to get your proof however, really in my mind you have just one thing to do, search the park keeper's bungalow, and hope," he advised.

"I'll have to check what our powers are regarding that Ron," Chris replied. "In August 1914, at the start of the War, the police were given extra powers, I might be able to use one of them," Chris added.

"You should be able to search a house if it's holding evidence," Ron remarked.

"Quite so," Chris replied. "But an Englishman's home is his castle, and we are quite a free people. One has to be absolutely sure that they would find evidence in the house, unfortunately the belief of that is often just an assumption."

Ron shrugged his shoulders. "The rights of law-abiding citizens then, are beneficial to the criminal?"

"That's the way of the world Ron, but I might find a way in?" Chris answered.

Ron and Chris left the house at twelve to go to the pub as Olive standing outside the front door with a smile on her face.

Chapter Eighteen

Because Elizabeth had to be at work a little earlier on the Monday morning, Chris found himself in an empty office. Having discarded his top coat and trilby, he sat behind his desk, took out his pipe and lit it, before taking up the sheet of handwritten writing. It was about the interview that George had with Mr Light on Saturday morning. Puffing on his pipe, Chris read the report twice before putting it down, shaking his head. He picked up a large envelope that was addressed to him, he was just about to open it when George and Cam entered.

"A day off do wonders for you Chris, what happened couldn't you sleep?" George remarked.

"Elizabeth had to be in early, and that makes me early," Chris replied.

"Morning Cam," Chris greeted him.

"Morning Chris," Cam replied making for his desk.

"I have read your report about Mr Light number one at Gordon Road," Chris remarked as he watched George sit at his desk. "Are you satisfied?"

"I can only go on what I am told," George replied. "He told me he had rented the house, but had not furnished it yet, he is living in a bed and breakfast for the time being, the address is there."

"I noticed," Chris replied.

"He said he did have friends there on Sunday night like housewarming party, they had a few drinks, and they left, he was unable to give me exact times, he gave me the names however, they are in the report," George remarked.

"He never heard a gunshot then?" Chris asked.

"He said he did not, but as he said, they were having a housewarming party, and they were not quiet and would have to apologise to the next door neighbour when he sees them," George explained.

"What's he like?" Chris asked.

"Smart well groomed, pleasant I suppose, I have no idea what a woman calls handsome," George smiled. "Around mid thirties I would imagine."

"I can vouch for the drinks they had, when I looked through a slip in the blinds, I saw glasses and bottles on the table," Chris commented.

"It was early enough for you to go to the morgue?" Chris asked curiously.

"Yes they came in about mid morning, all the Morris family came to the morgue, it was upsetting, they seem to be a close family," George replied. "They identified the body."

Chris puffed on his pipe a few more times, then laid it in the ashtray and picked up the envelope again. "Any luck with the travel agent?" he asked.

George shook his head. "Not yet, but we are waiting a couple calls from paper adverts."

Chris opened the envelope and took out a photograph, with a note attached.

"Dear Chris," it said. "This is the photo of Mr Wright, it may be of use to you, don't forget if you see him, let me know," Fred Willett.

"Is this your Mr Light?" Chris asked George passing over the photo.

"That's him," George replied, there was a surprised, puzzled look on his face. "Where did you get it?"

"Inspector Fred Willett sent it to me," Chris answered.

"Then that means, he is Mr Wright, the guest from the hotel," George replied a little amazed and passing the photo to Cam.

"That means Mr Wright using a false name under the Mr Light," George murmured to himself look of confusion on his face.

"Afraid so George, which means we have to visit him, good job you have his address at the moment, otherwise we would be waiting. Did he tell you where he was working now?"

"He's not working, although he did have a job lined up for when he is settled in Gordon Road," George replied. "I feel like a fool now, he did have identification on him, I had no reason to think he was anyone else but who he said he was."

"Not your fault George," Chris replied. "We can only go on what people tell us, pity we did not have this photo earlier, Cam you will have to take charge of the office, George and myself have a visit to make, we need two bikes."

Chris knocked on the bed and breakfast door along St Cross road and waited. The door eventually opened by a stout pleasant looking woman. "Gentlemen," she smiled. "Are you looking for bed and breakfast, if so I am afraid I only have one room vacant."

"We have called to see one of your guest madam," George informed her. "Mr Light."

"Oh yes, well he is in, he has just had his breakfast, not an early riser you see," she smiled. "Step into the hall, I'll call him."

Chris took off his trilby, and followed by George stepped inside.

The landlady took her leave, returning in a few moments. "Mr Light will see you gentlemen," she said as she reached the bottom of the stairs. "First right on the first landing," she smiled, and she watched Chris and George take the stairs. "Would you like a cup of tea?"

"That is kind of you to offer," Chris replied. "But we will only be here a short time, but thanks anyway."

Mr Light was at his bedroom door, and welcomed the detectives inside. "Please," he said. "This is only a bedroom, you will have to sit where you can."

Chris took the only chair in the room, George sat on the edge of the bed, Mr Light remained standing.

"I never expected a visit from you so soon Sergeant," Mr Light said to George. "There must be other questions?"

"I am Detective Inspector Hardie Mr Light, or shall I call you Mr Wright, I need to ask you questions," Chris interrupted, he spoke with a scowl.

Mr Wright's body seem to go limp, and a worried look showed on his face. "How did you find out?" he asked leaning against the bedpost.

Chris produced his photo. "The Bournemouth Police are looking for you, your wife has reported you missing."

"Why would she do that, she knew I was leaving her, it's been on the cards for months," Mr Wright's eyes widened.

"I have no idea Mr Wright," Chris replied. "But I am investigating three murders," he said in a loud authoritative voice.

"Murders!" Mr Wright almost shouted before Chris could finish. "What am I to do with murders, I only left my wife?" he shook his head, he looked at the inspector in total surprise.

"You were a guest at the Suffolk Hotel in Winchester Mr Wright," Chris remarked.

"So was a lot of other people," Mr Wright said, alarmed.

"But you were having an affair with one of the victims," Chris remarked.

Mr Wright slapped his sides, as he moved around the room.

"OK, let's have it, what have people been saying, and who was the victim?" he asked, a look of horror and alarm spread slowly over his face.

"It has come to our notice that you had affair with both Mrs Crompton a room maid, and Mrs Wedge a barmaid during your stay at the Suffolk."

"Come Inspector," Mr Wright gave a weak smile as once again he leaned against the bedpost looking at Chris. "We are men of the world, what a couple of flings to do with murder?"

"I am not a man of the world Mr Wright," Chris replied not caring for his attitude. "You admit then that you had affairs with both these ladies?"

"I suppose I did, if they say I did, I've had a lot of affairs, you see Inspector, I am a man who should never have got married, I cannot be true to one woman, I'm sorry but there it is, but I don't go around murdering them," he replied, looking worried.

"You have not been accused of murder," Chris corrected.

"You hinted," Mr Wright replied.

"Mr Wright, I am investigating murder, and your name has cropped up, please cool down and answer my questions, or you will be arrested on suspicion."

Mr Wright slapped his sides again, moved to the door and leaned against it. "No need for threats Inspector, I'm all yours, what can I tell you?"

"You are an agent for a drug or medicine firm?" Chris asked, as he saw George busy with his pencil.

"I was, but no longer," Mr Wright replied.

"Did you carry samples?" Chris asked.

"I had to, you can't go into a hospital or a chemist empty handed," Mr Wright scorned.

"Do you carry barbiturates in your sample case?" Chris asked sternly.

"Of course I do," Mr Wright replied without thinking. "Why do you ask?"

"Answer me again Mr Wright, you did have an affair with Mrs Crompton and Mrs Wedge at the Suffolk Hotel?" Chris asked ignoring his question.

"Mrs Wedge and a young woman called Doris as far as I remember, Mrs Crompton was not that sort," he replied hesitatingly.

"Come Mr Wright, you made her pregnant," George spoke sharply.

"Mrs Crompton pregnant?" Mr Wright answered a shocked look on his face.

"I'm afraid that Mrs Crompton and her baby is dead," Chris spoke with a straight face.

Mr Wright seemed generally shocked. "She was a lovely woman, not appreciated by her husband," he said in a low voice. "But tell me how would you know it's my baby?"

"Her husband would have been unable, and you are the only other person she has been with," Chris replied.

Mr Wright walked the room, he was thinking hard. "OK," he said. "I did have an affair with all three but I had no part in any killing."

"Mr Wright, you left your wife because you were not getting along, as you told us one woman is not enough for you, but why pick this particular time and leave your employment, was it because you found your barbiturate missing?"

Both George and Mr Wright looked at Chris amazement on their faces.

"You seem to know everything Inspector, I might as well tell you the whole story," Mr Wright sat on the bed near George, he grasped his hands in front of him looking at the floor.

"With regards to my wife," he started. "As a traveller I am home for one or two half days a week if I'm lucky, while I am away, as you seem to know, I do have a fling on the side, but so did my wife, which I found out some months ago," Mr Wright sighed. "You might say that what's good for the goose, is good for the gander, meaning that if I had affairs, why should I punish my wife for doing the same, but I did, our love went into decline since I found out. However last time I was home over three weeks ago, she told me she wanted a divorce, strange but I was not upset, I packed my bags and left," he continued.

"Do you have any children?" Chris asked.

"Two boys at school," Mr Wright replied. "Both are very close to their mother, as I told you I am away a lot."

"If your wife accepted that you were leaving, why did she report you as a missing person?" George interrupted.

Mr Wright thought for a while. "I can only think that it's to do with the divorce, she do not know where I am, I had no intension of telling her, but she would need my signature for a quick divorce, perhaps it was the only way she had of finding me."

"Run me through what happened after you left?" Chris asked.

"I am on the road all the time, I rarely go back to my firm, I have my rounds that covers all of Hampshire. I have always liked Winchester, so I came back here and started to look for a place to rent, I found one in Gordon Road, it was out of the way, a dead end, and seemed ideal to me."

"But you stole another person's identity to get it," George remarked.

Mr Wright smiled. "My God you have been busy, I have underestimated you, no I did not steal my friend's identity, before coming to Winchester I saw my friend at Beaminster, I told him everything also that I would need to change my name, he told me that both our names were similar and told me to use his name, even gave me a few paid bills in his name."

"Mr Light, Alfred Light was the name I used to rent the number one at Gordon Road."

"Well whatever Mr Wright, you falsified a rental agreement, and that is illegal," Chris remarked. "So you came back to Winchester found a house, but carried on staying at the Suffolk Hotel?"

"My expenses cover that," Mr Wright replied. "You see I had to get the house furnished, and decorated before I moved in, it's still not ready, but I'm getting there."

"So you stayed at the Suffolk, while you were there you had affairs," Chris went over what had already been said. "Then you found your sample of barbiturates short or missing."

Mr Wright looked at Chris. "I have no idea how you could know that Inspector?" he replied with a surprised tone."But you are right, that is why I sent in my notice regarding my job, you see some of the samples we carry are very dangerous when used wrongly," he paused for a second,there was a worried look on his face but he continued.

"We sign for the samples, and pay for them, but should any be stolen we are supposed to report it to the police. I was in a difficult position, I was trying to hide, so I sent back my last order from Basingstoke, then I disappeared."

"That was after the affair that happened in your hotel room between Mrs Crompton and Mrs Wedge and yourself," Chris remarked.

"You never cease to amaze me Inspector," Mr Wright smiled as he replied.

"After I had left the hotel I found my barbiturates samples missing, I was unable to replace them, I had only one course, tell me inspector why are you so interested in barbiturates?"

"Two victims were found with barbiturates in their blood stream, as you say, you cannot just buy them over the counter, if I was a betting man, I would bet that the victims were fed with the barbiturates that you lost," Chris informed him.

"Has anyone asked you for any?" George asked.

"If they had, I certainly would not have given them, in the wrong hands they are dangerous," Mr Wright replied.

"Then who could have taken those that you lost?" George asked.

Mr Wright stood up straight and slapped his sides. "My case is with me all the time," he explained. "Not only that but locked."

"Even in your room?" Chris asked.

"I suppose if I needed something from my case, in my room I might leave it open," Mr Wright replied looking very worried. "I do remember several weeks ago showing Mrs Crompton the contents and explaining them, but normally the only time my case is open in front of people is when I am selling."

"What about the other women you had affairs with in the Suffolk, was your case unlocked while they were in your room?" Chris asked.

Mr Wright slapped his side as he walked towards the door. "I don't know, I suppose at one time or another it could have been, look," he said as he turned back to the bedpost. "Are you saying that I gave barbiturates to these people who you found dead?"

"Just trying to get to the truth Mr Wright," Chris replied. "You have to admit it is a quite coincidence that you travelling with drugs and having an affair with one of them, later to be found dead with the drug you lost found in her blood stream."

"I can't explain that Inspector, I can say I did not have any part in their deaths, what possible motive could I have, I make love to women, I don't kill them."

"Mrs Crompton was pregnant," George replied.

"You tell me it was mine, I'm not sure yet how you know it was mine?" Mr Wright asked.

"I'm afraid we did mislead you on that Mr Wright," Chris admitted. "But you are the most likely one."

Mr Wright stayed silent for a while before he spoke again. "You know when we are questioned by the police we are expected to tell them the truth, don't you think that courtesy should also be given to the person being questioned, however as for being the most likely, you should check the other hotel staff."

"I apologise to you Mr Wright, you are quite right," Chris replied feeling a little embarrassed. "Are you saying Mrs Crompton was having an affair with someone else in the hotel?"

Melanie told me she was, but did not name the person," Mr Wright answered.

"Really!" Chris spoke deep in thought. "Just one more question Mr Wright, the list of housewarming guest that you gave to Sergeant House, mentioned Mrs Wedge and Mr Webb."

"That's right Inspector, I know just a few people in Winchester, I invited Mrs Wedge and Mr Webb, also Mrs Crompton and her husband, who she did not appear, and I now know why."

During the ride back to the Police Station, George found Chris very quiet.

"That was a turn up for the books," Chris remarked when they were both seated at their desk.

"It lets him out, don't you think?" George asked.

"House number one at Gordon Road has been dismissed by me since Friday George," Chris answered. "I have studied the house from all sides, no way would anyone risk taking two bodies from there to the park, I had thought that the bodies could have been handed over the side wall, but there is a river in between, I know it's narrow, but getting two bodies across I can't see it, when you confirmed the photo being Mr Wright, I was sure."

"You never considered Mr Wright as a possible suspect then Chris," George asked.

"Only the barbiturates came from him one way or another," Chris answered.

"I'm in the dark here," Cam remarked who had been keeping silent.

Chris gave a little grin. "Sorry Cam," he said. "Then looking at George who related their interview with Mr Wright."

"What charges will he get?" Cam asked.

Chris leaned back in his chair. "You tell me Cam."

"Well he's using another name," Cam replied.

"In itself not a crime," Chris replied.

"He signed a contract with a false name," Cam argued.

"Yes, you can call yourself whatever name you want, but once you sign a document, it becomes forgery intending to mislead," Chris replied. "I have given him today to put it right."

"He might lose the house?" Cam replied.

"That's life Cam," Chris replied. "You have to take the consequences if you are found out doing something that is dishonest."

"What about his wife?" Cam asked.

"If he has committed a crime, it would be a civil crime, I have told him that I would have to inform Bournemouth Police, by the time I have done that this afternoon, I expect he would have already got in touch with his wife," Chris answered.

"Mrs Crompton's baby could still be his?" Cam argued.

"Agreed," Chris replied. "But unless the baby becomes the motive or part of it, who's going to mention it, only five of us know about it."

"Don't you think it should be?" Cam asked.

"Only if as I said becomes a part of the motive," Chris replied.

George listening to the debate smiled to himself, he knew Chris would not blacken a woman's name on purpose, even if she deserved it, Chris had a soft spot, which even the Chief Constable realised.

"You see Cam," Chris continued. "Every thing Mr Wright has done wrong, has been self inflicted, he left his wife his own choice, he took another name his own choice, he signed a document in that name his own choice, but illegal, he tried to hide his identity his own choice, he went with lots of women his own choice, but all of what he did is now out in the open, he may have to appear in court should we solve the case but apart from that, unless Mr Dodd the estate agent who rented him the house wants to take further action, he is more or less in the clear."

"Now," Chris remarked. "I think we were all thinking that the house in Gordon Road was connected to this case, we now know this to be unlikely," Chris paused for a while laying his pipe in the ashtray.

"The bodies had to get to the park somehow, they were not taken there by horse and cart, someone would have seen that?"

"You mean that they had to come from another house in Gordon Road?" Cam asked a little bewildered.

"If we discard number one at Gordon Road, we have to discard the other houses Cam," Chris replied. "There is one house we could consider," Chris spoke as rolled his eyes at Cam.

"Where's that?" Cam asked with excitement.

"The park keeper's bungalow," Chris answered.

"I thought his alibi was solid?" George replied, there was a surprised, puzzled look on his face.

"His alibi is," Chris agreed.

"But give a little thought, no one would see you carrying two bodies out of his bungalow, and he is just across from the bandstand, it could have been done quite easily, I believe they were drugged and stripped before taken to where they were found."

"We haven't found their clothes yet," Cam interrupted.

"No Cam," Chris pressed. "If as I believe the bodies were stripped before hand, no one would have been carrying a sack of clothes as we once thought, the clothes could be right under our nose when we find the house, apart from destroying them, the best place to hide clothes is in a wardrobe."

"That could explain it Chris," George remarked. "Mr Jarvis who was not at the bungalow on Sunday night, how come Mr Wedge and Mrs Crompton who we believe did not know each other, both entered the bungalow."

"When I know that George I will tell you, we know however that the bungalow was occupied while Mr Jarvis was in the pub," Chris answered with certainty.

"How?" Cam asked with eagerness in his voice.

Chris smiled. "Cam you must read about my meeting with Mr Taylor of Gordon Road."

"I have," Cam replied, wondering where he had slipped up.

"Then you must know that the bungalow lights were burning after the park had been closed, and while Mr Jarvis was in the pub," Chris replied in all seriousness.

Chris turned to George. "I have read Bob Harvey's report on Mr Morris again, he explains the death of Mr Morris as a struck to the neck with a hard object, like a chop of the hand," Chris explained demonstration with a chop of his own hand.

"He also reported that the chin had been split, and the blood was soaked up largely by the high neck woollen jumper he was wearing, he also admits that he is unable to say whether the body was removed to where it was found, and there was no barbiturates in his blood."

"Not related to our double murder then?" Cam remarked after a moment of thought.

"Don't jump to conclusion too quickly Cam," Chris replied. "At first we assumed there was a connection because we know he was carrying a shotgun which is still missing, I know he was found at the back of the park on ground that was overrun with bushes and trees, unkept so to speak, and out of view, but we also know that at the time of his death, thirty yards away there was a cricket match with plenty of people around, I have also asked myself what was he doing where he was found, it's not a spot people would walk to without reason."

"What have you come up with then Chris?" George asked.

"If he was killed where he was found, he had to lured there," Chris replied. "And I can't see a man doing that?" he smiled.

"You mean a woman?" Cam butted in.

"If I wanted to talk to a man, even if I was rowing or fighting with him, would I walk into that patch full of brambles and such to be out of sight, my answer is no, I might however go there if a woman came on to me?" Chris commented.

"I understand what you are saying Chris, but you don't believe that do you?" George asked bewildered.

Chris smiled. "You know me well George, no I believe his body was removed there, have thought so ever since Cam found him, I'm more sure."

"Could he have been killed with the other two?" Cam asked.

"I wish we knew that Cam," Chris replied. "George I want you to concentrate on Mr Ronald Morris murder, it will mean that you will have to visit them again."

"No problem Chris," George replied happy at the thought of seeing Rosemary again.

"Find out everything you can about the love life of the daughter and the son, there might be something?" Chris advised.

"Cam, if what Mr Wright told us this morning is right, then your friend Melanie Roberts might know the names of other men, who Mrs Crompton had affairs with, so meet her if you can," Chris gave his opinion.

"I can do that Chris," Cam replied. "I'll call on her tonight."

Chapter Nineteen

George had already left the office as Chris finished tidying his desk.

"Right Cam, you come with me, we have a couple of calls to make," Chris rose from his chair.

"Do we need bikes?" Cam asked.

"No it's not a bad day, the walk will do us good, first we are calling on Mr Jarvis at the park."

Mr Jarvis open the door to the knock. "Inspector," he said with a surprised look on his face. "I am having my dinner, but please come in, I won't take any notice," he smiled.

Followed by Cam, Chris entered the bungalow. "Nice place you have here," Chris remarked as he took a chair.

"Comes with the Job," Mr Jarvis replied. "Would you like a cup of tea?" he offered. "I have just made a pot."

"Thank you no," Chris replied looking at Cam. "I have just a few questions to ask, you carry on."

"It can wait," Mr Jarvis replied. "I only eat a hot meal at nights when I have more time to cook, now how can I help?"

"I'll come straight to the point Mr Jarvis, last Sunday week, did you allow anyone to use your bungalow?" Chris asked straight out.

Taken back a bit, Mr Jarvis forced a smile. "Why would you want to know that?" he asked, he had a confused look on his face.

"You will have to admit that the bodies you found on the Monday morning had to come from some where?" Chris remarked sharply.

"Perhaps they were carried," Mr Jarvis replied nervously, after a moment's thought.

"From where Mr Jarvis, dead bodies cannot just be carried through the streets, not forgetting they were both naked," Chris replied in a stern voice.

"I take your point Inspector," Mr Jarvis replied slowly his mind racing. "I did as a fact allow Susan to use the bungalow from six that night, do you think she had anything to do with what we found the next morning?"

"No way of knowing Mr Jarvis," Chris answered excited by the answer. "We have to build up a picture, and need to know everything before we can answer that."

"I see," remarked Mr Jarvis, then he smiled weakly. "Come Inspector you are having me on, you don't really believe that those two were murdered in my bungalow do you?"

"No, Mr Jarvis," Chris replied. "We know they were killed where they were found, but I believe they were drugged and stripped before taken to where we found them, they had to come from some place near the bandstand, this bungalow of yours do seem an ideal place."

"Oh dear," Mr Jarvis remarked his face worried and serious.

"Susan asked me if she could use my place from six to around nine that Sunday, she said she would make it worth my while, I have told you I was taken by her, and I allowed it, but I still can't believe she had anything to do with those murders."

"Why not run by me how all this came about?" Chris asked.

"I have told you how I first met Susan," Mr Jarvis replied. "Sunday morning I saw her sitting on the bench as usual, it was barely eight thirty, so I asked if she would like a cup of tea, so I brought her back here. While we were here, she told me that she was seeing a man, but was going to finish it once and for all. She asked me if she could use my bungalow just for a couple hours. I asked why, and she told me that the only time she saw him was in the park on a Sunday evening, she did not want a row outside where all could hear, and that was the reason."

"You agreed to it then?" Chris asked.

"Not at first, my mind was a bit suspicious, I didn't want her using this place for sex," Mr Jarvis smiled. "She assured me that it was not, so eventually I agreed, and she offered to give herself to me before she left."

"How was it to take place?" Chris asked smiling to himself.

"She wanted the place from six, not sure of the time this other man would turn up, she told me that if I went for a drink for an hour or two, she would join me when all was done, as you know I waited in the pub until almost nine, but she did not turn up."

"Where did you go when you left the Foresters?" Chris asked.

"Well it was late and dark, I was sitting by the window hoping to see Susan come out of Hyde Abbey Road, I did think I saw her, and rushed out, but when I caught this other woman up, it was not Susan, disappointed, and with a feeling that she would not be turning up, I decided to drown my sorrow, so I went to the Catherine Wheel Pub in Lower Brook Street. I got home after closing time, my place was clean and tidy, better in fact than I left it, I have not seen Susan since."

"Just a couple of questions Mr Jarvis then we will leave you in peace," Chris said. "How often do you look into your wardrobe?"

Mr Jarvis smiled at the question. "I don't know," he shrugged his shoulders.

"Not very often, I have the uniform I am wearing which I wear almost continuously, I wear it for about two or three months then have it cleaned, I have a spare one in the wardrobe, I do not need to dress up when I go out only going to the pub," Mr Jarvis answered.

"I hear you have a twelve bore shotgun Mr Jarvis?" Chris asked.

"That's right, I showed it to your Sergeant," Mr Jarvis replied. "Would you like to see it?"

"Very much so, also if you will allow, I would like to look into your wardrobe," Chris answered.

Mr Jarvis led the detectives into a back room, it was a bachelor bedroom, a double bed, wardrobe, a dresser drawers and a washstand. Mr Jarvis went to the wardrobe and brought out his bore gun and handed to Chris. "I have not used it for years," he said.

Chris studied the gun then passed it to Cam. "Your opinion Constable?" Chris asked.

Cam took the gun then broke it, the cartridge chambers were empty. "It needs a good clean," Cam advised. "I should give it a coating of oil if I were you Mr Jarvis, it's an expensive weapon."

"I have had it for years, can't remember the last time I used it," Mr Jarvis replied as Cam handed the gun back to Chris, who satisfied handed it back to Mr Jarvis.

"While you have the wardrobe open Mr Jarvis, would you check your clothing?" Chris suggested.

"Of course," he replied as he started to pull various items, then stopped.

"How did that suit get in here?" he asked aloud to himself, taking out a brown colour suit on a wooden hanger. "This is not mine Inspector," he remarked handing the suit to Chris.

Chris took the suit, looked at it, then searched the pockets which were empty.

"It's just what I thought Mr Jarvis, this suit probably belong to the male victim you saw that Monday morning under the bandstand," Chris laid the suit on the bed, keep looking Mr Jarvis. "What about shoes or ladies clothing?"

"I only have two pair Inspector, I am wearing one pair, and the other pair is here, no others, and certainly no women's clothing," Mr Jarvis answered.

"I will need to have this suit at the police station Mr Jarvis, I will get it picked up, have you any objections?"

Mr Jarvis gave a weak smile. "It would be no use to me Inspector, but I am not completely a fool, this suit prove that the male was stripped as you put it from this house."

"I'm afraid so," Chris agreed.

"Oh dear," replied Mr Jarvis. "What is the council going to say?"

"This house go with the job as you said Mr Jarvis, surely you are allowed to have guest," Chris replied.

"I suppose," Mr Jarvis answered. "But this bungalow being involved in a double murder, they are bound to hold me responsible, oh why did I fall for that woman?" Mr Jarvise said with a trembling in his voice.

"Cheer up Mr Jarvis, don't be hasty," Chris wanted to calm him down.

"I'll keep you informed about the case, and should the time come I will speak to the council on your behalf, in the mean time I'll have that suit picked up later today, but before I leave tell me again about the Salvation Band that was playing here that Sunday."

Mr Jarvis hesitated. "I am afraid I told you a little lie, the band stopped about five that afternoon, not later as I told you, I cleared the chairs, I have a truck similar to a railway porters truck, I can load a couple dozen chairs at a time on it, a few trips and they are all cleared, twenty minutes or so."

"I see," Chris replied. "And then?"

"It would have been about five thirty, I promised to be out of the bungalow by six, so I pop over here, rinsed my face combed my hair, then left. It was too early to close the park, so I went to the far end and watched the cricket match," Mr Jarvis continued.

"When the game finished about six thirty, I hung around and watched the people leaving, then I went to the main gate and locked it, then made my way to the Foresters from the Park Avenue, where I stayed until almost nine," Mr Jarvis concluded.

"Thank you Mr Jarvis, you will keep an eye open for a constable to collect this suit."

"Well we found a suit that I believe belonged to Mr Wedge, we will go to the Suffolk Hotel now," Chris said to Cam as they left Mr Jarvis's bungalow.

"I wonder where Mrs Crompton's clothes are?" Cam remarked.

"Women's clothing are very thin, not bulky like a man's can be, a woman could put the clothes she is wearing into a brown carrier bag, a man's suit and everything would be difficult," Chris replied. "It's the gun that worries me."

Mr Wood the manager welcomed Chris and Cam as they entered his office and offered them a chair.

"How are things going?" the manager asked with a smile.

"We are getting there Sir," Chris replied. "It takes a little time."

"I'm sure it do Inspector, now how can I help you?" Mr Wood asked.

"I was hoping to see your under manager Mr Roger Webb?" Chris answered.

"Ah, then you are unlucky today, our Mr Webb is on a three day course, he left early this morning, won't be back until Thursday I'm afraid," Mr Wood replied.

"That's a pity," Chris replied feeling disappointed.

"Perhaps I can help inspector?" Mr Wood offered.

"You told me that Mr Webb has a room in the hotel," Chris reminded. "Would he have to come through the hotel to get to his room?"

Mr Wood answered without hesitation. "No, he has also an entrance in St Georges Street."

"I was hoping to get his permission to see his room," Chris spoke. "It's a routine that all those who might be involved are requested to allow."

"Is our Mr Webb involved, Inspector?" Mr Wood asked with a look of surprise.

"He was at the park that night, and the crime is in a way centred around this hotel, suspect or not, we have to check upon him, just to eliminate him."

"I think I can understand that Inspector," Mr Wood replied. "Oh dear, this is all new to me, never since I have been manager have I had to enter a employee's room without permission," the manager murmured.

"I have no authority either Mr Wood," Chris replied. "However this is a treble murder investigation, with your presence, a look at his room could save us hours of investigation, I realise your position and very thankful of your past help, so perhaps I better wait the three days before he returns," Chris said with a disappointed look upon his face.

"You really want to search his room Inspector?" Mr Wood asked.

"Just look in a couple drawers, perhaps the wardrobe, nothing too serious, he would never know we have been in there," Chris replied hoping.

"Very well Inspector," Mr Wood replied having made up his mind. "I cannot say I like doing it, but in such a case, and if it clears our Mr Webb of any involvement, I'll take you there."

"Thank you very much Sir," Chris replied watching Mr Wood take a bunch of keys from his desk drawer. "I cannot thank you enough."

"If you follow me then," Mr Wood remarked. "We can get to his room from inside the hotel."

The room was a hotel single, containing a single bed, wardrobe and a chest of drawers, a washstand with a bowl and jug standing next to it. "This is Mr Webb's room," Mr Wood pointed.

Cam found a large brown bag, which he brought to the bed and emptied it, two wallets and a wristwatch, a set of cufflinks and three rings fell out. Chris examined the rings, one was a wedding band, one was a signet ring, the other was a ring with a oblong blue stone in it, Chris looked in the wallets, both were empty. He looked at Mr Wood, who was watching wondering.

"I'm sorry Mr Wood, but it seems that Mr Webb is certainly involved, this ring alone belonged to Mr Wedge, one of the victims," Chris said holding up the blue stone ring. "I am afraid I will now have to search the room thoroughly."

"Oh dear, oh dear," Mr Wood moaned. "I would never believe it of Mr Webb, he is such a charming young man."

"We have the gun here Sir," Cam shouted looking inside the wardrobe. Cam brought the cloth gun case to the bed. "The gun is inside," Cam pointed.

Chris unbuttoned the case, and saw the gun, then rebuttoned the case up without touching it, he was satisfied seeing the initials RM on the case.

"I believe this is the gun that killed Mrs Crompton and Mr Wedge Sir," Chris said to Mr Wood. "I will have to take them, I will sign for anything I take."

Mr Wood did not answer, he looked as though he was in shock.

"What about clothes, shoes?" Chris asked seeing Cam back at the wardrobe.

"Can't be sure Sir," Cam replied. "Shoes here three pairs, no woman's clothing."

Chris looked at Mr Wood. "I am sorry Sir, but this room will have to remain closed for a while, Mr Webb will be arrested, I shall need the address where he has gone."

"Dear oh dear," Mr Wood choked on his words. "Perhaps we should retire to my office."

"I agree," Chris nodded his head in agreement.

Back in the office, Mr Wood slumped in his chair. "Just can't believe it of Mr Webb," he said rather confusedly. "This will certainly not be good for the hotel I'm afraid."

"I will list what we are taking Sir," Chris remarked. "And sign for it, your presence will assure the court that the items were found in Mr Webb's room," he remarked as he made out the list and signed it before passing the slip to Mr Wood.

"I have no idea what head office will say?" Mr Wood murmured taking the slip.

"It's not your fault Sir," Chris replied. "You are not to know what your employees are up to when off duty?"

"When we employ their character is supposed to be beyond reproach, Mr Webb is on an upgrade course, he would naturally take my place when I retire," Mr Wood murmured.

"I am sorry if letting me into his room comes back to you, you can however give your head office my name, and I will explain that I am investigating three murders, that might help," Chris said in a very convincing voice.

"When head office know the situation, they will accept my part in it, but thank you anyway, now I will have to phone them and put them in the picture, then see about getting a new under manager," Mr wood said a sad expression on his face.

"I shall need the address where Mr Webb has gone?" Chris requested.

Mr Wood took a card from his desk. "This will show his address, it is one of our top hotels at Southampton as I told you he is on an upgrade course."

"Please Mr Wood, do not let Mr Webb know that he is to be arrested, I will have him brought back now I know where he is, I do not want him to abscond," Chris asked as they shook hands.

Chris carrying the brown bag, with Cam carrying the gun, the detectives left the hotel to make their way back to the Police Station.

"You were quiet this morning Cam?" Chris remarked. "No questions offered, I was surprised."

Cam grinned. "I was listening to all your questions, I often asked myself would I have asked this or that, I am learning, still we did get a result didn't we?"

"We certainly did," Chris remarked with a smile as they entered the station. "I do not usually arrest anyone until I am sure they committed the crime, but with all this evidence, I have no option."

"Is the Chief Inspector in?" Chris asked seeing sergeant Dawkins at the desk.

"I believe so Sir," came the reply.

Takes these into the office Cam, I need to see the Chief Inspector," Chris said giving Cam the brown bag he had been carrying.

Cam was copying a report from his notebook when Chris returned.

"Well that's that," he remarked. "A constable will collect the suit from Mr Jarvis, and you Cam will go to Southampton with Sergeant Bloom and arrest Mr Webb, and bring him back here, all have been arranged."

Chris took out his pocket watch. "It's two now, you will catch the four o'clock train, you may be back late, you have nothing on tonight have you?"

"Not a thing," Cam replied a little excited. "Apart from seeing Miss Melanie Roberts."

"I forgot that Cam," Chris replied. "Still this is more important at the moment, you will be able to see Miss Melanie Roberts when you get back, now let's get this gun out of its cover," Chris remarked seeing the gun laid across his desk.

"Now the way I am thinking Cam," Chris remarked as he watched Cam unbutton the cover. There are three things we have to think of, first we have to be sure that Mr Webb did not buy this gun."

"How do we do that?" Cam asked bewildered.

"If Mr Webb did buy the gun, there is a chance that several fingerprints will be on it," Chris looked at Cam.

"If Mr Webb did not buy the gun and committed the crime, only his fingerprints and perhaps Mr Morris's fingerprints will be on the gun," Chris commented.

"We use a cloth to wipe the gun after a shoot," Cam spoke. "Then again I used to load for my dad, both his and my fingerprints would have been on the gun."

"Really!" Chris remarked knowing very little about the subject.

"Mr Morris as you say, he could have wiped the gun after the shooting had finished, meaning his fingerprints would not be on the gun," Chris thought for a moment. "If Mr Morris did wipe his gun, then let's hope we find Mr Webb's fingerprints, what about the trigger Cam, do you think we can get a fingerprints from it?" Chris added anxiously.

Cam showed Chris his open palm. "The trigger finger is next to the thumb," he said wriggling the finger. "Now the fingers has three bones in each, which divides the finger into three by creases you see," Cam explained bending his fingers.

"The fingerprints comes from the front of the finger, and many use just this part to pull the trigger, but some like myself use the centre part of the finger, or pulls the trigger around the first crease, however there might be a partial print on the trigger," Cam spoke with confidence.

"Well let's see, you must have been studying," Chris replied impressed.

Cam smiled as he opened up his detective bag, taking tin of white powder and a soft brush from it. "After seeing George do it I have practiced at home," he said.

"Really!" Chris replied. "Let's see then what you have learnt?"

Chris sat behind his desk watching Cam at work, it was several minutes before Cam gently blowing the white powder off revealed that the gun was clean of all prints, even on the trigger.

"Well it was a hope Cam," Chris said disappointedly.

Cam held the gun pointing it towards the office door, he pressed the release, and the barrel fell. "The cartridges is still in here," Cam almost shouted.

Cam shook the gun, the empty cartridges fell onto the desk.

"Fingers crossed," Cam remarked as he poked the pencil into one of the empty cartridges, which enabled him to lift without touching it by hand. "I'll powder this one," he remarked.

Chris watched him, and grew anxious as Cam blew the powder away, he saw a smile on Cam's face.

"We have at least four fingerprints on this one," Cam remarked excitement in his voice as he gently laid the cartridge down.

"Let's see what this other one show," he said picking it up with his pencil. "The same," Cam eventually said his voice raised a little. "We have two sets of prints in good condition," he confirmed.

Chris felt relief, all he hoped for now was that the prints would match the persons he suspected.

George walked in as Cam was carefully putting the two cartridges on a sheet of blotting paper.

"Well how did you get on George?" Chris asked. "Learn anything?"

"Not much," George replied. "I sat with Mrs Morris and Rosemary in the kitchen, had tea and cake," he smiled. "But one thing did come up, it seems that Rosemary's brother was friendly with Mr Jarvis the park keeper, through the park is a short cut to their home, Mr Jarvis turns a blind eye on him using it when the park is closed."

"That's interesting," Chris replied.

"Rosemary also told me that he probably would have used it that night, as a rough guess she said about eight."

"More interesting," Chris remarked. "Cam and Sergeant Bloom are going to Southampton to arrest Mr Webb in a very short time from now," Chris added taking out his watch. "Yes, you will soon have to go and catch that train Cam it's just gone three."

Sergeant Bloom entered carrying a suit as Chris put back his watch.

"A constable brought this suit in for you Sir," sergeant Bloom said laying it across the interview chair. "I understand I'm going to Southampton, any last orders?" he smiled.

"Just arrest him on suspicion of murder, he will have to stay in the cells for the night, tell him he is entitled to have a solicitor when he is questioned tomorrow," Chris advised.

"Very good," sergeant Bloom replied, then looked at Cam.

"We better be off young man," he smiled.

Chapter Twenty

*C*hris watched as George photographed the prints on the cartridges, knowing it might be a complete day before they were developed, still he was happy in his mind, almost sure that the case would be solved within the week.

"Why did you search Mr Webb's room?" George asked. "I had no idea he was in the frame?" he asked, surprised.

"It was after I spoke to Mr Jarvis that I thought of it, you see Mr Webb told me he was at the cricket match last Sunday week, and that he left about six fifteen, he said he saw chairs around the bandstand as he left, Mr Jarvis told me he had cleared the chairs by five thirty, then after he had a wash, spent time at the cricket match until he locked up, then going to the Foresters," Chris replied.

"Then Mr Webb went to Mr Wright's housewarming party," George remarked.

"I doubt it," Chris replied. "It was far too early and light, if the chairs were still out when he left the cricket match, he must have left between five and half past, not at six fifteen," Chris added.

"Do it mean anything?" George asked.

"Perhaps he was keeping an eye on Mr Jarvis, perhaps he was a little confused as to the time," Chris replied.

"We will see what he says tomorrow?" George replied. "There that's all finished," he added putting away his box camera, I will take them for develop tomorrow morning, it's too late now I think."

Chris looked at his watch. "Good God it way past six, Elizabeth would have gone home."

George smiled. "Pubs are open," he remarked.

Chris answered him with a grin. "Well I feel very happy at the moment, we have done good work today, a pint would be an award don't you think?"

"I agree entirely," George laughed loudly as he stood up.

The following morning Chris anxious to start work, received his usual kiss from Elizabeth outside the police station.

"Will you be late tonight?" Elizabeth asked with a smile.

Chris smiled back at her. "Yes I was a bit late last night, I'll try to be on time tonight, but I am near solving this case, it's difficult to know at this stage."

"Don't worry darling," Elizabeth replied giving Chris an extra kiss. "I accepted the ups and downs of a policeman's wife when I married you," she smiled.

Elizabeth was still smiling as she walked away from him, secretly hoping that her happiness would never end.

Cam was at his desk when Chris entered. "Good morning Cam," Chris greeted. "How was yesterday?"

"Got back about eight thirty last night," Cam replied.

"Mr Webb did not come easy, he kicked up saying he was on a course, and could get the sack, however Sergeant Bloom told him he had no choice."

"He moaned all the way back, saying that he would sue for wrongful arrest," Cam continued. "Anyway we got back about eight thirty, and he was put in a cell, where he is at the moment."

"It's only to be expected," Chris replied. "He had no idea he was a suspect?"

"Nor did I," Cam remarked. "Never thought of him being one?"

"Every one involved is a suspect until the case is solved Cam," Chris replied. "We will wait for George before we see Mr Webb."

"He's late, unusual for George?" Cam asked worrying.

"George should have called in early this morning to take Mr Webb's fingerprints, he will be having them developed on a photograph with all the others," Chris replied.

"You were unable to see Miss Melanie Roberts last night I take it?" Chris asked.

"I did as a matter of fact," Cam answered. "We spent the last hour in the Fox, in Water Lane."

"Really!" Chris replied.

"She did not have much more to tell us, but she did say, a couple months ago she saw Mrs Crompton come from Mr Webb's office, and she was dabbing her eyes as though she had been crying, although she tried to find out why, nothing was said about it."

"That's interesting Cam," Chris remarked.

"This was at least two months ago, that's what Melanie told me," Cam said.

George entered with a smile. "Managed to get them developed very quickly," he said putting an envelope before Chris.

"Good," Chris replied picking up the envelope.

"We will now have to study, see if any matches with what we have?" Chris remarked taking out the photos and studying them.

"They look good," he muttered. "I am going to see Mr Webb," he said handing the photos back to George.

"You're going to question him?" George asked wanting to be in on the questioning.

"No, we will all take part in that, I just want to make sure he is OK?" Chris replied leaving the room.

Sergeant Williams opened the cell door for Chris to enter, he saw Mr Webb who was sitting on his bunk.

"Have you had breakfast Mr Webb?" Chris asked in a kindly voice.

"Forget the breakfast Inspector, and the niceties, I hope you know what you are doing, bringing me back from Southampton while I was in the middle of a course charged with murder," he replied with a sarcasm in his voice, his face flushing with anger.

Chris sat on the only chair in the cell. "You were not charged with murder Mr Webb, just suspicion of murder there is a difference."

"Could you not have waited until tomorrow when I would have finished my course?" Mr Webb asked, temper in his voice.

"I searched your room yesterday," Chris informed him as a shocked expression showed on Mr Webb's face.

Chris continued. "I will tell you, yours was not the only place we searched, and before you ask, I did have permission from your employer."

"You had no right, nor did my employer," Mr Webb responded angrily.

Chris ignored his outburst. "You can understand why you were arrested, you know what we found in your room?"

Mr Webb did not reply.

"I am not here to question you Mr Webb, we must wait for your solicitor, I'm here just to enquire whether you are being treated alright, you will however be questioned, with your answers we will decide whether you will be released or not, do you want a book or paper to read?" Chris asked.

Mr Webb sat quiet and shook his head. "How long am I going to be kept here?" he talked eventually.

"As I said," Chris replied standing up to leave the cell. "It will be up to your answers, but you will be charged or released by tomorrow night."

Chris entered the office and went to his desk, George and Cam who were studying the photos looked at him.

"He's angry, I told him he was arrested because of what we found in his room, he didn't say anything, he knows he will either be released or charged by tomorrow night, anyway have you found anything yet?" he asked.

"I think we have two sets on the photos that match on the cartridges," George replied getting up and handing them to Chris. "Perhaps you could double check?"

"Well done," Chris remarked taking the photos and cartridges.

Chris took his magnifying glass from his desk drawer and settled down to study. Much later, Chris put down his magnifying glass and leaned back in his chair with a smile on his face. "I agree, we have two sets, we know for sure now who killed Mrs Crompton and Mr Wedge."

"What about Mr Morris?" George asked.

"I know who killed him, at least I think I do," Chris said with confidence.

"But don't ask me who, before I am sure, now Cam, go to the Suffolk Hotel, I want Mrs Wedge here at eleven tomorrow morning, Mr Wood will allow her, I also want Mr Jarvis and Mr Crompton here, also Mr Wright who now lives in St Cross, so you will have to make sure you see all of them, if you get any trouble, tell them, their failure to be here an arrest warrant will be issued."

"I can do that," Cam replied excited. "Do this mean we have solved the case?"

Chris looked at George and gave a little grin. "We must wait and see Cam."

As Cam left the office, Sergeant Williams poked his head into the office. "The solicitor is with Mr Webb Sir."

"Thank you Sergeant," Chris replied. "We will give him a little time to talk to his client before we interview."

"We will have to play this by ear George," Chris stated. "So feel free to ask questions."

Chris leaned back in his chair, took his pipe filled it and lit it. "I have time for a puff before we have him in," Chris smiled taking a deep draw of the pipe and blowing out clouds of smoke.

"It will be interesting to know how he was in possession of the gun and other articles," he remarked as he brushed away the smoke with his hand. "It might be a good idea to lay them out on your desk, so that he can see them," Chris remarked.

"I have them in the cupboard," George replied getting up and going to the cupboard where he took out the gun and brown bag, and laid them on his desk. "He can't miss them now," George replied.

"Good," Chris replied, putting his pipe in the ashtray, and tidying his desk. "Let's have him in," Chris lifted the receiver.

A few moments later, Sergeant Williams entered holding Mr Webb by the arm, and took him straight to the interview chair, and made him seat.

Chris looked at the well dressed man around fifty, that followed them into the office.

"I am Mr Melcher, solicitor," the man introduced himself, looking at Chris.

"I have been retained by the Suffolk Hotel to represent Mr Webb, you must be Detective Inspector Hardie," he said offering his hand.

Chris took the hand with a slight smile. "My colleague Detective Sergeant House," he said indicating George sitting at his desk, who nodded with a smile.

"Not much room in this office I'm afraid Mr Melcher, use my desk to rest your briefcase and bowler, please take the chair by your client," Chris offered.

"Your client Mr Roger Webb has been arrested on suspicion of murder," Chris informed.

"So I understand Inspector," Mr Melcher replied. "I take it you had reason for doing so?"

"Those articles, the shotgun and articles on the brown bag on Sergeant House's desk, all belong to three victims that were murdered at the park last Sunday week, they were found in Mr Webb's room at the hotel," Chris replied.

"I have spoken to Mr Wood the manager, he told me he was in the room when you found them, can I ask why you needed to search my client's room?"

"As a matter of course, his room was not the only place has been searched, for instance we searched Mr Jarvis's bungalow at the park, just routine," Chris explained.

"I see," Mr Melcher replied. "My Client has no idea how these articles got into his room?"

"That is why we are here Mr Melcher, to try to find out," Chris replied.

"Now Mr Webb can you explain to me how that gun, and those articles, wallets, rings etc belonging to three murdered people got into your room?" Chris asked his voice now full of authority.

Roger Webb swallowed. "I left Winchester Monday morning by seven am train for Southampton, those articles were not in my room when I left."

"Do you have an explanation for them being in your room?" Chris asked.

Roger Webb shrugged his shoulders. "They must have been planted," he suggested with a worrying look on his face.

"How many people knew that you were going on a course?" Chris asked.

"It wasn't a secret, nor was it broadcasted," Roger replied. "Who knows?"

"Did you tell anyone outside the hotel, say, when you were having a pint or such?" Chris asked.

"I might have done, I knew I was going on the course several weeks ago," Roger replied. "But I can't say for sure."

"Then it could be that only those in the hotel might have known?" Chris replied.

"The manager obviously knew, and perhaps some members of the staff, but as I said it was not a secret," Roger remarked.

"You have two entrances to your room Mr Webb," George spoke up. "One back entrance from St Georges Street, and one within the hotel itself, you keep your keys, I mean they are not held at reception like the hotel guest keys, as neither of the doors were forced, perhaps you lent your key to someone?"

"That would have been against hotel rules, bad for security," Roger Webb denied.

"Then Mr Wood the manager has the only one got the key to your room, do you suspect him?" George asked.

Roger Webb smiled weakly and looked down at his lap. "I am in the dark as well as you, but you are the detective?" he answered.

Chris decided to change the questioning. "You told me when you left the park that Sunday, it was six or just past, and you saw chairs around the bandstand."

"If I told you that, then yes," Roger Webb replied.

"Mr Jarvis the park keeper assures me that the chairs were put away by five thirty."

Mr Webb shrugged. "I might have been mistaken with the time, then again so could this park keeper?"

"The park keeper had an appointment that night, we have checked and believe his time to be correct," Chris remarked.

"Then I was wrong," Roger hesitated a moment before answering. "I just made a mistake about the time, it's not a crime," he said rather angrily.

"The time that my client left the park, is it relevant to the case?" Mr Melcher interrupted.

Chris smiled at the solicitor. "You must know as a solicitor every little detail is important, you could lose or win a case just on the times not fitted properly."

"Exactly Inspector," Mr Melcher agreed. "But as I understand these murders were not committed until after eight that night, my client had already left the park by then."

"Which entrance did you leave by?" Chris asked to Mr Webb, for the moment ignoring the solicitor's remarks.

"By the front entrance of course," Mr Webb responded.

Chris nodded. "OK Mr Webb you left by the front gate just after six that night, why did you use that gate?"

"I think I told you Inspector, I called at the Wagon and Horses for a pint," Roger Webb replied.

"You did, that's true," Chris admitted. "But you forgot to tell me you were at housewarming party number one at Gordon Road some time after seven having drinks with a regular guests of your hotel, a Mr Wright, you remember Mr Wright don't you, if you left the park gone six that night why did you not use the path by the park keeper's bungalow to go to number one at Gordon Road?"

"It was early for the housewarming party, I was passing the time," Mr Webb replied rather quickly. "I am sorry, I thought I had told you."

"You saw Mrs Wedge and Mr Crompton at the house-warming party?" Chris asked.

"Yes I saw them, I saw Mrs Wedge," he quickly corrected himself. "Can't remember Mr Crompton being there," Mr Webb replied.

"What time did you leave party?" Chris asked.

"God knows," Mr Webb replied. "I did go to the Wagon and Horses afterwards about nine I would guess."

"The landlord don't remember you," Chris replied.

"Really Inspector?" Mr Melcher said forcing a smile.

"Do you know Mr Ronald Morris of Worthy Road Farm?" George spoke again.

"Should I?" Roger Webb asked bewildered.

"His twelve bore gun was found in your room, the case has his initials on RM," George replied.

"Can't say I've met him," Roger Webb murmured.

"Inspector, have you any more of these questions for my client, they do not seem to go anywhere?" Mr Melcher advised. "I think you should let my client go."

Chris leaned back in his chair, the interview was not showing results.

"Mr Melcher I shall be keeping your client overnight, I am interviewing several people tomorrow morning at eleven who could be involved in these murders, if Mr Webb would agree to attend, you can be sure that if he is proven innocent, you can take him with you."

Mr Melcher looked at Mr Webb, who nodded.

"Fair enough Inspector, I will be here to represent my client tomorrow."

"That went as I expected George," Chris remarked when the office had cleared.

Chris looked at his watch. "It's almost midday, fancy a liquid lunch at the Standard Public House, I have sandwiches in my pocket," he suggested.

"This afternoon I will spend getting my case ready," Chris rose from his chair.

"Sounds good," George agreed with a smile.

They crossed the room, and took their trilbies from the hat stand before leaving the office.

It was striking twelve as Chris and George entered the saloon bar of the Standard Public House.

"Inspector, Sergeant," the landlord greeted them. "More questions?"

Chris smiled. "Not today landlord, we have our sandwiches, and decided to have one of your pints to wash it down."

"Sensible," replied the landlord. "Is the case getting solved?" he asked.

"Getting there," George replied. "Two boilers if you please, and one for yourself."

"Thank you Sergeant," the landlord said with a smile, as he took two bottles of brown ale from a grate behind him and started to pour them in pint glasses. "I'll have a half."

George watched as the landlord filled the glasses on top of the brown ale with beer.

"Get a table, I'll bring them over to you," the landlord smiled. "You are always welcome to have your lunch here," the landlord remarked placing the pints on the table where

Chris and George had decided to sit. "No one uses the saloon bar during the dinner time."

"That's very kind of you," Chris replied. "You do serve a good pint."

"Thank you and enjoy," the landlord said with a smile as he walked away.

Chris put his package of sandwiches on the table and opened them. "Cheese," he laughed. "Help yourself George."

"Don't knock it Chris," George remarked as he took a sandwich. "What goes better with a pint?"

Chris smiled as he took one. "Elizabeth always make sure these are in my pocket before I leave home."

"You married well there Chris," George commented. "I'm a bit jealous."

Chris grinned. "What about this Rosemary Morris, she is a stunner?"

"I know," George replied. "When this case is over, I may not see her again having no excuse to go there, I have been tempted to ask her out, because we seem to get on well, but being so close to her brother, it is too soon."

"You like her then?" Chris asked curiously.

George nodded his head in agreement.

"Well you never know what's around the corner?" Chris replied.

"When you have these interviews at the end of each case, you usually have some idea who the murderer is?" George asked chewing on his sandwich.

Chris took a drink of his pint. "One thing I do know that the murderer or murderers will be in our office tomorrow morning."

"It means you have a good idea?" George stated.

"Having an idea and proving it, it's a different thing, I do usually have an idea when I have these interviews, we know everything we are likely to know, I am never happy unless I get a confession I would hate to send someone to prison who is innocent."

"I can't say I'm much help in this case Chris," George remarked emptying his glass. "I know what you know, and I agree the murderer has to be one of those attending tomorrow, otherwise we are up the creek without a paddle."

"It's a complicated case, to me it seems far fetched," Chris spoke. "Anyway we'll have one more, then back to the office."

The landlord brought the pints to the table, as Chris checked his watch.

"Your clock landlord, is that the right time, it's faster than mine?" Chris remarked putting his watch back and from his trouser pocket taking change to pay for the pints.

The landlord grinned. "The law is very tight around here Inspector," he said, not even allowed music, the Cathedral you see, I keep my clock fifteen minutes fast for drinking up time.

"That explains it landlord," Chris replied with a smile.

Cam was in the office when they returned from pub.

"How did it go Cam, did you see everyone?" Chris asked as he put his trilby on the hat stand, and walked to his desk.

"Saw them all, had to wait a while for Mr Wright, he had gone out, but his landlady made me a cup of tea, she's a very jolly woman, anyway Mr Wright had no objections in attending, he is moving into Gordon Road next week, it seems that Mr Dodd the estate agent accepted his plea, made him sign a new contract in his own name."

"What about Mrs Wedge how did she take it?" George asked curiously.

Cam smiled. "I saw Mr Wood the manager at first to explain to him, he was willing to cooperate, Mrs Wedge however wondered why she had to attend, after all she remarked you have the killer in custody."

"You are telling me she knew we had Mr Webb in the cell?" Chris asked a little surprised. "I'm sure Mr Wood would not have broadcasted it?"

"It seems there's been talk in the staffroom about coming and going police action, Mr Wood however is more concerned with the good name of the hotel," Cam replied.

"I'm sure he is," Chris remarked. "There is no way of keeping the hotel being named, if Mr Webb is guilty, his name and address has to be given and at the moment his address is the Suffolk Hotel."

"I had to go to St Thomas's School to see Mr Crompton, he started work after taking a week off, he was not too happy, wanted to know if he should have a solicitor, I told him he was not under arrest, it was just an interview between all parties involved, however I told him he could if he wanted to have one, Mr Jarvis just smiled and said he would be here," Cam concluded.

"Good," Chris remarked. "We can expect all to be here tomorrow morning, George," Chris said looking at him.

"Cam is not used to our routine, so I'll leave it all to you, we want chairs and the typist, Mr Melcher will also be attending he can sit by the side of me."

The afternoon went quick for Chris who settled down studying all the reports he had on the case, and it was coming to six when he looked at his watch.

"Time to pack up," he remarked. "Can't keep Elizabeth waiting tonight."

"Well all is ready for tomorrow," George replied.

"Should be exciting," Cam remarked a grin all over his face.

"I hope you will think so afterwards Cam," Chris replied a slight smile on his face. "Anyway I'm off, see you both tomorrow," he said taking his hat from the stand, and leaving the office.

"Do you think we will solve the case tomorrow George?" Cam asked with excitement.

"We have always done so far," George replied.

"Chris knows who murdered these people, but cannot prove it so he needs a confession, Chris has a quick mind, if there is a confession to have, Chris will get it."

"It's not easy being a detective George," Cam replied.

"Apart from blood test and fingerprints we have very little to help us, I do have my suspicions who done it, I am just hoping that I'm right."

"The murderer has to be among the five attending tomorrow, they all could have been involved, only questions will sort it out, usually by one making a mistake in his answers, or one panicking and loosing their coolness, anyway Cam I'm off, see you tomorrow," George said and rose from his chair.

"See you," Cam replied with a smile.

Chapter Twenty-One

*C*hris saw Elizabeth walking towards him, he saw her smile as she caught sight of him.

"Hello darling," she smiled planting a kiss on his cheek. "Had a busy day?"

"Tiring," Chris replied.

Elizabeth took his arm as they started to walk towards home.

"Been reading up all the afternoon, my old eyes are getting tired," Chris moaned with a disappointed expression on his face.

"You have lovely eyes darling, they are not old," Elizabeth replied.

"Well they feel old at the moment," Chris insisted.

"I have eye drops at home darling," Elizabeth remarked. "I'll put some in after we have eaten."

"I wonder what Olive have cooked for tonight?" Chris asked. "I can eat a meal."

"Mum is doing a midweek roast," Elizabeth replied.

Chris remained quiet as he ate the roast, his mind pondering over the forthcoming interview with all the suspects. Grinning a few times at the banter between Olive and Ron, finally he pushed his empty plate away from him, feeling so full that he declined the prunes and custard afters.

"I am absolutely full Olive," Chris said. "Ron is very lucky to have such a cook," he flattered her.

"He don't share your opinion Chris," Olive replied.

Ron who had already left the table to sit in his armchair smiled. "I have always said that being put into service was good for you my sweet."

Olive glared at him and she said nothing.

"Chris felt so full," he moaned eating too much.

"It's all those roast potatoes you ate darling," Elizabeth stated with a giggle. "When it comes to roast potatoes you are greedy."

Chris grinned. "Yes I am afraid I am a glutton for them, it's the same with anything that I like."

"I'm glad to hear that," Elizabeth giggled again.

"As long as you have had enough Chris," Olive said giving her daughter a stare.

"Sit back in the chair and have your pipe, while Elizabeth and I wash up," Olive smiled at him understandingly.

Doing as he was told, Chris relaxed in the armchair to the facing Ron.   "How's the case coming along?" Ron asked looking over the top of the newspaper.

"I have all the suspects coming in tomorrow, if I do not solve it then, I don't think I ever will," Chris replied.

"Difficult is it?" Ron asked.

"I have all the pieces, the difficulty is fitting them altogether," Chris replied. "Still an early night might clear my head a little by tomorrow?"

"A good sleep can do wonders," Ron remarked.

Chris nodded his head. "How's the war going anyway?" he asked.

"We are suffering a lot of casualties, I can't see the end of it yet," Ron answered.

"America could come in?" Chris remarked.

"It would certainly help," Ron replied. "But there is no signs of it yet, still can you blame them, they are no part of Europe."

"I suppose not," Chris replied as Olive and Elizabeth entered the room.

"I'm taking Chris home now," Elizabeth smiled. "He is tired, and he has a busy day tomorrow."

"Best thing for him," Ron agreed.

Chapter Twenty-Two

*C*hris entered the Police Station the next morning with a bounce, Elizabeth's eye drops seem to have done wonders, he decided to take her advice and get spectacles for reading, when he could find the time.

"Morning George, Cam," Chris greeted them with a smile hanging his trilby.

"You look cheerful," George remarked.

"I feel it George," Chris replied. "I want to close this case today, and I am feeling good about it."

"I have managed seven chairs," George remarked. "Should be enough, how do you want them to sit?"

"I'll have Mrs Wedge one end of four and Mr Crompton at the other end, in between Mr Jarvis and Mr Wright, Mr Webb can sit in front with his solicitor, it's best for the solicitor to sit with his client, the typist will as usual sit with you George, let's hope her typewriter is one of the silent type," Chris explained.

George smiled. "I'll get on with it then."

"We can all have a cup of tea before we start," Chris suggested taking out his pipe and tobacco. "Plenty of time yet."

By eleven the chairs had been arranged, the typist was sitting with George, Cam was sitting at his desk behind the line of chairs. Sergeant Williams entered with Mrs Wedge, Mr Crompton, Mr Jarvis and Mr Wright.

"Thank you Sergeant," Chris said. "You can bring in Mr Webb now."

Moments later all heads looked as Sergeant Williams holding Mr Webb by the arm entered followed by Mr Melcher his solicitor.

"Thank you Sergeant," Chris said with a smile. "You can leave us now, I am sure Mr Webb has no intention of trying to escape."

Mr Webb looked at his solicitor and grinned.

"Thank you all for coming," Chris opened the meeting. "Now do we know each other, Mrs Wedge?" Chris said looking at her. "Do you know everyone?"

Mrs Wedge looked along the line. "I know Mr Wright," she giggled. "I don't know the park keeper, but I have seen him, the man on the end I don't know him."

"That gentleman is Mr Crompton, the husband of the victim," Chris informed her.

"Oh," replied Mrs Wedge.

"Now Mr Wright do you know everyone?" Chris asked to Mr Wright who was sitting next to Mrs Wedge.

"I know Mrs Wedge, and Mr Webb sitting in front, but I am afraid I am not familiar with the other two men," he replied.

"You Mr Jarvis?" Chris asked. "How about you?"

"I might have seen them at the park, but can't remember."

"Thank you Mr Jarvis," Chris replied. "And you Mr Crompton?"

"My answer will be the same as Mr Jarvis, I might have seen them, but do not know them."

"Thank you," Chris replied. "However you do know each other now, so to get on, Mr Webb sitting in the front is under arrest charged with the suspicion of murder, he is represented here by Mr Melcher his solicitor."

"Do we need a solicitor?" Mr Crompton asked, he seemed to be worried.

"You are not under arrest Mr Crompton, however if you feel you are in need of one, one is standing by in the station," Chris replied.

"I was only asking," Mr Crompton retorted.

"If Mr Webb is arrested, why do you need us here?" Mrs Wedge asked nervously.

Chris looked at her before answering. "I need to clear up where each of you were during the evening on Sunday 14th May, now none of you are under arrest, but should any of you want a solicitor speak now, you must understand, I am investigating a treble murder, and in the undignified way the victims were left, I would say whoever is responsible could be hung."

"Well that's easy for me, I did not kill anyone," Mrs Wedge reacted, fidgeting in her chair. "I met Mr Webb in Gordon Road about sevenish, we were both on our way to Mr Wright's housewarming party."

"I can certainly vouch to that," Mr Wright said with absolute certainty.

"What time did you leave the party Mrs Wedge?" Chris asked.

Mrs Wedge considered the answer. "We had a drink, was introduced to the other guest, at a guess I would say between eight and half past."

"Alone?" Chris asked.

"No it was getting dark, Mr Webb offered to see me home," Mrs Wedge replied.

"Can you vouch for that Mr Wright?" Chris asked.

"Not really," he answered. "I was not looking at the clock every time a person left the party."

"So Mrs Wedge," Chris continued. "You can swear that Mr Webb was with you, let's say at least to nine pm that night?"

"That's right," Mrs Wedge replied with a giggle. "Much longer in fact."

"We know that Mr Wright was at his party, and we also know that Mr Jarvis was at the Foresters Pub until around nine, where were you Mr Crompton?" Chris asked.

"You know where I was, I was in the Standard Public House until eight, then went home to wait for my wife," Mr Crompton replied, worrying look on his face.

Chris noticed the worried look on his face. "This was not usual for you Mr Crompton was it, I mean you usually stayed until closing time, why did you leave at eight as you said that particular Sunday?" Chris asked.

"Just didn't feel drinking, no harm in that is there," Mr Crompton replied.

"Then you went back to your home and waited for your wife?" Chris remarked.

"I did, and when she did not return, the next morning I came to you to report it."

"Did you know your wife was having an affair with Mr Wedge?" Chris asked the straight question.

"I would have told you, had I known," Mr Crompton replied with a little sarcasm in his voice.

"You Mrs Wedge did you know your ex-husband was having an affair with Mrs Crompton?"

"It wouldn't have worried me had I known," Mrs Wedge giggled. "He was an ex-husband."

"Well now we know where everyone was during the Sunday evening, let me bring you up to date," Chris began.

"We can go back several months, during which time Mr Wedge had met Mrs Crompton, they became lovers, but Mrs Crompton wanted it to be kept secret, in herself she was a religious person, she knew she was committing a sin, but her love for Mr Wedge was so strong, that it took preference over her religious beliefs."

"How can you say that?" Mr Crompton interrupted. "If it was so secret, how do you know and why did I not guess?"

"Because Mr Crompton your marriage had been on the rocks for a long time, your marriage was so bad, that you even told her you were barren so that you would not have anything to do with her."

"You are amazing Inspector," Mr Crompton replied. "You could make a fortune reading palms, however what I told you was true, and told in confidence."

"In confidence yes, but not true Mr Crompton."

"I am sure that Mrs Wedge would not be having an affair with a man incapable?" Chris replied expecting the outburst he got.

"I hope you have evidence of what you are saying in front of witnesses," Mr Crompton responded in a angry tone.

"Me also," Mrs Wedge stormed. "I am not having an affair with this man, I reject what you imply," she gave her head a defiant shake.

"We have eye witnesses," Chris answered.

"Who and where were we seen?" Mrs Wedge almost shouted. "You believe lies rather than the truth."

"The Cathedral Close comes to mind at one place you were both seen together," Chris said with a stern look on his face.

"Yes you are right Inspector, I had forgotten it, it was just a brief encounter, I did talk to Mrs Wedge in the

Cathedral Close, I did not know who she was, and never seen her since," Mr Crompton quickly stated.

"Why do you cycle to Stanmore late at night Mr Crompton?" Chris asked hoping that he had guessed right.

"Who says I do?" Mr Crompton replied with anger in his voice.

"We know Mr Crompton," Chris answered. "But we are wasting time over your relationship, these things happens, you were having an affair with Mrs Wedge, and Mr Wedge was having a relationship with your wife, it is a big coincidence, both relationships were kept secret, you being a school master and your wife being religious, both you and your wife were committing adultery so let's leave that and get on."

Hearing no more questions, Chris continued.

"After you left for school Mr Crompton, your wife who did not start work until around ten at the hotel, took to sitting in the park, she eventually spoke to the park keeper Mr Jarvis, then after a few weeks became friendly and felt she was able to talk to him. She called herself Susan. It seems that Mr Jarvis took pity on her, and allowed her to use his bungalow Sundays evening after seven. She had been doing this for several weeks, Mr Wedge and herself had met in Mr Jarvis's bungalow."

"She was supposed to be at church?" Mr Crompton shouted angrily.

"She did go to church Mr Crompton, it was after that they met," Chris informed him and continued.

"It was on the Monday morning that Mr Jarvis found the corpses behind the bandstand, he had no idea who they were, and did not connect them to Susan and her boyfriend, he told me later however that he had only allowed them to use his bungalow for one week that was untrue," he said looking at Mr Jarvis who was looking into his lap.

"I'm sorry Inspector," Mr Wright interrupted. "Mr Jarvis could not identify this Susan, and did not know her boyfriend, we now know it was Mrs Crompton and Mr Wedge, but how do you know these are the same people that Mr Jarvis allowed to use his bungalow?"

"We did not at first," Chris replied, "It was after Mr Jarvis mentioned this Susan which for a while confused us. Mr Crompton reported his wife missing, it was her birthmark that allowed us to know who the corpse belong to. The identification of Mr Wedge took us longer, the corpse had a half finger, we eventually found a doctor who told us about a Mr Wedge who had lost half his finger we eventually found out his address, we asked Mrs Wedge and Mr Crompton to identify the corpses, they did."

"I understand that part Inspector," Mr Wright continued. "But if Mr Jarvis was unable to recognise them, how are you sure they were this Susan and her boyfriend?"

"We searched Mr Jarvis's bungalow, and in his wardrobe we found the suit belonging to Mr Wedge, it seems that Mr Jarvis do not open his wardrobe very often because he wears his uniform most of the time, and had not noticed the suit, we now believe that Mr Wedge and Mrs Crompton was killed in the bungalow, and transported to where they were found under the bandstand," Chris lied on purposely about the murder happened in the bungalow.

"You believe that I did it?" Mrs Wedge shouted.

Chris smiled. "Why would you think that Mrs Wedge, however I am curious as to why you would not look at your ex husband body when you identified him?"

"I didn't want to look at his face, all smashed up," she replied without thinking.

"How did you know his face was smashed up?" Chris asked.

"I don't know," Mrs Wedge replied a bit flustered. "You told me didn't you?"

"No I did not," Chris argued.

"Well I must have been told, perhaps by the doctor in the morgue before I went in?"

"I can assure you, the police surgeon did not tell you," Chris replied. "But you knew, tell me how you knew?"

Mrs Wedge looked across at Mr Crompton who eluded her glance.

"I'm sorry Inspector," Mr Wright interrupted. "I have been listening to what has being said, for the life of me, I cannot see why a finger is pointed at others while you already have a person arrested on suspicion?"

Chris looked at Mr Webb and his solicitor, whose faces were giving a blank look.

"Mr Webb has been arrested, because after searching Mr Jarvis's bungalow, we searched Mr Webb's room in the hotel, it was just a matter of routine, we found wallets and rings all belong to the victims, he tells us he knows nothing about the articles, but cannot explain how there were found in his room?" Chris commented.

"They were planted," Mr Webb shouted loudly.

"That is why we are all here today to find out," Chris answered.

"But let me continue with my story, I have already told you how Mr Jarvis allowed Mrs Crompton the use of his bungalow. Mr Wright, you were in a kind of bother at the hotel which involved Mrs Crompton and Mrs Wedge, you left the day after when you found out that the barbiturates samples were missing," Chris continued.

Mr Wright nodded his head. "That is correct, I have no idea how I lost them."

"Mrs Crompton took them," Chris informed him.

"But why?" Mr Wright asked with a tone of disbelief in his voice.

"Mrs Crompton knew she was pregnant," Chris answered. "I believe that with her faith, she would not have been able to bear the shame with the birth, and had decided to end her life."

"Also the life of her lover," Mr Wright remarked.

"He deserved it being the father," Mr Crompton voiced his opinion.

"Mr Wedge was not the father," Chris said in a stern voice."Was he Mr Webb?" Chris looked at him as he raised his eyebrows."Mr Webb was the father of the child," his voice was firm and his words were loud and clear.

Mr Webb looked at the Inspector with surprise. "How would I know, I have never been with her?"

"Mr Webb, you are a cricket fan, and when you have the opportunity you go along to the park and watch a match," Chris said sharply.

"Well yes, but that don't make me the father do it?" Mr Webb remarked.

Chris smiled. "No, but one of these times, by chance you saw Mrs Crompton enter the park keeper's bungalow with Mr Wedge."

"You don't have to answer that," Mr Melcher advised Mr Webb.

Chris continued without waiting for a reply. "The next day you had Mrs Crompton into your office, you threatened her by telling all, perhaps even with the sack, all of which would have been disastrous for Mrs Crompton, and she gave in to your sex demands."

"Really Inspector, that is just a made up story in your own mind, no evidence of any kind, do you really expect my client to answer?" Mr Melcher asked.

"I do have an eye witness who saw Mrs Crompton leave Mr Webb's office in tears," Chris replied. "But if I may go on, Mrs Crompton when she knew she was pregnant told Mr Webb of it."

"Really Inspector, we all have opinions, but the court needs facts," Mr Melcher replied. "I advise my client to ignore your opinions."

Chris looked at Mr Crompton. "Mr Crompton, I am going to ask you a question that I want answered truthfully, remember this is a very serious investigation involving three murders, I believe you knew your wife was pregnant, who told you, I am sure your wife did not?" Chris asked with temper in his voice.

Mr Crompton looked straight at the Inspector, in his mind he knew he had not killed anyone, and decided enough was enough, he had to save his reputation being a school master.

"Mrs Wedge told me my wife was pregnant," he shouted.

"You told them what for?" Mrs Wedge blurted out. "I told you in confidence."

"So who told you Mrs Wedge?" Chris asked, looking at her.

"Only one person who could have told me, Mr Webb of course," Mrs Wedge blurted out the secret.

Chris looked at Mr Wright. "Mr Wright, I believe that Mrs Crompton was going to end her life that night, would the barbiturates she stole, be enough to kill both of them?" he asked.

"The barbiturates she stole was enough to kill both," Mr Wright replied without any hesitation. "Very dangerous stuff in the wrong hands."

"Mr Webb, after you and Mrs Wedge left Mr Wright's housewarming party, you saw the lights of the park keeper's bungalow burning, and decided to have a look in the side window, which was partially covered with low bushes that grew outside the window, you saw two bodies laying on the floor of the bungalow," Chris continued.

"Inspector," Mr Melcher spoke up. "Mrs Wedge also works at the Suffolk Hotel, may I speak for her?"

"Of course Mr Melcher, I only want the truth," Chris replied.

"Thank you Inspector," Mr Melcher said.

"Mr Wright has told us that the barbiturates Mrs Crompton stole from him was plenty to kill both victims, you have suggested that both my clients saw two bodies laying on the bungalow floor, my clients should be allowed to know that there is no murder charge against shooting a dead person?" Mr Melcher wanted assurance that his clients would not be charged shooting a dead person.

"You are of course right Mr Melcher," Chris replied gratefully. "For myself, I have never been involved in such a case, but it is certain you can not hurt or injure, or even take a person's life, if that person is already dead."

Chris noticed the smile came to Mrs Wedge's face. "Perhaps now Mrs Wedge you can tell us what really happened?" Chris asked.

"You are quite right, Mr Webb and myself sneaked up to the window, and did find my ex husband and Mrs Crompton laying on the floor, they were holding hands," Mrs Wedge giggled.

"Then you went inside?" Chris asked.

"Not straight away, Mr Webb knew I was meeting Mr Crompton so we waited for him."

"Mr Crompton turned up about eight?" Chris asked.

"You know I was still in the Standard Pub at that time," Mr Crompton quickly interrupted.

"You left the Standard Pub when the clock showed eight did you not?" Chris demanded.

"That's right," Mr Crompton replied. "You know I did."

"The clock Mr Crompton was fifteen minutes fast, put on such, because the Standard is only separated from the Cathedral by a narrow road, no singing or row after closing time is allowed, the Standard and the other two pubs along that road are all under the same restriction, I have done the walk from the Standard to the park keeper's bungalow myself during the day with the pavement full of people, I did it in fifteen minutes, you of course used your cycle," Chris paused.

"You all went inside, would you like to tell me what happened inside?" Chris asked.

"Palm reading again Inspector," Mr Crompton submitted.

Chris continued ignoring his remarks. "When you saw the two bodies, Mrs Wedge had an idea, her ex husband had recently inherited a vast estate in Australia, Mr Crompton would have taken Mr Wedge's place, and claimed the estate in Australia, I believe it was Mrs Wedge's idea to strip both bodies, take them to under the bandstand, Mr Webb and Mr Crompton both helped her, no doubt with financial promise. That is what you did, you somehow got them across the playing field, and shot their faces to pieces so that they could not be recognised, however you forgot Mrs Crompton's birthmark and the half finger of Mr Wedge."

"You are a story teller Inspector," Mr Crompton remarked. "Very good one as well, I congratulate you," he said sarcastically. "However according to Mr Melcher and yourself, we did no hurt to dead people."

"I am only trying to get the truth," Chris responded. "For instance, I know either you or Mrs Wedge fire the shots into their faces."

"Very clever Inspector," Mr Crompton replied. "Of course you were there?" he teased in a sarcastic voice.

"Your fingerprints were on the gun the one we found in Mr Webb's room," Chris replied.

"I don't think so Inspector," Mr Crompton replied with a anger on his face.

"Oh, I'm sorry I said gun," Chris replied. "I should have said on the cartridges that were still in the chamber, yours and Mrs Wedge's fingerprints were on them."

"Let me also suggest that while you were getting the two bodies across to the bandstand, Mr Morris who uses the park as a short cut of getting home, caught you in the middle of it," Chris added with confidence.

"You know what we have done Inspector," Mr Crompton interrupted. "Mr Morris, his death was accidental, Mrs Wedge and myself had no part in it."

"Well tell us what happened?" Chris remarked.

Mr Crompton paused for a second before continued. "We were crossing from the front of the bungalow to the field with Mr Wedge's body when Mr Morris suddenly turned up, saw what we were doing and asked for an explanation. Mr Webb was just in the door way of the bungalow, he was going to carry my wife's body across. What happened then was very quick, Mr Webb came up behind Mr Morris and hit him with a cricket bat, where he got the cricket bat from I have no idea, but it was an accident, there was no intention of killing anyone."

"Then one of you carried Mr Morris's body, perhaps on your bicycle to the back of the park, where he was found a week later," Chris replied.

"Mr Webb did that, we had no part in it, we did use his gun however, it was the quickest and easiest way to disfigure the corpses," Mr Crompton answered.

Chris looked at Mr Melcher. "I have finished with Mr Webb, do you wish to say anything?"

"Not at this stage inspector," Mr Melcher replied.

Chris looked at Cam. "Constable Streeter, please take Mr Webb outside, read him his rights, and charge him with the murder of Mr Ronald Morris."

There was silence in the room as Cam took hold of Mr Webb's arm, and took him outside the office.

"Sergeant House," Chris said looking at George who had already risen from his seat.

"Please charge Mrs Wedge and Mr Crompton of the murder of Mrs Crompton and Mr Wedge together."

"You can't do that," Mr Crompton burst out. "You cannot be charged with shooting a dead man."

"That's right," Mrs Wedge added to the commotion. "Mr Melcher made that clear," she shouted.

"I am afraid when you shot Mrs Crompton and Mr Wedge, they were both alive,"
Chris replied.

"No, they were not," Mr Crompton shouted. "I felt for their pulse, they had none."

"They were both in a deep coma, but still alive," Chris said his face serious.

"I believe you knew this, other wise, why did you come up with this ridicules idea of trying to hide their identification. Had they been dead, it would have been best for Mrs Wedge position just to leave them in the bungalow. Mr Wedge would have been found dead, and his inheritance passed down to his sons without fuss. You murdered the partners of each of you for financial gains, and I believe out of hatred, Mr Webb perhaps did not intend to murder Mr Morris, but he did, the law is clear, it was murder."

Half hour later George and Cam had returned to the office, which had been cleared of the extra chairs.

"They are now locked up Chris," George informed. "You did well."

"Thanks George," Chris replied.

"I spent all yesterday afternoon going over the reports we have made, my eyes got tired, Elizabeth says I need glasses just for reading," he smiled.

"I don't think I shall be any good having an interview like that," Cam remarked.

"You do not have to do what I do Cam," Chris replied with a smile.

"I just follow my old Chief Inspector Noal, he was good at it, a lot better than I, he would never arrest anyone unless he was a hundred percent sure, I more or less knew by last night everything, I had to make sure, I had somehow to make them confess, and they did."

"You kept away from saying that Mrs Crompton and Mr Wedge was actually alive when they were shot?" George remarked.

Chris smiled. "Yes, and I am grateful to Mr Melcher, he related the law as it stands, one can not be charged with murder when the person is already dead, it is the law, but it was also a help to me, it relaxed those responsible, and they opened up believing they were safe, however I am convinced that they knew Mrs Crompton and Mr Wedge were still alive, as I said, had they been dead, they could just have left the bodies, and Mrs Wedge's sons would have inherited his estate in Australia without fuss, being alive however they had to get the bodies out of the bungalow, they could not kill them inside, wanting to hide their identification."

"Why was it that the gunshots were not heard?" Cam asked.

Chris shrugged. "That Cam is a good question, I don't really know, I do know that there were strong gust of wind that night, perhaps these gust took the noise away, I really don't know."

"Are you sure Mrs Crompton did take the barbiturates from Mr Wright?" George asked curiously.

"I spoke to Reverend Mace the priest of Holy Trinity Church, he told me she was a devotee Christian, I asked him questions about religious beliefs, he told me that adultery was a sin also committing suicide was a sin, one would never get into heaven if they destroyed the life that God gave them, devoted Christians believe this, and that had me worried," Chris commented.

"Mrs Crompton was in a no win situation, you see Cam, love can be wonderful, it can make you very happy and glad to be alive, it can also hurt, make you so full of despair that you do not want to live, perhaps that is why you cannot ask to be in love or loved, it comes with a feeling, if the feeling is there or it grows, nothing can stop it, it is powerful," getting no comeback Chris continued.

"Mrs Crompton in my opinion was a good person, happy in her marriage until Mrs Wedge came along, and seduced her husband, her husband was so taken by Mrs Wedge that he even lied to his wife about being impotent so that he would not have to touch her. Somehow later Mrs Crompton met Mr Wedge, they fell in love, and later became lovers which was against Mrs Crompton's belief, and also committing adultery."

"One hell of a coincidence," George interrupted.

"Yes George," Chris admitted.

"I don't as a rule believe in coincidences, but in this case it do seem that the four of them, each married the wrong partner. Anyway, already going against her faith by committing adultery, Mrs Crompton found herself pregnant with Mr Webb's child, who had raped her by blackmailing, she knew it did not belong to her lover Mr Wedge, women seem to know these things," he remarked. "She also knew she could not keep it a secret for long, as she would start to show."

"So do you think it was a suicide pact between the both of them or did Mrs Crompton poison Mr Wedge without him knowing?" Cam asked.

Chris thought for a while. "That's difficult Cam," he replied.

"Her sins already would not allow her in heaven, Mrs Crompton would rather die, and should her pregnancy come to light after her death, her lover would believe that the child was his, and would love her memory rather than hate it, I like to believe that when Mrs Crompton poured out the two glasses wine that night in Mr Jarvis's bungalow, one already laced with the barbiturates, Mr Wedge did not know, and took the wrong glass by mistake and drank it, falling into a coma, realising the mistake, Mrs Crompton then put the remaining barbiturates into her own glass and drank, laid down beside him, holding his hand," Chris said.

"That is rather a sad story," George admitted. "She must have been driven to it with all her worries."

"You were right last week George, when you said these murders happened because of Mr Wedge's inheritance, without that, I do not think we would have had any murder, I don't think while they were spying in the window they had any thought of murder, but the situation they found presented an opportunity, and they took it."

"What would have happened had we not identified them?" Cam asked.

Chris thought for a while. "I believe that Mr Crompton would have taken Mr Wedge's place, and claimed the estate in Australia, the true Mr Wedge would have been buried in an unknown paupers grave, and forgotten."

"Mr Webb, he will be charged with Mr Morris's murder?" Cam asked.

"He will be, even if I am wrong in saying that Mrs Wedge and Mr Crompton knew that their partners were still alive when their faces were destroyed, Mr Webb intended to kill Mr Morris, he really had no choice, leaving him alive was no option."

"So what do we do now?" Cam asked.

"We have three things to do Cam," Chris replied. Mrs Wedge has two children at school, arrangements must be made for them, and Mr Wood at the Suffolk Hotel must be told, he will be short of staff."

"Both already taken care of," George interrupted. "Mrs Wedge has asked Mr Melcher to see her parents, who will take care of her boys, he will also inform Mr Wood, that's two, what's the third?"

"You will have to see the Morris family, George," Chris replied looking at him.

"Or would you rather I did it?" Chris asked with a teasing smile on his face.

"No, no, I can manage that," George replied quickly. "In fact I better go now, the sooner they know the truth, the better it will be for them."

"I agree," Chris replied smiling to himself as he watched George leave the office, Chris knew George desperately wanted to see Rosemary.

THE END

BOOK TWO

INSPECTOR
CHRIS HARDIE

THE SINGING

BARROW BOY

Chapter One

*E*lizabeth clung to her husband's arm, as they made their way to their respective employment. It was a glorious August morning, the sun was already high.

"I really enjoyed yesterday darling," Elizabeth remarked as they passed the King Alfred Statue. "It was lovely and a complete change."

"I agree," Chris replied patting Elizabeth's hand.

Sunday had been a day off for Chris, and with Olive and Ron, all had cycled out to the Worthies, where they relaxed by a small stream, under the shade of a large oak tree, and enjoyed a picnic that Olive had prepared with great care.

"Olive and Ron enjoyed it very much too," Chris remarked.

"The cycling done them good," Elizabeth giggled. "They do not get a lot of exercise."

Chris smiled. "Apart from being a little sore, it did me good, I get little exercise myself."

As they stopped outside the Police Station, Chris smiled down at her. "I love you Mrs Elizabeth Hardie," he said.

"I love you Detective Inspector Hardie," she replied planting a kiss on his cheek. "Usual time tonight?" she smiled.

"I shall be here as long as it's quiet," Chris replied. "Keep on the inside of the pavements, a few motor cars are about, and they are incline to make the horses nervous," he added seriously, then with a smile as he let her go. "The soldiers can look at you and eat their hearts out, they deserve some reward, but you are not allowed to look at them."

Elizabeth smiled back. "I only have eyes for you darling," she said planting another kiss on his cheek. "But I must leave you now, I shall be late at the Bank."

Chris watched until she was out of sight before entering the police station.

Sergeant Williams looked up as he entered. "Morning Inspector, enjoyed your day off?" he greeted him.

"I certainly did Sergeant," Chris replied. "Anyone in yet?"

"Both," sergeant Williams replied with a smile.

Detective Sergeant George House and Detective Constable Cam Streeter were both at their desk, looked up and greeted Chris as he entered and hung his trilby.

"You look as though you had a good day off?" George remarked.

"I did as a matter of fact, we went on a picnic, it was a hot day," Chris replied.

"In-laws as well?" Cam asked.

"The lot of us," Chris replied. "Another day off would have been acceptable."

"Good job you didn't," George replied. "The body of a young lady was found at Winnall Moors, she was naked, and sliced up a bit, the police surgeon Bob Harvey believes she had been in the water a few days, you know there is a large pond there that freezes over during the winter months, which allows people to ice skate."

"I'm not familiar this part of Winnall Moors," Chris replied. "The river Itchen I suppose?"

"Well the Itchen runs along there, but this is more like a huge pond, reaches across to the Park," George answered.

Chris used his imagination for a moment. "A large pond," he murmured. "Must be static, not running, then the only movement of the pond water can only be made by the wind."

"Did Bob have any idea how long she had been dead?" Chris asked.

"A few days, was all he could say," George replied. "She was sliced up a bit, her buttocks and inner thighs seem have been cut off."

"Really," Chris murmured. "What age?"

"About twenty five," according to Bob. "He had no idea how she died."

"Have we have any young women reported missing?" Chris asked.

"I checked," Cam interrupted. "No recent ones, plenty old ones."

"Would there be many young women at her age living alone?" Chris questioned. "I mean she would not get a council house if she was single, if she was married, after a few days her husband would have reported her surely, did she have a ring on her finger?"

"She did," George replied.

"That at least tells us she was married," Chris remarked.

"She could have been divorced, widowed, or separated, therefore living on her own," Cam voiced.

"She could have indeed," Chris answered. "Did Bob say when he would be able to give us more details?"

"We were unable to contact you yesterday," George replied. "We did try, Bob said he would try to give you some information by today, he'll be working most of the night he said."

Chris smiled. "That's Bob," he remarked. "But all we can do at the moment is to wait for his report, if she was sliced up, it seems to indicate murder."

It was gone ten that morning, when a tired looking Bob Harvey entered the office, after greeting them all, Bob sat in the interview chair. "Been at it most of the night, only had a couple hours rest."

"Would you like a cup of tea Bob?" Chris asked.

"No, thanks Chris," Bob replied. "I have drank gallons of the stuff to keep me awake."

"Was it a murder?" Chris asked.

"She was suffocated," Bob replied. "I doubt if she could have done that herself, she also was sliced up a bit, her buttocks and inner thighs seem have been cut off."

Chris leaned back in his chair, he smiled at Bob. "Any meaning to that Bob?" he asked worriedly.

"The fleshy parts of her buttocks and the inner thighs were cut off," Bob answered. "Sliced off as one would when carving meat at a dinner."

Chris shook his head, not understanding. "Sorry Bob but I'm lost."

Bob grinned. "I am trying to tell you Chris, that I believe you have a case of cannibalism on your hands."

"Really Bob," Chris replied the shock showing in his face. "You can't be sure?"

"I remember reading story that happened in Scotland many years ago, I forget the date, it was about a family called Bean or Beam, I'm not quite sure," Cam interrupted. "There was several daughters and sons, grandchildren and parents, about thirty of them there was," Cam saw that the others was listening to him intently, he swallowed and carried on.

"This family lived at an isolated spot in Scotland, at a coastal cave where they lived undiscovered for some years, the cave was 200 yards deep and during high tide the entrance was blocked by water. They were never seen during the day, they only came out at night to rob and murder individuals or small groups, the bodies were brought back to the cave, where they were dismembered and eaten. Leftovers were pickled, and discarded body parts would sometimes wash up on nearby beaches. The body parts and disappearances did not go unnoticed by the local villagers, but the Beans stayed in the caves by day and took their victims at night, it is said they killed and ate one hundreds of people over the years."

"Were they caught?" George asked interested.

"Eventually the clan was captured alive and taken in chains to the Tolbooth Jail in Edinburgh, then transferred to Leith or Glasgow where they were promptly executed without trial, the men had their genitals cut off, hands and feet severed, and were allowed to bleed to death, the women and children, after watching the men die, were burned alive," Cam replied.

"That was a bit extreme," George replied. "It must have been centuries ago, not years?" he said in disbelief.

"I forget the date, I do remember that the Scots treated their crime worse than that of a traitor," Cam replied.

"That's all very interesting Cam," Chris remarked even though he himself was interested.

"Bob, how long has she been dead, and was she in the water long?"

"I would say just two days," Bob replied. "I would say she was left where we found her, at the edge of the water which lapped over her, she was not killed there."

211

"She was killed say during Friday evening?" Chris asked.

"I would say so," Bob confirmed.

"Was she raped?" George asked.

"There are signs that she had sex, but I would not say she had been raped, the water that was around her of course can bury certain facts."

"So, she could have had sex willingly with the person who killed her, which means she was close to him," George remarked.

"It seems that way," Bob replied.

"There is no houses around there, is there?" Chris asked.

"People, children mainly do camp around there," Cam interrupted. "Opposite the Gas House farther down there is a place with overgrown weeds that is called the jungle, children spends a lot of their school holiday down there."

"Let's recap on what we have?" Chris spoke. "We have a young woman, left at the water edge at the Winnall Moors. She has been dead about two days, but was not murdered there, she has been mutilated which gives concern about a possible cannibalism, cannibalism is not common, if she was not murdered there, obviously she was taken there."

"Like always we are up a gumtree," George replied.

"I do have her wedding ring," Bob said taking a envelope out of his pocket and gave it to Chris. "There are initials inside the ring, Love PM."

Chris studied the ring for a while. "At least we have a start," he remarked looking at Cam. "Cam take this ring around the Jewellers, she is not very old, so the ring can't be more than a few years old, one might remember or know their work."

"Do you know anything about cannibalism Bob?" Chris asked after Cam had left.

"Not a lot I'm afraid, I have heard of the Bean legend that Cam was on about."

"If we find out who she is?" Bob said. "We should keep it secret, when she is identified it will only be her face to look at, her body would be covered, anyway, best of luck with this case, and be prepared this body was dumped before it was completely eaten, usually only the bones are left, which are then thrown down a well, or thrown to a dog to chew," Bob said standing. "It's a gruesome business," he added leaving the office.

"Well George," Chris remarked after Bob had left the room. "Where to start is the problem, let's hope Cam gets a result, in the meantime, can you go back in our records of all persons missing and not found, say for about ten years back."

"Men or women?" George asked.

Chris shrugged. "Do cannibals only eat women, I don't know much about them, best to get both sexes."

"It's going to take time Chris," George remarked about to leave the office.

"I know George," Chris replied. "Even when you have the list, it won't help, but maybe it will, should we catch him."

Chapter Two

*L*eft alone, Chris pondered on the case, he knew he was dealing with a murder, that should it turn out to be cannibalism, he would be working in the dark, he decided to wait until the first opening came, and he was hoping that Cam would bear some results, somewhere to start.

Sergeant Williams knocked and entered. "I have a Mr Collins at the desk Sir," he said respectfully. "His daughter seems to be missing."

Chris sighed. "Really," he replied trying to hide his excitement. "Perhaps I should speak to him, show him in."

Mr Collins entered the office, Chris stood and offered his hand, Mr Collins was about fifty, obviously a labourer, he held an old brown trilby in his hand, his open neck shirt was covered by a red hanky around his neck, his coat and waistcoat were different colours, and around the knees of his thick brown trouser's string was tied.

"Please Mr Collins take the chair," Chris indicated with his hand. "I am Detective Inspector Hardie, how can I help you?"

"It's my daughter Sir," Mr Collins answered respectfully. "She seems to be missing."

"Really," Chris replied. "Since when?"

"She left her husband's house last Friday night late, she was supposed to come home to me," Mr Collins answered nervously.

Chris picked up his pencil. "Better to get your details first Mr Collins," Chris smiled. "Where do you live?"

"Water Lane, number 14, next to the Chester Road," Mr Collins explained.

"I know the road," Chris admitted. "There is a chapel built over the river there."

"Down a little from me, towards the Fox Inn," Mr Collins replied.

"Now Mr Collins," Chris added. "Your daughter been missing since Friday, how is it that you have just reported it?"

"Because I had no idea until this morning," Mr Collins replied twitching his trilby rim.

Chris tapped his pencil on the desk. "Perhaps you can tell me your story?" he asked.

"Well it's like this," Mr Collins begun. "My daughter Olive married Paul Marston who lives at 2 Chester Road, they had known each other since childhood, married five years ago, anyway, the marriage was alright for the first few years, but during the last year, they have been having squabbles, nothing serious, but my Olive is pig headed, just like her dear mother, and sometimes she will come home to me when one of these squabbles happens, then after a day, go back to her husband."

"Your daughter lives with her husband at number 2, Chester Road?" Chris interrupted.

"That's right, they don't have a place of their own, they live with Paul's mother, anyway to cut a long story short, I was on my way to work this morning, I met Paul who was also going to work, he asked how Olive was, I looked at him asking what he meant, and he told me that Olive had walked out Friday night after a squabble, he thought she had come to me."

"Do you have a wife and other children?" Chris asked.

"I have two daughters and a son, my wife died in childbirth with my son, who now lives at Shawford with his wife and two children," Mr Collins replied.

"And your other daughter Mr Collins?" Chris asked.

"She went missing about four years ago, never been found," Mr Collins answered looking down at his lap.

"I am sorry Mr Collins," Chris said gently. "Life has not been kind to you, you reported your daughter missing?"

"Yes I did, but she was never found, it's a mystery," Mr Collins replied.

"You had to bring up your children on your own then Mr Collins, no easy for a man who had to work all day?"

Mr Collins gave a weak smile. "I managed with the help of my mother, but sadly my mother died, but by that time my daughters were old enough to look after themselves and take care of Robert my son."

Chris could not help feeling for Mr Collins, realising that his life had not been easy, Chris took the receiver from the phone. "What number do your son live at Shawford?" Chris asked.

"Number 6, Shawford Road, opposite the Bridge Hotel," Mr Collins replied.

"Sergeant," Chris spoke into the receiver. "Contact the constable at Twyford, ask him to go to number 6, Shawford Road, and find out if a Mrs Marston is there as soon as possible, tell him to play it light, don't unduly worry who he sees, whether Mr or Mrs Collins."

Chris put the receiver back. "Well we will know soon whether your daughter went to her brother, now Mr Collins, what did your daughter look like?"

"She has dark hair like her dear mother," Mr Collins began. "She is about five foot tall, not fat nor thin, I would say an attractive figure, I consider all my children beautiful Inspector."

Chris could see that Mr Collins was keeping a tight grip on his emotions, but his eyes were watery.

"Would you like a cup of tea Mr Collins?" Chris asked feeling for him.

"Thank you no Inspector, I don't feel like anything at the moment."

"Out at work all day, do you see your daughter much?" Chris asked.

"Not a lot, she sometimes call in the evening or Sunday when she knows I am home, but she do call in when I am at work and tidy up the house a bit, I'm not a tidy man I admit, she's a good daughter," Mr Collins replied.

"I am sure she is," Chris murmured. "Where do you work?"

"For the last year I have been working with a group of men, digging trenches for electric cables," he replied.

"Really," Chris replied. "We will all have electric soon I believe, where are you working now?"

"Coming down Stockbridge Road," Mr Collins answered.

"Keeps one fit, I expect?" Chris smiled.

"Summers OK, but winter times not so good, easy to catch colds and flue," Mr Collins replied. "Still that's life, you have to take what life throw at you, no good fighting it."

The telephone rang. "That will be the Twyford constable, he is only five minutes away from where your son lives," Chris said to Mr Collins.

Lifted the receiver, a few moments later Chris replaced the receiver, and looked at Mr Collins. "The Twyford constable, saw your daughter-in-law, I am afraid your daughter is not there."

Mr Collins looked at his lap, made no comment.

"We at least know where she is not," Chris remarked. "We will now carry out our routine, you can be sure Mr Collins, we keep you informed."

Mr Collins stood. "I must get back to work, can't afford to get the sack, I know you will do your best, but it's not easy having already lost one daughter who was never found."

Chris stood. "I am sure it is not, but please Mr Collins, believe that I will do everything in my power to find your daughter," Chris said offering his hand. "As soon as I have any news, I will send a constable to you."

"You're very kind Inspector," Mr Collins remarked shaking the outstretched hand. "I believe you will."

George came into the office. "I have been through the missing persons files, going back ten years," he said going to his desk with sheets of paper. "We have sixteen young girls all no older than twenty, four older women, and two young boys."

"Quite a lot, none ever found?" Chris asked.

"No Chris, all gone without a trace, strange though, all the girls seem to live this side of the Brooks."

"Do you have a Miss Collins on the list, missing about four years ago?" Chris asked.

George checked his sheets before answering. "Yes a Miss Lucy Collins, missing in 1912, usual routine followed, but no trace found, lived at Water Lane, as I said most of these girls are from the bottom half of the town."

Chris then told George of his meeting with Mr Collins.

218

"Not looking too good Chris," George remarked. "Can there really be a cannibal walking around in Winchester?" he asked.

"I dread to think so George, but it looks as though we will have to take it seriously," Chris said as Cam entered the office.

"No luck with the ring," he said going to his desk. "I have been to all the jewellers in Winchester, not one recognised the description or the work."

"Well it had to be done Cam," Chris replied.

After Cam had been told of the morning happenings, Chris took out his pipe, lit it and puffed. "What are you doing tonight George?" Chris asked between puffs.

George looked at Chris with a grin on his face. "I have a date," he said.

"Really," Chris replied. "Anyone we know?"

"I have had an invitation from Mrs Morris, inviting me to dinner," George answered his grin remaining.

"Lucky thing," Cam remarked.

"Well some of us have it, some don't," George joked. "Why Chris have you something in mind?"

"It's OK, you go on your date, Elizabeth would give me hell, if she thought our work stopped you seeing Rosemary," Chris said smiling at Cam. "I'll take Cam with me, I want to see this Mr Paul Marston tonight, that's if Cam hasn't got a date?" Chris smiled looking at Cam.

"No, I'm free," Cam replied.

"Tomorrow George, can you visit those addresses of the missing girls, you said they were all this end of town, see if anything comes out that is common to most cases, we have to start somewhere."

"Plenty of the day left so I'll start now, if that's OK?" George replied.

"Good man," Chris said. "We will expect you when we see you, please give my regards to the Morris family."

The day seemed to drag on, he was anxious to see Mr Marston, he could not go before, as Mr Collins had told him he had seen Mr Marston going to work, and assumed that it would be evening before he returned home.

Chris checked his watched. "It's coming to six Cam, go home and have your meal, I will meet you at the entrance of Chester Road at seven thirty, that will give the Mr Marston plenty of time to have his meal."

Elizabeth was waiting when Chris left the station. "Hello darling," she said planting a kiss on his cheek. "I have missed you," she smiled.

"I missed you as well," Chris replied as they made their way home. "I have to go out after dinner," Chris informed her. "While we were having the picnic on Sunday, a body of a young woman was found at Winnall Moors, I need to see her husband when he gets home from work tonight."

"Of course you must," Elizabeth answered. "At least you will be able to have a meal before you go, is it far?"

"No only a Chester Road, it should not take long," Chris replied. "Oh by the way, George can't come with me." "Why not darling?" Elizabeth asked, knowing that George went on all interviews with Chris.

"He has a date," Chris replied a smile on his face.

"What are you smiling about?" Elizabeth asked. "Are you teasing?"

"No, but you will never guess who he is going to see?" Chris replied.

"Tell me darling," Elizabeth asked squeezing his arm.

"Rosemary Morris," Chris answered.

"I am so glad," Elizabeth sighed. "Rosemary is a very nice beautiful girl, she needs someone to protect her, I have you, it do seem that us girls are not safe walking alone today, do you know the name of the dead girl?"

"Not sure enough yet to name her," Chris answered as they reached home, and saw Olive waiting at the open door.

Chapter Three

It was seven thirty when Chris met Cam at the entrance of Chester Road. "Ask what you want, Cam, don't keep quiet," Chris remarked as he knocked the door of number two.

The door was opened by a stout woman with a pleasant face, wearing an apron over her dress, on which she was drying her hands.

"Yes?" she asked.

"I am Detective Inspector Hardie, and this is Detective Constable Streeter," Chris answered. "We would like to see Mr Paul Marston, I believe he lives here."

"I am his mother," the woman replied. "Is this about his wife?"

"We would like to speak to Mr Paul Marston," Chris replied ignoring the her question.

"Well you had better come in, I have just cleaned the table and I am doing the washing up, you will have to forgive the state."

Chris smiled. "Thank you Mrs Marston, we will not stay long," he said as followed by Cam he entered the house and was shown into the dining room, where a young man was reading a paper spread out on the table.

"Paul, these men are from the police," Mrs Marston said to her son, who was looking at them.

Paul folded the paper. "Is it about my wife?" he asked. "Her father told me this morning that she was not at home."

"Aren't you worried Mr Marston?" Chris asked taking a chair he had been offered.

Paul shook his head. "Should I be?" he asked. "Olive my wife is always storming out lately, don't know what's the matter with her?"

"I can vouch for that," Mrs Marston commented. "Silly girl, don't know where her bread is buttered, my son works all hours to keep her, she never goes short of anything."

"I take it she normally go to her father when she storms out?" Chris asked.

"As far as I know," Paul replied. "But she has brother at Shawford."

"When her father reported her missing, we did check her brother at Shawford, she is not there, can you think of any other places she might go?" Chris asked.

"Dear oh dear," Mrs Marston interrupted in a friendlier tone. "Do you really think she is missing?"

"It looks that way, but then again a missing person will often turn up, after staying with a friend," Chris replied.

"Her storming out don't happen a lot, apart from that we normally stay here and listen to the radio, you see I have to be at work early, and haven't the money or the energy to go out," Mr Marston spoke.

"Where do you work?" Cam asked.

"On the railway, track work, it's pretty hard work," Paul remarked.

I wheel a wheelbarrow, through streets broad and narrow, selling kindling and logs at three for a penny.

"Who's singing?" Chris asked looking at the window, I hear someone singing a song outside.

223

"That's Jason Keen," Mr Marston smiled. "He lives next door, at number one, that's his wood shed on the other side of the road."

"Really," Chris replied.

"Yes I have heard of him," Cam remarked. "Quite a character I believe he's called the singing barrow boy."

"Hardly a boy, he is passed thirty, but he works hard and harmless," Mr Marston replied. "Works most of the day cutting up wood in that shed, and at nights goes around the streets selling it.

"And sings," Chris remarked.

"It's his way of letting people know he is about," Mr Marston replied.

"Can you describe your wife?" Cam asked as the singing faded.

"She's pretty, about five foot something, not very tall, with dark hair, she is not fat," Paul remarked.

"About what time did she leave that night?" Chris asked.

Paul thought for a while. "It was rather late, we had tea, then we went to our room and messed about for a while, I would say around nine," he answered.

"What about jewellery, does she wear any?" Chris asked.

"Not much," Paul replied. "She is into shoes and dresses though, apart from her wedding band, she wear very little jewellery."

"Would the ring had a description on it?" Chris asked.

"Love PM," Paul replied. "Had it done when we were on our honeymoon at Southsea."

Chris looked at Cam, knowing that the body was that of Olive Marston, he looked at Mrs Marston and her son Paul who were sitting together.

"I have bad news for you I am afraid," Chris said as gentle as he could. "On Sunday a body of a young lady was discovered at Winnall Moors, she had been strangled, she wore a wedding band with the initials PM inside."

Mrs Marston put her arm around Paul, who seem to be in shock. "Are you sure Inspector?" she asked.

"She fits the description of your son's wife," Chris answered.

"What could she have been doing at Winnall Moors?" Mrs Marston murmured. "I had supposed she went to her father's house."

"When your wife left Mr Marston, did you see which way she went?" Cam asked.

"She went towards Blue Ball Hill," Mrs Marston interrupted. "But whether she went up or down, I don't know."

"Did your wife like a drink?" Cam asked.

Paul straightened himself up. "We would sometimes cross the road for a drink, there are at least nine or ten pubs from here all within five hundred yards, but only on occasions."

"She would not have gone in a pub on her own?" Cam asked.

"No," Paul said shaking his head. "She was not a drinker, just a shandy now and again, but is this getting us anywhere?" he asked.

"Just a thought she might have gone into a pub, perhaps met someone, as you said she stormed out after a row, women are sometimes vulnerable after a row, and will do things that is not normally do, did you go out after your wife left, perhaps looking for her to make it up with her?"

"No I did not," Paul replied. "Olive just wouldn't budge to give me a chance, she was stubborn, and needed a night to come round, I did expect her on Saturday, but I suppose I'm stubborn as well."

"You must understand Mr Marston, our questions are just routine, we are in charge with finding your wife's murderer, and we need to ask a lot of questions," Chris said. "Now I must tell you that your wife was naked when she was found."

"Good God," Mrs Marston gasped. "Was she interfered with?"

"If your son can tell us whether some sort of activity took place before his wife stormed out, we could be sure," Chris replied.

Paul looked at his mother before answering. "We did mess about a bit," he replied. "It was before that the row started."

"Thank you Mr Marston," Chris remarked. "I think you can at least rest assured that your wife was not interfered with."

"That's one blessing anyway," Mrs Marston replied. "But why was she naked?"

"We believe she was killed elsewhere," Chris informed her. "Why her clothes are missing, we will eventually find out."

"When can I see her?" Paul asked.

"I'll try and arrange it for tomorrow," Chris replied. "I will now have to go to her father who reported her missing."

"That will be the end of him," Mrs Marston remarked. "He has already lost one daughter, who was never found, I will call on him, he will be in a state."

"That was not a pleasant experience with Olive Marston's father, Cam," Chris remarked the next morning when both were in the office.

"It must have been devastating for him having already lost a daughter in the same circumstances," Cam replied. "I was thankful when Mrs Marston called."

"So was I," Chris agreed. "Situations like that needs a women, they seem to be able to control situations better than men."

George entered the office. "Finished already?" Chris asked.

George smiled. "No, done a few, just thought I would have a break for a half hour, the two missing boys both of them went to St John's School."

"I know the school," Chris replied.

"Both went missing after leaving the school, both five years old, both went missing in 1910, both just completely vanished. I have also checked on two of the older women, one living at Eastgate Street disappeared in1909, the other at Durngate Place disappeared 1912, both around fifty years old," George informed them.

"I am not being funny," Cam remarked. "But if we are dealing with a cannibal, would he eat the young and the old, I mean, humans must be like animals, the older you are the tougher."

"I know what you are meaning Cam," Chris replied. "But I am not an authority on cannibalism, I can't even imagine anyone wanting to eat a human, I know we are assuming that it is a man, but do we have women cannibals," Chris said with a shrug.

"Well if any of our missing persons are victims, then they started to disappear a decade ago, the first one went missing in 1906, she was a missing young lady of about fifteen, a Miss Neil Keen of number one Chester Road, next door to where you went last night."

"Really," Chris remarked. "It must have been her brother we heard singing Cam."

"The singing barrow boy," Cam smiled.

"Is it?" George remarked. "I have seen him a couple times myself in the Brooks, he sings all the time, my landlady buys logs from him."

Chris then went on putting George in the picture as what occurred the evening before.

"We had a time with Mr Collins, but thankfully Mrs Marston came in," Chris spoke. "Cam, I want you to collect Mr Marston and Mr Collins this morning and take to the morgue to identify the woman," Chris remarked.

"How did you get on with your date last night George?" Chris asked a smile on his face.

"Good," George replied. "Mr and Mrs Morris was there as well, we had a nice roast beef dinner, I was told that Rosemary cooked the meal, and I have tasted none better."

"How are they coping with their son's murder?" Chris asked.

"They seem to be OK, but their son was not brought up, I stopped about four hours, made very welcomed. Rosemary walked me to the road, we shook hands and said goodnight."

"Didn't you ask her out?" Cam asked.

"I lost my nerve," George confessed. "I wanted to, and I had a feeling she wanted me to ask, I suppose I'm just a coward."

"If Rosemary is for you George," Chris replied thinking of Elizabeth who would want to bring them together. "You will see her again?"

"I hope so Chris, she's a lovely girl, anyway, I have work to do, I must get off," George remarked standing up.

"George," Chris said. "It would be best to see Mr Jason Keen daytime, I understand that he works most of the day cutting up wood in his shed, only delivers at night, we should see him this afternoon."

"I have a couple call back to do," George replied. "I'll see you in the Blue Ball Inn, say at one thirty," George said with a smile.

"That will suit me fine," Chris replied. "I have sandwiches that Elizabeth made."

"What do you want me to do Chris?" Cam asked.

"Well you have to go to the morgue, Bob said he would be ready any time after ten, so I will leave it with you what time you collect Mr Collins and Mr Marston, but make it this morning," Chris replied.

"I can do that," Cam smiled.

Chapter Four

*C*hris and George sat in a corner of the Blue Ball Inn at a table that over looked the Blue Ball Hill. Chris drank from his glass, while George eating a sandwich that Chris had laid open on the table.

"I'm not having a good feeling about this case George, perhaps we are assuming too much." Chris remarked as he chewed.

"How come?" replied George after washing his food down with his beer.

"Well at the moment we have cannibalism on our minds, these missing people may not have any connection with it, they could all still be alive, perhaps some of them were kidnapped, who knows?"

"You are right of course," George remarked. "But what I wonder about is during the last ten years why all these missing people are from this half of the town, are we looking for someone who moved here ten years ago?"

"We will only be able to answer that question when we find who is responsible?" Chris answered taking another swig of his pint. "We just need a starting point, something we can build on, cannibalism seem to be almost perfect murders, they leave no bodies."

"They leave bones," George remarked emptying his glass.

"Yes," Chris agreed. "But there are far more ways of getting rid of bones than a body."

"We have time for another," George remarked picking up Chris's empty glass and going to the bar. "I've been thinking," George said as he came back to the table with fresh pints. "It's Mrs Olive Marston we have to concentrate on, she came from this part of the town, at the bottom of this hill, she was also found at Winnall Moors, a few hundred yards along Wales Street, what one might call a stone throw."

"That's good thinking George," Chris replied taking a drink. "We know she left home about nine that night, hardly time to go any place apart from her father's, would she have crossed the river into Union or Eastgate Street at that time of night, if she did not cross the river, then she only had a part of Water Lane and Wales Street left to be in. If you are right George, our murderer could be within a quarter mile from where we are now."

Chris took a drink of his beer and smacked his lips. "Soon after leaving her husband's house in Chester Road, she could've been abducted, she could've been taken into a house shall we say, where she was strangled, stripped, and also she was sliced up," Chris commented. "After that she was somehow transported to Winnall Moors where she was found."

George did not comment, just nodded his head, and finished his pint.

After Chris had talked to the landlord, George followed Chris out of the pub.

"She did not come in here," Chris remarked. "In fact the landlord did not know her," Chris added as they made their way down the hill to Chester Road. "We know she did not usually go into pubs on her own."

Turning into Chester Road, they looked at the empty patch, and saw the wooden doors of the shack open, they crossed over and stood before the open doors. Jason Keen was sitting on a stool chopping kindling wood on a section of a tree trunk about eighteen inches tall, he smiled when he saw them, and stopped chopping.

"I don't deliver until evenings," he said. "Perhaps if you leave your address, I come by tonight."

Chris followed by George took a step inside. "You are a busy man Mr Keen," Chris said with a smile.

"Don't have a lot of time to waste," Jason replied looking at them. "How can I help?"

"I am Detective Inspector Hardie, and my colleague Detective Sergeant House, we would like to ask you a few questions."

"I have done nothing wrong," Jason replied. "I work on my own, live on my own, and don't interfere with anyone."

"I'm sure you haven't Mr Keen," Chris answered. "Your neighbour Mrs Marston went missing last Friday, we are in the process of checking all missing persons going back ten years, and we find your name on the list."

"Who would want to harm Mrs Marston, she seems a nice person, my name being on your list, you must mean my sister Neil, she went missing years ago, and your men could not find her, that's why I am living alone."

"I never said Mrs Marston had been harmed Mr Keen, just she was missing," Chris replied. "And it's the younger Mrs Marston that is missing."

"I'm sorry," Jason replied. "I have hardly spoken to the younger Mrs Marston, she was out of my mind."

"Your sister Neil," George remarked. "I wonder Mr Keen, was there anything that you did not tell the police when they were investigating?"

Jason stood up. "Look I'm off across the road for a cup of tea, perhaps you would like to join me?"

"Glad to," George replied, watching Jason take off his leather apron and about to leave. "Don't you lock up?"

Jason smiled. "I am only across the road, anyway who going to steal wood. I do lock at night time, funny you mentioned that, I saw the lock had been tampered with last Saturday morning so I put a new one on, perhaps it was some poor beggar looking for a place to kip," he grinned.

"We heard you singing when you came home last night Mr Keen," Chris remarked.

"Did you?" Jason remarked. "I'm good aren't I?" Jason chuckled.

"Yes you have a fine voice," Chris flattered.

"I have enough practice," Jason replied. "I have been doing it for years, people hear me coming, and come out to me."

"Would it not be easier or even better for you to cut the wood night time, and deliver the wood day time?" Chris asked.

"No it wouldn't," Jason replied abruptly. "Only women are home during the day, I meet mainly men at night."

"Don't you like women Mr Keen?" George asked.

"Don't know much about them," Jason replied. "Mother would never let me or my sister know any person of the opposite sex, that is why when your men was investigating my sister's disappearance, I told them that she would never had gone off with a man, put it another way, the only man she ever knew was myself, and I was five years older."

"In the same way, your sister was the only woman you knew?" Chris replied.

"Put it like that, yes I was," Jason replied.

Chris and George followed Jason across the road, Chris noticed he was dressed quite well for the job he did, he had a decent pair of shoes on well polished, he stood about five foot eight inches, but looked lean as though he needed a good meal, however Chris felt there was strength in his body.

"We'll use the side gate," Jason said as he lifted the wooden gate latch.

"Is this the back way for all the houses?" Chris asked as he followed.

"No, I am the only one with a side entrance, perhaps being on the end," Jason replied.

The kitchen was like most others, there was a gas stove, a kitchen cabinet, and a couple wall cupboards, everything was clean and tidy, nothing seems out of place.

"Won't be long," Jason smiled as he went to the draining board, put four spoonfuls of tea leafs in the teapot. "A spoonful for each person and one for the pot," he smiled looking at them.

"You are a very neat and tidy man," Chris remarked.

"Mother's training," Jason responded with a grin.

Jason filled the teapot with boiling water, putting a cosy over the teapot brought it to the table, and sat himself. "I'll be mum," he joked. "Help yourself to milk and sugar."

"Don't you get lonely?" George asked as he sipped his tea.

"Don't get the chance, I work most of the day in the shed, and deliver during the evenings, knackered by the time I finish, I usually go straight to bed after I have eaten."

"Is that a homemade barrow you have in your shed?" Chris asked.

"Yes," Jason replied with a grin. "Made it myself years ago all out of tree wood."

Chris smiled at the humour. "Wheels are from a pram?" he asked.

"Plenty of barrow around, nearly every house have one, but most are made with two wheels, I decided it would be easier for me if I had four, so I found two pairs on the dump, I keep them well oiled, anyway, what are the questions you want to ask?"

"Your sister went missing about ten years ago?" George asked.

"That's right, a year after mother died," Jason replied.

"What about your father?" George asked.

"Father died about two years after we moved here, had an accident at work, it changed mother, she became hard and forbidden, Neil and myself were never allowed out, she just kept us working, would not even allow us to go to school," Jason answered.

"How did you get the vacant lot across the road?" Chris asked.

"Not sure," Jason replied. "Father bought it, he built the shed, for a work shed I believe, I was quite young then."

"How long have you lived here?" George asked.

"Came here in 1900," Jason answered. "Queen Victoria died a little later I remember."

"Now you are sure that your sister would never have run away with a boy?" George asked.

"Positive," Jason replied. "She went out to do a bit of shopping, never came back."

"You reported it straight away?" George asked.

"That same night I did, I waited a few hours, but when she did not return, I went to your station, I'm sorry, I did not find them much of a help."

"They do have a routine to carry out Mr Keen," Chris replied. "You were living here when Miss Lucy Collins number 14 Water Lane went missing about four or five years ago?"

Jason shrugged. "I wouldn't have known her," he replied.

"Now we have Mrs Olive Marston lives next door to you who went missing Friday, you did not by chance see her did you?" Chris asked.

"I'm usually back by eight or eight thirty," Jason replied. "I see many people walking, but take little notice, I just carry on singing," he smiled.

"You have a fine voice, what is your route Mr Keen?" Chris flattered.

"All streets from Middle Brook Street to St John Street, I even go down Bar End," Jason replied. "It's enough, I make a comfortable living, I have no rent to pay."

"So on Friday last, you were home about eight to eight thirty then?" George asked.

"Don't know about the exact time, I was out having a drink, it was after the pubs shut, but I did not see young Mrs Marston," Jason replied.

"Thank you very much Mr Keen," Chris said after seeing George shaking his head. "Thank you very much for the tea, you will have to come to the station and show the constables how to make tea, it was enjoyable."

"I'm good at everything I do," Jason remarked with a grin. "I see, I listen, I never forget."

"There was not much more we could asked him?" Chris remarked as the both stood at the junction of Chester Road.

"I agree," George replied. "He certainly a clean and tidy chap."

"I thought that as well," Chris admitted.

"He told me the same as the others I have been to, the missing person left home and never came back, all completely disappeared," George remarked. "But I still have a few to see, perhaps we might find something."

"That's all we can do George," Chris replied. "I'll get back to the station then, see you when I see you."

Chapter Five

Chris entered the police station, wondering just where he was going with this case, no leads, no nothing. "Inspector," sergeant Williams said seeing him enter. "I have a young lady here, she wanted to see someone in charge, I think you might be interested in her case."

Chris looked at the young lady who was sitting in the waiting space. "Very well Sergeant bring her in," Chris replied making for his office.

"I am Detective Inspector Hardie," Chris said as he offered his hand which she took. "Please, take a seat," he indicated with his hand to the interview chair.

Chris smiled. "Now Miss..?"

"Nelly Green," replied the woman.

"How can I help you Miss Green?" Chris asked with a smile on his face. "You seem nervous, please try to relax and tell me how I can help you?"

"I suppose I am nervous," Nelly replied. "I had no intention of coming here, my mistress told me to come."

"I see," Chris replied trying to make her relax. "Your mistress, what do you mean by that?"

"I work in service, in the Worthies," Nelly replied. "I told the cook what happened to me last night, she told the mistress, who told me to come here."

"I see Nelly," Chris said gently, using her Christian name hoping to calm her. "Just what did happen to you last night?"

Nelly blushed. "My mother was out, when a man came, said he was checking houses, because electricity would be soon taking the place of the gas lighting, I let him in as you would, and when he was inside, he jumped on me, I was so frightened," Nelly swallowed.

"Would you like a cup of tea?" Chris asked seeing her embarrassment.

"No, thank you Sir," Nelly replied. "It's just a little difficult for me to explain, you are a man."

Chris could see she was uneasy. "Are you uneasy speaking to a doctor?" he asked.

"No Sir," replied Nelly. "But my mother is always with me."

"Would you like your mother with you now?" Chris asked.

"Oh no Sir, I don't want her to know," Nelly replied nervously.

"Well then Nelly, try to look upon me as a doctor, you are in a police station, you have nothing to fear," Chris replied gently. "How old are you, and where do you live?"

"I'm nineteen Sir, I live along Beggars Lane number three."

"I know the Lane," Chris replied. "It's a bit isolated along there."

"Just six houses," Nelly replied.

"And fields opposite," Chris remarked as he imagined the area. "What time did this man enter your home?"

"Mother was shopping, she usually go night times, shops are incline to lower their prices just before they shut, she goes after I get home which is around six thirty, it must have been around seven Sir," Nelly answered.

"Did this man do anything against your wishes?" Chris asked gently.

"He made me take off all my clothes," Nelly said with her face blushing. "Then he made me lay down, and he straddled my belly I was so frightened I could not even scream."

"Did you recognise this man?" Chris asked.

"No Sir, he had a scarf across his face, I only saw his eyes, all he was saying was, I could eat you, I could eat you, I was so frightened."

"I'm sure you were Nelly," Chris replied with feeling. "Did this man do anything else?"

"Well Sir," Nelly replied. "I know now he had me at his mercy, I was praying all the time for mother to come home, I think he must have heard something, he suddenly got up and left without a word."

"When did your mother get home?" Chris asked.

"About an hour later," Nelly replied. "By that time I had dressed and had a cup of tea, and had settled a bit."

"You did not tell your mother?" Chris asked.

"No Sir, I decided to talk to the cook, we get on fine, I can talk to cook better than I can talk to mother, sex is never mentioned at home."

"What about your father?" Chris asked.

"Father died a few years ago, he was very young, it was his habit to sit out on the window sill and smoke his pipe, one day, he just slipped off the sill, he had a heart attack."

"I am sorry Nelly," Chris replied seriously.

"That's alright Sir," Nelly replied. "I missed father, I was his only child, but time do make it easier."

"I'm sure it do Nelly," Chris remarked. "So you did not tell your mother, you spoke to your friend the cook about it?"

"That's right Sir, then the cook took me straight to the mistress, you see I thought I might be having a baby, he did sit across my belly, until my mistress told me this morning where babies come from, I always thought they come out of the belly button."

Chris looked at the flushed face of Nelly, he did not find funny what she told him, he felt sadden, so many young women are kept in ignorance about sex, well brought up young ladies are not supposed to know anything about sex.

"Your mistress at least put your mind at rest Nelly, this man did not do anything else or did you see or hear anyone around after or before the man?" Chris asked.

Nelly thought for a while. "I did hear the singing barrow man, but my mind was in such a panic, I cannot say when before or after," Nelly replied.

"Do you know the singing barrow man?" Chris asked.

"Jason is his name," Nelly replied. "He do supply mother a few logs now and again, he don't speak much, but I like his voice."

"Was this man tall, small, did you see any distinguishing marks, or anything that might identify him?" Chris asked.

"He was taller than our front door," Nelly said. "He bent his head to get in, but most tall men do, even the singing barrow man has to bend his head to bring in the logs, if I saw any marks on him, I must have forgotten, my mind was in a panic."

Chris stood. "Thank you for coming Nelly, and thank your mistress for sending you, I take it at the moment you do not want your mother to know?"

Chris picked up a pencil and paper. "Give me the name of where you work Nelly, I will contact your mistress should I have anything to tell you."

Chris wrote the address, then offered his hand to Nelly as he opened his office door for her. "Don't be frightened any more," Chris remarked.

Nelly smiled with her thanks and left the station.

Later Cam entered the office. "The body was identified," he said sitting at his desk. "I am not sure I am happy with this kind of detail, it's very upsetting."

"It's all a part of police work Cam," Chris replied understandingly. "We have to catch the murderer, but first we must be sure who has been murdered, the only way to be sure of that is by identification of the body by those who know the victim."

"I guess you are right," Cam replied. "But all the same it is very upsetting."

Chris then related his meeting with Miss Nelly Green. "I have no idea whether this man is the cannibal, if he was, then Miss Green was a very lucky person, something made the man leave her."

"One question comes to mind Chris," Cam remarked. "Would a cannibal kill and cut a person up in their own home, I would have thought that the victim would be enticed into his own place, where he could carry out his craft in private, doing it in someone else's home seems to be taking a chance is it?"

Chris smiled. "You are beginning to see things Cam, I'm pleased, the way you put it, you are right, cannibalism is the act of humans eating the flesh or internal organs of other humans, he would need the body whenever he is hungry, it was what Miss Green heard her attacker say to her that made me think."

"It must have been frightening for her?" Cam replied.

"I'm sure it was," Chris replied. "Do you know Beggars Lane?"

"Yes I know it, just a half dozen houses, faces a field," Cam replied

"I suppose you better do some door knocking Cam, ask if anyone had seen a tall man hanging around, even Mrs Green herself she may have seen someone, but don't tell them about the attack, just say complaints have been made," Chris remarked.

"I can do that," Cam replied getting up. "Better start straight away."

"Good man," Chris replied with a smile on his face as he watched Cam leave the office.

Chapter Six

*I*t was late in the afternoon when George having completed his list returned to the office, where he found Chris studying the reports in front of him.

George went to his desk, and dropped the several sheets of paper on to it and sat down. "That seem to be a complete waste of time," George remarked. "All the same, no one saw anything, they all just vanished into thin air."

"Then we can forget that line of enquiry George," Chris replied. "I was hoping that just one person might remember something, nothing is really a waste, although you have gotten nowhere, at least now we can eliminate that line and carry on."

"Jason the singing barrow boy, seems to quite well known, several people remembered him around at the time of their daughter's disappearance."

Chris looked at George and smiled. "I had a Miss Nelly Green after you left," he said, and told him about the meeting. "Cam is already door knocking at Beggars Lane."

"Do you think he could be our man?" George asked interested.

"I started to think because of what he said to Miss Green, but Cam pointed out that if you are a cannibal, you would want the body in your home," Chris continued. "I think he was right, a cannibal lures an unsuspecting victim to his home and subdues him and attacks him."

"Prostitutes do it in their own way, they entice men to their home," George replied.

"Good point George," Chris responded. "I think we are dealing with a man, how would a woman carry a body to the Winnall Moors?"

"Wheel barrow," George offered.

Chris smiled. "You are thinking of Jason the singing barrow boy."

"Well he is single, has a home of his own, even has a barrow," George replied.

"I grant you all that, but if we are looking for a cannibal, Jason would have eaten his own sister?" Chris remarked. "It might be who we are looking for is not a cannibal just a plain serial killer."

"Then we have to ask ourselves why Mrs Marston was sliced up ?" George replied. "Usual killers do not normally slice up their victims do they?"

"I just wish we had something to lead us in the right direction," Chris remarked, as Cam entered.

"No luck I'm afraid Chris, no one saw or can remember anyone hanging around, the singing barrow boy was around during that time however," Cam remarked sitting at his desk.

"Well I do have one very slight lead," George butted in. "At least four missing girls had an appointment at the Mildmay Arms."

"Really," Chris replied looking at George. "Anything else?"

"They were all young women, between seventeen and twenty, they answered an advert for cleaners, however I am told the police did interview the landlord, but nothing suspicious was found," George looked at Chris.

Chris thought for a while. "As you know George missing persons are normally dealt with by uniform, only when a body turn up we take over, within the last ten years sixteen young girls, four older woman and two boys, they had all gone missing without a trace, this case is really mysterious to me."

"I know the Mildmay Arms," Cam interrupted. "I often have a pint in there."

"What the landlord like?" Chris asked. "I can't remember ever going into the pub."

"Pleasant enough," Cam replied. "In his late forties I would think, but he might be older, it is said he has been the landlord since the turn of the century."

"Married I suppose?" George asked.

"No I don't think so, but he do have a fancy woman, he calls her his housekeeper."

Chris looked at George. "What do you think?" he asked.

"We have no where else to go," George replied with a shrug. "Can't do any harm?"

Chris checked his pocket watch. "Well it's coming to five, when we leave, we will call in for a pint, that is if you have no other plans?"

"No, I'm free," George replied with a smile.

"Me as well," Cam said getting excited.

"No Cam, the landlord might know that you are a copper," Chris replied. "It's best you keep your distance for the time being, but you can go now to the local newspaper, try to find out as far back as you can, about the adverts have been put by the Mildmay Arms for the cleaner job, then we can check the dates with the list George has."

A little disappointed Cam, rose from his desk. "OK," he replied. "You will get a decent pint there," he added as he left the office.

Chris smiled at George. "The landlord might know that Cam is a copper, I want to go in as customers, ask a couple of questions if we can."

"What about Elizabeth?" George asked.

"She will be outside at six, I will explain to her she will understand," Chris replied.

True to his words, Elizabeth was waiting outside as Chris and George emerged from the station, Chris got his usual kiss. "Had a hard day darling?" she asked.

"So so," Chris replied a smile on his face.

Elizabeth looked at George. "You look well George," she commented. "Have you seen Rosemary Morris lately?" she asked smiling.

"I have seen her actually," George replied with a grin on his face. "She sends you her regards."

"I'm glad," Elizabeth replied. "She is a lovely young woman, just waiting for the right man," she giggled.

"That's enough of that," Chris scolded. "Anyway, we will walk you to Eastgate Street, then darling you will have to walk home on your own, George and I have work to do."

Elizabeth pretended to sulk as she grabbed both their arms and with Elizabeth in the middle they walked towards Eastgate Street.

Elizabeth smiled as she let go of their arms as they reached the King Alfred Statue, she kissed Chris on the cheek. "It's not often a girl is escorted by two very handsome men, even if it was only a hundred yards," she said with a smile taking her leave. "I'll be waiting for you at home darling," she said looking at Chris.

"I shouldn't be too late," Chris replied.

"Goodbye George," she said with a smile.

"Do you think all wives are like Elizabeth?" George asked as they crossed the road, and entered Eastgate Street.

"If they love each other," Chris replied. "All men like to think their wife is beautiful, but beauty is in the eye of the beholder."

"Elizabeth is certainly beautiful," George remarked as they entered the Mildmay Arms."

"Thank you George," Chris smiled looking around the empty small bar room. "I think that Rosemary Morris is a beautiful young lady," Chris smiled leaning on the bar.

George did not reply as the landlord greeted them with a smile.

"Gentlemen," he said. "How can I be of service?"

"Two pints of your best bitter please," Chris replied.

The land lord smiled taking two pint glasses from under the counter.

"There you are gentlemen," the landlord smiled as he placed two pints before them. "That will be four pence please."

Chris put the four pence on the counter.

"Are you from these parts?" the landlord asked taking up the four pence. "I don't think I have seen you before?"

"Been here a few years," Chris replied after taking a sip of his pint. "Never been in here before, you serve a good pint landlord."

"Thank you," replied the landlord with a smile.

"The trouble is," George said putting his glass back on the counter, this is a small city, of about twenty thousand people, and there must be two hundred pubs, one is spoiled for choice.

"You are right there Sir," the landlord agreed. "Two hundred pubs, with our small population, means one pub for every one hundred people."

"Must be a job to get rich being a landlord?" Chris remarked.

The landlord laughed. "One has a job to make a living, but at least you have a roof over your head, and you are your own boss, it wouldn't be so bad if all pubs were the same."

"How do you mean?" Chris asked.

"Well this is a beer house, I can't sell spirits, I have no licence to allow me."

"Really," Chris remarked. "I did not know."

"Yes if you wanted a whisky, you would have to go to another pub, that is why this pub is mainly for men, don't get many women in here, women like Gin and Vodka which I can't sell."

"That don't sound fair," George remarked, knowing that certain pubs did not have a spirit licence. "I suppose your wife likes a drop of Gin?"

"Not married Sir," the landlord replied with a grin on his face. "Never have been, came out of the army in 1902, had a few pounds which allowed me to take this pub."

"Very wise," Chris agreed as he took another drink.

"You do all your own cleaning then?" George asked.

"You could say that I partly do, but I have a house-keeper, a Mrs Quinn, she lives just across the Abbey Grounds, in Colebrook Street."

"It seems a large pub for just the two of you?" Chris remarked.

"Well we do try to get cleaners, but they are all young girls that apply these days, girls that want to keep out of service, but we don't get a lot of success, Mrs Quinn deals with that side of things."

"We will have the same please landlord," Chris put his empty glass forward.

"My turn," George remarked. "Have one yourself landlord."

The landlord put three pints on the counter. "Thank you Sir, that will be six pennies."

"You are right landlord," Chris remarked putting his glass on the counter. "You certainly serve a great pint."

The landlord smiled his thanks. "Forgive me for asking, but you gentlemen, dress differently to most of my customers, may I ask you what business you are in?"

"I am sorry landlord," Chris replied offering his hand. "I am Detective Inspector Hardie, and this is Detective Sergeant House of Winchester CID."

"Well, well, well," replied the landlord taking Chris's hand. "I do have a couple of your coppers in here now and again, I am very glad to meet you," he said.

"What is your name landlord?" George asked.

"Albert Watts," replied the landlord.

"Fear not Albert, we are having a drink after a hard day that's all."

"Do you get many soldiers in here?" Chris asked.

"Very few," Albert answered. "They tend to use the pubs uptown, still you are both detectives, you must know that when they have a few, they get a bit rowdy."

"Albert," Chris smiled. "I bet when you were off duty in the army, you were the same?"

"Of course I was, but at that time I was not the landlord," Albert smiled.

It was gone seven when Chris and George parted and went in opposite directions. Chris walked slowly with his hand dug deeply in his trouser pockets, as he pondered over the case. He had the body, knew who she was, knew how she died, knew what had been done to her, but what was the motive, she had words with her husband and had stormed out of the house, but this was not unusual, she and her husband often had these rows, Chris could not see any motive there. Her flesh had been cut from her body, which brought in the question of possible cannibalism, but the Cam's words came to mind, cannibals they can survive for one or two months just feeding on one body, so they need to live alone, and have his or her own place, so if that was the case, why was this young body dumped with just a few slices cut from her body. Chris could not answer these questions as he walked up the path to where Elizabeth was waiting with the door open.

Chapter Seven

Sergeant Williams smiled as Chris entered the station. "Nice morning Inspector?" he greeted respectfully.

"It is Sergeant," replied Chris. "Am I the first one?"

"No Inspector the last," the sergeant said with a smile.

"Anyway, I have a Miss Bell coming in this morning, she called in late last night according to Sergeant Dawkins who was on duty, who told her to call back this morning to see you, it seems her sister has gone missing, Sergeant Dawkins thought you would be interested before we start our routine."

"I certainly will be," Chris answered. "Let me know when she arrives," he added as he went into his office.

Chris put his trilby on the hat stand amid greetings from George and Cam, then sat at his desk.

"How did you make out Cam?" Chris asked leaning on the desk.

"The local newspaper was very helpful, I spent a good hour going back on the adverts, I only had time to go back five years, but during that time I found six adverts were placed in the paper for staff relating to the Mildmay Arms, I can go back and finish the ten years," Cam replied.

"I have checked the dates with my list," George remarked. "I have five missing on each of the advertisement week, three of them older women."

"Really George," Chris replied. "That makes it awkward, you see I had put the missing people in three groups, the two boys, well they could have been taken by gypsies, there are plenty passing through here."

"Almost six years ago, and at the same time," George remarked. "If they are still alive, they would be around twelve now, John Thompson was almost six, and Peter Shaw was almost the same age, both were friends and went same school."

"If those boys were abducted, they are now old enough to find their way home should they want to, if abducted they might have been kept prisoners for a couple years, but not all this time, however they could have been killed, perhaps buried, if so they will only be found by chance."

"That applies to the young girls as well don't it?" Cam remarked.

"Of course Cam," Chris replied smiling to himself. "But both these boys were pals, disappeared the same time, no other boy has been reported missing, the young girls and women however, seems to be continuously reported missing, we have another one today."

"Yes Sergeant Williams told me about that one," George interrupted.

"That will make twenty three over the past ten years, let alone any before that. The boys were a one off in my opinion, and I hope that rather their disappearance being more serious, they were abducted by gypsies," Chris added.

Cam nodded his head in agreement. "George told me about last night," he ventured.

"Well you were right Cam about one thing, he do serve a good pint," Chris remarked. "How well do you know his housekeeper a Mrs Quinn?"

"I've seen her a couple times, stout, not handsome, around fifty I should say."

"Would you say she is the mistress of Mr Watts the landlord?" Chris asked.

Cam screwed his face. "Could be, any old port in a storm," he laughed. "But she would not be my type, I don't find her at all desirable."

Chris looked at George. "He seemed cool enough when we told him who we were, didn't he?"

"I agree," George replied. "Had I been him and had something to do with these missing girls, I might feel a little nervous."

"My thoughts exactly same George," Chris replied. "Now Cam, that's your job today, get all you can on Mrs Quinn, she lives at the Colebrook Street, behind the Abbey Grounds," Chris added.

Cam smiled as he stood up. "I can do that," he replied. "I'll get straight on it."

Chris smiled at George as Cam left the office. "Any old port in a storm, where does he get these saying?"

"It's sailors lingo," George answered. "After they have been at sea for a long time, they get shore leave, and take the first girl they can get, regardless of what she looks like, it comes from that any old port in a storm, meaning."

"I get the drift," Chris interrupted with a smile. "Anyway where do we go from here?"

"Miss Bell is here Inspector," sergeant Williams entered the office.

"Thank you Sergeant, please show her in."

Chris looked at the woman sitting in the interview chair, she was what one might call plumpish, about fifty, and quite handsome for her age, she wore a floral dress under her brown top coat.

"Miss Bell," Chris said. "I am Detective Inspector Hardie, and my colleague Detective Sergeant House, I understand your sister is missing?"

"That's right Sir, my sister and I live together, since our parents died."

"You never married?" George asked.

"No, neither of us," replied Miss Bell with a weak smile.

"Perhaps I might have your sister's name and address?" Chris asked noting George had his notebook ready.

"I am Miss Ursala Bell, my sister is Miss Pamela Bell, we live at number 6, Wharf Hill, right opposite the Dog and Duck, being a man you might know the public house."

Chris smiled. "When was the last time you saw your sister?" he asked.

"Yesterday evening, it was a lovely night, Pamela wanted to go for a walk, I felt too lazy, and declined," Ursala answered.

"Did she have a favourite walk she likes to take?" Chris asked.

"She did," Ursala answered. "She loves walking along the weirs, the one reaching the town, she usually sits in the Abbey Grounds, I have no doubt she did the same last evening."

"Can you tell us what is your sister look like?" Chris asked.

Ursala took a photo from her handbag and gave it to Chris. "Like me, we are identical twins," Ursala replied a proud in her voice.

Chris looked at the photo before passing it to George. "You are certainly look so much alike, I would have a job to tell the difference," Chris remarked.

"It's been the same all our lives," Ursala replied.

"Tell me Miss Bell," Chris asked politely. "It was unusual for your sister to stay out?"

"It certainly was," Ursala replied. "When she did not come home last night at nine, I went looking for her, I searched through the weirs, she was no where to be seen, I was near this station so I popped in, a nice sergeant told me to call back this morning, he said if she did not return home we have an Inspector who would want to know, I take it he was referring to you Sir?"

"Have you any friends or relatives she could have gone to?" George interrupted.

"All our family are dead, we have no one left, just me and my sister," Ursala answered.

"I take it that you would at times accompany your sister on her walks, did you ever met anyone that you became friendly with?" Chris asked.

"We did speak to a few women while we sat in the Abbey Grounds, spoke to some of them many times, we of course never spoke to a man, you see our parents were how can I say, religious fanatics, we were warned off of the opposite sex from early childhood, it stuck with us, but there you are, it's the way your parents bring you up."

Chris felt sorry for her, he had often come across sadness, mainly brought on by over protective parents who were religious to the point of being a fanatic, that was one problem of the eighteenth century.

"Well Miss Bell, I thank you for coming in," Chris said standing. "You can be sure we will do all we can to find your sister, in the meantime, should you remember anyone or anything that might help us, please let us know."

Ursala Bell stood. "You can rely on it Inspector, and thank you for your kindness."

"Not at all Miss Bell," Chris said with a smile on his face. "It is our job to protect you," Chris offered his hand which she took.

Chapter Eight

"People just can not vanish into thin air?" Chris remarked looking at George. "I just hope that we will not find another body."

"If we had not found Mrs Marston's body, all these people on my list might have slipped passed us unnoticed," George replied.

"I agree George, anyway, I have to see the optician, get my eyes checked, Elizabeth made the appointment so I'll have to keep it."

"I'll go over this list of mine again, see if I can see any common factor," George replied. "I can't think of anything else to do?"

"I did order a blackboard months ago, still not here, I'll check on that, it could help us to keep in mind where we have been," Chris commented.

Leaving the optician, Chris checked his watch, which told him that there was plenty of the afternoon left, after a few moments thought, he decided to go and see Jason the wheel barrow man before returning to the station.

Chris entered Chester Road from the Blue Ball Hill end, the double doors of the shack was wide open, and as Chris approached he heard voices coming from the shack.

"Inspector," Jason welcomed with a smile as he saw Chris at the entrance.

"I don't mean to intrude Mr Keen," Chris replied.

"You are always welcome Inspector," Jason answered. "This is my friend Charlie Webster," Jason indicated with his head.

Chris offered his hand. "Pleasure," he said as Charlie took his hand. "Do you live around here?"

"In Water Lane by the Gasometer, my back garden is next to this shed," Charlie replied.

"You can't be that steam engine driver, I noticed as I came along," Chris asked.

Charlie smiled. "That I am," he replied.

"I have seen it before crossing from Chesil Street into Water Lane," Chris remarked.

"That would be me," Charlie replied. "I always bring it home with me, takes a lot to keep clean and polished, so in the light evenings it gives me something to do."

"I'm sure it do," Chris remarked. "They are fascinating machines."

"Everyone loves them," Charlie replied. "Where ever I go, the children as well as adults look us over with interest, any way, must get on, see you later Jason," Charlie smiled. "And good day to you Inspector."

"He'll go down his back garden next door," Jason remarked as Charlie had left.

"You could be taken for brothers?" Chris remarked as he leaned against the door. "He is about your stance."

"He's a couple years older than me," Jason replied. "He lost his parents before I did."

"Married?" Chris asked casually as he took out his pipe and tobacco.

Jason grinned. "He's too crafty for that, he is never short of a girl, in fact he is seeing a woman with a child now, she lives just along Wales Street, a house on the corner of Colson Road, she buys my logs."

"Really," Chris remarked filling the bowl of his pipe with tobacco and he lit it blowing out a cloud of smoke.

"You don't get much time for girls do you?"

Jason laughed. "Don't bother much about them, although I do have a few who talks to me on my rounds, no doubt wanting me to take them out."

"Don't you ever go out and enjoy yourself?" Chris asked lowering his pipe. "I mean you are still a young man?"

"I go out Saturday nights, sometimes on a Friday night," Jason replied. "I play the piano in a few pubs, so it don't cost me anything."

"You play the piano, did you have lessons?" Chris asked before taking another puff of his pipe.

"No never did," Jason replied. "Father bought an upright piano in the sale at five corners, the piano and stool I was told cost him four shillings, I still have it in the house, anyway, I banged about on it then found I could play a tune without music sheet, in fact, now I can play any tune without any sheet music in front of me."

"You play by ear then?" Chris remarked.

"I suppose I do," Jason replied touching his ears. "They are wearing away a bit now," he laughed.

Chris smiled at the humour. "Do your friend Charlie go with you on Saturday nights?"

"As a rule, sometimes he is baby sitting for the woman I told you about, she works sometimes at night in a nursing home, he do babysitting for her."

"Did he go with you last Saturday?" Chris asked as he took another puff of his pipe.

"He did," Jason replied. "He was babysitting on the Friday I remember."

"He stops all night at the house then?" Chris asked.

"I suppose, she don't get home until early the next morning," Jason replied smiling. "Are you interested?"

"No," Chris smiled. "Sorry it's just the detective in me, I was just wondering how he manages taking that machine to work should his girlfriend be late home?"

"I think he is given some leeway mornings, he has to take back the steam engine and he can't travel all that fast," Jason replied. "Anyway Inspector, let's go across and have a cup of tea, I am sure you came to ask me questions?"

Having knocked out his pipe, and taken off his trilby, Chris found himself sitting in the tidy kitchen watching Jason make the tea.

"What is it you want to ask Inspector?" he asked putting tea into the teapot.

"A couple of nights ago, a Miss Green living at Beggars Lane was attacked in her home while her mother was in town shopping," Chris stated.

"I know the Greens," Jason said bring the tea things to the table. "They buy from me."

"You were heard to be along there during that time," Chris remarked.

Jason poured the tea into the cups, and passed the milk and sugar towards Chris.

"A couple nights ago you said, yes I did come home that way if my memory serves me correctly."

"Did you happen to see anything?" Chris asked taking a sip of the tea with satisfaction.

Jason added milk and sugar to his own cup. "It must have been about seven or a little later, I had done well that night, had no logs left, I was nearing the steps that leads to Wales Street, I did see a man, or the back of a man coming out of one of the houses, couldn't be sure what number from that distance, however I never took much notice, I just carried on, but I can tell you he went up towards Alresford Road."

"Really," Chris replied.

"Yes I'm sure, it was still quite light."

"Could you recognise him?" Chris asked.

"He never turned his head, he had no top coat," Jason replied. "Was Miss Green hurt, I mean I haven't read of it in the papers?"

"You won't Mr Keen," Chris replied. "The attack is being kept under wraps, the girl's mother do not know, I hope you will treat what I say in confidence, one thing I can tell you, I believe your singing stopped him doing anything serious."

"That's my trouble," Jason said with a grin. "I just can't help it, I burst out in song all the time, no reason half the time, but what makes you think hearing my singing made him run?"

"It's only a guess," Chris replied. "Perhaps he thought you might be knocking the door, or you might have logs to deliver, either way, he could not take the chance of staying."

"Can you tell me Inspector, Mrs Marston, I know she was murdered, but was anything done to her?"

"She was not raped, I can tell you that," Chris replied trying hard to understand Jason who seemed more interesting than most people. "You know we are trying to trace the missing girls during the last decade," Chris continued. "Tell me Mr Keen, your sister, did you get on well?"

"When my mother died, Neil became my mother even though I was the elder, she fussed over me like a mother hen, it seems to be a part of a woman's nature, they need someone to look after, I adored my sister Inspector," Jason said almost silently with a serious face.

"You have been looking for the person who took her away ever since I believe Mr Keen?"

"No wonder you're an Inspector," Jason replied with a weak smile. "I am not a religious man, but I have enough faith to know that God will eventually lead me to him, how did you guess anyway?"

"It was what you said last time we were here, I see, I hear, I never forget," Chris answered.

Jason got up. "I am not breaking any law Inspector, but please come with me, I want to show you something."

Chris got up and followed Jason through the hallway to the stairs. "I want to show you Neil's room Inspector, I keep it just how she left it," Jason opened a bedroom door to the left of the landing and went in followed by Chris.

Chris saw that the room was well kept and clean, nothing out of order. "You keep it as a shrine," Chris remarked.

"Not exactly Inspector, have a look at these charts I have on the wall," Jason replied.

Chris looked at the chart, about a yard square, he noticed it was an enlarged map of Winchester from Middle Brook Street downwards. "What do these red marks represent?" Chris asked, amazed at what he was looking at.

"Since my sister disappeared I have kept all details about all missing people," Jason answered pointing to a pile of newspapers on the bed. "I have all their details from these papers, the red marks shows where the missing girls lived, as you can see Middle Books, Lower brooks, Lawn Street, Union Street, Eastgate Street and so on, all those missing people have come from this end of the town."

Chris studied the chart for a little longer before turning to Jason. "I am amazed Mr Keen, you are better equipped with this chart than we are at the station," Chris continued thinking of the blackboard he had ordered.

"Tell me have you come to any conclusion yet?" Chris asked.

"Well I did have, there is only one street from Middle Brook Street where no girl has gone missing, that is St John Street that leads into Beggars Lane."

"That remains the same Mr Keen, the girl in Beggars Lane was assaulted not missing, Mrs Marston next door she did not go missing, she was murdered."

"OK then," Jason agreed. "In my mind who ever is responsible lives in St John Street."

"To a policeman Mr Keen, your chart tells us you could have known each of these girls, you also work in the area selling logs which gives you the opportunity of knowing these girls. You live on your own, in a house that you own, you have a end house, out of view from the others in the street, in fact Mr Keen a good case could be put together against you?"

"You are joking Inspector," Jason replied in a nervous tone. "You don't really think I am responsible, what do you think I did with the bodies, we are talking about nearly twenty."

Chris smiled. "I have no suspects at the moment, but if I had, you would be top of the list, however just in case all these disappearances are down to one person, I would ask you to be very careful, that person could be very dangerous for you knowing what you are doing."

"I'm not really doing anything," Jason replied. "Just keeping score."

"I know, but have you told anyone what you are doing, say, to your friend Mr Charlie Webster?" Chris asked.

Jason shook his head. "I've told no one, don't speak to many people, only when I deliver logs, perhaps a few in the pubs, but I normally sit and listen rather than take part in conversations, but one thing I know whoever took my sister's life around here somewhere."

Chris stood up. "Thank you for the tea Mr Keen, and thank you for showing me that chart of yours, but please do as I ask you, keep what you are doing to yourself, but remember, we are always open to information, and I mean that."

"I get what you mean Inspector," Jason replied with a smile.

Chris entered his office, Jason was still on his mind. "Good God" he explained, as he saw George writing on a blackboard. "So we have it at last."

"Been in the store room for over a week," George replied. "I have set the easel stand between our desks, I thought it's the best place."

Chris hung his trilby, then came and stood in front of the blackboard.

"I'm entering all the streets where a person has gone missing," George remarked as he continued writing with chalk. "Not a lot of streets left, it's almost as though one person is being taking from every street."

Both detectives looked towards the door as Cam entered.

"Have a look at this blackboard Cam," Chris invited. "It will give you a good idea what we are up against."

Cam studied the board. "I see you put Mrs Marston there George," Cam remarked. "She has not gone missing, she was murdered and her body was found."

George looked at Chris.

"He's right George, she is not a missing person, perhaps in a colour chalk you can put her name on the right-hand side of the board," Chris advised.

"Now let's debate for a moment," Chris said after George had altered the board, and George and Cam were seated at their desk.

"I have seen Jason the singing barrow boy this afternoon, had a long talk with him," Chris told them of his meeting.

"He seems a candidate for the top suspect?" Cam remarked after Chris had finished. "Every thing fits."

"Fits what Cam?" Chris asked.

"All these missing people," Cam replied.

"I agree he had a chart, all the details he had was from the papers, which he still has, but what do we know about the missing people, did they leave on their own accord, were they murdered, or were they a victim of a cannibal, all we know is that they are missing," Chris commented.

"I thought we were looking for a cannibal?" Cam murmured.

"Yes I'm afraid we all did in a way, but in reality we are investigating Mrs Marston's murder, we have to look into Miss Green's attack, and we have a missing Miss Pamela Bell, those are the three crimes we have to concentrate," Chris remarked.

"What about this chap that Jason saw coming out of a house in Beggars Lane?" George asked.

"Jason was sure that he went towards Alresford Road, and apart from what the man said to Miss Green, we can't connect him to Mrs Marston's murder can we?" Chris argued.

"He could have come down Magdalene Hill when he reached Alresford Road?" Cam remarked.

"Which ever way he went," Chris remarked. "I believe, he heard Jason's singing and he must have thought Jason was following him."

George nodded. "So where do we go from here?" he asked.

"Let's hear what Cam found out about Mrs Quinn first?" Chris said looking at Cam.

"Mrs Quinn lives at 28 Colebrook Street, her house over look the Abbey Grounds from the back, from her bedroom window she can see most of the grounds, nature it seems have not been kind to her, she looks sixty, but in fact is only forty seven years old," Cam turned over a leaf in his notebook.

"She came to Winchester in 1906 from Southsea, bought her house where she lives today. In 1910, she started to work at the Mildmay Arms, but only mornings, her duties I believe is getting the landlord's meals, breakfast and preparing his dinner after the pub closed, and supervise the cleaner woman. She is not popular where she lives, hardly speaks to the neighbours, but I am told she do have women callers from time to time, I have not met one person who have been in her house," Cam closed his notebook.

"That's about all I'm afraid," he said. "Apart from the fact there is no record of her ever been married," Cam concluded.

"You done well Cam," Chris praised. "You mentioned she came from Southsea, if you remember where Mr and Mrs Marston went on their honeymoon there."

Chris looked at his watch. "I am going to meet Elizabeth in half an hour, but before I do so, another name was mentioned by Jason, that was Mr Charlie Webster, he lives by the Gasometer in Water lane, a steam engine driver, it seems he do babysitting for a girlfriend of his who has a young child. This girlfriend Jason said works at a nursing home on night duty, I don't know which one. The girlfriend, again what

Jason said lives in Colson Road, I don't know the number, but it must be the last house pass the First in Last out pub."

"That brings us back to cannibalism again," George remarked. "Are these people relevant to our case?"

Chris pondered for a while. "You said yourself George that whoever is responsible might live in the Water Lane or Wales Street area. Jason lives next door to the murdered Mrs Marston, Mr Webster lives in the same area and the only other name we have, he was baby sitting on the Friday, because Mrs Marston was sliced up we have to keep in mind the possibility of cannibalism, but there might be other reasons for her being found that way, we must concentrate on Mrs Marston and not on people who disappeared several years ago."

"I get your point Chris, this Charlie Webster needs checking," George replied.

"I agree George," Chris smiled. "Who is best at this job?" he asked smiling at Cam.

"Oh so I'm selected," Cam grinned.

"I'm afraid so Cam, see what you can find out about Charlie Webster and his girl friend, they might have nothing to do with our case, so be careful."

Cam left the office after tidying his desk. "I think he's getting good at it George?" Chris remarked.

"I think he likes it, but then it's all a part of police work," George replied. "How did the optician go, by the way?"

"The optician shone a light in my eyes, using special torches, did a full test, God knows what he saw, but eventually he told me I needed reading glasses, they will be ready sometime next week," Chris said as he got up and made his way to the hat stand for his trilby. "It's just a hunch George, can your list show when the first older person went missing?"

"I'm already trying to make group of missing persons, do you want me to carry on?" he asked.

"We are stuck at the moment George," Chris replied reaching the office door.

"With no where to go at the moment, it won't be a complete waste of time, see you in the morning," Chris smiled as he left.

Chapter Nine

Chris met Elizabeth outside the police station, he got his usual kiss on the cheek, and she hung on to his arm as they walked home.

"You have your case on your mind again," she smiled. "Are you going to share it with me?"

"Let's have a meal first and get a early night," Chris replied touching her arm.

Elizabeth giggled. "That's the best offer I have had all day," she replied.

Chris shook his head and smiled, as he playfully tapped her bottom allowing her to go first up the path, where Olive was already waiting with the front door open.

Olive dished up a meal of shepherd's pie, followed by a treacle sponge pudding, Chris with his mind still on the case, was the last to finish, and saw Elizabeth smiling at him.

"Aren't you hungry darling?" she asked as she collected his pudding dish. "You were very slow in eating."

Chris looked at Olive. "I'm sorry Olive, I was deep in thought, I'm always hungry for your cooking, and I was in fact very hungry."

"Take no notice of Elizabeth," Olive smiled. "Would you like some more?"

Chris leaned back and put his hand over his stomach. "Couldn't get any more down," he replied smiling. "I really enjoyed the meal."

Olive looked at Ron, who was already in his armchair, with the paper across his lap, looking at them over the top of his glasses.

Olive looked at her husband. "All I really want is a little appreciation with my cooking, it wouldn't hurt you to say things," Olive scolded Ron.

"You know I enjoy your cooking my sweet," Ron replied winking at Chris. "I have been eating it more than half a lifetime, do I ever complain?"

"No, but it would not hurt you to say sometimes, that was good, I enjoyed that, or thank you that was great, never any compliment from you," Olive remarked as she collected the plates. "Come Elizabeth, let's get these things washed and put away."

Elizabeth smiling at her father, left the table and followed her mother into the kitchen.

Chris changed the table chair for the armchair one side of Ron, he took out his pipe and sucked on it.

"Difficult case again Chris?" Ron asked.

"It seems the story of my life, I never seem to get an open and shut case, still every case gives me experience, and keeps my mind active."

"It's in the papers tonight Chris," Ron said. "A young woman found murdered in Winnall Moors."

"Really," Chris replied. "Do it say anything else?"

"Only that detectives are following several leads."

"I wonder why they make up these things, I haven't got one clue yet, I don't even know where to start?" Chris remarked.

"Well you know what they say, believe just a half what you read in the newspapers," Ron smiled.

"I have never heard that," Chris replied. "Still it seems about right."

Ron had no chance to reply as Olive and Elizabeth entered.

"Darling, I forgot to ask you, did you keep the optician appointment I made for you?" Elizabeth asked sitting at the table.

Chris smiled at her. "Yes I went, I need reading glasses, should be ready within the week."

"That's fine," Elizabeth replied. "I can't have you having bad eyes."

"It will be a good thing when we get this electric that everyone is talking about," Ron commented.

"I know the cables are being laid," Chris remarked.

"We can afford our gas lighting," Olive chimed in. "It's the poor I feel sorry about, they have to use candles."

"They are dangerous," Elizabeth replied. "A fire can easily start."

Olive sat near Elizabeth at the table. "If your father can shift himself to the table, we can all have a game of dominoes before you retire."

After four games, which Olive and Elizabeth was allowed to win two games each, Elizabeth decided it was time to make a move. "It's an early night for us mother," Elizabeth said as she helped her mother box the dominoes. "Chris needs his sleep, and I feel a little tired myself."

Chris laid in bed facing the ceiling his mind going over the case. Elizabeth was laying up close to him on her side with her arm across his chest. "Are you going to share your thoughts with me darling?" she murmured.

"It's a difficult case," Chris replied moving his head sideways so that he could look at her. "Officially I am investigating a murder of a young woman, also a disappearance of a older woman, however because of the condition of the

271

younger woman, I seem to be investigating at least twenty other missing people that happened over the last ten years, I do not know where to start."

"Oh dear," Elizabeth sighed. "It do seem complicated, what condition was the young woman in?"

"Some of her flesh had been cut off from her body," Chris replied.

"That sounds horrible, why would a murderer do such a thing, murdering the girl was bad enough without cutting her up," Elizabeth replied feeling disgusted.

"According to Bob, our police surgeon, he thinks the murderer is a cannibal."

"Good God," Elizabeth exploded. "Do you agree with him, I mean are there such people, I always thought cannibalism was a myth?"

Chris smiled to himself as he patted Elizabeth's arm laying across his chest. "I believe there have been cases, but it's not common thank God, anyway, I am not sure whether this is such a case, but it's the reason we are trying to discover where these missing girls are, most of them under twenty."

"You made me frighten now Chris," Elizabeth said as she eased herself closer to him.

"I don't think you have any worries darling," Chris reassured her. "At work or at home, you are never alone, these girls went missing just vanished into thin air, no one saw anything."

"It's still worrying," Elizabeth replied.

"Perhaps I should keep my thoughts to myself in future," Chris remarked. "You are like your mother you get upset."

Elizabeth did not answer, she wanted him to able to talk to her, two heads are better than one, but cannibalism, it was such a shock.

"I'm sorry darling," Elizabeth finally said. "I was being foolish, I want you to share your thoughts with me, it was just the thought of being eaten that got me, these other missing women, do you think they are victims?"

"They could all be alive and walking about in some part of the world, as I said they just vanished," Chris replied. "Although it's worrying to love ones, in itself it's not a crime, I mean if I was to walk out of here, and vanished, say went to Scotland, I have not committed a crime against the law."

"You better not," Elizabeth remarked. "I would find you."

"You have no worry there," Chris replied. "I would never leave you, anyway I have decided that I must concentrate in finding the murderer of Mrs Marston, perhaps succeeding in that, might just give us a clue to the other missing people, but I am not holding my breath."

"If there is a cannibal around darling, it's a horrible thought, but he can not eat all of the body, eats only flesh parts not the bones, let's say he has eaten the twenty missing, that's an awful lot of bones left, what would he do with them?" Elizabeth asked having got over her fears.

"I would think bones would be easier to get rid of than the whole bodies," Chris replied. "Bones, he could burn, bury them, perhaps crush them, even throw them in the river, apart from burying them, he can not do the same with a body."

Elizabeth thought for a while before answering. "You know darling, if the bones were thrown in the river, they would eventually show up, the water would eventually make them gleaming white, people would notice them even laying on the river bed, burning them, they would smell as some flesh would be left on them, it would take a big garden to keep burying skeletons, we are talking big numbers here, no I think if there is a cannibal about, he crushes the bones almost to dust, but he would need something very heavy indeed to do it, then all he would have to do is to throw the dust into the air, like they do with the ashes when one is cremated."

Chris turned on his side facing Elizabeth. "You should have been a detective darling," he smiled at her in the dark. "I will keep in mind what you have just said, but now, it's sleep time."

"Are you sure darling?" she asked as she squeezed him tighter.

"Well perhaps a little later," Chris replied, her warmth and closeness, having weakened him.

Chapter Ten

*C*hris said cheerio to Elizabeth with his usual kiss on the cheek before entering the police station.

"Good morning Inspector," sergeant Williams smiled as he entered. "The Chief Inspector Fox is in your office, Sergeant House is also in."

"Really," Chris replied wondering as he looked at his watch. "I'm still early," he grinned as he put his watch away. "Thank you Sergeant."

Chris entered his office wondering what had brought the Chief Inspector Fox out this early in the morning.

"Good Morning Sir," Chris said seeing the Chief Inspector Fox sitting in the interview chair. "Had I known you were coming, I would have been in earlier," he remarked sitting at his desk, and smiling at George.

"Sergeant House kept me company," Chief Inspector Fox replied without a smile. "How is this new chap, what's his name, Streeter, is he proving himself?"

"Constable Cam Streeter," Chris replied. "Yes Sir, he is a good man."

"Comes in late does he?" Chief Inspector Fox asked.

"No Sir, he is getting information for me, I don't expect him in until I see him."

"Darn it Hardie, the man is a learner, you let him out on his own?"

"I have every confidence in him Sir," Chris replied.

"What's this I hear about you investigating a case of cannibalism?" Chief Inspector Fox asked. "Darn it Hardie, I know there is a war on, but people are not going hungry are they?"

Chris looked at George who had a slight grin on his face, Chris himself smiled inwardly. "I am investigating a young woman's murder Sir," Chris replied. "Although the question of cannibalism came up, it is only a suspicion, can you tell me how you heard this rumour Sir?" Chris asked.

"Darn it Hardie, through the grape vine, you may not know it, but I know everything that goes on in my division," Chief Inspector Fox replied.

"I am sure you do Sir," Chris replied respectfully. "But at the moment my investigation is on the murder of a young married lady Mrs Marston, and even if a cannibal was involved, I would not have broadcasted it."

"How far are you on with that?" Chief Inspector asked knowing he had been rebuked.

"Early days yet Sir," Chris replied. "It will be a difficult case to clear."

"How far are you with the disappearance of Miss Pamela Bell?" Chief Inspector asked, which took Chris by surprise.

"I must say, your grape vine is excellent Sir, Miss Pamela Bell's disappearance has just come to our notice with her sister's report," Chris replied.

"Darn it Hardie, it wasn't the grape vine, the twin sisters are friends of mine, by chance I met Ursala in town, she told me about it, she was not complaining, in fact she praised you darn it," Chief Inspector Fox enlightened Chris.

"That was nice of her," Chris replied, allowing himself a smile. "Constable Streeter is already gathering information on her disappearance."

"Darn it Hardie, I can give you information, I know them and their parents well."

"I have no doubt on that Sir," Chris replied. "However I am more interested in the last two days."

Chief Inspector Fox cleared his throat. "Very well Hardie, I would be pleased if you would keep me up to date on this, I don't want your hundred percent record broken on this case, I am sure you will resolve the case as well as the murder, how is that charming wife of yours?"

"Very well thank you Sir," Chris replied.

"It's about time young George House here got married," Chief Inspector Fox remarked standing up and taking his cap and stick. "Darn it Hardie, the division is proud of you and your team, don't let me down on this case."

"I don't intend to let you down on either of my cases Sir," Chris replied standing.

Chief Inspector Fox grunted, nodded to George and left the office.

"I think he likes you Chris," George laughed.

"Only because of our success rate George," Chris replied. "It makes him cock-a-hoop amongst the other Chief Inspectors, and also gives him a good name when he meets members of the Winchester Council, he didn't remark on our new blackboard?"

"He did to me, he thought it's a good idea," George said.

"Done anything with that list of yours?" Chris asked.

"With Miss Bell, there are now five missing women over the age of forty, they started going missing about eight years ago, the first one in 1908, the last one this week Miss Bell. The younger women went missing ten years ago, it do seem that most missing people are from below Middle Brook Street, Mrs Marston however contradicts that, she would have gone missing either from Water Lane where her father lives or Chester Road where she lived with her husband."

"I get your point George, but unlike the others Mrs Marston did not go missing, she was murdered, sliced up and dumped at Winnall Moors, can we class her as a missing person?" Chris asked.

"Perhaps you're right Chris," George agreed. "We can't class her as missing."

"There is no nice way of saying this, but Bob said three steaks had been cut off from her body, if it is a cannibal, why did he just cut off three steaks from her body, then discarding the body at Winnall Moors, which could keep him fed for sometime, perhaps when we find the killer, he will answer these questions, anyway, we must put all our efforts into catching the murderer."

George shook his head. "So where do we go from here?"

Chapter Eleven

*C*onstable Streeter had started his door knocking from St Martin's Church, he knocked on the dozen houses without any luck and he ended at Colson Road, it was the second to last house that he knocked, an attractive woman answered the door, Cam told her who he was and what he was after, when a man's voice was heard from the inside of the house.

"Who is it Lilly?" the man asked.

"A policeman is here asking questions, why don't you come?" Lilly smiled at Cam. "That's my husband."

"What's the matter?" asked the man who appeared beside his wife.

"I am Detective Constable Streeter," Cam introduced himself. "I am making enquiries regarding last Friday evening, a body of a young woman was found at Winnall Moors, I was wondering whether or not you heard or saw anything out of the usual that night, it would have been rather late."

The man fingered his chin. "Last Friday night you say," he replied. "I always go to the First in Last out on Fridays, pay day you know," he gave a cheeky grin. "No, I can't say I saw anything, what about you Lilly?" he asked his wife.

"You know I was in bed, I don't wait up for you to come home, or should I say stagger home, I heard nothing during the evening, had the radio on, didn't even here you come in."

"Well thank you," Cam replied about to move on.

"Just a moment, last Friday night you say, I stopped behind the bar, helped the landlord tidy up," he grinned. "Always worth an extra pint, the next time I go in," he added hurriedly. "I do remember it was just gone eleven as I opened the front door, I heard a squeaky sound, couldn't see anything, but it was someone pushing a pushcart coming from Easton Lane direction. I didn't really take any notice, and came in, thinking it must have been the singing barrow boy."

"What made you think that Sir?" Cam asked politely.

"I suppose because he is the only one out at nights pushing a barrow," the man replied. "He was not singing however," the man grinned.

"You did not see him clearly?" Cam asked.

"No, just an outline of a form, of course it could have been a woman although I would doubt it at that time of night," the man answered.

"Thank you Sir," Cam replied. "Should you think of anything else, please get in touch with the station, it will be appreciated."

Cam crossed the road and knocked on the first of three houses that joined onto the First in Last out public house.

A smart woman dressed in a blue dress answered the door. "Can I help you?" she asked.

Cam introduced himself and why he was there.

"I can't help you much," the woman answered. "Friday night I was working."

"Oh," Cam remarked. "No one was here during Friday night?"

The woman smiled. "I am a divorcee, with a child just under five, I have a babysitter of course."

"I see," Cam remarked. "Can you tell me your name please?"

"Perhaps you had better come in, but please be quiet, I have just got the baby to sleep."

Cam entered the house and shown straight into the neat tidy front room. "I am, Mrs Margaret Bumstead, I work at a nursing home, part time mostly, but I did have to go in Friday Night, six pm until six am," she smiled as they both seated.

"Twelve hour shift, that must be tiring?" Cam remarked.

"One gets used to it," Margaret replied. "I have a babysitter, actually we are kind of going out together, but I am not quite sure now if it will continue."

"Why is that?" Cam asked a little puzzled.

"My babysitter is Mr Charlie Webster, lives just down the road in Water Lane, not sure of the number, but next door to the Gasometer."

"I see," Cam replied. "Why are you not sure about him?"

"After he left on the Saturday morning, I did a little cleaning, I found a hair comb under the sofa, it's not mine."

"You think he had a woman in here while you were at work?" Cam offered.

Margaret shrugged. "It's not mine, I don't wear them."

"There could be another reason?" Cam replied. "One should not jump to conclusions, have you told him yet?"

"No, I have not seen him since Saturday morning," Margaret replied.

"Can I see the hair comb Mrs Bumstead?" Cam asked.

Margaret got up and went to the sideboard, where she opened a drawer and took the comb out and handed it to

Cam before sitting again. "I have had no woman visitors for several weeks constable," Margaret added. "But I am sure it was not there Friday night, believe it or not I am a very tidy person."

"I think you have a really clean and tidy house Mrs Bumstead," Cam remarked looking around the room. "Do you have a back entrance?"

"Yes, in Colson Road," Margaret replied.

"Do you have a pushcart?" Cam asked.

Margaret shook her head. "No, never had the need, callers come to the door with everything I need."

"Like the singing barrow boy?" Cam smiled.

"Jason, yes, he calls, he sings quite well," Margaret replied.

Cam got up. "Thank you for being frank with me Mrs Bumstead," Cam said. "Would you mind if I borrow this comb, I will see that you get it back."

Margaret hesitated. "I need it to confront Charlie with," she remarked.

"I will get back to you very soon," Cam promised. "Is Charlie a violent man?"

"Why would you ask a question like that?" Margaret asked worriedly. "I can't say he has ever shown violence towards me."

"Perhaps not Mrs Bumstead, but you have never accused him of seeing another woman before, he might lose it, if he had been with another woman while you were at work and confronted with the evidence," Cam remarked, taking an instant liking to her.

"Are you saying that I should just let it pass?" Margaret asked a serious look on her face.

"Are you serious about your relationship with him?" Cam asked.

"It could turn out that way," Margaret responded. "I just don't know what you are saying?"

Cam felt a bit awkward, he did not wish to alarm her, he was looking for the murderer of a young woman that took place not far from where she lives, this Charlie might have nothing to do with it.

"Perhaps it would be better for the moment to just ask him if he had a woman in the house last Friday, without showing him the evidence," Cam advised.

"I can't see why?" Margaret replied. "You don't think Charlie has anything to do with the death of that young woman do you?" she asked after a moment thought. "You can't seriously believe that?"

"I don't know your Charlie," Cam replied wondering how he was going to get out of this line of conversation that he had unintentionally started.

"I would doubt it, but it is unusual that your babysitter had a woman in the house, and we found the body of a woman the same night, and within a short distance, I would prefer for the moment that you said nothing about it to him, any doubts we have now, will be cleared up when we catch the person responsible."

"So you do have doubts?" Margaret remarked a worried look on her face.

"No, I don't," Cam replied a little angry at himself. "If this Charlie had anything to do with it, he would have had to leave your child alone in the house, he would have needed a pushcart to carry the body in, which you do not have."

Margaret smiled. "Charlie would never leave my child alone, and as you say, he would have needed a barrow," Margaret shrugged. "Very well then, I don't expect to see Charlie for a couple of days, I am not on night duty until Sunday."

"Just one more question before I go Mrs Bumstead, how long have you lived here?"

"My daughter is almost five, we moved here two years before she was born, close on seven years I would say."

Cam left the house still angry at himself, for Margaret he had put doubt in her mind, and perhaps worry, after all a hair comb do not make her boyfriend a murderer even if he was cheating on her. Cam reached the junction of Water Lane with Blue Ball Hill, he decided to go to Chester Road, twenty yards up Blue Ball Hill, where he knocked on number two, Mrs Marston's house.

Mrs Marston senior opened the door, she recognised Cam straight away.

"Constable," she said. "Please come in," she offered standing to one side allowing him to enter. "Have you got some news?" she asked as she closed the front door and followed Cam into the front room.

"I'm afraid not Mrs Marston," Cam replied as he sat. "But we are investigating, I'm sure it won't be long before we know something."

"Would you like a cup of tea Constable?" Mrs Marston offered. "As you know my son is at work."

"No to the tea, thank you," Cam replied. "With your son at work perhaps you can tell me, did your daughter-in-law have hair combs?"

Mrs Marston grinned. "She loved them, she had plenty of them in her room, you can see them if you want?"

Cam took the hair comb from his pocket handing it to Mrs Marston. "Would you be able to say that this was one of hers?"

Mrs Marston studied the comb. "Constable, Olive as I said had many all shapes and sizes, this could be very well one of hers, but I can't say for sure, you see the lot without taking particular notice of any one of them, no constable I can't say, was it found on her?"

"No, it just came into our hands, it was found not far from where your daughter-in-law was found."

"Well I am very sorry, as I said it could have been hers, and then again I could be wrong, so many of them about, you will probably find one like that in many houses."

Cam left the house disappointed knowing that the hair comb would prove nothing, he crossed the road, and saw the double doors of Jason's shed open, and walked to the front of them.

Jason who was chopping and making kindling wood, stopped as he saw Cam, he smiled. "Anything I can help you with?" he asked.

Cam stood idly against the open door. "I am Detective Constable Streeter," he replied. "You have met my bosses Inspector Hardie and Sergeant House."

"I have indeed," Jason replied. "Are you working on the same case?"

Cam nodded his head. "Been knocking doors."

"Got no where?" Jason remarked.

"Why do you say that?" Cam asked.

"It's written all over your face constable, you look depressed," Jason replied. "I could make you a cup of tea if you like?"

Cam smiled. "No thanks, Mrs Marston offered, just don't feel like one, I spoke to a Mrs Bumstead this morning, she has a boyfriend a Mr Charlie Webster, I believe you know him?"

"Yes, Charlie is a friend of mine, can I help you with anything?" Jason offered.

"No, I need to speak to him myself," Cam said. "Any idea when he will be home?"

"Not for a few hours yet, he normally gets home by six," Jason stood up and stretched himself. "You don't suspect Charlie do you?"

"We have no suspects at the moment, but we have to eliminate all names that come forward, and your friend was in the vicinity that night, babysitting."

"There you are then he wouldn't leave a baby on her own?" Jason smiled.

"You know Mrs Bumstead then?" Cam asked. "You know she had a daughter."

Jason smiled. "I will have to be on my guard with you constable, no I don't know Mrs Bumstead, apart from delivering logs to her, but Charlie told me she had a daughter."

Cam nodded. "We know someone was pushing a barrow around eleven that night coming from the Moors direction, would that have been you?"

Jason smiled. "Sorry constable, I was in the Mildmay Arms that night playing piano, I played the piano until ten, then I had a cheese sandwich, finished off my pint, and came home, I was tucked in my bed fast asleep by eleven."

Cam smiled. "I have been in there, he serves a good pint."

"You should try one of Mrs Quinn's meat sandwiches, she only makes them now and again, I am told they are great but I'm not a meat eater, I am a vegetarian."

"Well thanks for your time Jason, my boss will be wondering where I am."

Jason watched as Cam walked away, a smile played on his face, without locking the shed door, he walked across the road to his house, and went straight to his sister's room, where he studied his chart.

286

Chapter Twelve

Chris and George sat silent for a half hour as Cam reported his findings, as Cam came to the end and closed his notebook Chris looked and smiled at George.

"It's a pity what Mrs Bumstead found was not a bit of jewellery such as a broach or an earring, I can't see what the hair comb is going to prove?" George remarked.

"My thoughts are exactly same," Chris replied. "But it do give us something to think on and Mrs Marston did say her daughter-in-law was very keen on them."

"We will have to talk to Mr Webster, and ask him if he had a woman in the house?" Cam remarked. "Mrs Bumstead keeps her house spotless, she said the comb was not hers and it was not there the Friday night when she left for work and I believe her."

George looked at Cam and smiled. "What's this Mrs Bumstead like Cam?" he asked.

Cam screwed up his lips. "Nice looking, slender, about my age."

"You took a fancy to her then?" George teased.

Cam felt himself blush. "She has a boyfriend, Charlie Webster," Cam replied. "I doubt if she noticed me in that sense."

"Well we will be seeing Mr Webster tonight," Chris remarked. "If what you say turns out to be true, she won't want him if she has any pride."

"Do I come with you?" Cam asked a little excited.

"Well you are doing the checking on him, I suppose you better," Chris smiled. "You don't mind George do you?" Chris asked.

"As a matter of fact, I am seeing Rosemary tonight," George replied with a grin.

"Really," Chris smiled. "Going out somewhere?"

"Early stages at the moment, might have a walk around the farm, the weather is quite good, I like being with her."

"Elizabeth will be pleased," Chris said with a grin on his face. "Now Cam we will see Mr Webster about six, I don't have to worry about Elizabeth tonight, she will be leaving the bank early, you have plenty of time to get your report written."

George looked at his list, then at the blackboard. "You know Chris, studying this list of mine, the older ladies have no pattern to it, they came from all over Winchester, all disappeared while shopping in town."

"Miss Bell wasn't, she was taking a walk," Chris remarked.

"I know," George replied slowly. "But perhaps she was in town, like all the others, I don't accept that someone is walking the city and somehow snatches these women just like that."

"Perhaps they all went to a special part of Winchester, who knows, it could be a church, a café?" Chris offered.

"Even the Abbey Grounds," Cam interrupted as he was writing his report.

"The Abbey Grounds were closed when Miss Bell went for a walk," Chris replied. "But it's a thought, without

288

knowing each other, these women could've visited the same place for some reason, we will be lucky if we find out."

Both Chris and Cam looked at the gleaming steam engine as they opened the small gate to Mr Webster's house. Chris knocked the door. "It looks great," Chris said as they waited.

"He certainly keeps it gleaming, most drivers are proud of their engines" Cam replied as the front door opened.

Charlie Webster opened the door, and stared for a second, then a grin came to his face.

"Inspector," he said. "I met you talking to Jason a couple days ago."

"I remember Mr Webster," Chris replied. "I am Detective Inspector Hardie, and my colleague Detective Constable Streeter, we would like a few words with you."

"By all means Inspector, come in," he offered standing to one side allowing them to enter.

"Go right through," Charlie remarked as he closed the door behind him. "I'm in the scullery, I was about to get my dinner ready, I've just got home, perhaps a cup of tea?" he asked as he offered them a chair each.

"No thank you Mr Webster," Chris replied as he sat by the table. "We are off to have our meal, we will not keep you longer than necessary."

"Fire away then," Charlie remarked with a grin on his face. "Whatever it's about, I don't think I have been speeding?"

"Nothing like that Mr Webster," Chris replied. "You know we are investigating the murder of Mrs Marston who lived in Chester Road."

"I do," Charlie replied. "I knew Olive before she got married, as you know she lived with her father a few yards down."

"How long have you been here Mr Webster?" Chris asked.

"I was born here," Charlie replied a grin still on his face. "My parents came to Winchester in 1879, looking for work, so I was told."

"Really," Chris replied. "Where did your family come from?"

"Southsea," Charlie replied. "Although I have very little knowledge of the place, spent weeks holidays there when I was young, but have not been back since becoming an adult, Winchester is my home."

"When I saw you with Jason, he told me you were his best friend," Chris remarked.

Charlie rested his arms on the table. "Jason is a bit of a loner, I'm just a couple years older than him, when his family moved here about fifteen or so years ago, their house at the top of my back garden, we just became friends and have been ever since."

"You knew his sister then, the one that disappeared?" Chris asked.

"Yes, she was younger than Jason, looked after Jason like a mother when both their parents had died, I don't think Jason has got over it," Charlie replied, the grin gone from his face. "I really do feel sorry for him."

"You go out together?" Chris asked.

"Weekends sometimes," Charlie replied. "He plays the piano around the pubs."

"Anywhere special?" Chris asked.

"No, where ever we are, he is always welcomed."

"What about the Mildmay Arms?" Chris asked showing an interest.

"Sometimes yes," Charlie replied.

"Speaking about the Mildmay Arms, when you are in there, do you see many young women?"

Charlie screwed up his lips as he thought. "You already know Inspector, unless you are eighteen you are not allowed in a pub, so I take it that you mean ladies past eighteen, well yes, on a weekend in most pubs you will find young women in them, all accompanied by their parents or boyfriends of course. Weekends is when the whole family go and have a drink together, they all sit together around a table, can't say I see many on their own though."

Chris smiled. "I suppose you are wondering why we have called?" he asked.

"I was wondering, yes," Charlie answered. "I'm sure it was not about teenage girls going into pubs, I rarely go out during the weekdays, I have my engine to polish."

"I'm sure you have Mr Webster," Chris replied. "But let's get to the point, Constable Streeter here has been knocking doors, those past the First in Last out, in relation to our investigation regarding Mrs Olive Marston's murder, he knocked the door of a Mrs Bumstead, she told him you were babysitting that night that Mrs Marston was killed."

"That's right Inspector, I was there between five thirty Friday night and six thirty the Saturday morning, is there a problem with that?" Charlie replied his grin having left his face.

Chris looked at Cam indicating that he could have a go.

"Did you by chance have a woman in the house while you were babysitting Mr Webster?" Cam asked.

"No, I did not," Charlie replied a little angry. "Is that what she is saying?"

"No, nothing at all, but cleaning up the next morning she found an article that only a woman would have, she said it was not hers, so you see Mr Webster, we have to ask you, was there a woman in the house while Mrs Bumstead was at work?"

"I have told you, no," Mr Webster replied still a little hostility. "What was this article anyway?"

"It was a ladies hair comb," Cam replied.

Charlie sat looking at Cam for a moment, then a grin spread over his face, of course he said getting up and crossing the room to where his jacket was hanging, he searched his pockets, and eventually brought a packet with three other hair combs in it to the table.

"I bought these for Margaret, and forgot to give them to her, she is always in a rush, I have not seen her since, but one must have dropped out of my pocket," Charlie remarked as he sat again at the table, his hostility gone. "Did you really think it belonged to Mrs Marston?"

"No Mr Webster, we did not think that, we just wanted to eliminate you, you see we already know that a person was seen pushing a handcart from the direction of the Moors, eleven or just after that night. Mrs Bumstead assured us that you would never leave her daughter alone in the house, we also know Mrs Bumstead do not have a pushcart, while all this eliminates you we still wanted to know about this woman should you have had one in the house."

"I understand Inspector," Charlie replied a little more relaxed. "But I'm glad I was able to prove that I was not cheating on Margaret, I am quite taken to her."

"She never spoke against you Mr Webster, she was surprised to find the hair comb," Cam remarked a little doubt niggling him.

Chris left Cam at the bottom of Blue Ball Hill.

"My day off tomorrow Cam, Saturday, you will have to fill George in, I will see you Sunday."

"Do you believe him?" Cam asked.

"We can only go on what people tell us Cam, truth or lies, however lies can sometime bounce back on you, one have to be clever when they lie, they need to have a good memory, then again once a lie is told, you have to lie again to cover the lie before."

"Complicated," Cam remarked.

"Do you think Mr Webster lied Cam?" Chris asked.

Cam shrugged. "I don't know, I felt a little niggled," Cam replied.

Chris laughed. "That was because he proved he was not cheating on Mrs Bumstead."

"I suppose so," Cam admitted. "I'll put George in the picture."

Chapter Thirteen

*C*hris enjoyed his lay in on the Saturday morning, Elizabeth was already up when he opened his eyes to a warm and sunny morning, he stretched his arms and yawned as Elizabeth entered the bedroom.

"Breakfast is ready darling," she said before kissing him tenderly. "It will be on the table once you have had your wash."

Chris still half asleep, managed to smile. "I had a good night sleep," he muttered. "I must have needed it."

"Of course you did darling," Elizabeth commented as she fussed about the room. "That's why I left you alone," she giggled.

"I'm going to have a pint with Ron this morning, do you mind?" Chris asked as he tucked into his English Breakfast. "I haven't had one with him for some time, I know he likes one when he gets the chance."

"It will do you both good," Elizabeth replied pouring out the tea. "Dad loves his pint, but mother is not all that happy, she is only thinking of his health."

"Ron is a social drinker, not a boozer," Chris replied. "I can't see what he drinks will effect his health, anyway, it's said that drinking beer with moderation, softens the tempter, cheers the spirit, and promotes good health, and is as good as having a healthy meal."

It was half past eleven, as Olive and Elizabeth stood at the front door seeing Chris and Ron off. "Your dinner will be on the table at two, don't be late," Olive said in the form of a order to her husband.

"Don't fret my sweet," Ron replied with a smile. "I won't be under your feet while you are cooking."

"At least I know where you are, when you are," Olive replied. "Are you sure you are warm enough without a jacket?"

"It's a beautiful day," Ron replied.

"Get along with you, enough of your cheek," Olive replied keeping a straight face.

"You don't really mind dad going for a drink with Chris do you?" Elizabeth asked her mum as she closed the front door.

"Of course not darling," Olive replied. "I am glad he has Chris to go out with, they have taken to each other, but you must never let a man know your true feelings, or they will take advantage of them, it comes natural to a man."

"Chris know my feelings," Elizabeth replied. "I am happy that he is happy."

Chris and Ron walked down Magdalene Hill towards the Rising Sun. "Take no notice of Olive," Ron remarked. "If I am not home until three she will still have my dinner ready."

"I have no doubt of that Ron," Chris replied.

"I allow Olive to believe she has complete control of me, where I go or what I do, I don't mind one bit, I have a happy life, no rows, she keeps the house clean, and looks after me in every way possible. I like teasing her, but in a funny way, I believe she likes it, most of my teasing flatters her," Ron laughed.

295

"They say if you want to know what your wife will turn out like, take a look at her mother, well I shall be quite happy if Elizabeth turns out like Olive," Chris smiled.

"Thank you Chris, I would be lost without Olive, but for these kind words, allow me to buy the first round," Ron grinned as they entered the Rising Sun.

A few customers were in the Rising Sun, most of them around the dart board, Chris however was glad to see that his favourite seat at the window overlooking Bridge Street was vacant.

"Gentlemen," Alfie the landlord greeted them. "Long time no see, I was about to phone the undertakers to see if they had seen you."

Chris smiled at his morbid humour. "I'm afraid I am too busy to go to places like that."

"Yes, I heard you were on another case, but business first what can I get you?"

"I'm having a boiler Chris," Ron remarked.

"I'll have the same," Chris replied as he watched Alfie pick up two pint glasses placing them on the counter, then taking two brown ales from a case behind him poured one in each glass. "How are you keeping Chris?" he asked as one by one he filled the glasses up with beer by pumping away at his pumps. "Marriage seems to agree with you, you look well."

"A day off and a lay in do you good," Chris replied.

Alfie put the filled glasses before them. "Fourpence please," he said.

"Have one yourself Alfie," Ron said digging into his trouser pockets for change.

"I'll have a pint of Guinness, that will be fivepence please."

"Usual seat Chris?" Ron asked picking up both pints.

Chris nodded, and followed Ron to the seat under the window.

Ron and Chris was almost ready for their second pint, when Alfie joined them at the table. "I have five minutes, everyone is filled unless someone comes in," Alfie smiled. "Your man came in last night, Cam they call him, he don't come in much, just for a pint then gone, but last night he was asking about a couple blokes, discreetly of course."

"Really," Chris remarked looking at Ron. "Who was he asking about?"

Two chaps as a matter of fact, Charlie Webster who drives the steam engine, and Jason Keen the barrow boy."

"What did you tell him?" Chris asked interested.

"Well Charlie comes in now and again, he's friendly, don't cause any trouble, he seems alright."

"Jason?" Chris asked.

"Because he is a customer even though it's rare, I buy logs from him, even through the summer like now, I store them up," Alfie remarked.

"Does he play your piano when he drinks here?" Chris asked.

Alfie smiled. "No I have a pianoforte, it plays itself, although a person will sit in front of it sometimes pretending to play it."

"What are you able to say about Jason?" Chris asked.

"Not much I'm afraid, but he is strange boy, he keeps asking questions about the Mildmay Arms, as it happens I know Albert Watts the landlord, he's an OK chap."

"What sort of questions does he ask you?" Chris replied more interested.

"Just about his housekeeper mainly, do I know her, have I ever had her sandwiches that she is famous for, that sort of things."

"Do you know her?" Chris asked.

Alfie shook his head. "She might have been in, but I don't know her."

"Thank you Alfie for letting me know, the constable will no doubt tell me later," Chris replied draining his pint.

"But that is not all," Alfie replied. "About a half hour after Cam had left, speak of the devil, Charlie came in."

"Really," Chris remarked.

"My wife Liz was in the bar at that time, she will sometimes come down for a drink," Alfie said with a smile on his face. "She spoke to him, it seems he was telling her about the police visiting him regarding the murder of the young lady in Chester Road last week."

"And?" Chris asked.

"Well it seems that the police thought he was involved, but he had proof that he was not."

"Thank you for telling me Alfie, I did interview him yesterday, and what he told your wife was true," Chris pushed his and Ron's glass in front of Alfie. "Same again, and a pint for yourself," he said a grin on his face.

"Any good for you?" Ron asked who had been listening.

"Not really Ron, just a bit curious as to why he would mention it, I mean the police questioning you about a murder, would you go around telling people, even though you are innocent?"

"Not me," Ron replied. "I would want to keep it secret, mud sticks as they say."

"I agree," Chris replied as Alfie brought over their other pints.

The Sunday morning Chris was on duty alone, George and Cam were having the day off. Chris read through the reports of the happenings of Saturday, there was not much that interested him, Saturday seemed to have been quiet.

Sergeant Dawkins entered with tea. "Thought you would like a cuppa," sergeant Dawkins remarked putting the cup in front of Chris. "It looks like a hot day again."

"It is," Chris agreed. "It's a pity that some of us have to work."

"You can say that again," sergeant Dawkins replied. "Still one has to think of the boys in France, it's only through the grace of God that we are not out there with them, so I suppose we can't really grumble."

"Your words are a credit to you Sergeant," Chris replied. "We moan about having to work, while our boys are being killed having no choice."

"We have a young soldier in the cells now, he was in a fight outside the Mildmay Arms last night, he was drunk, and Sergeant Williams had him put in the cell for him to sober up."

"Really, what was the fight about?" Chris asked.

"Haven't got the full story yet, I've taking him a cup of tea, he did not want any breakfast, so I shall let him go soon with a warning," sergeant Dawkins replied.

Chris smiled. "I suppose, we do have to go easy on the soldiers, they are fighting for us, but let me know if you find out what was the fight about, the Mildmay Arms is a part of our investigation at the moment."

It was gone ten when Sergeant Dawkins entered again. "I'm letting the soldier go in a few moments although he still seems wobbly," he said. "His name is private West, a Winchester man, on a seven days leave before going over seas."

"Really," Chris remarked. "Did he say what started the fight?"

"It seems he was talking to a man, who was a bit older than himself, all he knew about him was his name was Jason, who said his sister had disappeared some time ago, Private West then told him his mother had vanished and he had been looking for her ever since."

Chris got up and studied the blackboard. "There is a Mrs Violet West on here that vanished some six years ago," he remarked returning to his desk. "Perhaps Sergeant I should have a word with him before you release him."

"I thought you might," sergeant Dawkins replied. "I have seen your blackboard."

"Thank you sergeant, very observant of you," Chris remarked.

"That's uniform for you, eyes and ears always open," sergeant Dawkins remarked as he left.

Chris felt himself excited, it could be a lead, and once again got up and looked at the blackboard. Chris was still studying the blackboard when Sergeant Dawkins entered with Private West, Chris saw that he was a well built man, about five foot, six or seven inches not too tall, was wearing his army uniform and carrying his peak cap. Chris welcomed him with the offer of the interview chair as Sergeant Dawkins left.

"You don't feel too good do you?" Chris said with a smile as gently as he could. "You had a night out last night I hear."

"You could say that, but I have felt like this before, it will pass," Private West replied looking around the room.

"What is your Christian name?" Chris asked.

"Edward, Edward West."

"You are a Winchester man?" Chris asked.

"All my life, born here, Nuns Road," Edward replied.

"Are you married?" Chris asked.

"No I live with my sister," Edward replied.

"Well Edward, I hear you are on leave before going to France," Chris replied.

"That's right," Edward answered.

"I don't blame you enjoying yourself while on leave, I would if I was going overseas," Chris spoke gently. "Can you tell me what the fight was about?"

Edward thought for a while. "It's not all come back to me yet, I do remember talking to the bloke who was telling me his sister went missing and was never found, I told him about my mother who also disappeared and never been found. Then the call came for him to play the piano, I have accepted in my mind that I shall never see my mother again, and I am living with it, but this bloke bringing up about his sister brought it all back again, I suppose I brooded about my mother while he was playing the piano, I perhaps had one or two too many because of my brooding, anyway," Edward went on with a sigh. "He eventually came and sat by me again, he started to ask questions, questions that were personal."

"You were offended by his questions?" Chris asked.

"No, not really, but another bloke came and sat at our table, it was him who seemed to get offended."

"Really," Chris remarked interested. "Who was he?"

"No idea," replied Edward. "He seemed to know Jason, the bloke I was speaking to."

Chris thought in his mind that this other bloke could be Charlie Webster. "How did the fight break out?" Chris asked.

"God knows," Edward answered. "One moment I was talking to Jason, the next minute this bloke lashed out, we have been training very hard for the last two months, I suppose that came in handy to me, I dodged, and gave him a punch, after a while the police turned up, that's all I can remember."

Chris was about to ask him another question, but saw Edward staring at the blackboard. "You have my mother's name there," Edward said pointing to the board.

"Your mother went missing some six years ago Edward," Chris replied his voice calm. "A case is never closed until it is solved."

"You are never going to find her after all this time," Edward assured Chris.

"We shall still try," Chris replied. "Tell me Edward, could your mother have gone off on her own accord, I mean would she have left her family for some reason?"

"My mother would never have left her husband, my sister or me, we were a very close family, I had a good life up to 1910, when my mother disappeared."

"Living with your sister, I take it your father has died?" Chris asked.

"About a year after, if there is such a thing, he died of a broken heart," Edward answered his eyes looking at the floor.

"I am sorry to hear that," Chris replied. "When is your leave up?"

"Next Wednesday, I have to report back by ten am," Edward replied. "Just three full days left," he said with a weak smile on his face.

"I'm sorry to harp on it, but every little bit of information helps, have you got any opinion as to why your mother disappeared?" Chris asked.

"I was only fifteen at the time, never really knew what was happening, father spoke to the police, we were not allowed in the room, one thing I do know, she had an invitation by letter, she went and never returned."

"The invitation, do you know what happened to it?" Chris asked now excited.

Edward shook his head. "I never saw it, I just heard father and the police talking about it, I suppose the police kept it."

"Well if I don't see you again, I wish you all the best, just one more thing, you can't remember what you were saying when this other bloke lashed out at you?" Chris asked.

Edward shook his head again. "Sorry, I must have said something, but it don't come to mind."

Satisfied that he knew all that Edward could remember, Chris stood up and offered his hand. "Try not to get into more fights while you are on leave, enjoy the rest of it, but always rest assure, we will find out where your mother went."

"Will my commanding officer be informed about this?" Edward asked a worried look on his face.

Chris smiled. "No, not this time, we did not arrest you, just gave you board and lodging for the night."

Edward smiled as he took Chris's hand. "Thank you Sir," he said as he left.

Chris spent the next half hour writing out his report then went out to the sergeant's desk.

"Sergeant, can you dig the reports out of the missing women, the dates are on the board, only the older woman for the time being there are just five, if I am needed I shall be at one of three places, Chester Road, Water Lane, or the Mildmay Arms."

Sergeant Dawkins smiled. "It will take a little time, I can't leave the desk very long."

"Well you have all day Sergeant," Chris replied. "Just do your best."

Chris decide he would first see Jason, and within the ten minutes he was knocking on his door.

"Inspector," Jason said as he opened his door. "I have been expecting you."

"Not chopping wood today?" Chris asked as he followed Jason into the scullery.

"Not after last night, which I take it you are here about," Jason answered offering Chris a chair. "Want a cuppa?"

"Never no to one of your cuppa," Chris replied with a smile.

Jason started to make the tea, his back to Chris while he stood at the sink. "How is the soldier?" Jason asked.

"He's fine," Chris replied. "He is on leave before going to France."

"He seemed a nice bloke," Jason replied. "I did not know he was going to France, I feel a little guilty now."

"Why?" Chris asked. "From what I hear, you did not start the fight, it was Charlie Webster."

"You know that?" Jason asked a surprised look on his face. "Oh I take it, you have already been to the Mildmay Arms."

"As a matter of fact I have not," Chris replied. "It was just a guess on my part."

"No wonder you are CID," Jason flattered bringing two cups of tea to the table and seating himself opposite Chris.

Chris took a sip of his tea, and smacked his lips as he replaced the cup. "You certainly know how to make a cup of tea," Chris said. "Tell me what did Private West say that made Charlie lash out?"

304

"I am not sure Inspector, honestly, Edward and I, that's his name was talking about my sister and his mother, both who had gone missing. Charlie came in the pub, saw me, and naturally came and sat by us. Edward was still asking questions, then Charlie tried to hit Edward who ducked the blow, and punched back. Tables went over, glasses smashed before the police came, Charlie and I were let off because we had a home to go to, and the landlord decided not to press charges. Edward was taken away as he was a soldier, he did however seem tipsy."

"You can't remember what was said that made Charlie angry?" Chris asked.

"Afraid not Inspector," Jason answered. "I would surely tell you if I could remember, but everything went so fast, what was said went completely from my mind."

"Well never mind, perhaps Charlie will remember?" Chris said with a grin, as he sipped his tea.

"I doubt that, he was in a bad way when I took him home, he will have a black eyes this morning I expect," Jason replied. "I have never seen him like that before, he is not usually violent."

"So his behaviour was uncommon to him?" Chris asked.

"As far as I know him yes, I have never seen him in a fight before."

"Strange," Chris muttered as he drank his tea.

Chris left Jason, he turned left into Blue Ball Hill, then left again into Water Lane, then left again past the Gasometer, stopping by the steam engine outside where Charlie Webster lives.

"I saw you coming Inspector," came a voice that made Chris look up where he saw Charlie polishing some brass work. "Are you here about the fight last night?"

305

Chris stood by the back wheel of the steam engine, the wheel about a foot wide, made of solid iron, was about the same height as Chris. "These wheels are tall," Chris remarked as he watched Charlie descend from the engine.

"Has to be, these steam engines are heavy and very powerful, flatten anything apart from iron, what the front roller don't get, the back wheels will," Charlie replied standing by Chris wiping his hands in a bit of cloth.

"You do have a nice eye there Mr Webster," Chris said with a smile on his face.

"Yes I got punched and have a black eyes," but next time I'll be prepared Charlie replied.

"I doubt if there will be a next time, the soldier will be in France this time next week," Chris remarked. "I am told it's unusual for you to get into fights."

"I had no idea he was on embarkation leave?" Charlie replied, stuffing his bit of cloth into his overall pocket. "I really don't know what got into me, as you say, I am not normally a violent type."

"I'm sure you're not Mr Webster," Chris replied. "But what did the soldier say to make you so angry?"

"I'm not sure, I was in a bad mood when I went into the pub, I had a bad day you see nothing went right what ever I did, so I thought a pint might make me feel better, I did not go out until late, wish I hadn't gone at all now," Charlie grinned touching his eye.

"Anyway I saw Jason talking to this soldier and joined them, Jason was talking about his sister, and the soldier was talking about his missing mother, my mood seemed to get deeper, then they started to talk about who could have killed them and the killer must live in the vicinity," Charlie sighed. "Somehow I could not stop myself and I said, because someone go missing, it don't mean that they are dead, if they are dead where are the bodies I asked?"

Charlie took out the piece of cloth from his overall pocket and started to wipe his hands again.

"The soldier ask me if I had anyone missing, I replied No, then he told me that I should mind my own business, and that was it, I snapped and threw a punch, but got one instead."

"That was it, was it?" Chris asked.

"That's all I know what happened," Charlie replied. "Perhaps Jason can tell you more?"

"I'm not investigating it as a case Mr Webster," Chris remarked. "As far as I know there is no case, the landlord would not press charges."

"That's good of him," Charlie said once again putting his cloth into his overall pocket. "I'll apologise and ask him how much damage I caused, everything went bad for me yesterday dogged by bad luck."

"Are you superstitious?" Chris asked.

"I think most of us do have some beliefs one way or another," Charlie replied. "Anyway would you like a cup of tea, I am just about to make one?"

"Thank you no, I will be having a pint and a bite to eat very soon, but thanks again for the offer, and keep out of fights," Chris remarked as he took his leave.

It was half past twelve when Chris entered the Mildmay Arms, there were quite a few customers, some playing darts, others playing push half penny, and one or two playing skittles. "You have enough games for your customers," Chris remarked as the landlord came up to him.

"Hello Inspector," Albert Watts the landlord smiled. "Yes it keeps them happy, no singing or music on a Sunday, we are only open as you know from twelve till two pm, then they will all be full of beer, going home to enjoy their Sunday roast, what can I get you?"

"I'll have a pint of your best bitter I think, do you have a sandwich?"

Albert took a pint glass and started to fill it. "I have no grub on Sundays, it would not sell if I did, as I said most of these in here will have a Sunday roast," Albert said having filled the glass and putting the pint before Chris.

"Have one yourself," Chris offered.

"Thank you, I'll have half a bitter, can't drink too much, unlike most of my customers I can't hold it."

Chris smiled as he put coins on the counter. "How do you get on for a Sunday Dinner?"

"My housekeeper brings me about two thirty, allows me to brush around and clean the glasses, are you here about the fight last night?"

"No, not really, you did not press charges, so there is no case, I was just interested how the fight started?" Chris said after taking a sip from his pint. "You see the soldier boy was on embarkation leave, he will be in France by the end of the week, I did not want him to get into army trouble."

"That would be a shame, our lads have plenty to worry about without the army on their backs, is he alright?"

Chris took another sip before answering. "Yes a bit wobbly but he's OK, has he been in here before, he is a Winchester man."

Albert shrugged. "Didn't recognise him, perhaps it was his uniform, but I can't really be sure."

"You know Mr Keen and Mr Webster I take it?" Chris remarked.

"Well Jason plays the piano for us, he is a quiet chap, mainly keeps to himself, he must be an intelligent chap."

"Why do you say that?" Chris asked.

"He is always asking questions, that's what intelligent chaps do isn't it?" Albert smiled.

"An inquisitive mind, I suppose would make you more knowledgeable," Chris agreed. "What about Mr Webster?"

"Never had any trouble with him before, he comes in here sometimes late at night, has a pint and a sandwich then goes home, he do come sometimes during the weekend with Jason."

"You have no idea how the fight started?" Chris asked taking up his pint.

"I was over here, never heard a word they were saying, just heard the table go over and saw Charlie sprawled on the floor."

"I saw Mr Webster this morning as I was walking past his house, he has a lovely black eyes now," Chris remarked a slight smile on his face.

Albert smiled. "That will teach him to keep his fist to himself, but as I said, I have never had trouble with him, that's why I did not press charges."

Chris finished his pint. "I have time for another, do you mind if I eat my sandwich, my wife insists that I eat midday, and always puts a sandwich in my pocket."

"That's the advantage of having a wife," Albert said taking the empty glass to refill. "I sometimes wish I had a wife around, but still my housekeeper looks after me, and she is a very good cook, but she cannot give me the company that a wife gives you."

"Chris took his sandwich out of his pocket, and started to eat, while the landlord was filling an order.

"Has your housekeeper been with you a long time?" Chris asked after rinsing down his food with a drink.

"About six years I would say," Albert answered. "She looks after the staff, she cooks for me, provides all the sandwiches, but we do not go out with each other if that's what you're thinking?"

"I'm not thinking that," Chris grinned. "Never crossed my mind."

"Well most of my customers do," Albert replied grinning. "She is a big help to me, don't know what I would do without her, but I find her strange, can't put my finger on it, but she is certainly strange."

"Don't you ever have a night off?" Chris asked changing the subject. "You must feel like a night out with the boys now and again?"

"I have one night off every week," Albert replied as he watched Chris take another drink. "Not a regular one, I choose the nights, usually when I am bored to death or for some reason feel down in the dumps."

Chris finished his sandwich, and washed it down with the remainder of his pint.

"I must go now landlord," he said. "I will see you again."

"Always welcome," grinned the landlord.

Chris entered the police station, it was almost two pm, sergeant Dawkins looked up as he entered.

"Enjoy the pint did we?" he asked with a smirk on his face. "Uniform is not allowed to drink on duty."

"I was on my break," Chris replied taking no notice of his disrespect for rank. "How's my files getting on?"

"I have managed to spend half an hour looking for them, but the room is piled with reports, none of them in order, I will look every time I get a chance."

"Sergeant House got the names of all the missing people over the last ten years quite quickly," Chris remarked.

"Sergeant House was looking for the names, he got those names from the yearly ledgers, I understood you wanted the records of each investigation?" sergeant Dawkins replied.

"I do sergeant, perhaps you could organise and have the record room put in alphabetic order, or would you like CID to do it?"

Sergeant Dawkins smiled. "I will spend as much time as I can, searching and I will get the room sorted out," he promised.

Chris smiled to himself as he entered his office, after disposing of his trilby he sat at his desk writing out a report of his mornings work.

An hour later, Chris leaned back in his chair, he took out his pipe and filled it, and after lighting it blew out clouds of smoke, it settled him, and his mind started to focus on what Mrs Olive Marston might have done when she had left her mother-in-law's house that night after a row with her husband. He knew she went towards Blue Ball Hill, away from where her father lives at Water Lane, but did she go up Blue Ball Hill or down into Water Lane. Had she gone down Blue Ball Hill into Water lane, she could have turned left, towards her father's house, that would have taken her pass Mr Webster's house, but then he thought Mr Webster was not at home he was babysitting. Had she turned right, there was two ways she could have gone, where Wales Street carried on from Water Lane she could have cross the bridge by the old Mill into Durngate, or she could have carried on towards Colson Road. Chris puffed on his pipe, a gut feeling told him she had carried on walking towards Colson Road, perhaps the only reason he said to himself was because that way took her towards where she was found.

Sergeant Dawkins, knocked and entered the office, which broke Chris's line of thought.

"There is a gentleman here to see you Inspector, he said he was asked to call by the Chief Inspector Fox."

"Really," Chris remarked putting his pipe in the ashtray. "We better have him in then."

Chris was standing when Sergeant Dawkins ushered the gentleman in, Chris saw at a glance that he was tall and thin, wearing a three piece blue pin stripe suit, wearing glasses, carrying a bowler hat.

Chris offered his hand. "I am Detective Inspector Hardie Sir."

The gentleman took his hand and shook it warmly. "I am Mr John Crowley call me John, I work for Scotland Yard in London."

"Really," Chris remarked wondering. "Please take a seat," he offered pointing to the interview chair. "How can I help you?"

John gave a smile. "It's not how you can help me, it's if I am able to help you, let me explain, I was invited a few days ago to the Chief Inspector Fox meeting at Bognor, during the break in the meeting your Chief Inspector Fox spoke to me, he said that you were investigating a case which might involve cannibalism, he asked me if I was down this way to call in and see you. Well I am in Winchester for the day, I know it's Sunday, really had no hope of seeing you, but I thought I would give it a try."

"I'm very glad you did John," Chris replied. "It is thoughtful of the Chief Inspector Fox, but how exactly can you help me, I'm not yet sure if I am dealing with cannibalism."

"I am a Criminologist," John replied. "I am supposed to understand the criminal mind, and why a person commits a crime, I think Chief Inspector Fox thought I could help you with advice."

"You have taken the trouble to call in, for which I thank you, but first would you like some refreshments?" Chris asked.

"No, no, no, I had dinner only an hour ago, I'm perfectly alright."

"Well," Chris started. "Last Friday week a young woman by the name of Olive Marston, let her home after a row with her husband. She was found on the Sunday following at Winnall Moors not far from here, she was found strangled, naked, and her body had been sliced off, the buttocks and inner thighs, it was the police surgeon that put the thought into my head that it might be cannibalism. My sergeant has a blackboard with all the details of missing people, mainly women for the last ten years on," Chris remarked looking at the board.

John got up and looked at the board which he studied for a while. "This is a board of missing people, why did you start making this list, after all missing people we all know can be dead, or still walking around, it's only when a body is found or the actual person is traced that we know what happened to them."

"I agree," Chris replied. "But Mrs Olive Marston was the daughter of Mr Collins, his younger daughter Miss Lucy Collins disappeared a few years ago without trace, so we thought we would compile a list of all missing people for the last ten years, just in case."

"OK," John replied. "For now let's say we do have a case of cannibalism, even though it might not be, looking at this board, I would say you have more than one, perhaps two, three or even four cannibals, you see, if I am reading

313

this board correctly, one young woman was taken from each street, within a very narrow area, that is how these cannibals work, take two person from one street, it prompts more police action in that street," John smiled. "And also, these cannibals are superstitious, they believe taken two person from any street is bad luck for them."

"I see," Chris replied. "What makes you think we have more than one?"

"Sometimes, or though it's very rare, a cannibal, will marry one, perhaps a distant relative, you have heard the story of Sweeney Todd," John smiled. "He was a barber, slitting his victims throats with his straight razor, his victims fall backward down a revolving trapdoor into the basement of his shop, and his partner in crime assists him in disposing of the bodies by baking their flesh into meat pies and selling them to the unsuspecting customers of her pie shop. In your case seriously these older women seem to be taken at random, no pattern at all, it means another cannibal operating, the two are not the same person."

"Good grief," Chris blurted out.

"Do you have any suspects?" John asked, leaving the board and taking his seat.

"Got a couple names, but all with alibis for that Friday night, the missing women are a side issue, I have to concentrate of Mrs Marston."

"Of course you do, but let's ponder a moment, this Mrs Marston lived in a street where her sister had already disappeared?" John asked.

"Yes and no," Chris replied. "Mrs Olive Marston lived at Water Lane with her family before her marriage, her sister disappeared without trace, Olive eventually married to a man who lived in a street above her Chester Road, she lived at her mother-in-law's house, who lived next door to where another young woman had disappeared some years ago."

"Double bad luck then," John replied. "Mrs Marston lived at two streets where a woman had disappeared in the past."

"What are you making at that?" Chris asked.

John shifted in his chair. "You have obviously looked into Mrs Marston's murder."

"Without any luck at the moment," Chris interrupted.

"Early days yet Inspector," John replied. "Go along this line, Mrs Marston was killed by mistake, it was only after she was killed that the mistake became apparent."

"I'm not fully with you John," Chris remarked.

"Well Mrs Marston lived at two streets where a woman had disappeared, she might have been killed believing she lived at a street where no woman had disappeared before, she was probably dragged into a house in the dark, and then only in the light the killer did realise his mistake, he could not eat her, it would bring him bad luck, so he had to get rid of the body."

"Flesh was cut from her body," Chris remarked.

"Perhaps he could not resist a slice," John replied. "You see a cannibal will eat all the soft fleshy body parts, they will also eat the organs."

"It has to be messy," Chris remarked.

"A bit," John replied. "But without the heart pumping the blood around the body, blood will clot, you cut yourself, blood will run, because it is kept on the move by the heart pump, once outside the body it will clot and dry, but there are other liquids in the body besides blood, water for instance which will not clot, cut a body deeply this water will run out, and mixed with the clotted blood looks just like it."

"How do they keep the flesh?" Chris asked. "You know I'm really ignorant, but a body will smell after a couple of days."

"Most people are ignorant," John replied. "Keeping the flesh from rotting, they have to be cut up more or less straight away, slices and the organs can be kept fresh for some time, but they have to be kept cold or frozen, look for someone who orders a lot of ice, it could help, winter time is perhaps the best time for cannibals."

"It's summer time now, and we just had a older lady go missing, just two or three days ago," Chris remarked.

"Then perhaps she has been cooked and eaten already," John replied.

"What do they do with the bones, that must be a problem?" Chris asked feeling a bit sick.

"Most houses has a chopper and a fire going, using logs, coal, or coke, the skeleton would burn with a hot enough fire, but there are many ways, they can be crushed or buried, it's the heads that could be difficult, it would be a job to burn a scull properly with its teeth, they are usually buried, or thrown in the sea, if there is one near by."

"Don't really know what to say," Chris replied. "I have seen some terrible murders, some bodies cut up, some unable to be identified, but eating it's gruesome."

"Don't forget Inspector," John said a little smile on his face. "Your case may not turn out to be cannibalism, you might find some of the missing people, or their bodies in time, what I have just told you may be worthless to you, but if it should be, then I hope I have helped you."

Chris walked home that night feeling sick, he could not get out of his mind what he had been told by John Crowley, but he realised if he was dealing with cannibalism he had a better outlook than he had before.

Chapter Fourteen

It was Monday morning a new week, Chris was still half asleep as with Elizabeth hanging on to his arm, they approached the King Alfred Statue on the way to the Police Station.

"You know darling," Elizabeth remarked. "With you getting up late and getting ready for work, with the rush I forgot to ask you why you were so restless in bed last night, you twisted and turned most of the night, and at times you groaned."

"Did I darling?" Chris replied patting her hand that was hanging on to his arm. "I did have some sort of nightmare."

"Tell me," begged Elizabeth.

"No, you will only laugh," Chris replied remembering his dreams vividly.

"Honest darling, I won't," Elizabeth implored.

"I dreamt that I was being eaten by cannibals," Chris replied looking straight ahead, not daring to look at Elizabeth.

"Honest darling," Elizabeth asked looking up at Chris. "They say that dreams come from your subconscious mind of something you have heard or talked about before, it's this case you are on, it must be getting to you."

"Perhaps," Chris replied as they stopped out side the police station.

Elizabeth fussed with his tie, she smiled. "Anyway darling, they say you should always reverse your dreams, so you don't have to worry, that is apart from me," she giggled. "I could eat you."

"You will probably find me a bit tough Mrs Hardie," Chris replied with a grin.

"I know you are tough and hard Mr Hardie," Elizabeth grinned cheekily. "I must get on now I shall be late," she said as she kissed him on the cheek. "See you tonight, here or at home," she smiled as she walked away.

Chris watched her until she went from view before entering the police station, Sergeant Dawkins looked up. "Morning Inspector," he greeted him with a smile.

"Morning Sergeant, have you any luck?" Chris asked.

"I stopped behind after Sergeant Williams took over last night and found them, they are on your desk, just four files, there were none for the latest Miss Pamela Bell."

"Thank you very much Sergeant," Chris replied amazed. "You must put in for a hours overtime, it was good of you."

"No need Inspector," sergeant Dawkins replied. "We uniforms are dedicated people, our job is more important than money."

"I am sure it is Sergeant," Chris replied trying to show his appreciation" "Very well Sergeant, but thank you all the same," Chris smiled.

George and Cam was already at their desk when Chris entered.

"You two, don't you ever get in late?" Chris smiled as he got rid of his trilby.

"We have said it before Chris," George remarked as he watched Chris seat himself.

"We are not married, we don't expect you in before us, should you be, then we will have to consider whether you have had a row with Elizabeth," George laughed.

"Can't imagine that," Chris replied seeing the files on his desk. "Anyway Mrs Marston has now been dead for over a week and we have no leads on that, nor on Miss Nelly Green, nor on Miss Pamela Bell who has gone missing," Chris said leaning on his arms across his desk.

"When I left you Friday night," Cam begun. "I went home had a meal, then I went to a few pubs in the area."

"Yes I know Cam, I was in the Rising Sun Saturday dinner time with my father-in-law, Alfie told me you had been in, did you go anywhere else?" Chris asked.

Cam smiled. "A couple more, I went to St Johns Tavern in St John's Street, I went to the Cricketers Inn on the corner of Water Lane, and ended up in the Fox Inn in Water Lane."

"You got drunk?" George grinned.

"No I only had a pint in each," Cam replied.

"Any results?" Chris asked.

"Only character references," Cam replied. "Mr Webster it seems pops in them all from time to time, while Mr Keen only pops in during the weekends, both are considered well behaved customers, they cause no trouble."

"As I expected," Chris remarked. "Now when I arrived here on Sunday, there was a young soldier in the cells, he was involved in a fight in the Mildmay Arms Saturday night with Mr Webster," Chris looked at George then Cam who was listening.

"I spoke to the soldier, a Edward West on embarkation leave before he goes to France," Chris continued. "That Mr Webster went into the Mildmay Arms late and saw Jason and this soldier talking to each other, so he sat with them,

Jason was talking about his missing sister, and the soldier was talking about his missing mother, her name is on your board George," Chris indicated the board with a turn of his head.

"Yes I can see it," George replied. "That was a stroke of good luck."

"It might turn out to be," Chris replied. "Anyway, no charges were brought by the landlord, and as the soldier was on embarkation leave, he was let off, but I wanted to know what made Mr Webster attack the soldier."

"Did you find out?" George asked.

"No, I went to see Mr Webster and Jason, also had a pint in the Mildmay Arms, but got no result, not one of them was clear as to how the fight started?"

"What about the soldier?" Cam asked. "Could he supply any help regarding his missing mother?"

"All he remembers was that his mother was missing after she was invited to someplace, he said she had been invited by letter, I asked about the letter, he told me that perhaps the police kept it, that is why I asked sergeant Dawkins to get me these files, the letter should be in Mrs Violet West's file, but let's remember the soldier was only fifteen at the time," Chris paused for a moment before continuing.

"However before we look at these files, I had a Mr John Crowley in to see me Sunday afternoon, he was asked to come by the Chief Inspector Fox."

Chris then related what took place, and by the time he had finished, both George and Cam was feeling sick.

"Fingers crossed that our case is not so," Cam said. "It makes me feel sick."

"I dreamt of it last night," Chris admitted. "Anyway, let's look at these files."

Chris took hold of the files, looking through them he selected Mrs Violet West and passed the others to George.

"Are we now concentrating on the missing persons?" George asked taking the files.

"No," Chris replied. "At the moment I haven't got a clue where to go, I do however believe that when Mrs Marston stormed out that night, she walked along Wales Street. I have walked the distance from Chester Road to the First in Last out pub and back, I was walking slowly, I believe Mrs Marston was killed or at least abducted within a half hour of her leaving home."

"That is in line with our thinking," George replied.

"If I am right about the route she took, she had to be taken into a house, she wasn't strangled in the middle of the road, but she could have been enticed into a house," Chris remarked.

"If Cam is right about your meeting with Mr Webster Friday evening," George said as he handed Cam a file. "His explanation seems acceptable."

Chris knew that George was right as he opened the file which contained reports of what was carried out in order to find missing four older women, then he came to a letter, handwritten.

Dear Violet, it began.

Please meet me tomorrow evening around seven, you will find me at our favourite cafe. Pam.

"Well I have the letter inviting her out," Chris said. "It was sent by a woman name Pam, I suspect that to be Pamela."

"I have one as well," George remarked holding the letter up. "Also sign Pam."

"Not one in this file," Cam replied shuffling through the pages inserted.

"Nor in my other file," George remarked.

"So we have two letters, each inviting one of the missing women out," Chris looked again at the paper the letter was written on. "I have a sort of logo on mine."

"Same here," George replied. "Looks like a rose."

"Who would use a logo like that?" Chris asked. "If it is a logo, it's a pity the letter did not include a return address, letterhead or name and address on it, these letters have been written on addition pages, that could be a business note paper?"

"Could be," George answered. "Find the firm, we might get who wrote the letters."

Chris looked at Cam with a smile on his face. "Sorry Cam, but you have another boring job, go to the council, in fact any authority, that might be able to tell you whose logo this is, and let's hope they are in Winchester."

"I can do that Chris, don't know how long it will take though," Cam replied.

"No one is rushing you Cam," Chris replied.

Cam grinned. "I'll get right on it, I need to take one of the letters."

"Don't let anyone have it Cam, it's evidence, take the one George has," Chris advised.

"What do we do?" George asked as Cam left the office.

"First study these files, see if we can find a common factor, though I have my doubts," Chris remarked. "I wish we had someone in the frame by the name of Pamela."

"I have been wondering that too," George grinned. "We do assume that the missing girls, because they are missing from this particular area, have been abducted by someone in this area, can we be so sure about that with the missing older women, there is no pattern."

322

"I get your point George," Chris answered. "The older women comes from all over, also where is this cafe, could be anywhere in town even just outside Winchester, who is Pamela, but with two letters out of four, I believe their disappearances are linked, I wonder if Miss Pamela Bell received a letter?"

"The only link I see in these files, is that all the missing are getting on in age," George remarked.

"Who would put a rose as a logo, that is, if it is a logo?" Chris asked.

George looked up. "I suppose a florist comes to mind at first, though I expect other businesses might use a flower."

"As far as I know we have only one florist in Winchester, apart from the women selling them on the street corners, by the way George," Chris commented as he studied the file in front of him. "How did your date go on Friday?"

George looked up from his file with a grin. "Fine just fine, Mr and Mrs Morris were very polite, I had a evening meal, a roast dinner cooked by Rosemary again, we strolled around the farm later that evening, we seem to get on well," his grin becoming broader. "I am taking her for a meal next Saturday, it's my day off."

"I can see that we shall be soon looking for a house for you George?" Chris remarked his eyes smiling.

"It's a bit early for that Chris, I don't even know how Rosemary feels about me?" George replied.

"Well she is obviously interested, otherwise she would not be going out for a meal with you," Chris remarked. "Don't forget if she accepted your invitation she would have known that her parents would not have objected, so they must like you."

"Yes perhaps you are right Chris," George smiled contentedly.

"Within a year we will all be married," Chris remarked as he still studied the papers in his file.

George laughed. "That's a bit early perhaps, but Cam is not even courting yet."

Chris looked up his eyes smiling. "Cam has a secret liking for Mrs Bumstead, you know Mr Webster's girlfriend, I saw how annoyed he was Friday night when Mr Webster explained the hair comb, he was really disappointed."

A knock came on the office door, and Sergeant Bloom entered.

"Hello Sergeant," Chris said. "Anything wrong?"

"There is a Miss Ursala Bell wishing to see you Sir," sergeant Bloom said respectfully.

"Really Sergeant," Chris replied. "She must be here about her missing sister, better show her in."

"It has just struck me, her missing sister is Pamela," George remarked as the sergeant left.

"It struck me at the same time," Chris replied, as he stood up when sergeant Bloom ushered Miss Bell into the room.

"Miss Bell," Chris said offering his hand which she took. "Please be seated, you of course know Sergeant House?"

Miss Bell looked at George and smiled, and nodded her head. "I have been wondering about my sister," Miss Bell said. "I miss her terribly, I enter her room and sit on her bed for hours, have you any idea as to her whereabouts yet?"

"We are investigating her disappearance Miss Bell," Chris spoke kindly. "It takes time, but as yet we do not have any idea where she might be?"

"Oh dear," Miss Bell muttered. "I pray every night that she is safe."

"That is our hope as well," Chris replied gently. "When you went to town, I mean both you and your sister, did you ever visit a local cafe?"

"Just the Eastgate Hotel," Miss Bell replied. "We would often stop and have a cup of tea there, it's only five minutes from where we live, we found it's a pleasant place, and friendly."

"Did you ever become friendly with anyone in there?" Chris asked hopping.

Miss Bell shook her head slowly. "As I said everyone seemed friendly, most people around our age, but come to think of it, Pamela was quite friendly with a woman who had the same Christian name."

"What about yourself, were you friendly with her?" Chris asked.

"I was of course polite," Miss Bell answered. "I could never be rude to anyone, but Pamela took to her, my sister Inspector was a kindly soul, she felt for people, I considered this other Pamela to be rather a strange woman perhaps because nature had not been kind to her, I mean in her looks, but then as we all get old, our looks fade and distorts our young looks."

"What age would you say she was?" George asked.

Miss Bell turned her head towards George. "I am not very good a judging ages Sergeant," she replied. "But my guess would have been that she was between forty five and fifty."

"You said your sister was a kindly soul Miss Bell," Chris remarked. "Was, means the past?"

"Please Inspector," Miss Bell replied, and Chris saw her eyes moisten. "It has been in my mind since my sister disappeared that she might be dead, I do pray that she is not, but my mind plays tricks on me, leaving me no peace, was, was said because of my mind."

"Don't upset yourself Miss Bell, we know that the mind can be your worse enemy at a time like this, in some cases if you allow it to, the mind can drive one to suicide," Chris replied as kindly as he was able. "I am sure we will find your sister."

"Thank you Inspector," Miss Bell replied with a sniff.

"Do the singing barrow boy come round your area?" George asked.

Miss bell looked at him for a while, then a smile appeared on her face. "You mean Jason, oh yes, he was around yesterday as a matter of fact, I bought some logs, three logs for a penny, he was very apologetic regarding Pamela being missing, I was feeling down, and lonely so I gave him a cup of tea, someone to talk to for a few moments, he in return gave me a extra log."

"Really," Chris replied.

"Jason is a good man, he told me of his own sister that went missing, it worried me when he told me she was never found," Miss Bell replied.

"Going missing do not mean that they are dead Miss Bell," Chris replied. "People go missing for many reasons, some people want to get away and just make up their mind and go, some are missing because they have loss of memory, others are persuaded to leave by a boyfriend, there are many reasons."

"Some end up dead," Miss Bell added.

"In those cases Miss Bell we usually find a body, we have only found one body during the last fortnight, we know who it belongs to, certainly not your sister."

"I know Jason told me about her, lived next door to him," Miss Bell said.

"Apart from her looks, this Pamela you met at the cafe, was she fat, thin, did she tell you where she lived?" George asked.

Miss Ursala Bell looked at George. "I would say she was neither, more like matronly type, just slightly plump, as for where she lived, I have no idea, I know she often sat in the Abbey Grounds however."

"Did your sister receive a letter before she went missing?" Chris asked.

Miss Bell shook her head. "We only get bills Inspector, we are quite alone regarding relatives, no one writes to us, however had my sister received one she would have told me, we have no secrets from each other."

"Miss Bell, I know it's been a week now since your sister disappeared, but everyone at this station is working on it, I'm sure it won't be much longer before we have news of her."

"You are very reassuring Inspector," Miss Bell replied standing ready to leave.

Chris offered his hand which she took. "Please feel free to call at any time."

"Thank you Inspector," she replied, and with a smile at George, she left.

"I'm glad she came," Chris said to George after Miss Bell had left.

"You gave some rest to her mind," George remarked.

"What else could I do George, she is frightened almost out of her mind that her sister is dead, at least we have a name of a cafe," Chris replied.

"Strange her sister's Christian name being the same as the name we have on the letters," George commented. "Coincidence?"

"Don't really believe in them George," Chris remarked. "Not in our game."

"Apart from the name, her description puts Mrs Quinn in mind," George remarked.

"Yes it do," Chris admitted. "However we only have Mrs Quinn's description second hand, I have never met her."

"There is that," George agreed. "Miss Bell said Jason had been round, still asking questions."

"Yes that man seems to get everywhere," Chris replied.

"I bet if we could track Jason's movements for the last ten years he would be somewhere around when all these people went missing," George added.

Chris looked at George. "I remember when we first met him George, you were not to happy about him, your mind still not changed."

"As you always say a person is a suspect until proved otherwise. As far as I can see he is the prime suspect, he has his own home, on the end of a row, very private you could say, he has a wood shack just across from where he lives, very handy I would say, he is always chopping up wood, people expect him to have a bonfire, burning all the saw dust, which could be getting rid of bones. You yourself have seen a chart he is keeping, that is strange anyway. He is known always to be wheeling a barrow, which is large enough to hide a body in, I could go on."

"But he has an alibi for the Friday night George," Chris replied. "He was around the pubs."

"They shut at ten thirty, he could have got home early, don't forget it was gone eleven when someone was pushing a barrow coming away from the Moors, it could have been him?"

Chris thought on what George was saying. "Don't let yourself be held back George, if you come up with a line we can investigate, we will certainly do it."

George shook his head. "I haven't the faintest idea Chris," George smiled. "It's just a possibility rather than a feeling."

Chapter Fifteen

*I*t was nearly midday when Cam returned to the office, much sooner than expected. His face showed that he had at least got some information.

"The council keeps a ledger on all business owners in Winchester," Cam remarked as he sat behind his desk. "We had to look through years of ledgers, the chap that ran the department was very helpful, we went through them together, or I would have been still there."

"So you got a result?" Chris asked.

"It was the logo that helped," Cam replied. "This chap was almost sure that he had seen the logo before, he had the impression that it was a florist, so we checked all the florist, fortunately there was only four, three of them closed, only one left in Winchester."

"I know the one that is left, in Parchment Street," Chris stated.

"That's right," Cam replied. "However the one we wanted is the Rose Florist at high street Winchester, just below the Westgate, closed in 1901."

Chris looked at Cam. "So we have the florist that went out of business fifteen years ago, but someone is still using their stationery."

"It seems that way Chris," Cam replied. "According to the ledger, the business closed because the owner died, the shop was rented from the council," Cam added.

"So the council cleared the shop out, which means if there were business note papers around, anyone could have taken them," Chris remarked.

"What about employees?" George asked.

"If there was any, they would be getting on now should they still be alive," Chris replied. "But we must check," Chris looked at Cam his eyes smiling.

"It's OK, I quite like the work," Cam smiled back.

Cam stood up to leave. "I think I will have a bite to eat then later I will call at the tax department, hoping that they keep their records for fifteen years back."

"That's a wise move Cam, you're a good man," Chris praised.

"Can we do anything to help?" George asked.

"You heard Cam, he is quite happy," Chris replied. "We can however knock a few doors around Colebrook Street this afternoon, just to see what this Mrs Quinn looks like."

"She works during the mornings," George remarked.

"I know, it gives us time to have lunch first," Chris smiled.

"Sandwiches with the compliments of Elizabeth?" George asked.

"Exactly," Chris replied standing up and moving to the hat stand.

Chris and George entered the Mildmay Arms, there was just two men in the bar.

"Gentlemen smiled the landlord, you are becoming my regulars."

"Anymore trouble?" Chris asked his eyes smiling.

"No, no more, it was just a one off, what can I get you?" the landlord asked.

"Two pints of your best bitter landlord," George replied.

"That will be fourpence please," the landlord said as he started to fill up the glasses.

"Have one for your self," George offered.

"Thank you Sir," the landlord replied. "I'll have a half of the same."

George put the fivepence on the counter. "Not many in here?" he remarked.

"Dinner times," the landlord said. "Hardly worth the paraffin that I burn, still I have nothing else to do, tonight will be different however, we don't do a bad trade."

"Glad to hear it," Chris remarked. "I see you have no food on sale, any objections if we eat our sandwiches?"

"No, not at all, we sale grub on Saturday dinner times, this weekend we will have venison sandwiches on sale," the landlord continued.

"Really," Chris replied. "I had no idea that people sell venison, I have never tasted it."

"Nor me," George remarked.

"It's a treat, my customers soon polish them off, we only get them now and again, it seems that Mrs Quinn my house-keeper buys it from one of the mobile butchers."

"Your housekeeper lives in Colebrook Street I believe landlord?" Chris asked.

"Yes, I forgot the number at the moment," replied the landlord.

"It makes no difference, we will be knocking every door this afternoon," Chris replied.

"Serious," replied the landlord.

"Most people believe that a Detective work is thrilling, but I can assure you half the time it's just boring, knocking doors can be very boring, but it has to be done."

"Can I ask why?" the landlord asked.

"A few days ago a elderly lady left home, and have not returned," Chris replied. "We have trace her movements to the top of the weirs, she might have gone into Colebrook Street?"

"She might also have gone up town, or turned the other way towards Cheese Hill Street?" the landlord said with a smile.

"She could have, but we are talking about late at night, after all the shops even the Abbey Grounds were closed," Chris replied. "In any case we will be knocking all doors in the vicinity."

"I take it you are talking about a Miss Bell from Wharf Hill?" asked the landlord.

"You know about her being missing?" George asked.

The landlord smiled. "When you run a pub, sooner or later you hear of all that goes on in town, as a matter of fact it was Jason the wood man who brought it to my notice, also it was in the local paper this weekend."

"Yes it was," George replied. "Just a small paragraph."

"Well let's find a table George," Chris said picking up his pint.

They sat at the small table. "That Jason certainly keeps abreast of things, specially missing people," George remarked.

"Help yourself to a sandwich," Chris offered. "I only hope that Jason do not get himself in trouble," he added.

"How do you mean?" George asked taking a half sandwich.

"Well all these questions he asks, everywhere he goes," Chris took a bit of his sandwich.

George did not comment, he was sure that Jason was involved in someway.

"These are nice," George remarked holding up a part of his almost eaten sandwich. "Thank Elizabeth for me," he smiled.

"Elizabeth is like a mother hen," Chris replied his face happy.

"You got a good one there," George replied.

"How are you really getting on with Rosemary Morris?" Chris asked after taking a drink.

"I'm happy," George replied. "She is a good cook, although she is little, she is as strong as an ox, I would love to marry her, but I have no way of telling how she feels."

"She is strong, being brought up on a farm," Chris replied, and for the next half hour the talk was about Rosemary, before Chris stood up to get another pint each.

"Got time for one more landlord," Chris said putting the two empty glasses on the counter.

The landlord smiled as he took the glasses to fill. "Enjoyed your sandwiches?" he asked.

"Very much," Chris replied. "Sometimes we go all day without time to eat."

It was half past one when Chris and George left the Mildmay Arms.

"We'll enter this end," Chris said as they stood outside the Great Western Hotel situated at the Bridge Street junction with Colebrook Street. "I have a feeling it's going to be a drag."

By the time Chris knocked on number 28, Colebrook Street, Mrs Quinn's home, both Chris and George was beginning to think their afternoon was wasted, no one so far had any idea, had seen nothing, had heard nothing regarding the missing Miss Bell, although several had said they had read about her being missing from local newspaper.

"Well at least we will see what Mrs Quinn looks like," George murmured as Chris knocked the door.

Chris had no time to answer as the door opened, a woman stood before them, and Chris thought she looked like a hospital matron, serious face which looked stern all the time.

"Can I help you?" she asked. "I am just making my dinner."

Chris introduced himself and George. "We are making enquiries regarding a Miss Bell that went missing in this area some time last week, we wondered if you heard or saw anything out of the ordinary during that time?"

"Since when have they been sending Inspectors enquiring over missing people?" she asked sternly. "It's usually Sergeants in uniform."

"You are humm..?" George asked.

"I am Mrs Dorothy Quinn," the woman replied.

"How would you know who deals with missing people, have you been involved before?" George asked.

"I work at the Mildmay Arms in Eastgate Street, in the past the police have enquired in the pub about missing girls," Mrs Quinn replied, with her face still serious.

"Why would they make enquiries in a pub?" George asked. "Are young girls allowed in the Mildmay Arms?"

"Not to drink, but for work in the house, yes they are allowed," she answered sternly. "I am afraid I am unable to help you with this latest missing person, this is a quiet street, very little happens around here, why do you assume she went missing in this street?"

"We don't Mrs Quinn," Chris answered politely. "We are knocking every door in every street in this area, we know she was in this area when she disappeared."

"Well she must be important to have an Inspector on her case, but I am sorry, I cannot help you," Mrs Quinn answered.

"You have a nice view of the Abbey Grounds here," Chris remarked.

"It's a view, you begin not to notice after a time," Mrs Quinn replied.

"You have been here some time?" George asked.

"What is that to do with a missing person?" Mrs Quinn asked.

"Just polite conversation," George replied.

"Well I do not have time for polite conversation with you or anyone else, but to satisfy your curiosity I have been living here for the last ten years," the woman replied with a angry look on her face.

"Why are you so aggressive Mrs Quinn?" Chris asked. "We are only making enquiries."

Mrs Quinn took a step back, and slammed the door in their face.

George looked at Chris. "I don't think she is going to invite us in?" he remarked a slight smile on his face.

"This has never happened to me before, it shows disrespect for the law, "Chris spoke a little angry.

"At least we have seen her," George remarked. "Her attitude matches her looks, it's a good job she don't serve at the Mildmay Arms, there would be a shortest of customers if she did."

Chris smiled as they started to walk making their way to police station. "I feel angry, yet I feel sorry for her, especially her being a woman, woman needs to look pretty, it's a big part of their life, what makes her attitude problem is because of her looks."

"Would you employ someone like that?" George asked.

"She could be good at her job, in fact I am sure she is, Mr Watts seems to trust her."

Chris replied as George suddenly cut him off.

"Listen," George said as they were about to enter the Passage.

"*I wheel a wheelbarrow, through streets broad and narrow, selling kindling and logs, at a penny for three.*"

"That's Jason," Chris remarked with a slight smile

Both detectives looked towards the top of Colebrook Street and saw Jason appear pushing his handcart.

"We will wait for him," Chris said. "He has a nice voice."

"Well, well Inspector," Jason smiled as he approached. "This is where you hide yourself, I never expected to find Winchester's Ace Detectives leaning against the wall of a girls school."

"Waiting for you," Chris replied.

"Heard you're singing," George remarked.

"How can I help you Inspector, do the police station need logs?" Jason asked.

"Nothing like that Mr Keen" Chris replied. "How often do you come along Colebrook Street?"

"At least once a week, I normally sell a barrow load along here, you have been to Mrs Quinn's house," Jason added

"Been to them all," Chris replied. "Do Mrs Quinn buy logs from you?"

"At times," Jason replied. "Although it's summer and quite hot, people still need the fires."

"Do you ever go inside?" George asked.

Jason smiled. "Oh no, I have to put the logs on the door step, she takes them in, I know of no one who has been inside her house."

"Why would you say that?" George asked. "You only come around here once a week."

Jason gave a broad smile. "It's the truth, I don't know anyone who has been her house, no doubt she has visitors, but I don't know them, of course I might hear about them."

Chris lowered his head looking at his shoes, wondering what logic there was in what Jason was saying, or was he trying to tell them something.

"You are saying that you do not know who enters Mrs Quinn's house, but you may in time come to know them, that Mr Keen, is a strange answer?"

"Well it's true," Jason replied. "When my sister went missing many people who did not know my sister came to me and told me not to worry, she would turn up, they did not know my sister, but later heard of her."

"I believe you are trying to tell me something," Chris replied. "Are you holding anything back that could be useful to us?"

"Inspector," Jason replied. "What would I know, I'm just a barrow boy selling logs."

"You ask a lot of questions," George remarked.

"I'm the inquisitive type," Jason replied. "I like to know things and ask questions, in fact as detectives, how many cases would you solve without asking questions?"

Chris smiled at the answer. "Any case Mr Keen, be careful who you ask questions to," Chris advised him.

"I will," Jason smiled. "But I must get on."

"What did you mean when you asked Jason if he was trying to tell you something?" George asked.

Chris walked for a while in silence before answering. It's just a feeling I have, his remarks seem strange to me."

"It has been known that people who can't stop committing crimes do sometimes give the police clues, hoping to be caught," George remarked.

"Yes I have heard of such cases," Chris replied. "Jason I think has some idea as to who may be responsible, he has been searching since his sister disappeared, he must have learnt something with all the questions he has been asking."

"Or he could be doing it so that he would come to the attention of the police," George remarked as they entered the Police Station.

Sergeant Bloom looked up as the detectives entered and smiled.

"Constable Streeter is in," the sergeant informed.

"Thank you Sergeant," Chris replied as he followed George into the office.

Cam smiled as Chris and George entered, he watched as Chris disposed of his trilby, and watched as Chris and George seated themselves at their desk before speaking.

"I spent the whole morning at the tax office," Cam begun. "I might have something, it seems the owner of the Rose Florist died around the turn of the century, he did however have a business partner, a Mrs Rose Balding. Then I went to the council I wanted to see the street lists, I found only one Rose Balding, living in a bungalow at number 4, Stoney Lane."

"That's good work Cam," Chris replied.

"If it is the same Mrs Rose Balding that was the partner, then she would be over seventy according to the old income receipts," Cam continued.

Chapter Sixteen

aving left Cam in charge back at the office, Chris and George who had cycled to Stoney Lane, opened the wide iron gate that led to Number 4, took off their cycling clips and parked their bicycles inside the gate, before walking the twenty yard gravel path to the front door on which Chris knocked.

"Come in," said a voice. "The door is open."

Looking at George, Chris opened the door.

"First door on the left, I'm in here," came the voice.

Followed by George, Chris entered the room, and found a little old lady sitting in an armchair with a blanket over her legs.

"Sorry I can't get up, bad arthritis," she explained. "I saw you coming down the path."

"Are you Mrs Rose Balding who once kept the Rose Florist?" Chris asked gently.

"Yes, I am," Rose replied. "I don't know you, who are you?"

"I am Detective Inspector Hardie from Winchester CID, and my colleague Detective Sergeant House, we would like to ask you a few questions if you have no objections?"

Rose chuckled. "I don't mind, but no handcuffs, my arms are so thin they will slip off."

"Nothing like that Mrs Balding," Chris smiled.

"Call me Rose," she interrupted. "And sit down, it hurts my neck keep looking up at you both."

Both Chris and George found a chair and sat.

"You have bad arthritis?" George asked with concern on his face.

"Since I caught the disease," Rose replied.

"Really," Chris remarked. "What disease was that?"

Rose chuckled again. "You don't need to worry, it's not contagious, it's called old age."

"I see," Chris remarked smiling at her humour. "I understand Rose at one time you were part owner of the Rose Florist in the high street."

"That was a long time ago Inspector, some sixteen years ago, I did pay my income tax and rent and rates, I don't owe any do I?"

"No, everything is how it should be Rose," Chris said with a smile. "You retired after your partner died."

"I was getting on, I'm seventy-two you know," Rose remarked with a proud look on her face. "I have outlasted all my friends which is sad, I have no one to visit me now."

"You have done well Rose," Chris replied. "But you really should be careful about inviting strangers into your home."

"I have a woman who comes in several times during the day, no fix hours, she cleans a little each day, gets my food, and comes around six and gets me to bed, I lock the front door when I go to bed, but during the day it's left open, I can walk around, holding on to the furniture as I go, but it's getting up from this chair that's difficult and painful. I can't bend enough to sit so I need a high seat, I have cushions under me now."

"This bungalow is just right for you no stairs," George remarked.

"I am glad I sold my house in the town to come here, it's out of the way a bit, but then I don't go anywhere," Rose replied.

"You had your own letter heading at the shop, could this be a continuation page Rose?" Chris asked showing her the paper with a logo on it.

Rose put her glasses, she looked at the paper and smiled.

"Yes Inspector one of ours, I designed the logo."

"Is it possible some of your letterheads still be in use?" Chris asked.

"I don't see how Inspector, after sixteen years, I would have thought they were all used up or destroyed, but wait a moment," Rose said after an afterthought. "I remember I brought all the business note papers home with me, before the council took over, I could have left some at my old home."

"Where was that Rose?" Chris asked feeling excited.

"Number 28, Colebrook Street," Rose replied.

Chris looked at George, a smile was around his eyes. "Who did you sell the house to Rose?" Chris asked.

"A widow from outside Winchester, my memory is not what it used to be, I forgot her name."

Have you got your document of the house sale Rose?" George asked. "Her name and address should be on it."

"The left hand drawer of the sideboard," Rose said pointing at the sideboard with her bend fingers. "It will be in there, I don't throw anything away."

George stood and went to the sideboard, he pulled out the drawer, and eventually found the deeds. "This must be them," George said turning to Rose. "Do you mind me looking at them?"

"They are in your hand young man," Rose replied grinning. "I cannot stop you can I?"

Chris saw a smile come to George's face as he studied the deeds, then he handed them to Chris.

"It seems that a Mrs Dorothy Quinn bought the house from you Rose," Chris remarked.

"That's it, Mrs Dorothy Quinn bought the house," Rose replied.

"Lived at Seaview Street, Southsea," Chris added.

"Did she, I had completely forgotten, whatever you are investigating, am I involved?" Rose asked.

"No Rose, but you have supplied the information we needed to know, one more thing Rose, would you mind us borrowing these deeds just for a little while, we will sign for them," Chris asked.

"You have not shown me any identification yet," Rose replied.

"I'm sorry Rose, we should have shown you," Chris said taking his police card from his pocket, showing it to Rose, with George doing the same.

"Well," Rose remarked after seeing the cards. "If you can't trust a policeman, who can you trust?"

"In the winter, what do you burn to keep the house warm?" George asked.

"I never let my fire go out, in any season Sergeant," Rose replied. "I have coal and logs delivered, during the night, my woman damps the fire down, only needs a poke in the morning to bring the flame back into it."

"You get your logs delivered?" George asked.

"Yes a nice young man brings me a barrow full whenever I want them, he lives the other end of Winchester, so it's a long way to come, but I always order enough to make his journey worthwhile, he's a lovely young man, always have a cup of tea with me and a chat."

"Would his name be Jason?" George asked.

"So you know of him," Rose replied.

"I live near him," George replied with a grin. "We call him the singing barrow boy."

"Well he is hardly a boy," Rose replied. "But yes he sings sometimes when he comes up the path."

"Thank you very much Rose, I will personally see these deeds returned to you as soon as possible, now before we go, do you want anything, a cup of tea perhaps?" Chris asked.

"Thank you no, my woman will be here within the hour to get my tea," Rose replied. "You will have to see your own way out, arthritis you see," Rose grinned.

"By the way Rose, Jason the log man, how did you get in touch with him, I mean his area is the lower part of the town?" Chris asked as he was about to leave.

"He used to call on me at Colebrook Street, when he knew I was leaving, he offered to deliver to me, as long as it was worth it, so I buy a full barrow at a time."

Chris and George took their bicycles to the shed behind the police station before entering their office, where they found Cam engrossed in paper work.

"How did you get on?" Cam asked with a smile.

George related to Cam what had taken place at Stoney lane. Chris took the house deeds from his pocket and started to study them until George had finished.

"You did well Cam," Chris remarked looking up. "We may have an important opening here, at least I am hoping so."

"That Jason seems to be everywhere?" George remarked.

"Yes," Chris remarked. "I'm a bit curious, I mean Stoney Lane is not his area of work, still Rose did say he called on her at Colebrook Street."

344

"Do the deeds help us?" Cam asked.

Chris smiled. "A lot really, we have Mrs Quinn's signature, that we can match with the invitation letters sent to the missing women, and we have her address at Southsea, my problem is what we do next, go and see Mrs Quinn or first find out about her life in Southsea?"

"Go to Southsea, or phone them," George advised.

"I'm sure if I phone the Southsea Police, they will do their best, but sometimes there are questions you have to ask face to face, I think I will phone them and tell them I am sending someone just to check out the address, of course who ever goes would have no authority in Southsea," Chris remarked.

"Well I don't mind going," George replied. "It's about time I use my motorbike out, it will go rusty soon."

Chris looked at Cam who had a anxious look on his face. "I am sorry Cam, but this job needs someone at least with the rank of Sergeant."

"I understand," Cam replied a little down hearted.

"Still if it had not been for your good work Cam," Chris flattered. "We would not be where we are now, I believe we are getting closer, however you will be with me tomorrow, we will call on Mrs Quinn, should she prove difficult, we will have her here."

"How was the deeds signed?" Cam asked.

"Mrs Dorothy Quinn," Chris replied.

"The letters were signed by a Pam," Cam remarked.

"I know that's annoying," Chris turned to George. "Cam found out that there is no record of Mrs Quinn being married, you might find something out when you go to her old address in Southsea, there must be someone there that knew her, also find out if she has any relatives?"

"I'll do what I am able," George responded.

"I know you will George," Chris said standing up. "I'll go and see the Police Inspector now," Chris said, leaving the office.

"He seems happy George," Cam remarked.

"He is, you yourself done very well, are you a betting man by the way?" George asked.

"I bet on the Grand National or the Derby, that's all," Cam replied. "Why?"

"I'll bet you two shillings that by the end of this week, Chris will have the missing women case solved."

"Well, I'll take that bet, however what about the murder of Mrs Marston?" Cam asked.

"Chris thinks that her murder is somehow mixed up with the missing girls, honestly I don't know how, but I believe that Chris knows it, if he ever clears that mystery up, then I believe he will have Mrs Olive Marston's murderer," George replied.

"Will he clear it?" Cam asked.

"No idea," George replied with a grin. "But he's a canny chap, his record is a hundred percent, he don't want that ruined, by the way don't let on to Chris about our bet."

"It should be an exciting day tomorrow," Cam remarked. "Seeing Mrs Quinn."

"Perhaps," George replied. "But Mrs Quinn is not a pleasant woman."

It was six fifteen when Chris re-entered the office.

"Sorry to have kept you waiting," he apologised. "The Police Inspector knew the number of police station at Southsea, he spoke on the phone, you will be given a uniform to take you wherever you want to go, Sergeant Bloom is getting you the address of the station now."

"I leave first thing in the morning then," George remarked.

"Well now I am late, Elizabeth must've gone home, so, as I am in happy frame of mind, how about a pint at the Rising Sun?"

"Suits me," Cam replied with a smile.

George nodded his head grinning. "I will only have a couple, I shall be driving tomorrow."

"Good man," Chris replied getting his trilby.

"At the Sergeant's desk, Sergeant Bloom gave George the address of the Southsea Police Station. "Have a nice holiday," sergeant Bloom smiled.

"I wish," replied George with a grin.

"Any trouble tonight Sergeant," Chris said as they were about to leave, don't call George out, according to the seriousness call either Cam or myself.

"I'll leave a note Sir," sergeant Bloom replied respectfully.

At around six thirty pm the three Detectives entered the Rising Sun, it was empty, which was not unusual at that time, Alfie who was wiping glasses smiled.

"Chris, George," he welcomed. "And Cam, we are being honoured tonight."

Cam smiled. "Well as we are off duty, I suppose I can tell you that being a mere constable, one can't drink with the bosses?"

Alfie looked at Chris. "It seems that this sniper snapper, has no respect for RHIP."

Chris winked at George. "You are right Alfie, and anyway, this constable is not off duty, only George here is off duty."

"Disrespect to one's superior is a serious offence," George added keeping his face serious.

"It must be," Chris agreed.

"Just a moment," Cam said. "What do RHIP stand for anyway?"

"Rank Has Its Privileges," Alfie confirmed.

"That's true Alfie," Chris agreed.

"I suppose we could forgive him just this once," George remarked. "I'm sure he would appreciate it."

A smile came to Cam's face. "OK I get the first round, what are we having?"

"Mine is a pint of bitter," George said quickly.

"Mine is the same Alfie," Chris said.

"I suppose I better have the same," Cam remarked. "Though I usually drink only a wine," he smiled as he lied.

George looked at Chris and pulled a face. "He got his own back."

"Yes I heard," Chris agreed. "I can't see Cam drinking wine can you?"

George was shaking his head as Alfie asked for six pence. "You have one yourself Alfie," Cam offered.

"I'll have a bitter then," Alfie smiled taking the extra penny. "Well it's nice to see all three of you, working on Mrs Marston's murder are we?" Alfie asked.

"Did you know her Alfie?" Chris asked.

"She would pop in now and again, always with her husband, didn't really know them, but they seemed alright, she was quite attractive."

"Seen Jason lately?" George asked.

"Not for a couple days, he should be able to tell you more about them, when they are in here they always sat together."

"Really," Chris remarked. "I always thought Jason was a loner."

"Well he talks to most people, so he is not a recluse," Alfie replied.

"How is that lovely wife of yours?" Chris asked.

"So so," Alfie replied turning his hand over a couple of times. "Women are all the same, changes mood whenever they feel like it."

Chris smiled as he took his pint to carry over to his favourite seat. "You would miss her Alfie if she was not here."

Alfie smiled. "That's the trouble, I would."

All three detectives sat around the table, and took drinks of their pints. "Now forget about work," Chris said. "Relax your minds, now Cam, how are you getting along with Mrs Bumstead?"

Cam almost choked on his pint. "I have only met her once," he stuttered. "Anyway she has Mr Webster, why would she want me?"

"Come Cam, if you had a chance you would take it," George teased.

"Well I did take a fancy to her, I don't get on well with women, I seem to be a bit shy," Cam replied. "But yes if I had a chance, I would hope to take it."

"You suffer with a lack of confidence Cam," Chris replied after taking a drink. "Being a detective constable gives you a certain amount of authority."

"It's different when it comes to women," Cam replied.

Chris felt on top of the world for some reason, he knew in his mind that he was on the right track in solving the mysteries that he was investigating, and knew also that it was team work, Chris was usually a serious type of man, not given to teasing like he had just now with Cam, it was out of his character, but he felt light hearted and happy.

"I can relate to you Cam," Chris remarked. "George here is different, all the girls go for him."

"That would be a wish rather than reality," George replied with a smile.

"Come off it George," Chris teased with a smile. "You have one of the loveliest girls in Winchester attracted to you."

"Rosemary is as you say a lovely girl, I'm not yet sure where I stand with her," George answered his thought imagining her. "Anyway Chris you have Elizabeth."

"Elizabeth is certainly beautiful, but beauty alone is no good, beauty will not stand the length of time if you do not love her," Chris paused to take a drink. "I know beauty can at first attract you to a woman, but it's her personality, plus many other things, that one falls in love with, such as her being a caring type of person, her honesty, her trustworthiness, and oh so many things that makes you love her, woman on the other hand might love you for the same reasons, but not always, some woman falls for the tall handsome dark hair type of man, these women are ruled by their hearts, which are often broken, because tall dark handsome men are usually womanisers, they know that women are attracted to them."

"That makes me out then," Cam remarked.

"I think you would make a good husband Cam," Chris replied. "Just have a little confidence in yourself."

"When did you fall in love with Elizabeth?" Cam asked.

Chris looked at Cam, and then at George, then a grin appeared all over his face.

"I fell for Elizabeth the first time I set eyes on her, she was in hospital, she looked ill, not at all very attractive, she did not look her best but the moment I saw her I loved her, and wanted to spend my life with her."

"You are a very lucky man Chris," George stood up. "Now it's my turn, the same again, then I must get going, I have a busy day tomorrow," he grinned.

Chris felt a little light headed as he walked home, after wishing George good luck on his trip to Southsea in the morning.

Chris climbed the path towards the front door, which opened to a smiling Elizabeth. "You look happy darling," she said as she kissed his cheek, had a pint?"

"Yes," Chris replied. "Saw George off, he is off to Southsea tomorrow to do some researching."

"Well, your dinner is ready," Elizabeth replied as she watched Chris hang his trilby on the wall peg. "It's your favourite Cottage Pie."

Chris holding Elizabeth around the waist entered the dining room where Ron was reading the paper sitting in his favourite armchair, and Olive was putting a dinner on the table where Chris usually sat.

"It's had to be warmed up a bit Chris," Olive said with a smile on her face. "But not enough to spoil it."

"Thank you Olive," Chris replied, letting go of Elizabeth's waist and sitting at the table.

"I am sorry I'm late again, but when I am on a case, I am on duty twenty four hours, not knowing where I shall be?"

"Don't apologise Chris," Olive replied. "We understand."

Chris started to eat, he felt a little hungry, he always did enjoy his food after a pint.

"How's the case going Chris?" Ron asked looking over the top of his glasses.

"I'm getting there," Chris replied as he chewed. "I hope to have it solved very soon now."

"I'm sure you will darling," Elizabeth remarked. She was proud of her husband, and it showed in her eyes.

"Don't bother Chris while he is eating," Olive rebuked Ron.

"I only asked," Ron replied winking at Chris.

"It's alright Olive," Chris replied.

"Well you should be able to eat your dinner before you begin interrogating," Olive remarked smiling at Elizabeth.

"I was doing no such thing Chris, I was just asking a question," Ron replied as he looked at his paper and muttered.

"What did you say?" Olive asked.

"Nothing my sweet, just doing what you ordered, keeping quiet," Ron replied with a grin on his face that Olive could not see.

An hour later after saying Olive and Ron goodnight, Chris and Elizabeth entered their own house.

"How good are you at judging handwriting, I mean at times you have to judge signatures on cheques don't you?" Chris asked moving to the dining table where he sat.

"Often, we have to be sure that each signature on each cheque is genuine," Elizabeth replied sitting at the table with Chris. "Why darling?" she asked.

Chris took out the invitation letter written to Mrs Violet West and the deeds to the house sold by Mrs Rose Balding from his inside pocket and placed the them on the table. "Tell me what you think about these, could the invitation letter be written by the same person who signed the house deeds?"

"It will take me time," Elizabeth replied. "I only check signatures, but I'll have a go," she offered first reading the deeds. "Is this woman a suspect?" Elizabeth asked.

"The signature on the invitation letter is Pam," Elizabeth remarked.

"I know," replied Chris. "Anyway, do your best, I'll make us a nice cup of tea while you are doing it," Chris smiled getting up and going into the kitchen.

In order not to distract Elizabeth, Chris had a pipe while in the kitchen, then made the tea, it was some time later when he returned to the dining room.

"I am no expert," Elizabeth said looking up, as Chris looked over her shoulder.

"But I would say both were written by the same person, you see on both documents space between certain words is larger than between other words," Elizabeth continued.

"I see," Chris replied. "So you think both these documents could have been written by the same person?"

"What makes me more certain," Elizabeth added. "Is the writing, you look at the letter, the joining of each letter is widely spaced," Elizabeth added. "If we look at the deeds, we find the same widely space writing."

Chris picked up the letters, studied them for a while, then agreeing in his mind with Elizabeth placed them safely in his jacket pocket. "You are a gem darling," Chris remarked as he kissed her neck.

"I know, but have I helped you?" Elizabeth asked smiling.

"I think you have," Chris replied.

"A positive help?" Elizabeth asked.

"If you are right darling," Chris replied looking at Elizabeth seriously. "It will help in solving this case of mine."

"I'm glad darling," Elizabeth replied.

Chapter Eighteen

With George away, Chris explained to Cam what Elizabeth had said about the writing.

"Elizabeth feels that both documents were written by the same person, she may not be an expert, but she has a certain knowledge working on signatures of cheques, I myself agree with her after pointing out certain points in the handwriting," Chris remarked.

"Well I'm no expert, never studied writing before, but I tend to agree," Cam remarked.

"We will see Mrs Quinn this afternoon, she will be at work during the morning Cam," Chris remarked. "I want you to go from the bottom of the town to the top, call in every shop that might sell ladies hair combs, find out how many is sold in a packet?"

"I can do that," Cam replied. "Any particular reason?"

Chris smiled. "Just a piece of the jig saw that might fit in later on."

Chris and Cam, stood outside number 28, Colebrook Street at two in the afternoon. Chris knocked the door, and Mrs Quinn answered.

"Oh," she said. "What do you want?"

"I need to speak to you Mrs Quinn regarding our ongoing investigation," Chris replied.

"Well I have nothing to say to you," Mrs Quinn replied about to shut the door.

Chris put his hand on the door to stop it closing. "Mrs Quinn, if you close this door on us, I will have you arrested interfering in the coarse of police work," Chris said commandingly.

"I will respond about harassment and police brutality," Mrs Quinn replied without slamming the door.

"Nevertheless Mrs Quinn, either you ask us in to speak to you, or you will come to the station, it is up to you," Chris replied.

"What can a poor defenceless woman do against threats," Mrs Quinn replied as she opened the door wider to let them in and led them along to passage to the back kitchen. "You had better seat yourselves," she said as she sat herself at the kitchen table. "I would not want to regarded as a bad host."

"Why are you so aggressive Mrs Quinn?" Chris asked as Cam and himself took a seat. "We are only here believing that you may be able to help us in our investigation."

"Perhaps you better enlighten me just who you are, I know you called yesterday, but I have forgotten your names, they were not important enough for me to remember," Mrs Quinn replied ignoring the question asked by Chris.

"I am Detective Inspector Hardie, and my colleague Detective Constable Streeter of Winchester CID." Chris looked at Cam shaking his head. "You are I believe Mrs Dorothy Quinn?"

"You are right," replied Mrs Quinn.

"You are a widow?" Chris asked.

Mrs Quinn smiled. "I have never been married Inspector," she answered.

"But you have just admitted that you were Mrs Dorothy Quinn," Chris replied a little unsure of himself.

"That is my name Inspector, I can assure you I have never been married, and to the best of my knowledge I have never told anyone that I had been," Mrs Quinn replied a slight smile on her face.

"But Mrs imply that you are a married woman?" Cam interrupted.

Mrs Quinn shrugged her shoulders. "I cannot be held responsible to how people think, my name is Mrs Dorothy Quinn, I do not break the law using this name," she responded angrily. "I really cannot see why my name is so important to your investigation."

"Mrs Quinn," Chris remarked agreeing with her for the moment. "We have spoken to the past owner of this house, a Mrs Rose Balding, she was part owner before she retired of a florist called the Rose Florist. Apart from the business note papers of the florist their additional pages also carried a logo of a rose on it, I was wondering did she leave any such writing material here when she left?"

"Inspector, that was eight years ago, did she say she did?" Mrs Quinn asked.

"She said she might have done," Chris replied honestly.

Mrs Quinn smiled. "Eight years is a long time, to be honest there was a bit of rubbish here when I bought the house, but I got the wood man to clear it for me, perhaps he would be the better one to ask, his name is Jason I believe, I buy logs from him."

"So Jason cleared the rubbish out?" Chris remarked.

"That is what I said Inspector," Mrs Quinn replied.

Chris looked at Cam his mind turning over, wondering. "Do you ever go to the Eastgate Cafe Mrs Quinn?" he asked.

"It's next to where I work, I have been in there," Mrs Quinn answered.

"Would you have met a Miss Pamela Bell while you were there?" Chris asked.

Mrs Quinn shook her head. "I have very little to do with anyone, I do not make friends easy, so I ignore everyone."

"Then you would not know a Mrs Olive Marston that lived at Chester Road?" Cam asked.

"Young man," Mrs Quinn again turned upon him. "You do not listen do you, I have just told you that I ignore people, and besides I do not know Chester Road."

"Thank you Mrs Quinn for your cooperation," Chris said standing. "We will leave you in peace now."

"You will not be calling again tomorrow then," Mrs Quinn replied.

Chris gave a weak smile. "No Mrs Quinn I shall not be calling again, but I would like you to call at the police station tomorrow morning around eleven, just to sign a statement about the writing material."

"Is it so important?" Mrs Quinn asked.

"To our investigation very," Chris replied. "We will see ourselves out, good afternoon Mrs Quinn."

"Do you really want her for a statement about the writing material?" Cam asked as they walked Abbey Passage towards the Police Station.

Chris smiled. "No not really, I believe that Mrs Quinn is a very clever woman, I believe also that she altered her name to Mrs, so that people would think she was a widow, perhaps she had a reason for it, I don't know, another thing she involved Jason, he seems to be a very big part of our investigation, his name always popping up, anyway, I need her at the station tomorrow, I am hoping that George will contact me before then."

Sergeant Bloom looked up as Chris and Cam entered the station. "Inspector," he said looking at the clock. "I have had a call from Sergeant House, I told him you were out, he will be phoning you around four, he said it was important."

"Thank you Sergeant," Chris replied with a smile. "I'll wait for the call."

"Did we learn anything today?" Cam asked Chris once they had both seated themselves behind their desk.

"We learnt she is not married, we learnt that she has been in the Eastgate Cafe where Miss Bell often went," Chris replied. "Most of all we are dealing with a very clever person."

"That don't make her a suspect do it?" Cam asked.

"No," Chris replied slowly. "It just makes one suspicious, there is nothing to connect her to our case really, no hard facts," Chris replied. "George may have some answers to my suspicions," he added.

It was quarter past four when George phoned, anxiously Chris picked up the receiver. "Hello George," Chris spoke. "Hope you have good news for me?"

"Hello Chris," George replied. "I have been treated very well, I have a uniform sergeant with me taking me where I want to go, anyway Chris I went to the address on the deeds, no one around knew of a Mrs Quinn, the name of the family living at the address was Watts."

"That makes it interesting," Chris replied.

"It seems the family lived here for many years, after the parents died, around 1870, a son and two daughters were left, the son the youngest have joined the army, the eldest daughter Grace married and moved away, she had no children, the other daughter Pamela moved away some eight or nine years ago, no one knows where?"

"Was she married?" Chris asked.

"Not married, when she moved," George replied.

"You have done good work George, in my mind things are starting to come together, what about the daughter Grace, anything else on her?" Chris asked.

"Not a thing Chris, trouble is, many of the people who were here thirty years ago, have either died or have just moved away, one thing I did learn that Pamela had some sort of accident before she moved, I shall try to find out more before I return."

"That's certainly good work George, anything else?"

"I checked missing people, there were several people missing, mainly women, but a man called Mr Anthony Quinn went missing around nine years ago, I thought that might interest you?"

"It certainly do George, it certainly do," Chris repeated himself. "Find out if he had a sister by the name of Dorothy, and where she is now if he had one?" he asked. "This Mr Quinn was he ever found?" Chris added.

"Not according to the police records," George replied.

"Where are you stopping tonight George?" Chris asked. "I take it you are not ready yet to return?"

"I have a bit more checking to do, I don't want this to be a wasted journey, I'm going to stop at a pub, I'll be back sometime Saturday."

"Thank you George, you have given me a lot to think about, see you when I see you."

Chris replaced the receiver, looked over at Cam with a smile, and told him what George had found out.

"Watts is the name of the landlord of the Mildmay Arms," Cam remarked.

"Yes it is, what is more, he is an ex army man, I don't believe in coincidence, I wonder who this other sister Grace could be or where she is?" Chris muttered.

"If she was married as George said, her maiden name would have change," Cam remarked.

"That's the difficulty Cam," Chris replied. "My thoughts have gone to Mr Charlie Webster's mother who has past away, just an off chance, I mean could the whole family have moved to Winchester?"

"George told you that the married daughter did not have any children when she moved," Cam replied.

"Yes I know, but Cam we also know that Charlie Webster was born in Winchester about thirty odd years ago, the timing might match," Chris remarked.

"I have time I could pop up the death birth and marriages department and find out," Cam offered.

"It won't help Cam, Charlie's birth certificate will not have the mother's maiden name on it, just her married name," Chris replied. "Let's hope George find out more about her while he is there."

"So what are we going to do now?" Cam asked.

"Tomorrow, you and I will see Mr Watts at the Mildmay Arms, then after we will question Mrs Quinn again," Chris replied. "The rest I will leave until George gets back, you see none of what we have don't seem to have anything to do with Mrs Marston's murder, I wonder why would a whole family uproot and move to Winchester, and why would Pamela change her name if she did, why she start calling herself Dorothy."

"Mrs Quinn might be the sister of the missing Mr Quinn?" Cam remarked.

"Whoever Mrs Quinn might be Cam," Chris replied. "I am sure that she wrote those letters, anyway, I am sure that Mr Watts at the pub will tell us tomorrow whether or not Mrs Quinn is his sister?"

"That's strange as well," Cam remarked. "Mr Watts told us he employed Mrs Quinn as his housekeeper, why didn't he just say he employed his sister."

"That's been worrying me as well," Chris admitted. "Anyway Cam it's almost six, if you get off now, would you go to Wharf Hill and see Miss Ursala Bell, I would like her here tomorrow morning about ten thirty."

"I can do that," Cam replied as he stood ready to leave.

"Explain to her that I want to know if she recognise Mrs Quinn when she arrives, I'll let Sergeant Bloom know what I want," Chris added.

Chris was waiting as Elizabeth appeared. "You look as though you lost a penny and found sixpence," Elizabeth said as she kissed Chris on the cheek before clinging to his arm. "You are happy?" she asked.

"Pleased, if that can be called happy," Chris replied as they started walking. "I am getting nearer to finding a solution to the case I am investigating."

"I knew you would darling," Elizabeth replied. "I have every faith in you."

"What would you say if I asked you to pop in the Rising Sun for a drink on our way home, I want to ask Alfie something," Chris asked.

Elizabeth giggled. "Try to get me drunk and have your wicked way with me," she teased.

"I did not know I had to get you drunk," Chris smiled as they approached the Rising Sun.

"I should phone mother if we will be an hour late," Elizabeth remarked.

"Alfie has a phone, he won't mind you using it," Chris replied as he opened the pub door allowing Elizabeth to proceed him.

It was five minutes past opening time, Alfie was behind the bar looked up as they entered.

"Mr and Mrs Hardie, it's very nice to see you both," he smiled.

"How are you Alfie?" Elizabeth asked as she reached the counter. "You look very well yourself."

"Thank you for those kind words Mrs Hardie, I do feel well, I have no complaints."

"Please call me Elizabeth, do you think I could use your phone, I need to let mother know that we will be a little late getting home."

"Be my guest," Alfie replied. "Go through that door," Alfie pointed to the private door at the end of the counter. "You will see the phone in the passage."

"Thank you Alfie," Elizabeth replied as she moved towards the door.

"What will you have?" Chris asked her.

"I think a small sherry would be nice," Elizabeth replied as she went through the door.

"That will be a bitter and a small sherry then," Chris remarked with a smile.

"Coming up," Alfie remarked as he started to fill the bitter glass.

"Tell me Alfie," Chris asked as he watched the bitter glass being filled. "I know Mr Watts at the Mildmay Arms is a friend of yours, do you know any of his history?"

Alfie placed the pint of bitter before Chris, then turned to the small counter behind him where he fill a small glass with sherry.

"I know he was in the army," Alfie remarked as he placed the sherry before Chris on the counter. "I never knew him at the time, but he was in the Boer war the same time as me. I know he left home at a early age joining the army, and saw action in several places, he did tell me he had two sisters, one he has lost contact with, the other one was married, that's about all I know."

"Have one yourself Alfie," Chris offered.

"Thank you Chris," Alfie replied.

"What's your general opinion of him?" Chris asked taking up his pint and taking a sip.

"He seems a nice enough bloke," Alfie replied leaning on the counter. "Has a good trade I believe, being a single man, he has a couple of young women working for him, but he do get a army pension, perhaps around ten shillings a week, that would help him with his staff."

"That's apart from his housekeeper Mrs Quinn," Chris remarked.

Alfie smiled. "I don't really know her, I believe she has been in here once, but as I said, I don't know her, but heard a lot about her not being very attractive."

"Yes I have heard that," Chris replied as Elizabeth made her appearance.

"Did you get through to your mother alright?" Alfie asked to Elizabeth.

"I did, thank you for letting me use the phone, how much do I owe you?" Elizabeth asked.

"Please," Alfie replied with a smile.

"Well thank you again Alfie," Elizabeth said with a smile.

"This is nice," Elizabeth remarked as they sat facing each other at the small table. "I like having a drink with my husband."

"We must do it again," Chris replied. "Was your mother OK with us being late?"

"You know mother," Elizabeth replied. "She is always happy for us whatever we do, dad of course was a bit jealous."

Chris smiled and took a drink of his pint. "Mother-in-laws are the butt of many a joke," he said as he placed his glass on the table. "I however have good in-laws and would not want to change them."

"You are sweet darling," Elizabeth replied. "Did you ask Alfie what you wanted?"

"I did, but he knows no more than I do," Chris replied.

"Can I help you when we are at home?" Elizabeth asked looking at Chris her eyes sparkling.

Chris looked at Elizabeth shaking his head. "You my darling wife are a brazen hussy, but I love you, in fact I love all I have, my in-laws, my job, most of all my lovely wife, we are not rich, nor are we penniless, we are able to live comfortable, thanks to my in-laws giving us a house, what else would a man want?"

"Oh darling," Elizabeth murmured, her eyes still sparkling.

"I do love you, so do mother and dad. If I am brazen I am allowed to be with my husband, perhaps I might be when we get home."

"Then let's drink up and get home," Chris replied with a smile.

Chapter Nineteen

*I*t was a little past nine when Chris and Cam went to the rear of the Mildmay Arms and knocked on the back door.

"Inspector Hardie," Albert Watts said with a surprise look upon his face. "This is a surprise, please come in," he said standing back to allow Chris and Cam to enter. "I have just made myself some tea, would you join me?"

"That would be very nice Mr Watts," Chris replied. "I apologise for calling so early, but later I have other appointments."

"Think nothing of it," Albert replied offering them a chair each at the table and pouring them both a cup of tea. "But how can I help you?"

"Mr Watts," Chris replied helping himself to two spoonfuls of sugar and stirring his tea. "As you know we are investigating the murder of Mrs Olive Marston who lived at Chester Road, unfortunately our investigations are being hampered with other missing people."

"I am not quite with you," Albert remarked.

"I realise it might be difficult for you to understand, and to keep it short, we have found a small link between a couple of the missing women, that link being a letter sent to them inviting out, by a woman who calls herself Pamela."

"I see," replied Albert making no other comment.

"Both these letters were written on pages that had a Rose Logo printed on them, the logo turned out to be that of a florist that's ceased business at the turn of the century."

Chris took a drink of his tea before continuing. "Fortunately a partner in the florist business still survives and we were able to talk to her. She told us that she might have left a box of work papers at her old address which she sold to a Mrs Dorothy Quinn some six or seven years ago."

"Mrs Quinn that is my housekeeper," Albert said.

"It has to be Mr Watts," Chris answered. "You see we saw the deeds of the sale of the house 28, Colebrook Street, that is where Mrs Quinn now lives."

"I'm not sure of the number, but yes she lives in Colebrook Street," Albert answered.

"Apart from that on the deeds Mrs Quinn's past address was Seaview Lane in Southsea."

"That's impossible," Albert blurted out. "That was my home address I was born and brought up there."

"We know that the Watts family lived there until Mrs Quinn moved to Winchester," Chris added.

"I don't get it, of course I have not been there since 1897, when I was on leave," Albert said with a worried look on his face.

"Perhaps you can run us through the details of your leaving?" Chris asked.

"Well, I was born there in 1871, but my parents died when I was about five, Pamela my sister a couple years older than me and myself were brought up by my eldest sister Grace, when I was about fifteen Grace married, and moved away, I never could get on with my sister Pamela, so at fifteen in 1886 I enlisted in the army. I never knew where Grace went to, but I did learn that she and her husband had died when I went back there in 1897 at that time Pamela was working in a textile shop in Portsmouth."

"So you have only been home once, some eighteen years ago since you joined the army?" Chris asked.

"That's right, after the Boer War, I had done sixteen years, I had a little money saved, I never married, then I came in here as a tenant," Albert replied. "However how Mrs Quinn's name came to sale my birth home is a mystery to me, that needs sorting out, as far as I'm aware, my sister Pamela still lives there."

"I shall have the answer to that later today Mr Watts, I am seeing Mrs Quinn at eleven," Chris replied

Cam who sat quietly butted in with a question that Chris was about to ask. "So Mrs Quinn is not your sister Pamela?" he asked.

A smile came to Albert's face. "Good God, is that what you are thinking, then you are way off the mark, I never got on with Pamela, but she was a very pretty girl, I am afraid Mrs Quinn do not look a bit like Pamela."

"Did you know of any families with that name?" Chris asked.

"As I said, I left Southsea when I was fifteen, only been back once, sorry, I know of no one by that name in fact," replied Albert shrugging his shoulders.

Chris finished his tea, the interview had not gone the way he expected. "Mrs Quinn has nothing in ways or her actions that could remind you of your sister Pamela?" Chris asked.

Albert shook his head. "As I said she was a very pretty girl, what she is like now I have no idea, getting on for twenty years since I saw her last, I would probably walk by her on the street without knowing her."

"Your sister Grace, you say you did not know where she lived, by chance do you know what was her married name?" Chris asked.

"There again you have me," Albert replied. "I was told by Pamela the last time I visited Southsea that Grace and her husband had died, so if you find Pamela she would know," Albert replied.

Chris looked at Cam, who seem to want to ask a question.

"Mr Charlie Webster, who caused you some trouble in the week, how well do you know him?" Cam asked.

"Just as a customer," Albert shrugged. "He did tell me once that his mother's name was Grace, I remember that because of my sister Grace."

"What time do you expect Mrs Quinn this morning?" Chris asked.

"I don't," Albert replied. "She did tell me she had an appointment."

Chris stood up. "Thank you for the tea Mr Watts, and I am sorry to bother you, but perhaps you can realise why we had to."

"Think nothing of it Inspector," Albert replied. "I would however like to know more, should you find anything out?"

"I can promise you that Mr Watts," Chris replied.

"Do you think Mr Watts was telling the truth Cam?" Chris asked as they left the pub.

"I am sure he was lying," Cam replied. "I mean even if you had not seen your sister or brother for twenty years you would still recognise them in some way, even though they would be older, Mr Watts is confident that Mrs Quinn is not his sister."

"That's my thinking as well Cam," Chris agreed. "But it has put me back a bit, I was sure Mrs Quinn was his sister after we saw the deeds, how can a Quinn live at a house that is known to be the Watts family?"

"Perhaps his sister Pamela died, and Mrs Quinn took over, we don't know how long she had been living there do we, and Mr Watts wouldn't know because he lost contact with his family," Cam offered an explanation.

Chris thought on what Cam had said, and agreed it could be an explanation, then disregarded it. "I wish I could agree with you Cam, it would make things easier, but don't forget, the writing on the deeds signed by Mrs Quinn, but the letters written to the missing women, signed Pamela, why would she sign the letters Pamela, she supposed to be a Dorothy?"

Cam dug his hands in his trouser pockets, unable to comment.

"Anyway Cam, it's not ten yet, so let's go and see this Jason, it's only a few minutes from here, I want to ask him some questions."

Chris and Cam entered Chester Road from the Blue Ball Hill end, and the singing came to their ears. "*I wheel a wheelbarrow, through streets broad and narrow.*" Chris looked at Cam and smiled. "At least he is in," he remarked as they eventually stood outside the open shed doors.

"Inspector," Jason smiled having stopped his singing as he saw the detectives standing in front of the shed. "What can I do for you?"

"Do you always sing in the mornings?" Chris asked.

"I sing all the time Inspector," he smiled. "I sit here chopping kindling and sawing logs, the time seem to go better and sometimes I get people looking in to see who is singing just like you are doing now, and they give me an order."

Chris smiled. "Would you mind answering a couple questions for me Mr Keen?" he asked.

"No, not at all, fire away," Jason grinned.

"You know Mrs Quinn at Colebrook Street?"

"I sure do," Jason interrupted.

"She informed us that you cleared her rubbish for her when she moved into her house at Colebrook Street."

"You are right Inspector, it was many years ago however, she had a couple of barrow loads, which I took straight to the dump at Winnall."

"Can you remember whether there were any boxes or piles of business writing material amongst that rubbish?" Chris asked.

Jason thought. "As far as I remember, it was mainly bits of broken furniture, bits of carpets, of course loads of newspapers and bottles, had there been any writing paper, I would have kept it for myself, you can be sure," Jason replied.

"Did you keep it for yourself?" Cam asked.

Jason stared at Cam. "I have just said had there been I would have done, but there wasn't, what's all this about anyway?"

"Just a line of enquiry Mr Keen, the paper had the logo of a rose at the top left hand corner," Chris explained.

"Paper belonging to the Rose Florist that used to be up town," Jason grinned. "You might like to talk to Mrs Balding she was a partner and still lives at Stoney Lane," Jason grinned again.

"You certainly get around?" Chris replied.

"Not to Stoney Lane," Jason replied. "It's too far, but I do deliver logs to her now and again, nothing wrong with that is there?"

"It just seems Mr Keen that you are always around where we investigate," Chris remarked. "Do you know anything else that we should know?"

"I don't know what you should know," Jason replied. "I know nothing about the murder of Mrs Marston that you are investigating, I just keep my eyes and ears open, just hoping that one day I shall find out where my sister disappeared to."

"I appreciate what you are trying to do Mr Keen," Chris answered. "But you should be careful, you have no authority or protection."

"I can take care of myself," Jason smiled. "One thing I can tell you, that who ever is responsible lives not far from where we are now."

Chris looked at Jason, what he just said, was his own thoughts, but that's all they were at the moment, he wondered what or how much Jason knew, after all Jason had been searching for years, where as he himself had only been on the case two weeks.

"Just be careful that's all I asked," Chris remarked. "And should you find out anything that could be useful to us, I would appreciate you telling us."

"Count on it Inspector," Jason smiled.

"Thank you Mr Keen," Chris replied smiling.

Cam and Chris entered the police station, it was later than he thought, and saw Mrs Quinn seated at the waiting area.

"I am so sorry to keep you Mrs Quinn," Chris apologised. "I had other calls to do, we did say eleven did we not?"

"Never mind about that, I am here now can we just get on with it," Mrs Quinn replied in her usual aggressive manner.

Chris turned to Cam. "Constable, please take Mrs Quinn in the office, make her comfortable, I need a word with the Sergeant."

"Please Mrs Quinn would you come into the office" Cam asked Mrs Quinn who got up and followed him.

Chris looked at Sergeant Bloom.

"Miss Ursala Bell is behind the door behind me Inspector," sergeant Bloom said. "She peered through the door while Mrs Quinn was sitting, she is certain that Mrs Quinn is Pamela who she met in the Eastgate Hotel Cafe."

Chris smiled. "That is great Sergeant, I can't see Miss Bell now, thank Miss Bell for me and tell her I shall be seeing her over the weekend."

"Sorry about the delay," Chris apologised as he sat behind his desk facing Mrs Quinn. "Now Miss Watts," Chris began.

Alarm showing in her face, Mrs Quinn looked at Chris. "What did you call me?"

"I called you by your proper name, Miss Pamela Watts," Chris replied.

"Then I am here wrongly, you have the wrong person," Mrs Quinn said standing up. "I am here to sign some sort of statement you wanted."

"Please sit down Miss Watts, we know who you are," Chris replied knowing it to be only a half truth.

Mrs Quinn re seated herself. "I don't know what your game is Inspector, I can assure you have the wrong person, and I would like to leave now," she emphasised.

"Miss Watts," Chris spoke rather sharply. "You are the sister of Mr Watts the landlord of the Mildmay Arms are you not?"

Mrs Quinn's face burst into a smile. "You are crazy, why don't you ask him, don't you think a brother would know his sister?"

Chris ignored the offer which he had already done, he opened his desk drawer and took out two invitation letters out plus the deeds of the house given to him by Mrs Balding and placed all three in front of Mrs Quinn. "You sent these letters Miss Watts to two women who disappeared, didn't you?"

Mrs Quinn glanced at the letters. "What makes you think that?" she asked.

"The hand that wrote these letters is the same hand that signed the deeds to the house you now live in," Chris explained.

"Most people's handwriting look like the same," Mrs Quinn said rejecting what had been told to her. "Anyway, why all the fuss about two letters?"

"Because Miss Watts," Chris kept emphasising Miss Watts. "Both these women disappeared after getting your invitation."

"What you are saying that I had invited these two women out, I am in someway responsible for their disappearance?"

"That is my opinion," Chris replied.

"Then before I say another word, I want a solicitor present," Mrs Quinn replied.

"Have you one you can call?" Chris asked feeling a little annoyed at the request. "Or would you like one provided by the police?"

"Why would I trust a police solicitor, they would be in league with you wouldn't they, no thank you I will call my own."

"Very well," Chris replied gathering the letters and deeds and putting them back in his drawer. "You can call your solicitor."

"I do have a job to go to," Mrs Quinn replied aggressively. "I will do it at the Mildmay Arms, when I get there."

"I am sorry Miss Watts, but you will be kept here until your solicitor arrives," Chris said.

"You can't keep me by force," Mrs Quinn stormed, standing up. "It's police brutality."

"I'm sorry Miss Watts, but you will stay in a cell, I am arresting you without charge at the moment, only for questioning regarding the disappearance of these two women who you invited out, constable," Chris said to Cam.

"Please take Miss Watts to the desk where she can call her solicitor, then ask the Sergeant to place her in a cell."

It was ten minutes later when Cam returned to the office. "Her solicitor will be here this afternoon, Sergeant Bloom has put her in a cell with a cup of tea," Cam confirmed. "Did we do right in arresting her?"

Chris looked at Cam as he took out his pipe and tobacco, he fill the pipe then lit it blowing out smoke. "I had no other option Cam if she is Miss Pamela Watts, then she knows we know, I don't want her disappearing, anyway," Chris continued puffing his pipe. "When her solicitor gets here and she can explain all to my satisfaction, then perhaps she can go, I hope however George gets back before her solicitor gets here."

"I was just thinking that arresting her without any definite proof of missing women that happened many years ago was a bit harsh," Cam replied.

"Cam sometimes in this job you have to do things that you really don't want to do," Chris paused for a while sucking on his pipe.

"One has to see the whole picture, I have Miss Pamela Bell missing at the moment, I know that Mrs Quinn is the Pamela that became friendly with Miss Bell in the Eastgate Cafe, her sister Ursala who was with Sergeant Bloom when

Miss Watts entered she has recognized her, anyway Cam, I have not charged her with anything yet," Chris added.

Cam did not comment on the subject in his mind he thought Chris had gone a little too far. "I had better get on with our report for this morning," he said getting out his notebook.

"You don't like my arresting her do you Cam?" Chris asked as he reached over putting his pipe in the ashtray.

"I'm the apprentice," Cam replied. "You are the boss who I am learning from."

"Things might look better to you by the end of the day Cam," Chris remarked. "Although I am the higher rank we are a team in this office, always open to a debate with each other, I am not always right, but Miss Watts is a very aggressive woman, a few hours in the cells will cool her down a little I hope."

"We seem to going off our investigation regarding Mrs Marston's murder," Cam voiced his opinion.

"I have a feeling Cam that once we have settled the missing women, we will also clear up Mrs Marston's murder, this is a funny sort of investigation I agree, we started out looking for a murderer and end up with missing women that happened years ago, apart from Miss Bell, I have a real feeling that both are connected."

The office door opened and George entered. He smiled at Chris then at Cam.

"Good to see you George," Chris smiled. "Did you have a good trip?"

"The old motorbike done me proud," George grinned. "Not one break down, stopped the night in a pub, so I had a few last night."

"Well sit and tell us what you found out?" Chris said a little impatiently wanting to know. "We have been busy as well, we have Mrs Quinn or Miss Watts in the cells, waiting for her solicitor to call."

"I'm glad of that," George replied making Chris and Cam look at him.

"Really," Chris asked with surprise in his voice. "Why would that be?"

"That accident that Mrs Quinn had, I told you about it on the phone," George said seriously. "Well this morning I visit the hospital where I was told she was taken to, it seems she was standing in front of a horse drawn milk cart, when for some reason the horse reared up onto his hind legs and thrashing out with his front legs, one of the horses front hoofs caught the Mrs Quinn in the face, broke her jaw a couple times, flattened her nose, and distorted her face, she was unrecognisable. She did spent months being treated, but at the end she was still unrecognisable, however she never changed her name, but it definitely Miss Pamela Watts that lived in the house."

"Well done George," Chris replied with a grin on his face. "You have made my day, what about her sister Grace?"

George bowed his head looking down at his desk. "That's a sticking point, Grace married and moved away, not many seem to remember her, or her married name or where she went, sorry about that."

"No need George, you have found out enough," Chris smiled. "Now all we have to do is wait for Miss Watts solicitor, did you get the medical reports by the way?"

"Copies," George replied as Sergeant Bloom entered the office.

"Mrs Quinn's solicitor is here Sir," he said respectfully.

"Thank you sergeant, allow him a half hour with his client, then bring them in."

Chris looked at George and Cam as the sergeant retreated.

"Now perhaps we will get to the bottom of this sorrowful business, Cam, while Mrs Quinn and her solicitor is in this office, you and Sergeant Bloom go to her house in Colebrook Street, search it but keep it tidy."

"I can do that," Cam replied a little surprise. "Can we do that legally?"

"There is a war on Cam, if a person is suspected of hiding someone in their house, we have the authority to enter, it could be a German spy."

Cam laughed. "Is she hiding someone in her house?" Cam asked not believing a word of it.

"Could be Miss Bell," George answered. "Who knows Miss Bell could be a spy?"

"Come off it," Cam laughed loudly. "You don't really believe that?"

Chris smiled looking at Cam. "All I want you to do is walk through the house and check every room I want to know where Miss Bell is, and Mrs Quinn's house is the only place I can think of, also Jason has mentioned several times about the venison sandwiches she sales now and again, should you find any meat cut up ready, bring a slice, I have already asked Bob Harvey to have it checked, so should you find any get in touch with him at the mortuary where he will be today."

"Venison is the meat of the deer, it can be eaten," Cam replied.

"I know Cam, I just want to settle my mind about it, Jason is always harping on about it, just go when Mrs Quinn is shown into the office."

Cam got up to leave as Sergeant Bloom ushered in Mrs Quinn and her solicitor.

"I am Mr Charles Gibson from Gibson and Gibson Solicitor of Southgate Street, the man carrying a bowler hat and a thin leather case under his arm approached Chris who was already standing. "I am here to represent my client."

Chris looked at the man, in his fifties he thought, he wore glasses, with a heavy moustache, and stood about five foot, ten inches, and well built. "Nice to see you Mr Gibson," Chris greeted him offering his hand which Mr Gibson took.

"I am Detective Inspector Hardie, and my colleague Detective Sergeant House," Chris replied indicating George with his hand. "Please have a seat."

Chris sat behind his desk, facing Mrs Quinn who sat in the interview chair, and Mr Gibson by her side.

"You have arrested my client," Mr Gibson begun.

"Arrested but not charged," Chris replied.

"Before we get down to the nitty-gritty of the reason you have arrested her, I have advised my client to come clean," Mr Gibson smiled. "My Client now wishes to let you know that she is indeed Miss Pamela Watts from Southsea as you suspected."

"It is not an offence to alter your name should you wish as long as if it's not for dishonest reasons, however as you wish to be called Mrs Quinn, I shall do so, but can you tell me why you changed your name?" Chris asked.

"I did not want my brother to know," Mrs Quinn replied.

"How would your brother not know you were his sister?" Chris asked already knowing but wanting Mrs Quinn to tell him.

"When my brother last saw me, I was a young pretty woman, but about ten years ago I was in an accident with a horse, his hoof completely destroyed my looks, after several months in the hospital, no one recognised me, I looked as I do now ugly."

"It's not always looks that people go by," Chris replied as gently as he could feeling a little sorry for her. "It's the inner self, their attitude, some of the loveliest people around have not been blessed by nature as far as looks go."

"That might be so," Mrs Quinn replied. "But they were born so, when you were born pretty, then all of a sudden you are made ugly, your whole attitude to life changes, you never lose the anger in yourself."

"I can understand that Mrs Quinn, but why did you not just tell your brother, I am sure he would have been understanding."

Mrs Quinn gave a rare smile. "My brother and I never got on, we had little to do with each other, however after my accident, I knew that I would be needing a job to live, no one would employ me because of my looks, you see the only thing I knew was selling material, no one would want a woman as ugly as I am in their shops."

"But your brother did, even without knowing who you were," Chris remarked. "Run me through how that happened."

"After I came out of hospital, as I told you I was unrecognisable, people who knew me would look at me in a queer way and more often avoid me, so I decided I would have to leave the area, I had a little compensation money and savings, and I heard that my brother had a pub in Winchester, I decided to come to Winchester, perhaps with the idea that should my brother recognise me he would look after me."

"You have the job of his housekeeper, did he recognise you?" Chris asked.

Mrs Quinn shook her head. "Not at all, I did go into his pub occasionally, but there was no recognition, then he advertised for a housekeeper, I am a very clean person, so I applied for the job."

"I can vouch for your cleanliness Mrs Quinn having been in your house, but your looks did not stop him giving you the job."

"Perhaps it was because I told him I knew his sister Grace and I had just moved from Southsea, Grace and Albert were very close."

"Your sister Grace got married and left Southsea, what were their married name?" Chris asked.

Mrs Quinn looked at Mr Gibson who just nodded before answering. "She married a Mr Johnny Walker, they moved up north, County Durham, somewhere like that, he came from there, but they are both dead."

"I see," Chris muttered not believing the story. "Did they have any children?"

"Not as far as I know," she replied.

Chris knew her story was plausible, although he had his doubts, he looked at Mr Gibson who seem to be contented and at ease.

"Very well Mrs Quinn," Chris said taking the letters and the deed from his desk drawer and placing them in front of her. "Do you still say these letters are not written by you?"

Mrs Quinn again looked at Mr Gibson, who again nodded. "I did write those letters, they were just invitations to have tea with me."

"Were they accepted?" Chris asked.

Mrs Quinn nodded her head. "Yes if my memory serves me correctly they were."

"These letter were an invitation to Mrs Violet West, did you ever send out other invitation?" Chris asked.

"Inspector, I might have done, do you really expect me to remember who I once invited out?"

"What about Kate Mitchell, Mrs Johnson, or Mrs Stanley, Miss Bell?" Chris asked.

"Inspector, I do remember Miss Pamela Bell, two weeks ago I was speaking to Miss Bell in the Eastgate Café."

"Do you remember sending these three women an invitation?"

"If I could remember Inspector I would have told you, but I can't."

"Not even Miss Pamela Bell who only went missing two weeks ago?" Chris asked.

"I never sent Miss Bell an invitation letter," Mrs Quinn replied. "Surely her sister would have seen it had I, they were joined at the hip."

Chris looked at George who had not interfered but was listening intensely. Chris did not want to close the interview before he got the telephone he was expecting, but so far Mrs Quinn had explained things that he knew would not allow him to charge her with anything, it was quite within reason that she could have had a cup of tea with the missing women, then gone their separate ways, but Chris did not believe in coincidences of this nature.

"You were good friends with Miss Pamela Bell?" he asked.

"She was kind to me, her sister never seem to like me, which I understood, but Pamela was very kind, I am sorry to hear that she is missing, I really am."

"Mrs Quinn," Chris finally gave up. "You have caused the police a lot of time wasting because of your dishonesty, Sergeant House here has spent two nights at Southsea checking, do you know I could charge you with wasting police time."

"I'm sorry Inspector, I just wanted to keep my real name a secret, I suppose my brother will have to be told now," Mrs Quinn replied.

"That is not my worry Mrs Quinn," Chris replied a little angrily as the phone rang. "Please excuse me," he said lifting the receiver.

Chris said very little as he listened. "Oh, yes, yes, good," he said, before replacing the receiver.

Chris looked at George who could see he had a smile around his eyes and knew it was good news he had just heard.

"Now Mrs Quinn before we finish, can you tell me why you picked the name of Quinn as an alias?" Chris asked staring at her.

Mrs Quinn stared back at Chris before answering. "You are a bastard," she blurted out. "It was that telephone call wasn't it?"

"Just please tell me," Chris asked, he saw the face of Mrs Quinn soften, her eyes became moist. "Just tell me."

"What would my client taken the name of someone else be anything to do with missing women in Winchester?" Mr Gibson asked. "Whatever name you wish to be called you can choose."

Annoyed Chris turned to Mr Gibson. "Mr Anthony Quinn went missing a few months after Mrs Quinn came out of hospital."

"So," replied Mr Gibson. "What is the connection?"

Chris did not have an answer, then decided to take a long shot. "Mrs Quinn was in love with him."

looked at Mrs Quinn who was almost in tears. "You don't need to answer that question Mrs Quinn," Mr Gibson advised her.

"It's alright I can answer it," Mrs Quinn almost sobbed. "Yes I was in love with Anthony, and still am," she reached for a hanky in her pocket and dabbed her eyes. "I was nineteen working in a material shop, my best friend was Dorothy Quinn. One day her brother came to pick her up, and that was it, I loved him the first moment I saw him."

"You became lovers?" Chris interrupted.

"No not at all," Mrs Quinn tried to smile above her tears. "He did not notice me, you see he lived in Portsmouth, he was a womaniser, out with a different girl every night, having a good time."

"You must have got together at some time?" Chris remarked.

"Eventually we did, I believe because Dorothy kept on to him, she knew I worshipped him, I waited for him almost fourteen years, never went out with another man in all that time, then one day he asked me out, I almost fainted."

"Then what happened?" Chris asked interested.

"We saw each other many times, even had sex, I thought he was going to marry me, then I had the accident, he saw my face after the accident and told me he wanted nothing to do with me."

Chris waited until she had dabbed her eyes once again. "Then he suddenly disappeared," Chris said.

"Yes he did, but looking as I do, I could not blame him, after all he was handsome and could get plenty of beautiful girls."

"Was Mr Gibson's body found?" Mr Gibson asked.

"Not as far as police records," Chris answered.

"Then why bring this up upsetting my client for no apparent reason, he could be anywhere, even still in Portsmouth," Mr Gibson replied.

"I think if he were in Portsmouth, or anywhere else he would have got in touch with his sister," Chris responded. "What we know about him is that he relied on his sister, much like a child relying on its mother but she has heard nothing of him."

"I think my client has explained a plausible reason why he disappeared," Mr Gibson replied. "Unless of course you are hinting she might have killed him, but as no body has been found Inspector, and she has explained her friendship with two of your missing women, also with no bodies having been found, I think we should leave, you have no charges against her."

Chris clasped his hand in front of him, ignoring Mr Gibson, he looked straight into the moist eyes of Mrs Quinn. "While you have been here Mrs Quinn, your house has been searched."

Mrs Quinn looked at Chris, her tearful eyes did not hide the fury in them, she looked at Mr Gibson.

"Really Inspector, you have crossed the line, what was your reason for doing so?" Mr Gibson asked.

"I thought she might be hiding someone in her house," Chris replied without taking his eyes from Mrs Quinn.

"Who?" Mr Gibson asked.

"A missing woman named Miss Pamela Bell," Chris answered.

"Did you find her?"

"We found no one," Chris replied still staring into Mrs Quinn's eyes.

"You had authority?" Mr Gibson asked.

"Of course," Chris answered.

"Inspector, I do not know why this meeting took place, I see it as just assumption on your part without the slightest proof, and no bodies, I shall look into the fact that you searched my client's house, now have you finished?" Mr Gibson said

"There is just one thing," Chris replied still keeping his eyes on Mrs Quinn. "We did find plates of meat in your kitchen covered with a damp clothe."

"That is venison for sandwiches I make, I hope your men did not steal or contaminate them," Mrs Quinn burst out with anger in her voice. "And would you please stop staring at me?"

"I am sorry Mrs Quinn I did not realise," Chris apologised turning his head to George who was busy writing. "Tell me where do you get your venison from, I hear that you only get it now and again and that your sandwiches are sold in the Mildmay Arms, do you have a regular supplier?"

"No I do not, a couple mobile butchers sell it when they are able to get it, dears are not killed every day Inspector."

"Really," Chris remarked.

"What do you do with the bones?" Chris asked his eyes now firmly fixed on her face.

Mrs Quinn smiled. "One thing Inspector I do not buy the bones, it is already sliced venison meat."

"Would you be surprise to know that the venison you have in your house is in fact human flesh," Chris dropped the bombshell.

Mrs Quinn sat up in her chair, the anger in her face changed to fear, she looked at Mr Gibson.

"Really Inspector, what are you insinuating now?" Mr Gibson asked.

"Not insinuating Mr Gibson, but a fact, the meat found in Mrs Quinn's kitchen was human, tested by our Police Surgeon who is also a coroner."

Mr Gibson for the first time was unsure in his reply. "I really do not know what to advice," he stammered looking at his client. "Mrs Quinn did you know what you were buying was human meat?" he asked.

"Of course not," Mrs Quinn replied anger showing in her voice. "It has to be venison."

"Then please tell me who you bought it from Mrs Quinn?" Chris asked.

Chris could see that Mrs Quinn was trying to control her fear.

"I don't know," she replied. "I bought this lot from a traveller, I had not seen him before, and did not ask him questions like who he was or where he worked, he sold me the deer cheap, so I bought it."

"As it was a whole deer Mrs Quinn, then what did you do with the bones?" Chris asked.

"I burnt them," Mrs Quinn muttered her mind dizzy with fear trying to find answers.

"Where did you buy this deer, I mean outside your home or in town?" Chris asked, knowing that Mrs Quinn was struggling with her thoughts.

"I don't know," she almost screamed, tears coming to her eyes. "You have muddled my mind, I am unable to think clearly."

"Well did this traveller carry it in doors for you or did you carry it?" Chris asked without a pause in his questioning.

"I carried it, no, no he carried it, yes that's right he carried it to my kitchen," Mrs Quinn stammered.

"And you were able and have the enough experience to carve the animal up were you?" Chris continued.

Mrs Quinn did not answer, she bowed her head looking at her lap, and keeping her hanky to wipe her eyes.

"Mrs Quinn, everything you have told us about buying a deer, is a pack of lies," Chris waited a moment for her reply, which was not forth coming before continuing. "The human flesh at your house is that of Miss Pamela Bell?"

"I'm afraid Inspector that my client is not in a fit state to be questioned any more, I would suggest a break."

Chris looked at George who nodded his head. "Very well Mr Gibson, she will go back to her cell, shall we say ten o'clock tomorrow morning."

"It is Saturday tomorrow Inspector," Mr Gibson answered.

"I know, but I am sure you understand the seriousness of this crime."

Mr Gibson gave a tired grin he had never represented a case concerning human flesh before. "Very well Inspector," Mr Gibson said.

George got up and open the door of the office beckoned Sergeant Bloom into the room.

"Take Mrs Quinn back to her cell Sergeant," George said. "This time lock the cell door, but she must be kept an eye on throughout the night."

"Leave it to me," answered Sergeant Bloom, entering the office and taking Mrs Quinn by the arm led her without a murmur or struggle from the office to her cell.

By the time the office had settled, Cam had entered. "Did we do alright?" he asked.

Chris smiled at him. "We are getting there, mainly thanks to the meat you found."

"Bob did not have time to test it properly, but he told me to tell you it is human flesh, and said he would get in touch."

"Bob's word is good enough for me," Chris remarked. "Did you find anything else there Cam?"

Cam shook his head. "No not really, she seems to collect handbags, there was at least a half dozen different handbags."

"Really," Chris remarked, his mind working overtime. "Perhaps she has a thing about handbags and could not bare to throw them away, what about clothing?"

"Don't know," Cam replied. "I am not sure, all the clothes in her wardrobe could have been her own."

"Miss Bell is the latest victim," George remarked. "Can we get her sister to see them, she might be able to pick out something that belonged to her twin."

"I was having the same thoughts George," Chris agreed "Tomorrow George is your day off, but I take it you will want to be in on the interview?"

"I would not miss it Chris," George responded.

"Right," Chris said. "I will see Mr Charlie Webster tonight, I want to talk to him, I want you Cam to collect the handbags, take them to Wharf Hill and show them to Miss Ursala Bell, see if she can recognise any of them, if she cannot, just replace them back in the house, if she can recognise any, bring them back here."

"Can we do that?" Cam asked.

"At the moment we are treating her house as a murder scene," Chris replied.

"I can do that," Cam replied accepting what Chris had said.

"Then I want you to go to the Mildmay Arms, perhaps you can do that on your way home, and ask Mr Watts to be here at ten tomorrow morning."

"If he can't?" Cam asked.

"You can tell him it's important, but nothing else."

"I can do that," Cam smiled.

"You better be off then," George grinned.

After Cam had left the office, George got down to his report on the interview.

"One thing Chris, how did you know she was in love with Mr Quinn that he disappeared?" George asked.

"I didn't," Chris replied. "It was a long shot, and for once it came off, you told me yourself that several women had gone missing without a trace, Mr Quinn stood out being the only man you mentioned, I just took a chance."

"You certainly kept on to her about buying the deer," George remarked.

"I did not want her to have time to think, I knew she was lying."

"Have we got her, do you think?" George asked.

"I hope so, but by tomorrow her mind will be clear, she will already have her answers worked out, that's why I was disappointed when Mr Gibson asked for a break, although I had to agree with him."

"It's a bit gruesome eating another person," George made a face of distaste. "You always thought that Jason was trying to tell you something, do you really think he knew?"

Chris shook his head. "More of a suspicion I would think, he told us he keeps his eyes and ears open and listens, he also told us he did not eat the meat, but when we were in his kitchen he had a lamb joint on the kitchen worktop, covered over with a clothe."

"Jason must have loved his sister, after all these years still looking for the reason of her disappearance."

"He did tell us she looked after him like a mother hen, but I don't think Mrs Quinn had anything to do with her disappearance."

Chapter Twenty

en minutes after Cam had left the office, the telephone rang, Chris lifted the receiver.

"Yes Sergeant?" he asked.

Chris lifted the receiver away from his face. "It's a Sergeant Appleby for you George."

George got up and took hold of the receiver. "Hello Sergeant," he said.

After a while he listened. "Are you positive?" he asked. "Well that is certainly what I wanted to hear Sergeant, thanks for all you have done for me, I might have some good news for you within a couple of days," George laughed as he replaced the receiver.

George went back to his desk. "That was the sergeant that was assigned to me by the Inspector at Southsea," he informed Chris who was looking at him. "This morning we both went to the hospital, after that I told the sergeant I wanted to check Grace Watts marriage certificate, anyway he told me to get on my motorbike and get back home, he would see to it and phone me."

"And?" Chris asked anxious to know.

"Miss Grace Watts married a Mr Charles Webster in 1885, Mr Webster was from Durham, he did not know where they might be now."

"So why did Mrs Quinn lie about the name," Chris said. "At least she told the truth about where he came from."

"We now have enough facts to question Mr Webster," George replied.

Chris looked at his watch. "Yes we do, and I think we can go and see him now, it's almost six."

"What about Elizabeth?" George asked.

"I have already phoned her, she won't be expecting me to meet her tonight," Chris replied getting up to collect his trilby.

Chris and George strolled along Water Lane. "At least he is in, his steam engine is there," Chris remarked looking ahead of them.

"Friday, perhaps he left work early," George remarked.

They both looked at the gleaming engine as Chris unlatched the small wooden gate and took three steps to the front door and knocked.

"He should be in," Chris remarked as the door was not answered.

"Perhaps he's in the back garden," George replied, we can go along Chester Road to see."

Agreeing, Chris closed the gate behind them, and made their way the short distance to Chester Road. "No singing," he remarked, as he noticed the doors of the wood shack open. "In doors I expect."

The detectives passed the shack, and looked over the fence of the back garden to Mr Webster's house.

"No one there," George said looking at Chris.

"Let's try at Jason's house," Chris replied already crossing the road to the wooden gate which he opened that led to the back door.

They saw Jason's wheelbarrow on its side laying in the pathway to the back door, which they noticed was also open, for no reason Chris had the feeling of caution, and put his finger to his mouth, telling George to be quiet. Followed by George, Chris inched himself along the wall of the house, passed the barrow, until he was able to peer into the window, the door of the house was the other side of the kitchen window. Chris saw the kitchen was empty, he noticed a upturned chair, and the door leading to the hall and stairs open. Chris made a face at George as he crossed the window, and stood at the door.

"I have a gut feeling that all is not well George," he whispered as he opened the back door further and stepped inside.

"Voices coming from upstairs," George whispered.

Chris entered the hall, and the voices became clearer. "Careful as we mount the stairs," Chris mimed with his lips, as he stepped on the first stair.

They both stopped as their heads became level with the landing, Jason sister's bedroom door was open, and to their surprise, they saw Charlie Webster sitting on the bed, his arms bound by a rope around his waist, he was looking at the wall.

"You won't get out from this house alive, if you don't tell me," said a voice from behind the open door, that both recognised as Jason.

"You have it all wrong," Charlie was trying explain. "I bought that ring from a jewellers in Parchment Street, we have been friends for a long time, how can you think I would hurt your sister."

"I have been watching you ever since you came out of Mrs Green's house in Beggars Lane last week," Jason replied. "I know it was you, but I kept it to myself."

"So you did recognise me, I thought you might, I realised after I went up Alresford Road, it was my scarf wasn't it."

"Where is my sister?" Jason asked with anger in his voice. "I know you were involved, you are the only one, my sister had a crush on you."

Jason showed himself from behind the door as he came into view and grabbed Charlie by his throat.

Chris decided to move, he rushed up the remaining stairs. "What's going on?" he shouted entering the room.

Jason moved his hand from Charlie's throat, Charlie grinned relief showing on his face. "How did you get in Inspector?" Jason asked anger still in his voice.

"Actually," Chris answered while George was untying Charlie. "We came for a word with Mr Webster, he did not answer his door, so we took a look at his back garden hoping he might be there, when he was not seen we thought about you, your back door was open."

"He was involved in my sister's disappearance," Jason said angrily.

"So he might have been Mr Keen, but you cannot go around abducting people, it's a serious offence."

"He's gone mad," Charlie interrupted. "I am his friend as you well know, he hit me with a log in the shack, then wheeled me over here in his barrow, he kidnapped me, aren't you going to arrest him?"

"I think you both had better come to the station," Chris replied. "We can then sort this out, had you any proof to your accusations Mr Keen, you should have come to us with it, now by taking things into your own hands, you are in trouble."

"Do you think I care," Jason responded. "I have been searching for years, and who do I eventually find responsible," Jason flapped his arms. "None other than who I thought to be my best friend."

"You are upset Mr Keen, now get whatever you want to wear and we will go to the police station, you can walk in front of us, but any trouble on the way, will add to whatever the outcome."

With Charlie between them and Jason walking in front, they made their way to the police station without incident.

Sergeant Bloom looked up as they entered, surprise was on his face, which turned into a grin. "Been busy I see Inspector."

Chris scratched the back of his head. "Unexpected I would say, is Constable Streeter back yet?"

"No not yet," sergeant Bloom answered.

"When he arrives keep him out here for a while will you?"

Sergeant Bloom nodded. "I shall be off in an hour, would you like me to hang around?"

"I would appreciate that, but it might be a waste of time," Chris answered.

"Anyway, you had better book these two in, and empty their pockets," Chris said in a low voice.

Charlie kicked up about having to empty his pockets. "I am not a criminal, I was the one assaulted and kidnapped."

"It's routine Mr Webster," Chris told him. "The contents will be given back when you leave."

Chris sat behind his desk facing Jason and Charlie, while George was already with his notebook. "Now let's get this sorted out, why did you assault and abduct Mr Webster?" Chris asked Jason. "I have told you before, you have no authority even though you are looking for your sister, what you have done is a serious offence."

"I don't care," Jason replied unable to clear his voice of anger.

"Just tell me why you think Mr Webster was involved in your sister's disappearance?" Chris asked.

"I was delivering wood last evening at Wales Street and Colson Road, around that area, Mrs Bumstead, Charlie's girl, wanted some logs, she knew I was friend with Charlie, she offered me tea or apple juice, I took the juice and as she handed me the glass, I noticed a ring on her finger and recognised it straight away," Jason looked at Charlie with hatred in his eyes.

"My sister Neil was given that ring by my mother, it must have been some king of family heirloom, handed down from mother to daughter, anyway I remember it was too large for my sister's finger, so she kept it around her neck on a chain."

"Then what?" Chris asked.

"Well I just said to Mrs Bumstead, that's an unusual ring, Mrs Bumstead smiled as she lifted her finger up, which allowed me to see it clearly, Charlie gave me it some time ago after we decided to become an item, she told me, I knew straight away it belonged to my sister."

"I bought that ring several years ago, I thought it was antique, I travel all over Hampshire, I always carry a fiver in my pocket, just in case if I see a bargain," Charlie interrupted. "I am being accused, beaten, tied and kidnapped, and I want something done about it."

"It will be Mr Webster, but first where did you buy the ring?" Chris asked.

"I can't remember now," Charlie replied. "It was a long time ago, could have been in one of a half dozen villages."

"I should try to remember Mr Webster if I were you," Chris replied. "This is a serious accusation, I did hear you say you bought it at Parchment Street, now you say you bought it at a small village, it would be better for you if you could remember?"

"I was scared when I said that, but I will give it some thought, anyway what happens now?" Charlie asked.

Chris looked at him. "It's up to you Mr Webster, do you want to bring a charge against Mr Keen?"

It was several moments before Charlie answered. "I was his friend, he knows I could not harm his sister, however we have been friend for a long time, and I don't want this advertised, so this time I'll let it go, providing I get no more accusations from him."

Chris looked at Jason. "You are lucky Mr Keen, although I sympathize with your desire to find out about your sister, you cannot go around taking the law into your own hands, as you know, had I not been there, you would have also had a charge of grievous bodily harm against you, so think yourself lucky that you have got off with just a warning. I want you back here tomorrow morning at ten, will you attend?"

"I will," Jason nodded realising that it was best for him to keep quiet.

"Can we go now?" Charlie asked.

"Mr Keen as no charge has been made against him now he can go, I am afraid Mr Webster, you will be arrested, Sergeant House and myself heard you confess that you were the man who sexually assaulted Miss Nelly Green of Beggars Lane, you will stay tonight in a cell by which time we shall know more about the ring you gave Mrs Bumstead," Chris spoke.

"You can't do that," Charlie replied violently. "Here I have just let a criminal off, and you are arresting me, what about my steam engine, children will be all over it if I am not there."

"I am quite sure no one will pinch your steam engine Mr Webster."

"I never sexually assaulted Miss Nelly Green of Beggars Lane," Charlie responded angrily.

"Wasn't she?" Chris replied a little anger showing in his voice. "Miss Green a young ignorant girl, who you forced to strip and then sat on her stomach, she was frightened out of her mind, you are looking at several years in prison."

Charlie laughed nervously. "That's silly, I didn't touch her, I did not rape her."

"Making her strip is sexual assault," Chris replied.

Chris looked at George, who rose and arrested Charlie and charged him with sexual assault after reading his rights.

As George led Charlie out, he looked at Jason who had a smile on his face.

"Smile as much as you like," Charlie snarled. "You won't ever find your sister, and I have changed my mind, I want you charged."

Chris looked at Jason taking no notice of Charlie's outburst. "Now you go home and watch your behaviour, be back here at ten tomorrow morning."

"I'm glad you were at my house Inspector," Jason replied apologetically. "I might have done something I would have regretted."

"We all do things in a fit of temper Mr Keen, you just have to control it, however I do not think you would have harmed him any further."

George entered as Jason left. "He is now in the cell, I told the sergeant to put him as far away from Mrs Quinn as he could."

"Is Cam out there?" Chris asked as Cam entered the office. "How did it go Cam?" he asked.

"I took all the handbags to Miss Bell, she broke down when she picked this one out," Cam said holding out a small handbag with a bone handle and a brass clasp. "She swears this belong to her sister."

"Any contents?" George asked.

"No, empty," Cam replied.

"Better put it somewhere safe then," Chris replied feeling a little tired. "It will help us tomorrow, would you call Sergeant Bloom in?"

Sergeant Bloom entered the office on call. "Are you on desk duty tomorrow?" Chris asked as he appeared.

"Until Monday," sergeant Bloom replied, but I can get covered if you need me?"

Good man, sergeant, I want you and Cam to search Mr Webster's house tomorrow morning, garden and all, don't ask me what you will be looking for, you will know should you find it, he left his keys I hope?"

"I noticed them as he emptied his pockets," sergeant Bloom replied with a smile. "What time are we talking about?"

"Early as possible in the morning, I have interviews at ten, but now we should all go home, we have had a busy day."

"An awarding one as well," George remarked.

"Just one thing before we go," Chris looked at Cam. "Mrs Bumstead it seems has a ring that Jason swears belonged to his sister, I know you won't mind calling on her tonight, ask her about how she got it, and try to get her to loan it to you."

"Then what?" Cam asked.

"When you have finished searching Mr Webster's house tomorrow morning visit jewellers, find out how old it might be?" Chris advised.

"I can do that," Cam grinned. "I just hope she is not at work."

"If that should be the case, then you will have to decide what to do?" Chris replied.

Chapter Twenty One

*C*hris crossed the junction with Blue Ball Hill into Alresford Road, he looked at his watch while walking it was almost eight pm. He felt tired, he had only eaten the sandwich that Elizabeth had put in his pocket this morning, and felt hungry. He looked towards his house which was about one hundred yards up, and saw Elizabeth standing outside waving to him, he waved back, and quickened his step.

"I was worried about you," she smiled as she stood before him kissing him on the cheek.

Chris looked at her and smiled. "You married a policeman, you knew my hours are controlled by events, not by time, anyway, it feels good to have someone worry about me."

"I have told mother and dad, that I am taking you straight home tonight," Elizabeth said grasping his arm.

"I am rather hungry," Chris replied wondering about his dinner.

"I took your meal to our own house, it's keeping hot over a saucepan of boiling water," Elizabeth replied. "You must be hungry you poor darling."

That night as Chris laid in bed staring at the ceiling, with Elizabeth snuggled up against his side. "If we were brother and sister," Chris spoke. "And one of us had our face altered so that it was unrecognisable, do you think we could recognise each other in other ways?"

Elizabeth raised herself on her arms. "I can't see why not," she replied. "We are all individuals, we all have our little quirks, from the way you dress, the tone of your voice, I could recognise you by your walk, you walk with your feet saying it's quarter past nine, also the way you hold your shoulders back, the way you tilt your trilby and suck your empty pipe, however if your handsome face was unrecognisable, there is one way I would be sure to recognise you."

"Really," Chris replied. "What you are saying is that you would be able to recognise certain ways about one person that you have known," Chris argued as he turned on his side facing Elizabeth. "How many times have you heard people say, you remind me of someone by their actions, but what about if you had not seen your brother for many years, and the face had been unrecognisable."

"I don't know," Elizabeth replied. "But if mum or dad became unrecognisable, I know I would know them."

"Even after about ten years?" Chris asked.

"I am sure darling," Elizabeth responded. "You see there must be some sort of feeling, also your face is altered, your speech, laugh, and other peculiarities, never really change."

"Perhaps you're right," Chris agreed turning back to look at the ceiling.

Chapter Twenty Two

Chris entered the office on the Saturday morning, and found George already there. "Morning George," Chris said as he hung up his trilby. "I see you have put the chairs out, let's hope we can get somewhere today with this case," he said rubbing his hands as he made for his desk. "I see Sergeant Williams is on duty."

"Covering for Sergeant Bloom," George replied.

"I keep wondering what he might find, if anything at all," Chris remarked scanning his desk.

"What do you expect him to find?" George asked.

"Not really sure, but if Jason is correct and Charlie Webster is involved in Jason sister's disappearance, it shows that he keeps certain articles, like keeping that ring."

"If it is really the family ring, we only have Jason's word, and with no one alive to prove the existence of it."

"As long as Mr Webster can tell us where he bought it?" Chris added. "Anyway think positive, at this stage we don't want negative thinking."

"The telephone rang, Chris lifted the receiver. "Inspector Hardie," he said.

"It's me Cam," came the reply. "I think you had better come now," Cam said. "We have found what I can only say is indescribable, you should be here."

"Where are you now, you know in a half hour I am interviewing," Chris asked.

"I already have Mr Bob Harvey here, we found a bottle of whisky in the front room, and with Sergeant Bloom we are having a tot."

"Drinking on duty?" Chris asked a little surprised.

"You will need one when you see," Cam answered.

"Very well Cam, give me ten minutes."

"That was Cam," Chris said as he replaced the receiver. "He wants us now, he has already got Bob over there, we better go," he said getting up.

Chris spoke to Sergeant Williams on the way out. "Sergeant, you know I have people coming at ten, put them in my office, give them tea, apologise for me, I have no idea how long I will be, can you get a constable to stay in the office with them?"

"Leave it with me Sir," sergeant Williams replied respectfully.

"Good man," Chris smiled as he left the station with George by his side.

Chris and George entered Mr Webster's house with the front door already opened, and found Sergeant Bloom, Cam, and Bob Harvey in the front room, a whisky glass in front of them all."

It was Bob Harvey that spoke as they arrived. "I see your look Chris, as a doctor I would suggest that you have a dram of whisky before we take you to the room."

"I need a clear head, I have an interview in a short time, it can't be that bad can it?" Chris asked.

"I'll take you up," Bob offered.

"We found a locked bedroom Sir," Cam informed. "We broke it open, I can't say anymore."

"If it's that bad Cam," Chris replied. "Perhaps it will be best for you to stay here," Chris added as he and George followed Bob up the stairs.

Bob opened the bedroom door. "In you go," Bob said without entering himself, waiting for the rush, which took only moments before Chris and George fled from the room holding their hands over their mouths.

"My God," Chris muttered breathless. "What have we got here?"

"A den of evil," Bob replied.

"How do you feel George?" Chris asked a couple minutes later. "We have to go in again."

"At least we know what to expect," George replied thinking that he could do with a dram of whisky that Bob had offered them.

"Well let's get it over with," Chris replied. "You coming in Bob?"

Bob nodded as all three once again entered the room.

Although their first entry into the room had been a severe shock, it was in no way reduced as they forced their eyes around the scene. Portions of female corpses were displayed around the room well preserved, lamp shade were made out of human skin, with one body carefully skinned keeping it as whole as possible.

"If he is really mad, he might have worn this skin around," Bob remarked indicating the skin.

"He's mad alright," George replied as he looked at a number of things had been made from human remains such as a tom-tom drum which had been covered with human skin, a soup bowl made from half a skull, and bracelets which were also made from human skin.

"This is hell on earth," George remarked through his mouth covered with his hand. "No one in their right mind could have done this?"

"How many women have gone missing Chris?" Bob asked.

"We have only gone back ten years, we have five women and sixteen young girls missing in that time," Chris answered.

"It's going to be difficult to sort this lot out, he has a portion of every bit of a female anatomy around, how he preserved them is a miracle?" Bob murmured.

"Would he be a cannibal or just someone who kills women for the sake of it?" Chris asked.

"It's hard to tell at the moment, I shall have to get a team down here, it's only parts of the anatomy that he keeps, if he ate the rest, he would cut slices off the corpses, and cook them with vegetables, it's sickening," Bob commented.

Having seen enough, the three soon found themselves back in the dining room, where Chris and George accepted a dram of whisky before saying another word.

"Cam," Chris said after draining that last of his whisky, that made him feel a little easier. "Did you see Mrs Bumstead last night?"

"I'm afraid she was at work," Cam replied.

"Then I suggest that you try to see her now, get yourself some fresh air, there is nothing any of us can do at the moment, should you get the ring, go around the jewellers."

Cam not wanting to stay in the house took a hurried exit.

"I don't care about the ring after what I have seen," Chris remarked after Cam left. "At least it will tell us if Miss Neil Keen is amongst the portions on display."

"That's going to take time, trying to find out what part belongs to one missing woman," Bob remarked. "But it is obvious that Mr Webster is responsible, after all he is the only one living here."

Leaving Bob in charge, and sending Sergeant Bloom home, Chris and George still feeling sick returned to the police station.

"I want a typist," Chris said to sergeant Williams as they entered. "Thank you for standing in for Sergeant Bloom, I have sent him home, he has had a bad experience."

"That's alright Sir," sergeant Williams replied. "He would do the same for me," he said without asking what sort of experience.

"Are the rest here?" Chris asked.

"In your office Sir," sergeant Williams answered. "A constable is with them."

"Good man, now when the typist gets here, bring in Mrs Quinn and Mr Webster will you?" Chris asked.

Sergeant Williams nodded his head.

Chris entered his office, George had already seated himself at his desk. Mr Watts and Mr Keen were sitting together and looked up at him as he entered.

"Thank you Constable, that will be all," Chris said looking at the constable who had stayed in the office.

"I'm sorry to have kept you waiting," Chris remarked as he got rid of his trilby and seated himself behind his desk. "I had a call out, it was unavoidable, have you had tea?"

"We have been looked after," Mr Watts replied. "But it is getting on, I have a pub to open."

Chris took out his watch. "Yes it's almost eleven, but I do need you here, and now I am waiting for a typist, things never do go according to plan do they?" Chris said with a weak smile.

"Where is Mrs Quinn?" Albert Watts asked. "She did not turn up for work at all yesterday."

"I'm afraid she was kept here last night," Chris answered. "Also Mr Webster was charged and kept here, all will be explained later, but Mr Watts let me ask you a question before they arrive, are you sure you did not recognise Mrs Quinn as your sister?"

"As I told you, my sister was a pretty girl, however after you had left, I did think on it, Mrs Quinn do have some of the peculiarities of my sister Pamela, but that's as far as it goes, I employed her mainly because she came from Southsea."

Chris looked at Mr Watts. "Well we do know now that Mrs Quinn is indeed your sister Pamela," Chris said.

"Impossible," Mr Watts replied. "Impossible."

"After your last visit to Southsea, your sister was in an accident involving a horse whose hoof smashed her face, distorted her face, she was unrecognisable, she did spent months being treated, but at the end she was still unrecognisable, people who knew her looked at her in a queer way and more often avoided her, so she decided to leave the area, she heard that her brother had a pub in Winchester, she decided to move to Winchester, she changed her name from Pamela Watts to Mrs Dorothy Quinn."

Dumbfounded Mr Watts could not answer.

Sergeant Williams knocked and entered the office followed by the typist. "Please sit down," Chris said to the typist offering Cam's desk. "I hope you have a silent one?"

"I have," replied the typist as he readied himself at Cam's desk.

Chris turned to Sergeant Williams. "Right Sergeant, we will have the prisoners in now."

Mrs Quinn was the first one brought into the office, she looked straight at Mr Watts as she was led to the interview chair, but made no comment. Mr Webster was then brought in and sat by Mrs Quinn.

Facing the four, Chris sat at his desk, wondering how to start, he looked at George who was watching him.

"Two weeks ago, a young lady by the name of Mrs Olive Marston was found murdered in Winnall Moors, her body had been mutilated. Now this case was strange because the first person we asked questions to apart from her kin, was Mr Keen here, through Mr Keen, Mr Webster became known to us, and through them both, Mr Watts and Mrs Quinn became known to us," Chris looked at the faces in front of him, they were blank of expression, only Mr Watts and Mr Keen was showing any interest.

Chris continued. "Then a lady by the name of Miss Pamela Bell went missing, and our investigation was now not only to find a murderer, but also a missing lady. Naturally we checked back records, and found that over the last ten years, there were including Miss Bell and some twenty one young and older women, plus two boys missing, vanished into thin air within Winchester, Mr Keen's sister and the sister of the murdered Mrs Marston were amongst those missing women. Mrs Marston's sister was living at Water Lane at the time she went missing, and Miss Keen and the murdered Mrs Marston lived at Chester Road, an area of about one hundred yards between them, so it was natural that there was a link in the area, which we concentrated on."

Chris paused and took a drink of water, the room remained quiet, no one interrupted, listening like children as though there were being told a fairy story.

"We did check as a matter of routine what you were all doing on the Friday night when Mrs Olive Marston was murdered. Mr Watts was serving behind his bar, Mr Keen was drinking or playing piano in the Mildmay Arms, Mr Webster was baby sitting at Wales Street for a Mrs Bumstead, Mrs Quinn had no alibi, she was at home, however we accepted this for several reasons, there was no reason or motive for her to kill Mrs Marston."

Chris saw a small smile appear on Mrs Quinn's face as she looked at Mr Webster who gave her a black look.

"We knocked on doors in the vicinity of Winnall Moors, and we got what seem to be a break. Mrs Bumstead who Mr Webster had been babysitting for her, she found a woman's hair comb in her front room, which was not hers. Knowing that Mr Webster had been babysitting for her, we called on Mr Webster, after first confirming that Mrs Marston had a thing about hair combs, she had many of them."

"At least you cannot pin her murder on me," Mr Webster interrupted. "I showed you a packet of combs that I had bought for Mrs Bumstead didn't I?"

"Yes you did Mr Webster, you showed me a new packet with three ladies hair combs, stating that one had some how fallen out."

"That's right I did," Mr Webster again interrupted.

"Chris leaned forward on his desk and clasps his hands. "I accepted your reason about the hair comb at the time, but wondered if one had fallen out why was the packet not undone, however, we checked the shops that sold hair combs, and found most packets of ladies hair combs comes with just three hair combs, you must have had the fourth one in your packet?"

"Perhaps I did, I did not count them, but if you are accusing me, remember I did not know Mrs Bumstead had found a hair comb, until you told me."

"That is not quite true Mr Webster," Chris replied. "You had been leaning over your back garden fence looking into Chester Road, you saw Mrs Marston's mother-in-law leave her house, you asked her was there any news regarding her daughter-in-law, she replied that we were asking about a hair comb, that had been found in a woman house, you then rushed up town and bought a packet, but fail to open it."

"That's a lot of made up rubbish, I did ask her if there was any news, but she did not say anything about hair combs," Mr Webster replied. "Besides that you know I was baby sitting that night, I could not leave a baby on its own, and beside you told me that a man pushing a barrow had been seen coming from Winnall Moors, Mrs Bumstead had no barrow, where would have I got one?"

Chris smiled. "Mr Keen here answered that question for me, although at the time I did not pay a lot of attention he told me that on the Saturday morning following Mrs Marston's death, he had to put a new lock on his shed in Chester Road someone had tampered with it, I believe you took Mr Keen's barrow to transport Mrs Marston's body to Winnall Moors."

"You mean I walked up and down Wales Street pushing a barrow, and no one saw me?" Mr Webster scowled.

"Wales Street or Beggars Lane," Chris answered. "Although I would say Beggars Lane was the less risky, however the streets were empty at that time, pubs were empty, no one about, it would have taken you no more than five minutes either way, we have checked."

"Rubbish," Mr Webster storm.

"Mr Keen," Chris asked. "Perhaps you can tell me the truth now, were you aware that your barrow had been used that night after the break in?"

"I did see a little mud on the wheels and a few blades of grass which puzzled me, I only keep to the road, I do not cross fields," Jason answered.

"How could I break into his shed with him just across the road?" Mr Webster asked his voice still showing anger. "Come off it, he would have heard me breaking in, and don't forget I had to get it back without him knowing, I did all this without being seen."

410

"Habit Mr Webster habit," Chris replied. "After Mr Keen goes for a drink, he goes straight home and straight to bed, you made him believe you were his best friend for years so you would have known his habits, all you had to do was to see his bedroom blinds being drawn, and you were safe."

Mr Webster flung his arms about. "But what reason would I have to kill Mrs Marston, she was a pleasant sort of woman, I had no quarrel with her."

Chris stared at Mr Webster. "I have realised for some days now that you killed Mrs Marston mistakenly, it was dark when you attacked her, believing at the time she lived in Colson Road, it must have been a shock to you when you realised you had killed a person from Chester Road."

"Now you have me," Mr Webster replied. "I have no idea what you are talking about?"

"Did your aunty not tell you that to kill two girls from the same street was very unlucky?" Chris asked.

"What are you talking about?" Mr Webster stormed. "God you are making no sense, who the hell is my aunty?"

"Come Mr Webster," Chris replied softly. "Mrs Quinn of course, Mrs Quinn sister's was your mother."

Mr Watts jumped up from his chair. "Inspector, one minute you are telling me that Mrs Quinn is my sister, now you are telling me that Mr Webster is my nephew, I just cannot keep up with what you are saying."

"I'm sorry Mr Watts to bring it out this way, but Mrs Quinn is indeed your sister Pamela and Mr Webster is your nephew, the only child of Mr and Mrs Webster who moved from Southsea to Winchester some thirty five years ago. Mrs Grace Webster had just one son Charlie, Grace was your sister."

411

"My mind is in a whirl, I can't believe it, Pamela did not tell me when I last saw her," Mr Watts murmured.

"She probably did not know at that time?" Chris replied. "But when she came to Winchester, and saw Mr Webster in your pub, she recognised him."

"How could she do that without knowing him?" Mr Watts asked.

"She may not have known at the time that Mr Webster was her nephew, but people with unnatural habits shall we say, are able to recognise each other, they can recognise each other without a word, it's the same with cannibalism."

"Cannibalism," shouted Mr Watts. "For God sake what are you saying now?"

Mrs Quinn looked at Mr Webster scolding him. "I warned you that your action would bring us down."

"That was the night you caused unrest in the Mildmay Arms Mr Webster, Mr West was talking to Mr Keen about his missing mother, when uncharacteristically you punched him," Chris interrupted. "You were in a bad temper, it was that night that your aunty found out that you had not only killed Mrs Marston, but had cut slices from her which you no doubt fried and ate before Mrs Bumstead arrived home from her shift."

"Guessing again," Mr Webster stormed.

"But what is this about cannibalism?" Mr Watts asked.

Chris looked at Mr Watts, felt sorry for him. "What I have to tell you Mr Watts will come as another shock to you."

"You have already given me two, another one will do no harm," Mr Watts sighed. "This is doing my head in."

Chris clenched his hands that he was resting on the desk. "Very well Mr Watts, you were supposed to be having venison sandwiches on sale in your pub today, I have to tell

412

you they would not have been venison, but human flesh, as all the venison sandwiches you have sold in the pub has been human flesh."

No sound came from Mr Watts who was sitting and staring as though in shock.

"That's not so Albert," Mrs Quinn turned and spoke to her brother for the first time. "I have told the Inspector how I bought the meat, but he don't believe me."

"Mr Watts, the flesh found in your sandwiches, I believe to that of Miss Pamela Bell who lived with twin sister at Wharf Hill, Miss Pamela Bell went missing just over a week ago," Chris said.

"How could you possibly know that?" Mrs Quinn asked a arrogant smile on her face.

"Miss Bell was the last one to disappear," Chris answered.

"Pamela Bell has never been to my house," Mrs Quinn replied forcefully. "Are you saying I killed her?"

"How was it then that her handbag was found at your home?" Chris asked.

Before Mrs Quinn could answer, Mr Webster stood up looking down at his aunty. "You stupid woman, you told me you destroyed all the clothes etc."

"Sit down Charlie," Mrs Quinn said quietly. "Do you realise what you have just said?"

"You Mr Webster kept the ring that belonged to Mr Keen's sister," Chris remarked.

"There you go again, I had nothing to do with Miss Neil Keen," Mr Webster exploded.

"You mean you do not keep anything from the women you kill?" Chris replied quickly.

"If I had kill women, I would not be such a fool," Mr Webster replied angrily.

"The reason I was late for this interview, because I was called to your home in Water Lane, we had it searched, it sickened me I can tell you when we entered the bedroom you had locked."

"Mr Webster jumped to his feet, his mouth was open about to respond, then his mouth closed, and he sat down without a comment, knowing he had been caught."

Chris looked at George, who had not interrupted all the way through. "Mr Webster, we saw corpses, how many I am not able to say, it will take time to discover what part belonged to what missing girl or woman."

"God almighty," Mr Watts moaned.

"You mean my sister might be there?" Jason asked looking at Mr Webster with hatred in his eyes.

"That I am unable to tell you Mr Keen, as I have already said the medical team will take some time trying to find out, but I will keep you up to date."

"I wish you could be hung a dozen time," Jason flung at Mr Webster his voice full of hatred.

"Calm down Mr Keen," Chris said. "At least you can say that you did help to bring this case to a conclusion, I'm sure your sister would be proud of you."

Jason sat back, his eyes moist as he thought of his sister Neil.

"Now Mr Webster, you are already charged with sexual assault, that will remain, but why did you attack Miss Green, did you intend to kill her as well?"

Mr Webster seemed very calm as he answered, no doubt knowing that his bedroom alone was enough to hang him, he had to accept it. "I decided only to frighten Miss Green, I wanted the police to think that there was a common link between Mrs Marston and Miss Green, I knew they knew each other, I had seen them talking together, however it was daft idea, Jason saw me and he had recognised me," Mr Webster took a look at Mrs Quinn who was staring ahead at the Inspector.

"That might have been the case," Chris replied. "Had you not mutilated Mrs Marston's body in the manor that you did, in fact it was that put the idea that a cannibal might be around, which in turn led us to find out about many missing persons."

"Exactly what I told you, you fool," Mrs Quinn shouted staring at her nephew.

"You Mrs Quinn, you will be charged with murder," Chris remarked.

"You can't charge with that, I never killed anyone, OK I did eat the flesh, but as far as I know there is no such crime in the English Law."

Chris had a weak smile as he replied. "Mrs Quinn, I am aware of British Law, you supplied the women to your nephew, knowing that they would be killed, you invited these older women to tea, then having already pre arranged with your nephew, you offered them a stroll along the river in Water Lane, eventually finding themselves in Mr Webster's house, from which they never left, you are as guilty as your nephew is."

"I have killed no one, you cannot prove that I have," Mrs Quinn shouted.

"Come Mrs Quinn, you aided and abducted with your nephew for your gruesome appetite while I might agree that you took no hand in the actual murder of these unfortunate women in Winchester, you did murder Mr Quinn at Southsea."

"Prove it," Mrs Quinn challenged Chris.

"Come Mrs Quinn, you know your game is up, it is far better to make a clean sweep," Chris replied.

415

Mrs Quinn dropped her head, her eyes became moist. "I waited for over a decade for him, when he told me after my accident that he was not going to marry me, I decided that he would marry no one else, do that answer your question?"

"It would Mrs Quinn if I knew where he was?" Chris answered.

"He's with me of course, I cooked him, and find them if you can, his bones are somewhere at the bottom of the sea, off Southsea."

Chris stared at Mrs Quinn, there was no remorse in her voice just venom, the room remained silent.

"Tell me Mr Webster, how did you get rid of the bones?" Chris asked with a feeling of complete disgust for Mrs Quinn.

"I put the bones in a coal sacks, then ran over the sack with my steam engine, my front roller can squash almost anything," Mr Webster looked as if he was almost pleased to be telling his story.

"With the bones in bits, I used them to steam up my engine ready to move, that reduced them almost to ashes, which I spread somewhere in the countryside or wilderness or spread over many a Hampshire roads," he said with a grin on his face.

At a nod from Chris, George left the office and fetched Sergeant Williams. "Take them both back to their cell," he said. "Make sure they are securely locked in, I can't bear to look at them."

Chris stood and shook the hand of Mr Watts as he was leaving. "I am sorry Mr Watts, you have had more than your share of shocks this morning."

"I'm in a daze, I still cannot believe all that have been said and happened," Mr Watts replied in a whisper. "I need to get someone to open the pub for me, I need some time on my own."

"I think that is wise, Mr Watts, I will of course keep you up to date."

"Well Jason," Chris said using his Christian name for the first time. "If you're suspicious in anyway of anything in future, come straight to us."

"I will" Jason replied his face serious. "At least I might be able to bury parts of my sister, and my long time stress in trying to find her, has come to an end."

Chapter Twenty Three

With the office clear, Chris looked at George. "You never interrupted?"

"No need to," George replied. "How you got it all together like that beats me, however should we get another case like this, I will ask for leave, I shall have nightmares over that room."

"I shall as well, it was gruesome," Chris replied as Cam entered the office.

"This ring," he said holding it out in the palm of his hand, is a fake, one like you would get out of a Christmas cracker."

"Really," Chris replied a little surprised. "Are you sure?"

"For the jewellers," Cam replied.

Chris looked at George. "It's hard to believe that a ring from a Christmas cracker really solved this case."

"How do you mean?" George asked.

Chris leaned forward on his desk. "We were going to see Mr Webster because we found out that he was the nephew of both Mrs Quinn and Mr Watts no other reason."

"That's correct," George agreed.

"Being out when we called, led us to Mr Keen's house, where we heard Mr Webster's confession of his attack on Miss Green, which enabled us to charge him and keep him in a cell over the night," Chris continued. "Because of this confession, we were prompted to search his house, where we found the remains of several women," Chris paused for a moment, leaned back in his chair.

"All this which would never had happened, had Jason not seen that ring on Mrs Bumstead's finger and took the law into his own hands, this ring although cheap, was at one time given to Jason's sister by her mother, which obviously the sister treasured by hanging it around her neck."

"Wouldn't Mrs Bumstead had known it was just a cheap imitation?" Cam asked.

Chris shrugged his shoulders. "Perhaps," he replied. "It is however unusual, perhaps she liked it, either way it was good thing that she wore it."

"But as it turned out, it was just luck that we went to Mr Keen's house, it was not our intention as you just said," George spoke.

Chris took out his pipe sand filled it, he sucked on his pipe, then took it from his mouth.

"I believe it wasn't just luck, Jason saw us, he knew we would not find Mr Webster at home, as he already had Mr Webster unconscious in his shack, thinking perhaps that his house would be our next port of call, Jason dumped Mr Webster in his barrow rushed across to his house, tipped Mr Webster out of the barrow and carried him upstairs to his sister's room where he sat him on the bed."

"Jason had to do it in a hurry, it would not take many minutes for us to walk to his house," Chris went on. "His shack left open, the barrow on its side in the pathway, back door and hall door left open, that's not Jason that we know his is very neat and tidy, I believe Jason did everything deliberately wanting us to walk into his house," Chris remarked.

"I agree with that," George remarked. "Then what we heard, more or less solved our case, but what would have happened had we not called upon Jason?"

"Can't really say," Chris replied taking his pipe from his mouth. "Perhaps Jason would have come to our notice with a charge of grievous bodily harm, he was angry enough, but one thing for sure, this case would have gone on and on, we would never had a reason for searching Mr Webster's house."

"You could say that Jason forced our hands?" Cam remarked with a smile.

"Whatever," Chris replied putting his pipe in the ashtray. "This has been a disgusting crime, and I am glad it's over." "I hope women will ignore the spiders offer when they go into house with a sole occupier."

George smiled. "What's a spider got to do with it?"

"*Will you walk into my parlour said the cunning spider to the fly,*" Chris replied as he got up and crossed the office to the hat stand, and taking his trilby.

"You off then?" George asked.

"While you two are making out your reports, I am off to get my glasses, they should be ready today."

With Chris out of the office, Cam put his hand in his pocket and counted out two shillings, which he offered to George.

"I have never been lucky in gambling," he said with a happy look as George accepted their two shilling bet.

THE END

BOOK THREE

INSPECTOR
CHRIS HARDIE

SINS OF
THE MOTHERS

Chapter One

The sky was dark and overcast, and the heavens opened in a downpour, thunder rolled across the sky, followed by flashes of lightning.

It was just after half past nine in the morning, Detective Inspector Chris Hardie, found himself along with Detective Sergeant George House, standing against the trunk of a tree, both trying to keep the rain off of them as they stared a body of a middle aged woman a few feet from them, who had been partly covered with a policeman's cape. Chris pulled his raincoat collar further up around his neck, he was irritated, as the water built up on the rim of his trilby, acted as a mini waterfall every time he looked down.

"Blasted weather," he said to George as he watched him brush the rain from his hair. "You should wear a trilby."

George smiled. "A good rub with a towel will soon dry it, but I don't know about your shoes, the rain coming off your trilby is soaking them."

Chris automatically looked down and another mini waterfall fell from his trilby and the water splashed over his shoes, Chris shook his feet in annoyance.

"I have another pair back at the station," he remarked. "I wish Bob Harvey would hurry up, Cam picked the right day to have off."

It was the first Saturday in August 1916, Chris and George were sharing the Saturday duty, Detective Constable Cam Streeter was having his day off. Just after eight thirty that morning, a body was reported to have been seen by the bridge at the end of Gardenia Road, a track by the river that led to Catherine's Hill.

"Have you alerted the police surgeon?" Chris asked Sergeant Williams who had brought them the news.

"I have Sir," replied the sergeant. "He didn't seem to happy."

"Nor are we in this weather Sergeant," Chris replied getting up and crossing to the hat stand.

"We will need our raincoats and a couple of bikes George, we may get wet on the bikes, but wetter if we don't take them, it would be quite a walk."

"I have already sent a constable to the scene," sergeant Williams remarked. "It's a woman so I'm told."

"Who reported it Sergeant?" Chris asked. "Who would be down that way on a morning like this?"

"I believe it was a dog walker," sergeant Williams replied. I have his address and phone number, he works for the Winchester College.

The thunder rolled across the heavens and the lightning flashed, Chris and George found it was hard work pedalling against the strong wind and rain, they were completely exhausted when they reached the scene.

Chris and George parked their cycles against the bridge, a constable was standing near the bridge.

"Constable, where is your rain cloak?" Chris said to him. "You are soaked man."

"I covered the body with it Sir," replied the constable. "I couldn't leave her like she was, I have not touched her, just covered her."

"That was commendable of you constable, now get in out of this, those trees will stop a little," Chris told him indicating a small group of trees opposite.

The constable was thankful to do what he was told, while Chris and George bent over the corpse.

"Been here a few hours, looking at the state of her," George remarked as Chris lifted the policeman's cape.

"It's been raining most of the night," Chris replied as his eyes took in the surrounding area of the body, annoyed with the rain coming off of his trilby.

"No way of knowing if there was a struggle, but we do have an axe," he remarked pulling the axe that was half hidden by the body. "With her head smashed like that, it won't take a genius to tell us how she was killed."

"Nor much blood," George muttered.

"Blame the weather," Chris hearing him, replied as he bent a picked up an object. "Looks like a school boys lapel badge," Chris said looking at it before putting the badge in his pocket.

"Her handbag is here as well," George remarked as he picked the handbag up. "Let's hope it will tell us who she is?"

Chris stood up, and covered the woman's body with the policeman's cape. "Can't do much here in this weather, let's join the constable under the trees until Bob gets here."

"How old would you say she was George?" Chris asked as they leaned against the trunk of a tree.

George puffed his lips. "I would say she is in her forties," he replied. "Although her clothes are drenched, she seems well dressed."

"I agree George," Chris replied taking his trilby off and giving it a quick shake before replacing it. "We will look into her handbag when we are out of this weather, it's too wet to empty it here."

"The morgue wagon is here," the constable who was standing nearby reported, making Chris and George look outwards along the road.

"I hope Bob is inside," George said with some concern, as he watched the black box type wagon drawn by a single horse pull up, and the two uniform porters who were wet through jump from the drivers seat.

"Is the police surgeon with you?" Chris shouted to the porters against the wind.

"Yes I'm here," Chris heard a shout come from the back of the wagon, and Bob appeared dressed like a fisherman, wellingtons, a heavy black raincoat, and a fisherman's hat.

"Can't say I like your choice of weather," he shouted against the wind. "You stop where you are, I will look at the body."

Bob Harvey spent just five minutes looking at the body, before moving to where Chris and George stood shaking his head.

"It do seem that this lady has been killed, her head has been bashed in, however I will know more later, I would say she has been dead about fifteen or sixteen hours," Bob spoke.

Chris worked out the time mentally. "That would make around seven or eight last night."

"About," Bob replied. "Anyway, I can't do much here, have you finished with the body?"

"We have her handbag, and we have an axe which might be the weapon used, fingers crossed we might find out who she is when we examine her handbag, it's too wet to do it here, the body is all yours Bob," Chris replied.

Bob turned to the porters and gave instructions, who straight away started to lift the corpse onto a stretcher.

"Your cape is soaked Constable," Bob remarked to the constable standing near by.

"That's OK Sir, I just could not see her lying there without a cover."

"It's called compassion Constable," Bob praised him. "It's a long walk back for you, you better ride with me in the back of the wagon, I will drop you at Bridge Street," Bob suggested. "You Chris and George, I see you have your bicycles."

Back at the police station, having got rid of their raincoats, Chris had changed his shoes, George being given a towel by Sergeant Williams to dry his hair, plus a nice hot cup of tea, that Sergeant Williams had made for them, their annoyance with the weather had almost disappeared.

Having drained their cups, Chris picked up the handbag. "Let's check this bag George," Chris offered. "Let's hope it will help us," he remarked as he tipped the contents out on his desk.

With George both checked the contents with interest. George picked up a small purse and opened it. "Just a few shilling in here," George said closing the purse and laying it to one side.

Chris flicked the rest of the article to the side with a pencil. "A powder case, comb, a wallet, hanky and a couple of keys," Chris said picking up the wallet and opening it. "The keys look like front door keys, a fiver in here, and a photo," Chris looked at the photo, it was a photograph of the dead woman, and three young children.

Chris looked at the back of the photo. "In luck here, we have a name and address," he said. "Mrs Doreen Ewing, 29, Bar End Road, Winchester," Chris read.

"That is a good start," George replied. "Unusual for us, what about the axe?"

427

Chris took the axe from the cloth he had covered it with. "I can't see that we shall get any fingerprints from it, it's been out in the rain all night, even the blood on the blade has been washed off."

"It will be difficult to find the owner, it's not a new one," George spoke. "Every house in the land must have a chopper of some kind."

"That is true George, but should we find the murderer, we may be able to connect the axe, anyway, you can start your blackboard going with what we have."

George chalked the details that they had on the blackboard.

"We will need our cycles again George," Chris stated seeing that George had finished. "We will have to call, there might be a Mr Ewing."

"Children as well," George voiced thinking of the photo.

"The rain has let up a bit," he murmured.

Chapter Two

*H*aving parked their cycles against the house wall, and taken off their cycle clips, Chris knocked the door of number 29,unbuttoned his raincoat and shook it.

A young woman with dark hair answered. "Hello," she smiled.

Chris smiled back at her. "I am Detective Inspector Chris Hardie, and my colleague Detective Sergeant House, I am looking for a Mr Ewing."

"That will be father," replied the young lady. "He is not in at the moment, but expected at any time, if it's important, perhaps you would like to come in and wait."

Thanking her, Chris and George followed her into a well furnished front room, on the sofa sat another young lady, who looked very much like the young lady who answered the door.

"I am Mr Ewing's daughter," the young lady who had invited them in informed them, I am June Ewing, born in June."

"I am May Ewing, born in May" the young woman sitting on the sofa added with a smile. "I heard you at the door, you are from the police, perhaps it would be best for you to discard of your wet coats."

"Both with the name of a month, what happened to April?" George joked with a smile as he took off his raincoat.

"April is our older sister, she is married and lives at the other side of town," June replied. "I am the youngest."

"I am in the middle," May added taking their raincoats from them. "I will hang these in the hall," she remarked leaving the room.

"Chris smiled as June offered them a chair. "Please be seated, father will be home for dinner."

"He is working?" Chris asked.

"No father is retired, he is sixty five," June informed him.

"Your mother?" George asked.

June and May looked at each other and smiled. "Our mother left us some two years ago," May replied.

"We take care of our father," June continued.

"A break up of Marriage," Chris murmured.

"You could say that, mother is so much younger than father, some twenty two years," May answered.

"Any reason for the break up?" Chris asked in the kindness voice.

"Mother wanted younger men, wanted men in her knickers all the time, father was not up to it," June added without embarrassment.

"That is if she ever wore any," May added with a grin.

Chris studied the two young women, who were now both sitting together on the sofa, they were both attractive, slender, and in a way very charming, but Chris wonder, when talking about their mother as they did, not a blush came to their faces, there was no shame.

"So you did not get on with your mother?" Chris asked.

"We don't mention her, it upset father," June replied.

"He still loves her," May added.

Chris thought he better change the subject until their father was present. "What line of work was your father in?"

"He is a master carpenter, and a wheelwright," June answered proudly. "His speciality is carpentry and church windows, he would travel all over when called."

"Really," Chris replied impressed.

"He can retire in comfort now," May said.

"What about you young ladies, do you work, in service perhaps?" Chris asked.

"We have no need to go into service," May added. "We both look after father."

"We can see you have a nice home," George praised. "All your doing, keeping it clean and tidy."

"We work together," June replied. "I mainly do the cleaning."

"I do the cooking," May claimed.

"Light the fire, chop the wood?" Chris questioned.

"Father normally do that," June answered.

"Your father must be very proud of you both," Chris commented.

"We hope so," they both said together grinning at each other. "Do you want to talk to father about mother?" June asked. "It will upset him."

Chris did not answer straight away, he had no intentions of telling these young ladies that their mother was dead without their father presence. "Did your mother move far away when she left your father?" Chris asked ignoring the question.

"We believe she moved quite a bit," June answered. "We never saw her much, just heard."

"Her moves would rely on who she sees at the time," May smiled.

They all looked towards the hall as a key was heard being put in the front door.

"That's father," May said getting up and going towards the hall. "He must be wet through."

Chris and George stood up as they heard the conversation in the hall.

"You are wet through father, you should not have gone out in this weather, you must remember your age, let me have your coat and hat, we have visitors."

Mr Ewing entered the front room, followed by May, who overtook him and pulled a chair out from the table ready for her father to sit. He was a well built man standing about five foot, ten inches, wearing a blue pin stripe suit, his jacket was open, and a gold chain was noticeable across the front of his waistcoat, one end disappearing in the bottom pocket of the waistcoat. His hair was grey, and was clean shaven, and one could tell that he had been handsome in his younger days.

"Gentlemen," he said, his voice soft and gentle. "I hope my daughters have treated you right, I am Mr Ewing, Frank Ewing," he said offering his hand.

Chris took his hand. "I am Detective Inspector Hardie, and my colleague Detective Sergeant House," Chris introduced themselves as in turn Mr Ewing offered his hand to George.

"Well then, please take a chair," Frank offered as he sat himself at the chair. "How can I help?"

"It's a rather sensitive matter Mr Ewing, perhaps it would be better if we spoke to you in private," Chris suggested looking at his daughters.

432

Mr Ewing smiled. "How long have you been here?" he asked.

"Ten minutes or so," Chris replied.

"Then," Frank smiled. "You will know that my daughters take charge in this household, we have no secrets from each other."

Chris looked at May and June who were sitting together on the sofa looking at him.

"Very well Sir," Chris realising he had no option. "What I have to say concerns the woman in this photo," Chris took the photo from his pocket and gave it to Frank. "Is that your wife Sir?"

Frank took the photo and looked at it, Chris could see that his eyes became moist, May seeing this jumped up and stood behind her father, holding her father's shoulders she also looked at the photo, instantly looking at June who remained seated.

"Yes it is mother," May confirmed "It was taken a long time ago, we sisters were all very young at that time."

"Why have you shown me this photo, how did you get hold of it?" Frank asked his eyes still looking at the photo.

"I am afraid we found her body this morning, she had been murdered," Chris replied as gently as possible.

"Oh my God," Frank replied with a sob in his voice putting his hands to his head still holding the photo. "Where did you find her?"

"By the track leading to Catherine's Hill," Chris replied. "We believe she was killed sometime between seven and eight last night."

Frank lifted his head and looked at Chris, his eyes looked sad. "My wife left me about two years ago, I have seen very little of her since, however I will answer your questions to the best of my ability."

"The place she was found is not very far from here," George remarked.

"We used to go swimming in Bull Drove that's in Gardenia Road," May remarked looking at June.

"About twenty minutes or so walk from here," June agreed.

"Her body will have to be identified Mr Ewing," Chris said gently. "Perhaps on Monday."

"June and I will do that, we don't want father to be upset," May interrupted still holding her father's shoulders.

"That will be in order," Chris agreed. "I will send a constable to take you, now," Chris continued. "I have to ask you some questions, they are strictly routine, but have to be asked."

Mr Ewing looked at his daughters, his face showing his sadness. "We will answer what we are able," Frank muttered.

"Can you tell me where were you, say between seven and eight yesterday evening?"

"I was here until eight," Frank began. "I then went across to the Heart and Hand where I stopped until ten, came home, had cocoa which my daughters had made for me and went to bed."

"That seems straightforward Mr Ewing," Chris said. "Is it a normal routine, or was it just last night that you went for a pint?"

"Every night," Frank replied. "I do not go to sleep easily, a pint helps."

"You leave at eight every night, this is normal?" Chris asked.

"It is, you see I wait for my daughters before I go out, they are always back by eight with the nights getting darker, summer time they can stay out a little later, but with all these soldiers in town I want my daughters in the house safe before I go out."

"That is very commendable Mr Ewing," Chris praised him. "Last night your daughters were home?"

"Came in about ten to eight as far as I can remember," Frank replied.

Chris looked at the daughters who were now sitting together on the sofa. "Can you tell me where you had been?" Chris asked.

"We were at our sisters April house," May replied.

"We often spend the evenings with her, her husband is away in the Army," June confirmed.

"Where do your sister live?" George asked ready with his notebook and pencil.

"Stockbridge road, just under the railway arch, number 15," May stated.

"Can you think of any reason why your wife, I take it that you are not divorced, would be at the place she was found dead?" Chris asked.

Frank shook his head. "No, to both those questions," he said.

"Perhaps she was out for a walk," May replied. "The weather was alright when we walked home wasn't it June?"

"Chilly but dry," June replied.

"Which way did you come home?" George asked.

"Straight down the North Walls, and home," May replied.

"Father have already told you he do not like us walking through town at that time of night," June interrupted with a slight frown on her face.

"I am sorry if my questions upset you Mr Ewing," Chris said gently. "But would you know any of her boyfriends, or where she would be living now?"

Frank looked at his daughters before answering. "I don't know."

"We know she was once with a man named Roger Webb," June offered. "Whether he is still with mother or where he lives we have no idea."

"Would you know where he works?" George asked.

Both daughters shaking their heads in answer.

"How did you know his name?" Chris asked wondering.

"We were with a friend who knew him," May replied.

"This friend, what was her name?" George asked.

"Linda Marston, lives somewhere alone Parchment Street," May answered.

"I understand that you do all the chopping of the wood Mr Ewing?"

"That's correct, I don't want accidents to happen to my daughters," he replied.

"Would it be possible for my Sergeant here to see your chopper?"

"That is a strange request?" Mr Ewing replied. "How did my wife die?" he asked.

Chris looked at George before answering. "It is our belief that she was killed with a axe."

"You think one of us is responsible?" Mr Ewing replied a little anger in his voice.

"At this moment we have no idea who is responsible, but every house we visit regarding this crime we will ask to see their axe, it is simple routine," Chris answered.

"They are outside," Mr Ewing replied not wanting to argue.

"I'll show it to Sergeant," June said jumping up from the sofa. "Follow me Sergeant," she said smiling.

George followed June out into the hall through the kitchen, where George noticed the table was spread, and out through the back door, next to the outside toilet there was a covered but open low building, well stocked with logs and kindling wood.

"You are well stocked," George remarked.

"We have a man Jason who delivers," June answered.

"The singing barrow boy," George added thinking of his last case.

"That's right," June agreed. "This is our chopper," June pointed at an axe that lay the front of the logs. George bent and picked it up, studied it, the chopper was old, and well used. "Thank you," he said replacing the chopper. "Is this the only one you have?" he asked.

June nodded her head. "Was mother really murdered with an axe?" June asked as they made their way back to the front room."

"I'm afraid she was," George replied.

With their return, Chris stood. "I am sorry I have been the bearer of news that upset you Mr Ewing, it's an unpleasant part of a detective's work I'm afraid. However we will leave now, I will of course keep you informed, and remember a constable will call you during Monday morning," he said looking at the daughters.

June who was still standing smiled. "I will get your coats," she offered.

"I must get father's dinner on the table," May added getting up.

June stood with the door open and watched until Chris and George had cycled away before closing it, in the hall she looked at her father in the front room, he had not moved.

"You alright father?" she asked.

Frank looked at her, and with a faint smile on his face nodded his head.

June went into the kitchen and found May preparing the meal. "It must have been a man," she smiled at May. "Killing with an axe is a man's weapon."

"A woman would use poison wouldn't she?" May asked.

June smiled. "We must see April tonight."

"You saw the axe," Chris asked George as they cycled back to the Police Station.

"Yes it was old and well used," George replied as they rode side by side.

"Just the one?" Chris asked.

"I did ask if there were any more, she shook her head," George answered.

"Did you see a wheel barrow?" Chris asked as they were passing King Alfred Statue.

"There was one up ended against the wall, looked like a well made one," George replied.

"Well he is a master carpenter," Chris commented as they dismounted outside the station.

Having discarded their top coats, Chris and George sat at their desk sipping a cup of tea that Sergeant Williams had brought in.

Chris put his cup down. "That was a most unusual interview," he remarked. "Polite, but in a way a little comical when you think of the daughters."

"Each one backed each other without being asked," George replied a slight smile on his face. "No contradiction, just completes each other's answers."

Chris looked at his clasped hand that lay on the desk before him. "They seem good daughters, the way they look after their father. "What do you make of him?"

George gulped the remainder of his tea down before answering. "We left a very upset and sad man when we left."

"He never had an alibi until his daughters returned home at around quarter to eight, was he at home during the time the daughters were at their sisters?" Chris wondered.

George thought for a while. "Where his wife was found is really quite close to where he lives, I mean it would only take him twenty minutes at the most to get home, and would not have to pass through town, if Bob is right and his wife was killed around seven, no later than eight, seven would give him ample time to get back home before his daughters arrived."

Chris agreed in his mind that it was possible. "Could he act with the sadness that was in his eyes?" he asked.

"If you killed someone that you loved, and Mr Ewing obviously still loved his wife, you could still feel very sad of what you had done, I would think," George replied.

Chris looked at his watch. "It's just past midday George, you have more to add to your blackboard, while I will have a smoke," he said taking out his pipe. "Then we go and see this Mrs April Marshall at Stockbridge Road."

"Anyway," he continued sucking on his pipe. "On the way we will stop at the Eagle and have a liquid lunch."

George smiled as he started to write with chalk on the blackboard.

Chapter Three

*C*hris and George felt very contented as they knocked the door of number fifteen at Stockbridge Road. The rain had stopped, they had enjoyed two pints and shared the sandwiches that Elizabeth had put in her husband's pocket.

A young woman answered the door, in her mid twenties Chris thought, although she was attractive, she did not resemble that of her sisters.

"I am Detective Inspector Hardie and this is Detective Sergeant House, are you Mrs April Marhall?" Chris asked.

"Oh my God," April gasped falling against the door. "It's my husband?"

Chris looked at George with a question on his mind, then he automatically held his arms forward to aid Mrs Marshall, he realised what Mrs Marshall was thinking. "We are not here about your husband Mrs Marshall," he said to her in a comforting voice.

April steadied herself, touching her breast with her hand. "I'm sorry," she gasped. "I thought you were bringing me bad news about my husband, he is in France."

"I am sorry we have shocked you Mrs Marshall, but we are here on another matter, which I am afraid is not good news, may we enter?"

April made way, and Chris followed by George was taken into a small but well furnished front room.

"Please find a chair," April invited still a little breathless. "I am sorry I acted as I did, you know I think of my Richard out in France all day and night, hoping he is safe, the worry of it all builds up a lot of stress, I sometimes feel that I would rather be out there with him than be stuck at home, wondering and worrying all the time, anyway you don't want to hear my worries, so what is the other bad news you have for me?"

"We are here about your mother Mrs Marshall, we have already seen your father and your sisters," Chris informed her. "I am sorry, but your mother have been found dead."

April looked at the two detectives, there was just blankness in her face, no sign of tears.

"You must already know then," April responded. "My mother left my father some two years ago, went off with another man, I am sorry of course that she has died, after all she was my mother, but she disgraced the family, which cannot be forgiven, but God rest her soul."

"When we said dead, we did not mean she died naturally," George said. "She was murdered."

"My God," April gasped, her face showing disbelief. "How, why?" she stammered.

"We have no idea why Mrs Marshall," Chris said gently. "But she was killed with an axe, a blow to the head."

"My God," April muttered. "Poor dad, he must be upset."

"I'm afraid he was, but your two sisters were comforting him when we left," Chris answered.

"Yes they adore dad, dad is a pussycat, he has no violence in him, he was absolutely broken when our mother left, it was a shock to him, although we sisters knew she was seeing other men, we had seen her."

441

"Really," Chris remarked. "I understand that your sisters were with you during the early hours of last night?"

"Yes they were, they often come up just to keep me company, they will be here tonight to let me know what is happening at home."

Chris smiled inwardly. "About what time did they arrive and leave?"

"Their usual time, arrived about five thirty, you see they get dad's tea ready before they come, and left just after seven, dad likes them home before he goes for a drink."

"That bears out what we know," Chris said still with a gentle tone in his voice. "Would you know a Mr Roger Webb?"

April looked at Chris, gave a faint smile. "I do not know him, he is in a different age group than me, I am only twenty six, I have heard that he is around forty, I have no idea what he looks like, but according to my sisters he is one of mother's boyfriends."

"So you would not know where he lives?" George asked.

April shook her head. "Why would I even be interested?" she asked.

"Don't get offended at my next question Mrs Marshall, our questions are just routine, also to eliminate any involvement in a crime," Chris said as gentle as he could.

"Ask what you like Inspector," April responded. "Anything that I can do or say that will help you catch who ever is responsible, I will be only to willing."

"You have an axe?" Chris asked.

April nodded, and looked at George. "If you will go along the passage to the back door, you will see it on the left."

"Tell me Inspector," April asked as George left the room. "Do you think this Mr Webb is responsible?"

Chris smiled. "I have no idea, I have never seen the man, I will know better when we find him, however, it might be a woman."

George returned to the room. "It's neither old nor new," he said.

"I bought it nine months ago when we moved in here," April informed him.

Chris stood up. "Well thank you Mrs Marshall, I shall keep your father informed, and no doubt your sisters will do likewise to you," he grinned.

"Yes, they will tell me everything," April agreed as she showed them to the door.

"Not much there," George remarked as they walked under the railway arch on their way back to the Police Station.

"She seemed genuinely shocked about her mother's death, but no tears," Chris replied. "It seems that only her husband had feelings for her," he added.

"Sad really when you think about it, sex is the cause of many things, most of our cases, sex plays a part," George remarked as they crossed the Andover road junction.

"I'm afraid it's life George," Chris replied.

Chapter Four

ack at the Police Station, George devoted his time to his report on the interviews that had taken place, Chris took out his pipe and puffed contentedly, while he turned over in his mind what he had been told.

"You know George," Chris said taking his pipe from his mouth. "Mrs Ewing was not the walking type was she, I mean as far as we have been told, she was more incline to be found in a pub than on a walk, but even if she did like walking, would she have gone walking at that time of night?"

George looked up from his writing. "No one has told us that she was a prostitute, but everything we know about her suggest she was an whore, perhaps she picked up someone and wanting a quiet place, decided to walk to Catherine's Hill."

Chris puffed on his pipe. "Hell of a long walk for that George, when there is the park even Morn Hill, both these places are much nearer, where they could get privacy," Chris studied the stem of his pipe.

"You're suggesting two things Chris," George replied. "If her escort was carrying an axe, the murder could have been intentional, or she was walking on her own, and someone in hiding waiting for the lone female to pass."

"For the moment I am discarding the theory that someone was waiting in hiding, we haven't heard of anyone being attacked in that area before have we?" Chris asked.

George shook his head.

"If someone was waiting for her to pass, then jumped out on her and killed her with an axe, what would have been his reason, as far as we know she was not interfered with in anyway," Chris continued.

"I am more incline to believe that she was there because of an appointment, I cannot see her walking there for a bit on the side, any way surely a man carrying an axe, would have been noticeable wherever he was, it is not an article one could hide on a person very easy," Chris commented.

"We know very little about her at the moment, we do not know whether she was at the moment living with someone, or she had a place on her own?" George remarked. "We have no idea how she made a living if she is on her own."

"So what are your plans?" George asked.

"I shall leave a note for Cam, he is on duty tomorrow, I shall ask him to find this Linda Marston and this one time boyfriend Roger Webb, we are told by the Ewing daughters that they live around the Parchment Street area," Chris replied. "What are you doing tomorrow?" Chris asked changing the subject.

"I am seeing Rosemary," George replied with a smile.

"How is Mr and Mrs Morris?" Chris asked.

"They are fine," George answered. "They welcome me as part of the family, they will never forget what happened to their son, but I think it becomes a little easier as time goes by."

"I'm sure it will," Chris agreed. "Please give them my regards, perhaps soon Elizabeth can arrange for you and Rosemary to dine with us."

"That would be great," George replied with a smile. "I will tell you that I am really taken with Rosemary."

"She is a lovely girl, and Elizabeth will be very happy," Chris replied grinning knowing she loved to matchmaking.

"All we need now is for Cam to find himself a woman," George smiled.

"I think he already have," Chris replied. "Still we wait and see."

Chris looked at his watch. "Well it is almost time for me to get home, Olive will have the dinner on," Chris said getting up and crossing to the hat stand, where he put on his raincoat and took his trilby. "You know I have left a note for Cam, let's hope he gets us some information," he said.

"I'll just finish this report," George replied. "I will see you Monday morning."

May and June Ewing placed their father's dinner before him.

"Do you need anything else?" June asked. "We are off to see April."

Frank Ewing smiled. "No, thank you, I have plenty here, give my love to April, tell her should she ever be lonely while her husband is away, her room is empty here."

"She knows that father," June replied.

"We will have to tell her about mother," May remarked.

"The police have already told her I expect," Frank replied, his face losing its smile. "Tell her I am sorry."

"What for?" asked May.

"For picking her mother," Frank replied, his eyes watering. "But I loved her mother, never the less, she may have been a bad wife and mother, but she did produce three beautiful daughters that I am very proud of."

May and June, looked at each other and smiled.

"We will be off now dad, we will be back by eight," June said.

"Go careful," Frank remarked as he took up his knife and fork.

The front door of 15, Stockbridge Road was open as May and June reached it.

"Come in you two," April shouted hearing the door being pushed open. "I expected you two tonight."

"We know that," grinned June.

"Meaning that the police have already been here?" May asked.

"Yes they came this afternoon, they were polite and considerate," April confirmed as she poured out tea for her sisters who were already sitting at the table.

"Did they asked you about your mother-in-law?" June asked as she sipped her tea.

"She only died five months ago," May added pouring milk in her cup.

"Why would they?" April asked looking at her sisters with a smile on her face. "Our mother it seems was murdered, my mother-in-law was not, she fell down the stairs and broke her neck, no police were involved in her death, they probably did not know, why should I tell them."

"Nothing they could do anyway," June replied.

"She is already cremated," added May.

April sipped her tea. "Strange though," she remarked a grin appearing on her face. "Our mother was found dead by the bridge at Gardenia Road."

"Where we threw the ashes of your mother-in-law," May interrupted.

"Only because your mother-in-law hated the place," June remarked.

"Not as much as I hated her," April muttered, offering a plate of cake to her sisters. "I suppose father is taking it badly?"

"It was a shock to him, but time will make it easier for him knowing that his wife is now at rest, no longer around town picking up Tom, Dick and Harry," June smiled.

"I suppose," April agreed.

"If the police do find out about your mother-in-law, won't the police wonder why her son was not allowed to come home for her cremation?" June asked looking at May then at April.

"Richard is fighting a war in France," April replied. "Anyway she was cremated before word of his mother's death got to him, it must have upset him, especially as he is fighting a war, but she was no good for him, she was a dominating mother, she treated him badly, treated him as a boy all the time."

"We told the police that our mother once went with Roger Webb," May remarked.

"They asked me if I knew him, I said I had heard of him but did not know him," April replied.

"You must not tell fibs to the police," June advised.

"Not really a lie," April argued. "In truth I did not really know him."

"I wonder who mother was living with?" May asked.

June shrugged her shoulders. "Some down and out, who was able to keep her."

"Mother is now history," April remarked.

"The stain will stay," June sighed.

"Only for a short time, memories fade," May remarked.

"Let's hope so," April smiled getting up to clear the table. "What else did you tell the police?" she asked her sisters.

"Not a lot," May replied.

"We did mention Linda Marston," June added.

"Last I heard she was living with Roger Webb," April informed them.

"It must have been a man who killed mother, a woman would not use a chopper would they?" June asked.

"A woman could have done, an axe is heavy, don't take a lot of strength to bring it down on someone's head," April remarked. "They checked mine while they were here," she added.

"Ours also," May said.

"Well we have time for Ludo before you go," April said getting the board game out of the sideboard drawer. "Always tell the police the truth, but do not add information they do not ask for."

"We will remember," June replied.

" If they ever call again," May added.

"I have a feeling they will," April replied as she opened the ludo board.

Chapter Five

Detective Constable Cam Streeter entered his office after talking to desk Sergeant Williams for a while, and sat at Chris's desk, where he picked up the note Chris had left him. Sergeant Williams had already told him of the murder of the day before, it was no surprise to him to find instructions. Picking up the note, he left the office to speak again to Sergeant Williams.

"I have to try to find these two people," Cam said to the sergeant. "A Mr Roger Webb and a Linda Marston, I don't suppose they are known to us?" he asked.

Sergeant Williams smiled. "Already been asked, the answer is no."

"Lives around Parchment Street it is believed," Cam continued getting the expected reply to his question. "Any idea, I mean have you heard of them?"

Sergeant Williams shook his head. "I might know them, but cannot place them, don't forget we have a population of about twenty thousand in Winchester, can't expect to know them all by name," sergeant Williams replied. "I am afraid it's door knocking for you, still it will pass the time."

"I suppose," Cam replied. "No better time than the present to start," he said with a smile as he made to leave the station. "I will be some where in the Parchment Street area if needed," he added.

Within a few minutes Cam found himself in Parchment Street, the first part of the street from the high street were mainly shops, which ended a quarter way along with the General Post Office, from there on there were bay window terraced houses, where Cam decided to start knocking doors.

The third house he knocked struck lucky for Cam.

"Yes I know both of them," a plumpish lady in a long colourful dress answered Cam's enquiry. "Linda lives at 32, this side, I believe she has a lodger but I am not sure of his name, I see them quite often together."

Cam thanked her, he was well pleased with the early success, and made straight for number 32. He knocked the door, which was opened by a woman Cam thought to be around middle forties, she had an attractive pleasant face and was neatly dressed.

"I am Detective Constable Streeter," Cam introduced himself. "I am looking for a Linda Marston and a Roger Webb, I have been told, that they both live at this address."

"You were told no lie," the woman replied. "I am Linda Marston, Miss, should you need to know."

"I would like a few words with you Miss Marston," Cam replied. "Can I come in?"

Linda shifted herself from blocking his entrance. "Certainly," she replied.

Cam was shown into a comfortable lounge, the bay window looking out on Parchment Street.

"Take a seat," Linda offered as she seated herself at the table.

Cam decided to sit opposite to her at the table.

"What is this about?" Linda asked. "Have I broken the law in some way, because if I have I have no idea what it could be?"

451

Cam smiled. "No Miss Marston, not as far as I know, I am told that you could put me in touch with a Mr Roger Webb, he is a man I need to contact."

"Can you tell me why?" Linda asked. "Is he in trouble?"

Cam smiled again. "No, not that I know of, but we are told he was acquainted with a woman known as Mrs Doreen Ewing."

Linda laughed. "We are all acquainted with that woman," she said. "She is well known around the pubs."

"You visit pubs as well Miss Marston?" Cam asked.

"Yes I like a drink, but I am usually escorted when I go in," Linda answered. "Anyway what has Doreen been up to?"

"Apart from being murdered, nothing," Cam blurted out which made Linda stared at him in disbelief.

"You can't be serious," Linda managed to said.

"I am afraid I am," Cam replied.

"I knew she would come to a bad end, she would go off with any man who would buy her a drink, she had no shame, anyone of them could be a murderer?" Linda replied feeling a little upset. "Although she was a friend, I had no time for her, but I would not have wished anything like this happen to her."

"Where is Roger Webb?" Cam asked.

Linda laughed. "You can't pin this on him, he was finished with her a long time ago, he lodges here, I will get him he is in his room," she said getting up. "I won't be long."

Cam passed the time while he was waiting by writing in his notebook, points of the conversation with Miss Marston, he did not want to forget, he dropped the pencil by the notebook as Linda entered followed by a tall slender man, who Cam thought was in his forties. He was quite pleasant in looks with dark hair greying at the temples that Cam thought was an added attraction to his looks.

"This is Mr Roger Webb," Linda introduced him.

Cam offered his hand. "Sorry to have bothered you Sir," Cam said apologetically. "I am Detective Constable Streeter, I expect Miss Marston have already told you why I am here."

"Yes she has," Roger remarked crossing to the table where they all sat. "It was certainly a shock to me, but how can I help you?"

"We were given your name by one of the daughters, who said at one time you were shall we say keeping company with Mrs Ewing."

"At one time is right," Roger smiled. "But that was years ago before she became Mrs Ewing, I was going out with Doreen up to about six months before she ditched me and married Frank Ewing, knowing how she turned out, I think Frank Ewing did me a good turn by winning her."

"When was the last time you saw her?" Cam asked.

"Difficult to say exactly, I often saw her around the pubs, never spoke to her, she always manage to be with a fellow, must have seen her last week at least."

"Where were you last Friday evening?" Cam asked. "I have to ask these questions, they are only routine."

"I was in the Fox Inn, Water Lane, with Linda," Roger replied. "So she was killed Friday night?" he asked.

Cam ignored the question. "Was Mrs Ewing in that pub on Friday night?" he asked.

"If she was we did not see her," Linda interrupted. "Where was she killed, and how?" Linda asked with a look of shock on her face.

Cam thought for a while before answering. "She was found dead at the bridge in Gardenia Road," Cam replied.

"That is a long way from here," Roger butted in. "Quite a walk to, what was she doing down there?"

"We have yet to find out," replied Cam. "Would you know if she had any enemies, was she in trouble with one of her male friends?"

Both Linda and Roger shook their heads. "Don't know of any, most men liked her, just for the night you understand, but they would keep in with her because should they see her without a man, they knew they were going to be lucky."

"As bad as that?" Cam asked a little surprise.

"Don't like speaking ill of the dead, but for a glass of stout she was anyone's," Linda replied.

"As far as Friday night, you were both together at the Fox Inn?" Cam asked again.

"You can easy check," Roger replied. "It's not far from your station, by the way have you seen Mr Ewing, I knew the marriage had failed, I just wondered how he was?"

"My boss saw him yesterday, I have not seen him," Cam answered. "Is there any thing you can tell me, it would be appreciated."

"Sorry," Roger replied, she was history to me long time ago, I would not want to know her or her business."

"That seems to be in order then," Cam replied. "Just one thing before I go, do you have an axe in the house?"

Roger looked at Linda who spoke. "No constable, I have a fortnightly delivery from Jason the barrow boy, logs and kindle wood, I have no need to keep an axe in my house."

Cam returned to the station, he was pleased he had successfully carried out his instructions, but was a bit disappointed that he had no information as to why Mrs Ewing was murdered. He was about to open the station door, when the Guildhall clock struck twelve, he let go of the handle, deciding to visit the Fox Inn.

Chapter Six

It was Monday morning, Chris stood outside the police station saying goodbye to Elizabeth.

"Should I not see you, I shall carry on home tonight darling," she smiled looking up to him.

"That is the life of a policeman, never being sure about keeping time," Chris answered. "I shall miss you."

"Me too darling," Elizabeth replied as she kissed him on the cheek. "I wish yesterday could be every day, it was lovely."

"Chilly but the rain kept off," Chris remarked keeping a straight face knowing what his wife was referring to.

"I do not mean the weather silly, you are teasing," Elizabeth scolded.

"You spent the morning cleaning the house," Chris said still teasing.

"I do not mean that darling," Elizabeth scolded again. "I want to keep our house nice, I am hoping that it will soon be a family home," she giggled. "We did have that extra hour in bed in the morning which was lovely keeping each other warm."

"I remember," Chris agreed with a smile.

"The best part was in the afternoon after we came back from mother's, when we got the tin bath in and both had a bath in the kitchen," Elizabeth giggled.

"It took hours for the water to boil enough to fill a bath," Chris replied trying to keep a straight face.

Elizabeth looked up at Chris, her face serious. "Is that all you have to say?" she asked with a look of disappointment on her face. "I thought it was beautiful, my legs turned to jelly."

Chris thought he had teased Elizabeth enough. "Darling it was a wonderful day, together in our own home, enjoying each other, how could any man ask for more, especially when he has the most beautiful wife in the world," he smiled.

"You say lovely things darling," Elizabeth smiled giving his cheek another kiss. "I must be off now, I don't want to be late on a Monday morning."

Chris watched until Elizabeth was out of sight, he was a happy man with a lovely wife, life could not be better for him. Yesterday was memorable, the case had hardly been on his mind, but now his mind is fresh and clear, he could concentrate on the case.

Chris entered the station, the desk sergeant was no where to be seen as Chris entered his office, where both George and Cam looked up as he entered.

"George, Cam," he greeted them as he hung his coat and trilby before crossing to his desk. "How was your day George?" Chris asked.

"Spent it on the Morris farm," George replied with a smile. "Had a great day, put my hand to a spot of farming."

"On a Sunday?" Cam asked.

"Farms do not stop working because of the Sabbath," George remarked. "However I don't think I will make a farmer, although some parts of it is interesting."

"Meaning the farmer's daughter no doubt," Chris replied. "Now Cam how was your day?" Chris asked.

"I carried out your instructions, I put the report on your desk," Cam replied.

Chris looked at his in-tray and saw the report. "I will read it later, just tell us what happened?"

Cam related his day to Chris and George.

"Did you ask him where he worked?" George asked after Cam had ended.

"Did not have to, I recognised him straight away," Cam replied. "Last winter our outside toilet busted, mum called a plumber, it was Mr Webb."

"I'm glad that you verified their alibi for Friday night," Chris remarked as once again he looked at Cam's report in his in-tray.

"As I said, the landlord of the Fox Inn did say they were both in there on Friday night, he could not say when they left, Friday Saturday and Sundays are busy nights for him, he employs extra staff on those nights, he do remember serving them earlier on, but that all he could say," Cam repeated his story.

"So it is an alibi, but not watertight," George remarked. "Jason the barrow boy is still with us," he smiled.

"When I finished in the Fox Inn, I went to see Jason, it was nearby, he confirmed that he delivered logs every fortnight to Miss Marston as a standing order."

Chris in deep thought nodded as the door opened and Sergeant Dawkins entered, seeing Chris he smiled.

"Did not see you come in," he said.

"Because you were not at your desk," Chris replied looking at him.

Sergeant Dawkins smiled. "I was in the filing room," he replied

"Really!" Chris replied wondering.

457

"Yes," replied sergeant Dawkins. "Speaking to Cam yesterday about the murder, he brought up the name of Mrs April Marshall, I thought the name was familiar, and last night before I fell asleep I remembered, her mother-in-law died a few months ago by falling down the stairs and breaking her neck," he said handing Chris the report he had found.

"Really!" Chris remarked taking the report. "Why were we not told, surely all accidental death come to us, we decide whether it was an accident or not."

A smirk came to Sergeant Dawkins face. "If you look at the date, you had other things on your mind," he said.

Chris looked at the date, the accident happened on the twenty third of April that year, he smiled to himself, he was on his honeymoon.

"I see what you mean Sergeant," he said with a smile as he looked at George.

"Were you informed, George?" he asked.

"I recall it now, I went there with the police Inspector," George explained. "It looked straightforward, the lady in her forties fell down the stairs, she lived alone, not found for two days. I did check the carpet which was a bit frayed on the landing, I tested her shoe in the tear of the carpet, I considered it fitted, and it was possible that it was an accident. Being two days old, according to Bob Harvey, without any other leads, no reason to believe it was anything other than a accident, the report was left in your tray."

"Was Mrs April Marshall interviewed?" Chris asked unable to remember reading the report.

"She was," sergeant Dawkins replied. "I did it myself, as she claimed the body, she told me she hardly seen her mother-in-law, and it had been a couple months since she had seen her, they did not get along. However with her husband just gone to France, she claimed the body and would take responsibility for her burial, she was cremated I believe," sergeant Dawkins added.

Chris who was reading the report as Sergeant Dawkins was talking, shook his head annoyed at the word cremation. "Was her son brought over for the funeral?" he asked.

"I have no idea," sergeant Dawkins replied.

"I wonder why she did not mention it when we saw her?" Chris asked looking at George.

"Perhaps she saw no need to," George commented. "Perhaps she never even thought of it."

"Still," Chris added as he put the report down. "All seems as you said, there is no reason to suspect foul play, were you satisfied George?" he asked.

"Bob Harvey said her broken neck was in line with a fall down the stairs, the carpet was torn where she could have caught her shoe, no issue came to light to make me feel otherwise," George replied.

Chris looked at Sergeant Dawkins, he smiled. "Thank you for your concern sergeant, I do appreciate it."

"No problem, uniforms are always on their toes," he smiled leaving the room.

"That man always seem to get the last dig in, even when he is being praised," Chris said to George grinning.

"Now George if I had been here," Chris continued. "My report would probably have been a copy of your own, but she is now involved again in a death, this time murder so we must do a little digging, are you OK with that?"

George nodded his head. "Let's go for it," he said.

Chris looked at Cam. "Some door knocking for you Cam," Chris said with a smile. "Mrs Marshall lived at six

Western Road, near the Red Deer pub, knock some doors around, find out what kind of woman she was, was she liked, did she make enemies that kind of stuff, ask in the Red Deer she might have liked a drink, but before you start that, you are to collect May and June Ewing, take them to the mortuary, they have to identify their mother, Bob is expecting you this morning, when you see Bob, ask him to give me a ring."

"Not Mr Ewing?" Cam asked.

"No, his daughters will not allow him," Chris smiled.

"I can do that," Cam replied getting up. "I get myself a bike," he said leaving the office.

"What is our next step?" George asked a smile on his face.

"We must find out where Mrs Ewing was living, it has to be some where?" Chris replied. "Nothing in her belonging with an address on, strange, a well known lady, no one know where she lives?"

"Leg work," George murmured. "She was well known in the pubs, perhaps that is the only way we will find out."

"If she had a house, perhaps the council would know, but then she could have rented privately, it means a lot of visits to do for you George, including pubs," Chris suggested. "However you could keep the pubs in the area of the town, if she went outside, I would suspect it was rare."

"Well the pubs are open, it's gone ten thirty, so I might as well start getting drunk now, what are you doing?" George asked.

"First I want to speak to Bob Harvey, then I will be seeing Mrs April Marshall again, then perhaps the Ewing girls."

"Do you suspect them?" George asked.

"They might know something which they have not told us," Chris answered.

Chapter Seven

With the office cleared, Chris put his glasses on and studied the two reports, one regarding the death of Mrs Marshall, and the other report that Cam had written regarding his interview with Mr Webb and Miss Marston. It was always a habit with Chris to read reports over and over, until he could almost recite every word from memory. Chris took off his glasses and placed them on the desk as the telephone rang, he lifted the receiver.

"Hello Chris," came the voice. "Bob Harvey here, you wanted me to phone."

Chris smiled to himself. "Hello Bob," he replied. "I take it the body has been identified."

"Yes, no problem there, the deceased is who it was thought to be, the young women are still here, they are having a cup of tea," Bob replied. "Strange girls however they showed no grief."

"When I interviewed them I got the impression they hated their mother," Chris informed Bob. "Still as long as we are sure who the dead person is, we can get on."

"Anything else?" Bob asked.

"Yes there is Bob, I want you to test your memory," Chris answered.

"Fire away then," Bob replied in a calm voice. "My memory is pretty good."

"Can you remember back to my wedding?" Chris asked.

Bob chuckled. "It's one day I shall never forget Chris, what do you want to know?"

"Can you remember while I was on my honeymoon, a Mrs Marshall living at Western Road dying by accident, my reports tells me she fell down the stairs, and broke her neck."

A few seconds later, Bob answered. "Yes I remember," he replied.

"What was your impression?" Chris asked.

"She simply tripped and fell down the stairs, her injuries were in line with such a fall."

"No foul play suspected then?" Chris asked.

"As I remember your sergeant and the police Inspector was there, they tested the carpet, which ran down the middle of the stairs, they found the carpet torn at the landing and assumed that she had caught her shoe in the tare, making her lose her balance, I personally agreed with them, of course," Bob continued. "She could have been pushed, but no one was in the house, nor had anyone been seen entering or leaving, don't forget those houses are high with a half dozen steps to mount to reach the front door, and anyone could be seen entering or leaving."

Chris thought on the words before answering. "Thank you Bob, who claimed the body?"

"Her daughter-in-law as far as I remember, there was no one else, her son was fighting the war in France."

"Did you meet the daughter-in-law?" Chris asked.

"I did," Bob replied. "Quite attractive, come to think about it I wonder why she did not show grief when she identified the body, children today are strange I must say."

"The daughter-in-law is the oldest sister of the two Ewing girls who are now having a cup of tea at your place," Chris informed him.

"Well it's a small world Chris, but now I realise why you are so curious about the death of Mrs Marshall," Bob replied.

"Two thing don't seem to sit right with me Bob," Chris continued. "First it took two days before she was found, she could have come down those stairs during the darkness, secondly, I do not see why she was cremated, surely a grave would have been more in keeping, so that her son could pay his respects when he returned from France."

Bob thought for a while before answering. "My opinion for her falling down the stairs is it was an accident, however I have to agree with you that cremation is not used a lot, but the ashes could be buried or thrown over a special place, or kept in an urn on the mantel piece, have you considered that?"

"I will do after I find out where the ashes are," Chris replied. "Anyway Bob thanks a lot, call in any time for a cuppa."

"I will," promised Bob as he replaced the receiver.

Chris thought over what Bob had said, Bob had experience in murder, he had dealt with a lot of it, being a police surgeon who also carried out autopsies, plus being a coroner. He was incline to believe Bob's own opinion, but the two days and cremation still bothered him. Chris decided to take a bike and cycle to where the body was found.

Quarter hour later, Chris was in Gardenia Road, on reaching the bridge, he dismounted, placed his bike against the bridge, and without removing his cycle clips, walked down to the river edge to the right of the bridge, where he had first seen the body.

"Mr Ewing what are you doing here?" Chris remarked with surprise in his voice, seeing Mr Ewing bent on knees at the spot. "I never expected to see you here."

Mr Ewing stood up, there was sadness in his face. "I often walk along here," he explained. "I just wanted to see the spot where my wife was murdered."

"I can understand that," Chris replied. "I myself thought I would have another look around, I am on my way to see your daughters, they identified your wife this morning."

Mr Ewing nodded. "Yes your constable called for them, they should be home by now."

"The weather that night was beneficial to the killer," Chris explained. "The rain washed away any clues that might have been left, but a second look even not finding anything, is always worth it."

"I suppose," Mr Ewing replied.

"If you are going home, I can walk along with you," Chris offered.

Mr Ewing shook his head. "No, not yet, I want to stop a while."

"Mr Ewing, your daughter April, I understand that she lost her mother-in-law six months ago in an accident."

Mr Ewing looked at Chris. "April has had a hard time, her husband sent to France, her mother-in-law fell down the stairs killing herself, now her own mother has been murdered."

"Yes it must be hard on her," Chris admitted. "Did she get on with her mother-in-law?"

Mr Ewing Shrugged. "Mothers of sons never look upon a daughters-in-law with favour do they?" he said.

"You must have met her Mr Ewing, you must have both been at the wedding, did you get on with her?" Chris asked.

"I had very little to do with her, but to be honest I never took to her, perhaps because I could see her resentment to my daughter, she should have been proud to have had a daughter-in-law like my April," he added.

"Your daughter had her cremated I believe," Chris said.

"So I believe," Mr Ewing replied. "I had little to do with it."

"So you would not know where your daughter put the ashes?" Chris asked as he searched the ground with his eyes.

Mr Ewing shook his head. "I was not interested, felt sorry for the son however."

"As your son-in-law, did you get on with him?" Chris asked.

"He was alright, pleasant, I am sure he loved my daughter, but he was controlled by his mother, I would have stopped the marriage, but April was well over the age of consent."

"I can't see anything here," Chris remarked. "Are you sure you want to stay, I need to see your daughters, to see how they got on this morning in the mortuary."

"No I will stay for a while, make sure my daughters make you a drink," Mr Ewing said with a forced smile. "They should know how to treat a guest."

"They do very well I assure you," Chris remarked as he left to get his bicycle.

Ten minutes later having parked his bicycle and taken off his cycle clips, Chris knocked the door of number 29, Bar End Road, June opened the door, and a smile crossed her face.

"Inspector Hardie," she said. "Please come in, we have not been back long."

Chris took off his trilby and entered the house. "Through here Inspector," he heard the voice of May. "Take off your coat first, or you will not get the benefit when you leave."

Chris smiled to himself as he did as requested, handing his coat and trilby to June who was waiting. Before entering the room May already had a chair pulled from the table for him.

"I have just been talking to your father," Chris said as he took the chair offered. "He knows I am calling on you."

"Where were you speaking to him?" May asked as she sat by June.

"Where your mother was killed," Chris replied. "He seemed very unhappy."

"He would be," June said looking at her sister.

"Just like him, he will spend hours down there now," May commented.

"Well how did you get on this morning?" Chris asked knowing what their answer would be.

"Mother was a beautiful woman," May answered. "She may have seemed gruesome when you saw her all wet and smashed up, but you should see her now."

"Washed and with her hair combed," June murmured.

"I am sure she was," Chris remarked. "You sisters get your looks from her, that should please you?"

Both sisters looked at each other and smiled. "As long as we do not have her ways," June remarked.

"Nor her desires," May agreed.

"Can I ask you both," Chris asked. "Why do you hate your mother so much?"

Both sisters looked at each other. "Oh, we don't hate her," June replied. "We just do not know her," she added. "She is a stranger to us, how can you hate a stranger?"

"But you were around twenty when your mother left, during your up bringing, she looked after you, fed you, clothed you, and did everything a mother is expected to do," Chris said in a calm voice.

"I do not know what was happening while we were still young, in our kindergarten stage," June replied.

"It was father and April who looked after us, mother was always out, coming home while we were in bed," May remarked. "April had an old head on her before she was twelve, she was like a mother to us," May added.

Chris had no answer to their remarks, he had not known the family long, and had no opinion. "I have to see April again, I told your father, it has come to our notice that her mother-in-law Mrs Marshall died by falling down the stairs some six moths ago, I suppose you have already seen your sister?"

"The day you called," May said.

"But you had already been to April," June added.

"This is a murder investigation, everything is going to be investigated, we'll leave no stone unturned whether good or bad," Chris replied.

"Everyone's a suspect?" June asked.

"That means all our family," May remarked.

"Until we find the right person, or persons," Chris replied.

"Why are you interested in Mrs Marshall, she was a nasty person," June asked. "Her death was an accident," June continued.

"She has gone to hell, she was burned," May added with a serious face. "Where she should be."

"Where her ashes were thrown?" Chris asked.

The sisters looked at each other, June turned to Chris. "April told us to tell you the truth what ever you asked, and we have been totally honest with you, holding nothing back," June answered.

"I am sure you have, your attitude tells me that, it was good advice that April gave you," Chris remarked.

"We were both with April when she threw the ashes over the bridge in Gardenia Road, just where mother was said to have been found," May continued.

"We knew she hated the place," June confirmed.

"Was your father present?" Chris asked, still shocked at their obvious but honest hate.

"We informed him," June replied. "Father had no liking for Mrs Marshall."

"He hated her?" Chris suggested.

The sisters laughed. "Father is too gentle to have hatred in him, he may dislike," May said with a slight smile. "But never hate," she added.

"So you sisters do not get the hate you feel for certain people from your father?" Chris remarked.

"Unfortunately we do get that from mother, we could see her hatred plainly in her eyes," June answered.

"Especially when father scolded her for always being out, getting drunk, and being a bad wife, but he still loved her," May added.

"What do you both do for fun, I mean do you go dancing, cinema?" Chris asked changing the subject.

"Father is very protective of us, with all the soldiers in town," June replied.

"I can understand your father being protective of you both, you are both very attractive girl," Chris praised them. "He is naturally worried."

"Mother would not care," June remarked.

"April would though" May added. "Mother would have encouraged us to go out with men."

"But you must have friends that you go out with, you are not nuns?" Chris remarked being interested. "Don't you know or have a boyfriend?"

June laughed. "We have friends, father don't mind as long as we are with other people that he knows, but we are way past twenty, father's trouble is that he trusts us, but not the men, he tells us he knows about men as he is one himself."

"I often wonder what he meant by that," May grinned.

Chris stood up, he did not think he would get much more from the sisters, he knew they were being honest, but in a way he was not getting the straight answers.

"Thank you for talking to me," Chris said. "Please give my regards to your father, oh just one more question," he smiled stopping in the hallway. "When April got married, was your mother invited?"

"Yes," June replied. "But not by our family, April's mother-in-law invited her."

"Mother brought shame to this family," May added who had also followed him to the hall.

"So your mother knew Mrs Marshall?" Chris asked.

"Became friends as well," June added taking Chris's coat and trilby from the hall pegs for him.

"When you see father again, please do not tell him we were bad host not offering you a drink," May smiled at him.

"We were so interested in our conversation that we forgot, but father likes us to be polite," June added as she opened the front door.

Chapter Eight

*C*hris cycled back to the Police Station, his conversation with the sisters is going over and over in his mind, he believe that the sisters were honest, but he wondered to himself did he get straightforward answers. He smiled to himself as he dismounted at Abbey Passage to put his bike away. Having done so, he patted his overcoat pocket, he felt the sandwich that Elizabeth had put there, he felt hungry.

Sergeant Dawkins smiled as he entered the station. "I was beginning to feel like a hermit," he said watching Chris discard his overcoat and trilby.

"No one else in?" Chris asked ignoring his remark.

"Been empty all morning," sergeant Dawkins replied.

"I have been busy all morning," Chris replied. "Would there be a chance of a tea?" he asked.

"I'll bring you one in," sergeant Dawkins replied. "It will take a little boredom away."

Chris smiled as he entered his office where he hung his coat and trilby, taking out his sandwich before sitting at his desk. He saw a large envelope in his in-tray, and recognised it as one from Bob the Police Surgeon. "Must be the autopsy report," he thought to himself as he picked it up.

Sergeant Dawkins knocked and entered the office. "Had one already made," he said placing the cup of tea before

Chris. "That came half an hour ago," he remarked seeing Chris holding the envelope.

"Autopsy report I expect," Chris informed him taking out his spectacles and putting them on. "Thank you for the tea," Chris said as the sergeant left with a smile on his face.

Chris read the report while he was eating, he read it twice before laying it on his desk, there was not a lot to go on.

The cause of death was a blow at the back of the head by a heavy object, as an axe was found under the body, the axe was presumed to be the weapon. Mrs Ewing had been killed between the hours of seven and eight pm last Friday night. Bob could not say whether she was killed where she was found, or if she had been killed elsewhere. Chris looked at her blood group, it was a common group of "O Rh positive." There was little else that could help Chris, apart from the daughters having identified their mother.

Chris gathered up the empty sandwich wrappings and threw them in the waste bin, and drank the remainder of his tea as Cam entered the office.

"Hello Chris," Cam greeted as he hung his overcoat before sitting at his desk. "George not in yet?"

"I have only been back a half hour myself," Chris replied picking up the autopsy report. "I have had Bob's report, nothing that can help us I am afraid, anyway how did you get on?"

"I had two conflicting opinions," Cam replied taking out his notebook and opening it. "I called on the houses around where she lived, most people said she was unfriendly and disliked, but it do seem she kept to herself, no one could remember seeing anyone entering or leaving her house around the time of her accident."

"No joy there then," Chris interrupted. "What was the other opinion?" he asked.

"Talking to people, the time seem to rush by, so after I had called on all the houses around the area, I thought I would pop into the Red Deer on the corner Western Road and have a sandwich before coming back."

"Glad you did," Chris smiled.

"I was the only one in the bar, I had a pint and a cheese sandwich. The landlord who was getting on in years was pleasant enough, he started to speak to me as I ate, and eventually I told him I was with the police, he did not seem to mind," Cam smiled. "Anyway one thing led to another, and Mrs Marshall's accident was mentioned so I asked him if he knew her, and he told me that he knew her very well."

Chris sat interested as he watched Cam flick a couple pages of his notebook.

"Anyway," Cam continued. "The landlord eventually told me she was one for the men, but she was not obvious, she did not flirt or leave with a man while in the pub, she would sit at a table by herself, if a man fancied her he would naturally go and talk to her, offer her a drink, after all he said, she was a very attractive woman. So I asked him if she was a whore, he replied that she hardly was a prostitute, don't forget her son was married, she had no income, she had to get money from somewhere."

"The landlord said she was quite frank with him, she once told him that without money she could starve, and be thrown out on the streets, why should she allow that to happen when she was sitting on a gold mine that could produce the money she needed."

"That means that Mrs Ewing and Mrs Marshall was in the same line of work," Chris remarked. "Perhaps there is a connection there."

472

"I did say to the landlord, that his opinion was way out according to the people living close to her, he told me it was all an act, she was a pleasant woman, he don't think she was unfriendly, it's just that she did not want neighbours getting too friendly with her, they would never see any man entering or leaving her house as she took them, she usually took them when it was dark, and usually late at night."

Chris thought on what Cam had told him. "Did you ask about the husband?" Chris asked.

"I did," Cam replied. "The landlord said he had been the landlord for over eight years and have always known her as a widow, she had never spoke to him about her husband, he assumed he died before he came."

"Any special man?" Chris asked.

"The landlord said that she was not in there every night, there were several pubs within a short walk, but as he said, she never left with a man, perhaps meeting outside."

"Well Cam you did fine work," Chris praised. "You have a full report to get on with now," Chris smiled.

George entered the office some half hour later, he was all smiles as he hung his overcoat, and greeted Chris and Cam who just sat and looked at him.

"Any success about Mrs Ewing?" Chris asked with a broad smile on his face.

"I would say," George replied. "I have been to every pub from where your Elizabeth works to the bottom of the town."

"Now tell us about your success," Chris asked.

"Mrs Ewing was well known in most of the pubs, the landlords seemed did not discourage her from going in, as she did according to some landlords bring in a bit of trade, men looking for a woman you know," George said with a grin. "However no landlord could pick any man that was special, she went with anyone. I do know who she was living with before she was killed," George remarked getting out his notebook. "Mr Toby Woods lives at 9, Symonds Street Winchester."

"Well that is cleared up," Chris replied. "You will have to call on him, perhaps tomorrow," Chris smiled.

"That's quite away from where she was found," Cam remarked.

Bob Harvey could not be certain if she was killed where she was found," Chris replied.

"You have had the autopsy report then?" George asked.

"It was here when I got back from seeing the Ewing sisters, nothing in it apart what we already knew," Chris said handing George the autopsy report.

"If she was killed elsewhere, she would have been transported," Cam said.

"Wheelbarrow or hand cart comes to mind," George remarked having read the autopsy report handed it back to Chris.

"Wheelbarrows and hand carts are seen every where, no one takes any notice of them," Chris said. "Also many of their wares are covered while moving, nothing unusual there, I have always considered that she was found where she was because of an appointment, but had she not, then I would say a wheel barrow, it is not so clumsy as a hand cart."

Chapter Nine

*C*hris stared at the ceiling as he laid in bed, Elizabeth who was resting her head on his arm and snuggled up close to him, was snoring gently, he smiled, her gentle snoring never did distract him or kept him awake, and in one way he was glad that he could hear her breathing. It was late, the only light in the room came through the partially opened blinds from the streetlights outside.

He heard the faint ring of the phone that was downstairs in the front room, he turned his head towards Elizabeth, and in order not to disturb her, he gently eased his arm from her, and was pleased that she had not awaken as her head touched the pillow. He got out of bed, and he immediately felt the biting cold of the room, he shivered with cold in his thin cotton shirt, he made his way out of the room and downstairs where he lifted the receiver.

"Inspector Hardie," he spoke onto the receiver.

"Inspector, sergeant Williams here, I thought I had better phone you, the body of a woman has been found in the Holy Trinity Church grounds," came the reply.

"Who found her?" Chris asked. "At this time of night?"

"A tramp looking for a place to sleep," sergeant Williams replied.

"Where is he now?" Chris asked.

"Having a decent sleep, I have put him in a cell for the night," sergeant Williams replied.

"Good man," Chris remarked. "I shall want to see him before he is released, now contact Sergeant House, and the Police Surgeon Bob Harvey," Chris instructed.

"All taken care of, Sergeant Bloom is there with a constable, they called at Sergeant House's lodgings on the way," sergeant Williams informed him.

"I have to put some clothes on, I go straight there, thank you sergeant," Chris said putting the phone down.

Chris went into the scullery, and washed his face under the tap, before going back into the bedroom to collect his clothes that were laying tidy on a chair, quietly he picked them up, took another look at Elizabeth who seemed to be soundly asleep, and crept out onto the landing, where he dressed himself. Having done so, he went back into the front room, scribbled a note for Elizabeth and left it by the phone, before quietly letting himself out of the house.

Having checked his pocket watch, Chris knew it was almost midnight, the streets were dark and empty, he pulled his overcoat collar up around his face, with the aid of his torch he hurried down Blue Ball Hill, into Water Lane, he crossed the river into Union Street walking towards North Walls. He knew that to the entry of the Church there was two gates, one in Upper Brook Street, and one in Middle Brook Street, he looked along the Brooks, and saw the beam of a torch playing on the ground, which decided the entrance he would take. The torch flashed into his face as Chris approached the entrance.

"Inspector," spoke the constable who lowered his torch. "Sergeant House asked me to stay here until you arrived, I will take you to the body, it's the other side of the church near to the North Walls."

"Thank you constable," Chris replied.

With both the constable and Chris playing their torches, they arrived at the body, where several torches was moving over the ground. George hearing footsteps turned towards them, and eventually recognised Chris.

"Inspector," he greeted. "Not the warmest of nights."

"Damn cold if anything," Chris replied. "What have we got?"

"A young woman, I would say in her forties," George replied playing his torch beam towards the body.

Chris recognised Bob Harvey bending over the body. "Bob is pleased no doubt," Chris remarked.

"He has just arrived," George replied. "I was knocked up by sergeant Bloom over there," George pointed his torch to the sergeant holding his torch for the benefit of Bob.

"No one is ever happy being called out this time of night, it do not happen a lot," Chris replied a smile on his face.

"The tramp who found her, was shivering, I sent him back to the station with the constable, he can be questioned later when we are able to see him clearly," George informed.

"Do we know who she is?" Chris asked accepting George's action.

"I found her handbag, she is Linda Marston, 32, Parchment Street, it must be the same person that Cam interviewed on Sunday," George remarked.

"Really," Chris murmured. "After I spoken to Bob, we will call on Mr Webb who lodges there, can't do much here tonight, cordon it off, we will go over the ground in the morning."

"Hello Chris," Bob said as he stood seeing Chris approach him. "Not the best of nights."

"Cold but dry," Chris replied. "Not like our last one."

"That's for sure," Bob agreed. "But this one was killed in the same way."

"Really Bob?" there was a surprised, puzzled look on Chris's face. "Axe murder you mean?"

"The back of the head has been smashed, killed by a single blow I would suspect, just like Mrs Ewing," Bob remarked. "I will know more when I have her in the light, the wagon should be here any time, do you want to look at her?"

Chris shook his head. "George would have done all that," Chris replied confidently. "No axe found?"

Bob shook his head. "Not as far as I know."

"This darkness beats us, we will have to wait until morning to give the grounds a good search," Chris suggested. "I better have a talk to Sergeant Bloom, still be thankful for small mercies, we do know who the victim is, we have her handbag," Chris said moving off.

"Not a nice night to be out Sergeant," Chris said as he torched his way to where the sergeant stood talking to the constable.

"Not for you Sir," sergeant Bloom replied respectfully. "I am on night duty."

"There is no path this side of the church Sergeant," Chris remarked.

"Not many people come this side," the constable interrupted. "The main path to the entrance of the church is from Upper Brook Street, the path however narrows and stretches along the other side of the church pass the vestry door, and out of the gate at Middle Brook Street."

"You know this church Constable?" Chris asked.

"I was a choir boy here Sir" replied the constable. "It is a high Church."

"Being a high Church, brought you more pay then lad?" sergeant Bloom smiled looking at the young constable.

"Shilling a quarter," the constable replied. "Sometimes I did get three pence extra when I carried the cross at christenings and the child's father would give us extra few coppers."

"You must have been rolling in money then," sergeant Bloom teased.

"Couple bars of chocolate and a ticket at a magic lantern shows," replied the constable.

"So you say this side of the church is not usually used?" Chris asked smiling at the banter.

"Only tombstones this side, not even a path," replied the constable.

"Could she have been with a man this side?" sergeant Bloom asked.

"Both gates are locked after the last service," the constable interrupted. "They would have climbed over the surrounding wall to get into the grounds."

"What time would the last service be then constable?" Chris asked.

"Can't quite remember Sir," the constable replied. "This time of year I would say at least by eight."

"The tramp who found her must have climbed over the wall," sergeant Bloom remarked.

"He could have been here before the gates were closed," the constable offered. "He would not have been seen on this side of the church."

"Thank you constable," Chris said his mind going over what the constable had said. "Now Sergeant how do we keep this part of the ground secure until morning?"

"Your guess is as good as mine Sir," replied the sergeant. "I shall pass this way several times during the night, I can get the constables on the beat to keep an eye on the grounds as well, at first light in the morning I could have men here to search," he added.

"That would be fine Sergeant," Chris replied. "I can not see anyone trying to search the grounds for something in the cold, tell your men to bag anything they find, but to be honest, after what the constable said, had it not been for the tramp, she could have laid here for a long time."

Chris went back to where Bob was talking to George. "Could she have been moved Bob?" Chris asked.

"Possible Chris," Bob answered.

"Any idea how long she has been dead?" Chris asked.

"Not long, I would say four or five hours," Bob replied.

"Around seven or eight last evening then," Chris commented.

"I will know better later on," Bob replied. "What about the body, can I take her?"

"Yes Bob, George and I are going to her address now," Chris replied. "Sorry to have dragged you out."

"You were both dragged out as well," Bob smiled. "However I can put in for overtime," Bob smiled.

"Some people get all the luck," George grinned.

Chris and George walked to number 32, Parchment Street, just a few minutes away from the Church.

"According to Cam, Mr Roger Webb lives here as a lodger," Chris said to George as he knocked the door.

"He won't be happy at this time in the morning," George replied.

Chris knocked the door again.

"I'm coming, I'm coming," Mr Webb's complaining voice came from inside. "Hell of a time to call, what is it?" a voice asked as the door opened.

Chris and George automatically covered their eyes as the beam of a torch caught their faces.

"What the hell do you want at this time of morning, you woke me up?"

"I am detective Sergeant House, and this is Detective Inspector Hardie," George replied. "Would you please lower your torch."

"What do you expect," replied the man lowering his torch beam. "This unholy hour."

"Are you the owner of this house?"

"No, I only lodge here, Miss Marston rents the house."

"Then you are Mr Roger Webb, a constable visited you on Sunday," George said his voice firm.

"That is clever of you," Roger replied angrily. "What is it that you want?"

"Is Miss Marston in?" Chris asked in a gentler voice, noticing that in the light of the torches, Mr Webb was in stocking feet, wearing an overcoat covering his body.

"She will be in her bedroom, we don't sleep together if that is what you are referring, even if it's, not any of your business," Roger replied.

"I am sorry Mr Webb, please see if she is in her bedroom?" Chris asked.

Roger looked at them for a while, then shrugged. "Oh very well if it means I can get back to sleep," he said leaving the front door open an disappearing inside the house.

"That is an angry man," George remarked in the darkness.

Chris smiled, but did not comment knowing that he would also have been angry at this time of night.

A few moments later, Rodger returned. "She is not home yet, her bed has not been slept in, she must be out with someone."

"Would that be a natural occurrence?" George asked.

"How would I know," Roger said. "I am not her keeper, I just lodge here, sometimes she don't come home during the night."

"Mr Webb, if what we know to be true, I do not think Miss Marston will ever be coming home," Chris spoke as gently as he could.

"I don't know what you are talking about," Roger replied nervously. "Has something happened to her?" he looked so confused.

"Better let us in," George replied. "We cannot talk here on the doorstep."

"Better come in then," Roger agreed. "Let me light the gas, it seems I am not going to get any sleep, you have really woke me up."

A light at the end of the passage lit the hall way up. "Come to the kitchen," Roger offered. "It's still warm in there."

"Now what is all this about?" Roger asked as they were all sitting at the kitchen table. "What did you mean when you said Miss Marston would never be coming home?"

Deciding to come straight to the point, Chris looked at Mr Webb wondering just what his feelings for Miss Marston was. "We have found a body, we believe that it is Miss Marston," Chris said.

"Oh no," replied Mr Webb, the anger gone from his voice, his face soften. "How, where, why?" he mumbled. "Are you sure?"

"She will have to be identified, we are pretty sure however, we found her handbag, which brought us here," Chris answered.

Mr Webb looked at his hands that were spread on the table in front of him. "I don't understand, who would want to kill her, she was quite popular."

"That is why we are here Mr Webb," George answered. "Did she have any enemies that you were aware of?" he asked.

Mr Webb shook his head. "Can't think of any, the people in the street spoke behind her back, being a single woman with a single male lodger, but that was only petty stuff, Linda took no notice of that."

"What about men friends?" George asked.

"She had a few," Mr Webb replied. "But she was a single woman, entitled I would say."

"We are not here to judge her Mr Webb," Chris interrupted. "We just need to know all about her, in order to catch the person responsible for her death."

"Do you know what time she left the house last night or where she was going?" George asked.

"Yes she left about seven or just after, she was going to the Barley Corn in Middle Brook Street as far as she told me, where was she found?" Roger asked.

"In Holy Trinity Church grounds," Chris replied.

"Yes she would use the short cut by going through the church grounds," Mr Webb confirmed. "It cuts the corner off."

"Did she go to the Barley Corn a lot?" Chris asked.

"She liked it," Roger replied.

"So it could be known that the church grounds was the route she would take?" Chris asked.

"I knew," answered Mr Webb. "I suppose other did as well."

"You would not know who she was meeting?" Chris asked.

"She never said, but I would expect it to be a man," Mr Webb replied. "As I said she was very popular."

"Did you ever have a fling with Miss Marston?" George asked.

Mr Webb smiled. "Of course I did," he replied. "But it ended when she met someone else, she could not handle a

483

long time relationship, a bit like me really, but we always remained good friends, as you know I am now her lodger, we do go out and have a drink together occasionally."

"So I understand, you were out with her last Friday night when a Mrs Ewing another of the women you had been out with was murdered?" Chris remarked.

"Yes your constable came to see us about Mrs Ewing," Mr Webb agreed. "Very little we could tell him, my affair with her ended when she met Mr Ewing, a very long time ago."

"Mrs Ewing was known to have been a regular visitor to the pubs around Winchester, you must have seen her sometimes?" Chris asked.

"Of course I did," Roger replied a smile on his face. "I said hello to her, may have even bought her a drink, after all we were once close, no need to be enemies with a break up."

"Did you never marry Mr Webb?" George asked.

"Never felt the need, I was never short of women company," Roger replied.

George smiled. "We have all heard about plumbers Mr Webb."

"I am not sure that myth applies to me," Roger smiled. "But yes I do get to know a few women," he boasted.

"Did you know a Mrs Marshall of Western Road?" Chris asked, thinking that Mr Webb was a very vain man.

"Might have," Roger replied. "I know a lot, many without knowing their surname, why, has she been murdered as well?" he asked grinning.

"We are not aware she was," Chris remarked. "Have you done any work in Western Road, or have you ever been in the Red Deer?" Chris asked.

"I have to say yes to both those questions," Roger replied. I have been in the Red Deer while working in the area, but it is too far to go when I am not working."

"You cannot remember meeting a Mrs Marshall in the Red Deer then?" George asked.

Roger shook his head. "As I said I might have done, if I had, she could not have made an impression on me, or I should have remembered."

Chris looked at George who shook his head, then turning to Mr Webb. "Are there any one we can get in touch with regarding Miss Marston, we do need her to be identified."

"I am the one perhaps closest to her, I know of no family that she had," Roger replied.

"Then perhaps you would be kind enough to identify her body for us?" Chris asked.

"Of course I would, it is the least I can do," Roger replied.

Chris stood up, followed by George. "Thank you Mr Webb, I am sorry had to wake you up, but you now understand the reason, you will be available tomorrow sometime afternoon, when you can identify Miss Marston, a constable will call to take you."

Chris and George made for the front door, George stopped and turned back to Mr Webb. "One question Mr Webb, did you go out last night, after Miss Marston had left?"

"No," Roger replied grinning. "I had a skin full during the lunch hour, decided to give it a rest last evening, had an early night."

"He did not seem unduly upset after we first told him about Miss Marston," Chris said to George as they made their way down the North Walls with the aid of their torches.

"I agree," George replied. "He answered all the questions though."

"Yes he did, cannot fault him there, but he will remain a suspect for me, he is a vain man, vain men can lose their temper when rejected, as much as a vain woman," Chris voiced his opinion.

"He is a good looking man, even at his age," George replied. "I was wondering what he is going to do now, he is only a lodger in the house, he might be kicked out."

"He will have to find another woman who will have him," Chris smiled. "After all he seems to know only one type of women."

They were walking pass the wall surrounding the Holy Trinity Church, Chris stopped and looked over, all was in darkness. "No one around, the body has obviously been taken," he remarked as they continued to Middle Brook Street junction.

"I'll leave you here George, you can get a couple hours sleep, don't come to the station tomorrow morning, go straight to Symonds Street and see this Mr Toby Woods, I have a tramp to interview," Chris ventured his opinion.

Chris walked home without hurry, his mind was going over the many questions and answers regarding the interview with Mr Roger Webb, his mind was not satisfied. He reached his house without really realising, and saw the light burning in the front room, Elizabeth must have woken up and found him missing, he thought, as he hurried up the front path, but the door opened before he had reached it.

A worried looking Elizabeth wearing just her dressing gown, flung herself at him in a hug. "I woke up and you were not there, I went downstairs and could not find you, I was worried sick, I was about to go to mothers when I saw your note by the telephone, oh, darling I was so worried," she sobbed with tears in her eyes.

Chris pulled away from her. "Come inside, you will catch cold," he smiled in the darkness. "I heard the phone go, you were sleeping soundly," Chris remarked as holding her waist they entered the dining room. "I did not want to wake you, I had a call out, an another woman was found dead."

"I am silly darling," Elizabeth smiled, sniffing and wiping her eyes at the same time. "I was so worried, please next time wake me, at least I would not worry, was it bad for you tonight?" she asked.

"I never looked at the body, it was too dark, George and Bob Harvey was there," Chris said as he hugged her again, his love for her hurt, he was very touched by her concern for him.

"I promise to wake you next time darling," he said gently. "I am sorry you were upset, but it do not happen much."

Elizabeth pulled away from him, she dabbed her tear-stained face. "I have made tea," she said forcing a smile.

"I could murder a cup," Chris replied.

"Then we can get to bed, you need a few hours sleep," Elizabeth sniffed again.

Chapter Ten

At quarter to seven on the Tuesday morning, George knocked the door of 9, Symonds Street. However it was not known whether Mr Woods worked or where he worked, George wanted to call early to catch Mr Woods at his home. The door opened by a man, he was a big, bully type of man in overalls, he looked around forty, George thought.

"I hope you caught the worm," the man said with a grin on his face. "What do you want at this unearthly hour?" he asked.

George was taken back a little, this big bully type of man was quite pleasant, he expected a little aggression from him at this time in the morning.

"I know it's early," George replied. "I am just glad I did not wake you, are you Mr Toby Woods?" George asked.

The man nodded. "You have got it in one."

"I am Detective Sergeant House of Winchester CID, I would like to ask you a few questions regarding a Mrs Doreen Ewing."

"Oh her," Toby replied. "Well you better come in, I haven't got long, I'm getting ready for work, want a cuppa, I'm having one myself?" he offered.

"I have not had one yet," George replied as he followed Toby into his kitchen. "Would love one."

"Sit yourself down then," Toby offered as he poured the tea out for himself and George.

"Help yourself to milk and sugar," he said bring the two cups to the table. "Now how can I help?"

"Do you know Mrs Ewing?" George replied after taking a sip of his tea.

"You must be well aware that I do," Toby grinned. "Why else would you be here?"

"Then you know she was found dead?" George asked.

"I have heard," Toby replied. "I have not seen her for over a week now."

"We understand that she lived here," George remarked.

Toby grinned. "On and off, she used this house a stop gap, no doubt she had other houses she could use."

"I am not quite with you," George replied.

Toby grinned again as he took a sip of his tea. "When Doreen left her husband, she lived with many blokes all single with a place of their own like me, you see she had no income, and no permanent place of her own," Toby took a drink of his tea and continued.

"Doreen however cannot stop with a man for a long time, she would get the itch to move on, normally when she met someone new and when she got tired of him, she would either have someone new, or call back for a while to one of her old haunts, such as here, in the past two years she has been back here at least five time, stopping perhaps for a fortnight or so, then off she would go again without a word."

"During which time you kept her?" George asked.

"Yes she ate my food, and at nights when she went out on her own, I gave her a few coppers to buy herself a drink," Toby explained.

"Never knowing if she would return," George remarked.

"I didn't mind, look at me Sergeant," Toby requested. "I am not exactly the type women go, Doreen was a very attractive woman, but two weeks with her left a man two months getting back his strength, sex was a driving point in her she would wear any man out."

George drained his cup. "I have to ask you Mr Woods, where were you last Friday evening?"

"That is easy," Toby replied. "I was in the Brewery Bar in St Thomas's Street, from seven until closing time, you can ask, we had a friendly dart match going."

"Mrs Ewing had left your house before then?" George asked.

"Several days before," Toby replied. "Otherwise I would not have had the strength to throw a dart, but seriously, I am sorry she died, especially if she was murdered, the time will come when I shall wish she was here, desire only fades for a while," he grinned.

"You would not know who she left you for?" George asked.

"Not entirely sure," Toby remarked. "I did hear she was with John Newman, he lives in those last few houses near the Bell Inn in St Cross, I don't know the number."

"As far as you know Mr Woods, she used her sex to get a living, but would you know, did she have any enemies?" George asked.

"I wouldn't think so," Toby grinned. "We were all bees around her honey pot, I think most men she lived with was like me, grateful for the two or three weeks she stayed but glad when she left, with no hard feelings, a man should never marry a woman like her, he could never trust her, I would think that the men she lived with accepted that."

"Do you know a woman by the name of Linda Marston?" George asked.

"Most men who drinks know her," Toby replied. "She is Roger Webb's bit, he lodges with her, she has never fancied me however."

"What about Mrs Marshall, lives at Western Road by the Red Deer?" George asked.

Toby shook his head. "Can't say I have ever been in the Red Deer, too far to walk from here for a pint, can't say I know her," Toby answered.

"Did you go out last evening?" George asked.

"Went for a pint in the Foresters on my way home, then came home and had an early night," Toby explained.

"Where do you work Mr Woods?" George asked changing the subject.

"On the railway," Toby replied looking at the clock in the kitchen. "And I shall be sacked if I don't get a move on, anything else?"

"Thank you for your frankness Mr Woods, sorry I have delayed you, should I need to talk to you again, what time do you get home at nights?" George asked getting up from the table and moving to the front door.

"Always home by seven, sometimes earlier," Toby replied following George to the front door.

George opened the front door and stepped out. "By the way Mr Woods, do you remember who told you about Mrs Ewing's death?"

"Last night, Roger Webb told me, I met him outside the church in Parchment street on my way home, must have been around eight o'clock, he paid me back the two dollars he owed me."

"Did Mr Webb borrow money from you?" George asked surprised, knowing that Mr Webb has reasonable work as a plumber.

"He has for the last few months, never used to, but he always pays back, he carries a list of all his loans, pay you back when he sees you, then almost immediately borrows it back," Toby smiled.

"Strange way to carry on," George remarked.

"Gambles a lot, he often plays card games all night, I don't think he is very lucky," Toby offered.

"Well thank you again Mr Woods, I hope you are not late for work."

Elizabeth kissed Chris on the cheek outside the Police Station. "At least you had a few hours sleep darling," she remarked fussing with his overcoat. "Try and be early tonight, we will get an early night, I will drive you to sleep with my warmth," she said with a giggle.

"You did last night," Chris replied with a smile. "I will do my best."

Chris watched Elizabeth out of sight before entering the station.

"Morning Sergeant," he greeted the desk sergeant. "The tramp still here I hope."

"Eating his breakfast," remarked sergeant Dawkins. "Never seen a man eat so much, apart from that I had a job to wake him, he slept like a log."

"Probably his first good night sleep in a bed, and I would predict that tramps are always hungry, I'll see him in a short time," Chris added. "Sergeant Bloom is he back?"

"Not yet, he has a couple constables searching the grounds of the church," Sergeant Dawkins replied. "My rota is all to pieces."

"I am sure you will cope Sergeant," Chris praised with a smile as he made for his office.

Both George and Cam looked up and greeted Chris as he entered and hung his overcoat and trilby before sitting at his desk.

"George, I take it you have seen Mr Toby Woods?" Chris said with a smile on his face. "You get very little sleep?"

"Yes to the first question and yes to the second," George replied. "I had to see him early as he might go out to work."

"Then how did you get on this morning?" Chris asked.

George related his interview with Mr Woods. "He is a bully type of man, over weight, but very pleasant, he has a nice attitude," George remarked as he finished.

"If Mrs Ewing flirts from man to man, living with them for a couple of weeks before going with another, does she carry a suitcase with her?" Cam asked. "She would need a change of clothing now and again I'm sure."

"Now there is a thought," Chris remarked.

"Never thought of that myself," George admitted. "Cam is right, she is said to be attractive, she would naturally keep herself so, Mr Woods said that she would go out one night and not return, but she can't walk around week after week in the same clothes, she must carry a suitcase, but if that is the case, when she went out, the man she was living with would know she would not return if she took her suitcase with her."

"Unless she did have a room somewhere?" Chris remarked. "Don't forget the men she lived with worked all day, what she did or where she went while they were at work, they do not know."

"Anyway, I cannot see Mr Woods as the murderer," George remarked. "He said he did not know Mrs Marshall, but knew Linda Marston who he had never been with, he freely admitted his association with Mrs Ewing."

493

"Remember though George," Chris remarked. "According to you, Mr Woods admitted speaking to Mr Webb around eight last night, a stone throw from where Linda Marston was found dead, remember also Mr Webb told us he had an early night after Miss Marston left, now we know he was out around eight, Mr Woods and Mr Webb must be both suspects, Miss Marston was killed around that time."

Mr Woods works on the railway, would he have been working that late on a Monday night in the dark?" Cam asked.

"It was a last minute question," George replied. "I asked as I was leaving and he was in a hurry to get to work, he did say he had stopped for a drink on his way home, to be quite frank, I was more interested in Mr Webb's borrowing."

"A lot of people borrow the odd half crown," Cam remarked.

"I know," George replied. "But it seems that Mr Webb has only just started to borrow."

"We all make slight slip ups when we are interviewing, the mind has to flick from one question to another, often asking the same question in a different way, we all make them," Chris remarked. "It is debating like this when we see the slip ups we made, anyway I'll leave it with you George."

"This Mr John Newman," Cam said. "He lives very near where Mrs Ewing's body was found, just a short walk."

"I was also thinking of that, I will leave that to you Cam," Chris smiled as he looked at George. "Find out what you can about him, the Bell Inn is close, you are good getting information from pubs."

"Well let's see the tramp," Chris remarked. "Cam pop out and ask the sergeant to bring him in."

Chris looked at George when Cam left the office. "Don't be down hearted George, I have probably slip up more times than you have, you did get a lot from Mr Woods, even another name which we never had, I would never have thought about Mrs Ewing's clothes, and even had I, Mr Woods may not have considered it himself."

"I certainly did not," George admitted.

"It's only through mistakes that we learn," Chris added as Cam came in the office with the tramp.

Seated in the interview chair, Chris looked at the tramp with a smile.

"Did you sleep well?" Chris asked, looking at him.

He wore a heavy looking overcoat that seem too long for him, what he had on underneath Chris could not see or guess, his trilby had seen better days, and he badly needed a shave, but Chris thought he look a healthy sort of chap.

"Like a bomb," the tramp replied resting his shoulder strap clothe bag on his lap.

"You have eaten?" Chris asked.

"Filled up," replied the tramp.

"Then perhaps you will tell us your name?" Chris asked.

"Collins," answered the tramp. "Most people call me Yorky," he added.

"Really," Chris replied with a smile. "Why is that?"

"I come from York," replied the tramp.

Chris smiled to himself, sounds logical he thought. "Well Yorky, I am Detective Inspector Hardie, to your right is Detective Sergeant House, and behind you is Detective Constable Streeter, we have a few questions to ask you."

"You're not running me in are you Gov?" the tramp asked. "I behave myself, I haven't done anything wrong."

"Let's first see how you answer our questions," Chris replied. "But first if you come from York, a long way from here, what are you doing in Winchester?"

Yorky smiled. "I come here twice a year, I do the round trip, I've been doing it for years, that's why people call me Yorky, I follow the same route, people begin to know me as I pass by."

"So you walk from York to Winchester then back to York twice a year?" Chris asked.

"That's right," the tramp replied. "Been doing it for years," he repeated.

"You must wear out some shoes or boots," Cam remarked.

The tramp shifted in his seat so that he could see Cam. "I get a lot of clothes given me as I passed by the villages, I do odd jobs you know to get a few pence for a drink, but I am particular about my shoes, I buy them in the second hand shops, I like boots," he added.

"Don't you feel the cold sleeping out especially in the winter months?" George asked interested.

The tramp shifted his position again so that he could look at George. "I have always lived in the open with the stars as they say my roof, weather toughens the skin, in the winter I don't have wash so much, the dirt keeps a little cold out, and I have a newspaper under my shirt keeps me warm," the tramp remarked patting his stomach.

"You walk long ways in all kinds of weather, you sleep where you are able, your clothes takes a beaten, do you wear the same clothes all the time?" George asked.

Again the tramp smiled. "I do a lot of odd jobs as I pass, I am often given shirts, pullovers, trousers that are being thrown out, being thrown out they are old, but to me they are new, I know the clothes will last me for a while, then I throw them away, I never wash them."

"That is how you live then?" Chris asked.

"I do have a few suitcases of clothes dotted about on my route, farmers allow me to keep the suitcases in their barns, if I need a change as I pass, then I can do so, if I have been given more than I need, the spares go into the cases."

"You seem to have it all organised," Chris remarked.

"What about having a wash?" Cam asked. "How do you get on?"

The tramp shifted in his chair again. "I pass a number of streams and rivers that I am able to have a wash, in the summer however I have a bath once a week, most larger towns has a bath in one of their gents toilets, only cost one and half pence, you have one just near here," the tramp remarked thinking of the gents in the Abbey Grounds. "And very nice it is, but in the winter, I like to keep the clean dirt on me as I said it keeps a little cold out."

"You seem educated Yorky," Chris said with a smile. "You have been educated?"

"Oh yes," Yorky replied. "I was educated at a Catholic School, my parents deal with horses, they are well off, but I am the black sheep of the family, I wanted the open life, and I have it, but my family disowns me."

"Well Yorky, let's get back to last evening, you reported a crime in the Holy Trinity Church grounds, we thank you for that," Chris said pleasantly. "Were you intending to sleep in the grounds?"

"I always do," Yorky replied. "The church entrance porch is large, and have a built in bench each side of it, either one makes a decent bed, but I have to wait until the grounds are locked so I usually wait around the side facing North Walls, no one ever walks around there."

"The porch has locked gates as well," Cam said.

"I know," replied the tramp with a smile. "But they are low gates, I am able to climb over, the gates make me feel safe as well," he added.

"So it was while you were waiting for the church grounds to be locked that you found the body?" Chris asked.

"Not exactly," replied Yorky. "I was crouching down by the church wall waiting, it was pitch dark, when I heard movement, I saw the outline of two people walked by me about fifteen feet away, lucky they did not see me, I watched them keeping quiet, then suddenly one went down and the other knelt over the one that went down, I thought at first that it was a courting couple, but then I heard a slight groan, the one kneeling got up and ran back passed me, I waited for a while, then went over to the one on the ground, even in the darkness I could see it was a woman, she was not moving."

"Did you touch her?" Chris asked.

Yorky shook his head. "No way, being a tramp I would always be suspected, but I did want to report it, then thought about how I would sleep that night if I reported it, I would perhaps be better off if I just moved off without anyone knowing I was there, I am not an aggressive hard person, and my up bringing got the better of me, I came here and reported it."

"It paid off," Chris smiled. "You got a bed for the night followed by a good breakfast."

"I did," smiled Yorky. "But have I put myself in trouble?" he asked.

Chris ignored the question. "Is there anything that you can tell me about the two persons you saw, I mean was it a man and a woman, or two women?"

"I only saw the outline of their heads, I can't say, however they both seemed to be the same height, I'm sorry," Yorky replied.

"When are you going to start your journey back to York?" Chris asked.

"Not for a couple of days," Yorky replied. "I am going to see a friend at Catherine's Hill, and another one who stays around the meadows before going back."

"My problem is Yorky," Chris said. "I might need to speak to you again, but you have no address, you could stop in the cells, where you would have a bed and food, but I could only hold you as a vagrant for one night, but I have no wish to do that," Chris looked at George.

George shrugged his shoulders, he understood Chris, but letting the tramp go was not clever, he could be the murderer, and he had no address, he could disappear, it's a case of whether trust him or not.

Chris thought for a moment before making his mind about Yorky. "He did report the crime, he could have just slipped off without reporting it, no one would have been the wiser," Chris thought, and he knew he had to trust him.

"I am going to trust you Yorky," Chris eventually said. "I want you to stay in Winchester until I tell you, you can go, I am investigating a murder here, will you report each day to the station?"

"My time is my own," Yorky replied. "So I can stay as long as I like, I will report each day," he promised.

"Very well, you have not been under arrest, so you can walk straight out of here, I hope you meet your friends, once again thank you for being law abiding," Chris replied standing.

With the tramp gone, Chris looked at George and Cam.

"I could not keep him locked up," Chris said. "I had no idea what to do, however I felt I could trust him."

"He did tell us that the victim and the murderer was about the same height," George voiced.

499

"That is well keeping in mind," Chris replied. "It's the damn darkness that beats us."

"Had it been light, who ever it was might have seen him," Cam remarked.

"But seeing him might have saved Miss Linda Marston's life," Chris replied.

Sergeant Bloom entered with a knock, Chris smiled at him. "Sergeant, how did you get on?" he asked seeing the sergeant carrying a large brown bag.

"We searched from Middle Brooks end to the Upper Brooks before we found this," he said putting the bag in front of Chris.

Chris looked into the bag, then emptied it on his desk. "It's another axe murder," he remarked looking at George. "You better try your skill at finger printing George," he said.

Chris looked at Sergeant Bloom. "You have done well, thank you, you were on all last night," Chris added. "Put in for overtime, I will authorise it."

"Thank you Sir," sergeant Bloom replied with a grin. "It's getting on, the good lady will be wondering where I am, so if there is nothing else."

"No you get on, you need sleep," Chris replied.

Chris and Cam watched as George dusted the handle of the axe. "I hope who ever found it picked it up with care," George remarked as he carefully dusted the handle before blowing the dust off.

"Not a sign of a fingerprints on this," George remarked. "It is safe to handle now."

"Expected," Chris replied. "Now George let's look at your blackboard, what have we on it?"

George got up and stood before the board. "We have Mrs Ewing, and Miss Linda Marston now, both murdered by an axe."

"You have to put Mrs Marshall up there," Cam said looking straight at the board from where he sat.

"I know," George replied. "She is a relation to the Ewing, but I have put a question mark beside her name, anyway," George continued. "In the frame of suspects we have Mr Webb, who knew both women, and I believe had an affair with both woman, we have Mr Woods, who Mrs Ewing as far as we know was the last man she lived with. I have added a question mark by Mr Newman, who we know little about at the moment," George paused for a moment. "Because the location of each death is wide a part I am unable to draw a plan, as for motive," George continued looking at Chris. "There is no apparent one, accept that all three women were known to many men, to put it politely."

"Then we have a sex murderer," Cam voiced.

"Do you believe that as a motive George?" Chris asked smiling to himself at Cam's excitement.

"Not really, apart from Mrs Marshall everyone involved knew each other," George replied.

"Mrs Ewing and Mrs Marshall knew each other," Cam remarked.

"I'm incline to agree with you George," Chris said. "But in this case the motive seem to elude us, but I do not see these murders as sex murders, there has to be another reason?"

George returned to the front of his desk, picked up the axe and placed it in front of Chris before returning to his seat. "What is our next step?" George asked.

Chris looked at Cam. "After lunch break Cam, you call on Mr Webb, and take him to the morgue to identify Miss Marston, he will be waiting for you."

"But all three of us have seen her is that not enough?" Cam asked.

"In some cases," Chris admitted. "But it is better on the report if someone close to her identifies her."

"OK, " replied Cam not really liking the job. "Then what?"

"First when you take Mr Webb, try to find out what he was doing out around seven thirty last night, he told us he had an early night and did not go out, before you see him however, get yourself down to the Bell Inn and the White Horse, in St Cross, see if you can find out anything about Mr John Newman, he lives close by these two pubs, he probably would use them, George and I will call on him tonight, you might find out some thing beneficial for us."

Cam stood up to leave without comment.

"By the way Cam," Chris added with a smile. "Do you ever see that nurse, Mrs Margaret Bumstead I believe, the one you met in our last case?"

Cam looked at Chris, then a George, a slight colour appeared on his face. "I have had a drink with her," Cam replied. "In fact I shall be seeing her tonight."

"Babysitting?" George asked.

"No, we shall go for a drink, she has a friend who babysits for her," Cam replied.

"How is she anyway?" Chris asked. "Has she got over her Charlie?"

"Don't think she ever will," Cam replied. "She shudders every time to think about him, she feels bad about him babysitting her child while she was at work, she blames herself for putting her child in danger."

"I hope you understand how it would effect her Cam, please give her my regards, and tell her that she is now safe, he will never walk the streets again," Chris said sincerely as Cam left.

"It must be a constant worry to her," George said when Cam had left. "Sleeping without knowing it with a cannibal would make anyone shudder when they found out."

Chris nodded. "You were not meeting Rosemary tonight were you?" he asked.

George smiled. "No, not tonight."

"We are both off this coming Saturday, would you and Rosemary like to come over to our house and have dinner with us?" Chris asked.

"I did mention your offer to Rosemary, she was all for it, yes I think that will be alright," George confirmed.

"There is just one thing, my in-laws will also be there, Olive has demanded that she would cook," Chris remarked a slight smile on his face.

"I will bring a drink," George replied accepting the situation.

"Well I have a report to make out about last night, also the tramp report," Chris said changing the subject as he took his reading glasses from his top pocket. We will see Mr Newman about six, he should be home by then should he work, it will be a long walk, too dark for bicycles with their flickering lamps."

"I will take you by my bike," George offered. "My lights are good."

Chris nodded. "That might be best if you don't mind George," Chris replied. "For now, I want you to call on the Ewing sisters, tell them that their friend Miss Linda Marston had been found murdered, see what you get."

Chapter Eleven

*I*t was a chilly morning, but not bitterly cold, George pulled his overcoat collar up around his neck, as without hurrying he made his way to Bar End. Rosemary came to his mind as he walked. He smiled to himself as he thought of Chris and Elizabeth, Chris had met Elizabeth during a murder case, he had met Rosemary during a murder case, and now seemed that Cam was seeing Mrs Bumstead, who he had interview during a murder case. Strange he thought how things turn out in life. To George, Rosemary was the most beautiful girl he had ever seen, he knew he loved her, and Rosemary's continued association with him, led him to believe that she felt something towards him. However Rosemary was a farmer's daughter, he had met her when her only brother had been murdered. Both parents were getting on, and George knew that Mr Morris had wanted his son to take over from him, but the son was dead, only Rosemary remained to take over the farm.

George had been invited to the house many times since, and hints had been made that who ever married Rosemary would also have the farm. This had worried George, he was not a farmer, had no knowledge of it, and was never really interested in farming, he had always wanted to be a policeman. George came to a halt outside number 29, Bar End Road and knocked the door.

The door opened and two attractive women stood smiling at him.

"Sergeant House," June said. "Lovely to see you, come in."

"Let me take your coat, you will find the benefit when you leave," June added as George stepped inside.

"I'll put the kettle on," May said leaving June to hang the coat.

"Thank you," George said smiling. "You're both very welcoming."

"Father has always been strict on politeness and manors," June replied. "Come into the front room and make yourself at home, May will have the tea here soon."

George had just sat at the table when May entered with a tray, on which was three cups, tea pot covered with a cosy, and a plate of biscuits, she placed the tray on the table.

"I'll get the sugar and milk," May said leaving the room again.

"May is the bossy one," June smiled as she started to pour the tea.

"That is because you are the youngest," May remarked as she brought the sugar and milk to the table.

George thanked them for the tea, as he helped himself to sugar and milk. "It amazes me," George remarked as he stirred his tea. "Both you young women are very attractive, yet you have no boy friends?"

May and June smiled at each other as they both sat at the table with their tea.

"That is not exactly true," June replied.

"We do know quite a few," May added.

"Boys were always trying to sit with us when we were at a mix school," June said.

"Those boys are now young men, the same as us being young ladies," May remarked.

"Lots of them are now married," June laughed loudly. "I suppose we are left on the shelf."

"I am sure that is not true," George replied. "You will both eventually find the right man, and looking at you," George smiled. "I think those men will be very lucky."

May and June looked at each other and gave a giggle.

"How is your father?" George asked wanting to change the subject.

"Father is out walking, he don't stop in doors a lot," May replied. "He will be by the bridge at Gardenia Road," May added.

"He is still upset then?" George queried.

"We hope he will eventually get over her," May replied.

"Was it father you wanted to see?" June asked.

"Actually," George said having just drained his cup. "I wanted to tell you about your friend Miss Linda Marston, I am afraid it is not good news."

"Linda is not the one we would call a close friend," May replied.

"But we were friendly enough, what about her?" June asked.

"I am afraid she is dead," George replied.

May and June looked at each other, this time the smile had left their faces.

"I am sorry," June replied. "How sad."

"I feel upset," May murmured. "She was a lot older than us, but we have known her for many years, mother I think introduced her to us."

"How did she die?" June asked.

George hesitated. "I am telling you of her death because she died as your mother did."

"You mean she was murdered?" June asked a shock look on her face.

"Not with an axe?" May asked with the same shock look on her face.

"I am afraid so," George answered.

"I do not know what to say," June remarked.

"Nor me," May added. "Can we help you in any way?"

"You say your mother introduced you to her, did you know she lived with Mr Webb, although he is said to be just a lodger."

"Mother's ex," June remarked. "No, we did not know, do you suspect him?"

George shook is head. "We are just gathering facts, if we were to suspect him of killing Miss Marston, we would have to suspect him of killing your mother, both killings were exactly the same."

"Why would he kill mother?" June asked. "Their relationship has been over for years, I see no reason why he would want to?"

"Perhaps Mr Webb was seeing mother again, after all she left us two years ago," May ventured her opinion.

"No, your mother was not having an affair with Mr Webb, we know the last two men she was living with, did your mother have any close friends that you can recall?" George asked.

Both girls looked at each other shaking their heads. "If we knew, then we have forgotten," May replied.

"Wait a moment May," June voiced. "Mother was very close to Mrs Hanks daughter Sylvia, in Vale Road, and after Sylvia's death, mother kept in touch with her mother."

"The Sergeant wanted to know who mother was close to, Mrs Hanks is twenty odd years older than mother was," June argued.

"Do you know the number in Vale Road?" George asked interested.

Both girls shook their heads. "We never visited the house," May replied.

"Would you know a Mr Woods or a Mr Newman?" George asked.

Both girls shook their heads again. "Are they the last two lovers mother had?" May asked.

"It looks that way," George replied.

"We do not know them," June added.

"Even mother would not have known all her lovers, or had forgotten them," May added. "She was a disgrace bring shame on us."

George felt he would not learn much more. "I am sorry that your father was not here, please give him my regards when he comes back."

"We will," May replied as George stood.

"Are we allowed to tell him why you called?" June asked.

"Of course," George replied.

"April as well?" May asked. "She will be interested."

"Would April have known Miss Marston?" George asked still standing.

"Of course she was with us when mother introduced us, we always went out together," May replied.

George left May and June at the door, and as he walked towards the town, wondered just what he had learnt apart from Mrs Hanks, who he intended to call upon before going back to the station. Vale Road, was the first turning passed the Heart and Hand Public House. He walked along the road about a half way, then decided to knock a door and ask where Mrs Hanks lived, he was fortunate, Mrs Hanks lived at forty nine, just two door up on the opposite side from the door he had knocked on.

The door to forty nine was opened by a little old lady about five feet tall, her hump back was plain to see. Her white hair was thinning, her creased lined face broke into a toothless smile as she waited for George to speak.

"Good morning," George said. "I am looking for a Mrs Hanks."

"What can I do for you?" Mrs Hanks asked showing the gums of her mouth as she spoke.

"I am Detective Sergeant House from Winchester CID, I would like to ask you a few questions."

"At last, I have been expecting you, you better come in," Mrs Hanks offered allowing George to enter. "It has taken you long enough."

A little bewildered George followed Mrs Hanks into the kitchen, where she offered him a seat at the table.

"Well," she asked as she sat by him at the table. "Did you get the little beggars?"

"I'm sorry Mrs Hanks," George answered bewildered. "I am at loss here, I am here to ask you about Mrs Doreen Ewing who I believe you know."

"So you are not here about the children, I should have known it, the police do not care about us old people living alone," Mrs Hanks replied.

George looked at Mrs Hanks, in a way he felt sorry for her, she was obviously getting on.

"I am sure that is not right Mrs Hanks, what is your complaint?" George asked wanting to get on the right side of her. "Tell me, I will promise to do what I can to get it sorted."

"I can't go out, every time I do, kids follow me and call me hunch back, it upsets me, I have made several complaints to the police, at least three times but it don't stop, I am seventy six you know," Mrs Hanks informed George.

"You certainly keep your age well," George replied flattering.

Mrs Hanks touched the back of her thinning hair, and gave a toothless smile.

"We all love children," she continued. "But children can be very cruel, I know they consider it fun, but I am an old lady living on my own, I get frightened."

"I am sure you do Mrs Hanks, leave it with me, I will get on to it when I get back to the station," George assured her.

Mrs Hanks gave another toothless smile. "You seem a nice young man, I trust you," she answered. "Now what can I tell you about Doreen?"

"When did you last see Mrs Ewing?" Chris asked.

Mrs Hanks screwed her toothless mouth. "Perhaps about four or five days ago, she comes here every two or three days, I am expecting her at any time now, she don't as a rule leave it this long."

"She's a good friend then?" George asked.

"I suppose you could say that, I never like her ways, but she was good to my daughter, I will always be grateful to her," Mrs Hanks replied.

"What happened to your daughter?" George asked gently. "Did she become ill?"

George thought he saw a tear in Mrs Hanks eyes as she answered. Sylvia my daughter and Doreen were best friends as they say from school days, they were always together, Doreen spent more time here than she did at her own home, but I didn't like her ways with men, I feared she would lead Sylvia a stray. But Doreen turned out to be a true friend when my daughter got TB, and for the last five years of her life, Doreen was an angel to my Sylvia, when you consider she was married with three young daughters of her own."

"Your daughter died of TB then Mrs Hanks, I am sorry," George said gently.

Mrs Hanks forced a smile. "Time has passed," she said. "One learns to live with the grief, the memory is never lost."

"I am sure it is not," George replied. "What did you mean by her way with men?" George asked.

"She has a lust for men, my Sylvia tried to stop her, but she couldn't, then she became pregnant, and married soon after, she was lucky as most of these type of women are, she married a good man, not far from here, but the same lust eventually ruined that marriage."

"So Mrs Ewing calls on you several times a week Mrs Hanks, would you know where she might have lived between times?"

"No idea young man," Mrs Hanks replied. "It might be best if you asked her these questions."

"Oh I am sorry Mrs Hanks, I took it that you knew, Mrs Ewing was found dead last Saturday morning."

"Good lord," Mrs Hanks muttered clearly shocked. "What happened to her?"

"I am afraid she was murdered," George replied.

Mrs Hanks shook her head. "I have always said, I didn't like her ways with men, and she would end up badly, now what do I do?"

"In what way Mrs Hanks?" George asked.

"Well she rents a room from me, she hardly ever sleeps here, but she calls several times a week, changes her clothes and washes what she takes off, I know she is sleeping with men, but long ago I accepted that she would never change, the five shilling a week she pays for the room is a big help to me, now I won't get it."

George felt excited, he had not expected this. "Would you allow me to look at her room Mrs Hanks, it might give a clue to who may have murdered her," he asked.

Mrs Hanks stood as she nodded. "I will show you," she said leading the way to the stairs. "What am I supposed to do with her clothes?" she asked as they mounted the stairs. "She has quite a lot."

George did not comment as she opened a bedroom door. "This is her room," Mrs Hanks said as followed by George she entered.

It was a large size room with the usual furnishing, wardrobe, washstand, and bed. George thought it looked clean and tidy as he searched the room with his eyes, before moving to the wardrobe which he opened.

"She certainly had plenty of clothes," George remarked as he eyed the contents.

"She likes to dress, she was an attractive woman," Mrs Hanks replied.

George moved to the chest of drawers, and opened each drawer, gently moving articles of clothing as he did, he found nothing that interested him.

Watched by Mrs Hanks, George searched the room, eventually giving up, the room offered no help to his investigation.

"Mrs Hanks," George said when they were back in the kitchen. "Thank you for your cooperation, I have to ask you not to touch that room for a while, we may need to look over it again, the room must now be accepted as a police scene."

"You don't want me to enter it?" Mrs Hanks asked.

"Not for the time being," George replied. "In the meantime I will see about the complaints you have made."

George left Mrs Hanks, he was happy with his morning work, but a bit disappointed the bedroom did not yield anything valuable to the case.

Chapter Twelve

It was almost midday when George entered the Police Station. He spoke to Sergeant Dawkins on his way to his office about Mrs Hanks complaint.

"The trouble is, Mrs Hanks do not know the children, she can't name them, and our beat bobby is never around when it happens, the beat bobby has been told to keep his eyes open, we have not ignored her complaint, but it is difficult," sergeant Dawkins explained.

"Well do your best, we are trying to keep Mrs Hanks sweet, she rented a room to our first victim Mrs Ewing," George said.

"I'll have a word with the beat bobby again," sergeant Dawkins assured George.

Chris who was writing as George entered the office. "You have had a good morning," Chris remarked.

"How can you tell?" George asked as he hung his overcoat, and went to his desk.

"There is a smirk on your face," Chris replied with a smile.

"I suppose in a way I did," George answered, then related his morning works, through which Chris did not interrupt.

Chris leaned back in his chair as George finished. "You have done well George," he praised. "Cleared a couple points up, one we know now where she changed her clothes, was your search complete?"

"As good as I could do with Mrs Hanks watching, I was wondering whether we could send Cam down there, he seems to be luckier than me at finding things."

"And me," Chris agreed. "Get him on to it, what interest me is what Mrs Hanks said about girls who get pregnant then marry, I am wondering did she mean these girls marry a man who did not know that their would be bride was pregnant?"

"There is a thought," George remarked. "It could mean that many men marry and bring up their first child without knowing that they are not the father."

"I know it's far fetched, and we have no reason to think it, but could Mrs Ewing have been pregnant when she married Mr Ewing?" Chris asked.

"Knowing what Mrs Ewing was like, I would say that she and Mr Ewing had sex before they married," George replied.

"I agree," Chris replied. "But she could have already been pregnant, don't forget she left Mr Webb to marry Mr Ewing."

"If true, that would mean that Mrs April Marshall was illegitimate," George replied.

"Silly idea really," Chris replied putting the question to the back of his mind. "I did phone Bob while you were out, Miss Marston was five foot, five inches tall."

"Do that help us?" George asked.

"Well Yorky said he was crouched down by the church wall looking at Miss Marston and who ever killed her," Chris answered. "He said both looked about the same height, I am incline to think that out killer is about five foot, eight inches tall, and no more."

"So we reject anyone in the frame over five foot, eight inches?" George asked.

Chris grinned. "I only said I am incline to think," Chris said. "But we will eventually know."

"Have you any idea who the killer might be?" George asked.

"I have one idea, but for the life of me, I cannot find any reason, we need to find the motive, what about you George any idea?"

George thought for a while, then shook his head. "The only motive I can see at the moment would be hate, all the Ewing sisters hated their mother."

"I agree George, but did they hate Miss Marston?" Chris asked.

George shrugged his shoulders. "They do not give that impression," he answered.

Chris checked his watch. "It's now just gone one George, tonight we go and see Mr John Newman, I have already phoned Elizabeth telling her I shall be late, have you had any lunch?"

George shook his head.

"I have had the sandwiches that Elizabeth put in my pocket, perhaps you better go and have some lunch," Chris suggested.

George smiled as he rose, crossed to the hat stand, where he put on his overcoat. "I'll pop across the road to the Crown and Anchor," George said. "You will know where I am," he said leaving the office.

Left alone, Chris thought on all what George had told him, he thought of the Ewing sisters, they all hated their mother, they could have done it, after all May and June alibi was their oldest sister, but they lived only a short distance from where their mother was found, they were young and strong. April on the other hand hated her mother-in-law as well who was also found dead at the bottom of her stairs, and said to be an accident. However with the death of Miss Marston, he could find no reason why they would have killed her, she might not have been a friend of the Ewing sisters, perhaps because of the age gap, but she was an acquaintance, and not hated by them.

Chris thoughts were interrupted as Cam entered the office. Chris watched without comment as Cam hung his overcoat on the hat stand.

"Cold out there," Cam said rubbing his hands, making his way to his desk. "Chilly riding a bike."

Chris grinned. "It's getting colder, summer is definitely over, anyway how did you get on?" he asked.

"I called at the White Horse first," Cam replied. "I did not learn a lot, but the landlord was quite friendly. The landlord told me that Mr Newman sometimes call in to his pub, mainly around nine at night as he makes his way home from the town pubs, he is friendly, causes no trouble, gets on with everyone, normally spend half hour or three quarters there, then moves to the Bell Inn, near where he lives. So I then went to the Bell Inn, being the last pub going out of Winchester on that road, it was empty, so I was able to talk to the landlord without interruption." Cam paused looking at his hands that were spread on the desk in front of him.

"Mr John Newman is a thatcher, and it seems he is a skilled and fully-trained roofer, most of his work in the villages surrounding Winchester, he keeps a horse and buggy in the grounds of the Bell Inn where there is a small stable. It seems that he uses this as his transport going and coming from work, apart from that, I got the same character for him as I got at the White Horse, friendly, causes no trouble, gets on with everyone like these things."

"That is not too bad Cam," Chris praised. "After all Mr Newman has a horse and buggy, easily can be used as transport, and he lives very close to where Mrs Ewing was found."

"I did ask both the landlords about last Friday and Sunday night," Cam continued. "Both seem to remember him on both nights."

"So they might," Chris replied. "But remember, Mr Newman only called at these pubs while making his way home from town around nine at night, Miss Marston we know was killed around eight Monday night, being in one of these pubs around nine at night, is no alibi for where he was earlier."

"I suppose not," Cam agreed.

"Mr Newman as far as we know was the last man Mrs Ewing lived with, now we are not sure whether she was killed where she was found, or was transported there, but we do know she was dead before his time in any of these pubs."

"Do you suspect him?" Cam asked.

"I will be seeing him tonight," Chris replied. "A case could be made against him, but without a motive," Chris shrugged.

"George back yet?" Cam asked.

"Yes gone for a lunch, he found out a lot," Chris added before relating what George had told him."

"I don't know how valuable they are, but little bits are beginning to fit," Cam remarked.

"Half of what we know will eventually be thrown out Cam," Chris explained. "But until they are we must check and double check each bit, that's why now I want you to go to Vale Road, you know the area, you were once the Beat Bobby."

"You want me to check the room Mrs Ewing has rented?" Cam asked with a grin.

"That is right Cam, George has already checked it, but we both think you do a better job than we do at searching," Chris smiled as he flattered.

"I'll get straight on to it then," Cam smiled as he rose, secretly hoping he would find something. "I will take my time, and may not be back tonight."

"I don't want you to rush Cam," Chris spoke up. "Should you find anything however, George and myself will be here until six, but before you rush off, how did you get on with Mr Webb?"

"Sorry that completely left my mind," Cam replied seating himself a slight embarrassed smile on his face.

"He had taken Mr Webb to the morgue to identify Miss Marston, which he had, he seemed genuinely upset with tears in his eyes," Cam explained.

"At least she has been identified," Chris replied. "It's no easy job is it?"

"No I am not fond of the duty," Cam replied.

"Not many of us are Cam," Chris replied. "Anyway off you go and see Mrs Hanks."

"I have sent Cam to search Mrs Ewing's room," Chris said to George as he entered the office from his lunch break.

"How did his errand go?" George asked discarding his overcoat and sitting at his desk.

Chris related what Cam had told him about Mr Newman. "He did not find out a lot but what he did find out makes me interested."

"I can see why," George answered. "A lot could be said against Mr Newman, we have to find out where he was earlier in the evening."

"That will be our job tonight," Chris remarked as a knock came and Sergeant Dawkins entered.

"I have a woman outside, she wants to see someone regarding the death of Miss Marston," he explained.

"Really," Chris said looking at him. "Then please show her in."

Chris was already standing as Sergeant Dawkins ushered the woman in the office, he saw at a glance that she was quite attractive, and well dressed, perhaps in her forties.

Chris offered his hand which she took. "I am Detective Inspector Hardie, and my colleague Detective Sergeant House," Chris said still standing. "Please, be seated," he indicated the interview chair.

"Thank you for coming in," Chris looked at the woman who seem to be nervous. "Try to relax, may I first have your name and address?" he asked.

"I am Mrs Withers, I live at number ten Union Street," the woman replied.

"I understand that you know of Miss Marston's death, can you tell me how you know?" Chris asked.

Mrs Withers shifted in her chair. "We work together at Dowlings, we have been friends for years," Mrs Withers explained. "When she did not turn up for work this morning, I thought she might be ill, I mean as friends you do don't you?" she tried to explain.

"I can understand that," Chris replied.

"I am on a late lunch break, so rather than have lunch, I called at her house, her lodger was there."

"Mr Roger Webb?" Chris asked.

"That is right, he told me she was found dead, and he had been interviewed by the police early this morning."

"It must have been a shock to you Mrs Withers?" Chris said gently.

"It was, I still cannot believe it, we had a good old chat when we left work Monday night."

"Is that why you are here?" Chris asked.

"Well yes in a way, you see she told me the police had called on her during Sunday, concerning the death of a Mrs Ewing, I think that is the name, I never knew her, you see I am married and don't drink, not like Linda," Mrs Withers forced a smile.

"What is it that Miss Marston told you that you thought we should know?" Chris asked looking at George who was showing interest.

"Well it could be nothing," Mrs Withers answered. "She told me that after the police had call on her on Sunday, she thought she knew who might have murdered Mrs Ewing."

"Did she name who she thought?" Chris asked getting excited.

"I begged her to, but she would not, she thought it would have been dreadful had she be wrong, but she did say she would talk to the police about it," Mrs Withers replied giving Chris disappointment.

"Is that all she said?" Chris asked.

"I am afraid so," Mrs Withers replied. "I hope I did the right thing coming?" she asked.

"You have done well Mrs Withers," Chris thanked her.

"She did say she would give him his marching orders," Mrs Withers added.

"She definitely said this?" Chris asked.

Mrs Withers nodded her head. "That is what she said," she added.

"What about boy friends?" George asked. "Did she have any?"

Mrs Withers shifted to look a George. "Linda was an attractive woman, and single, and she liked a drink, she must have had several admirers."

"But do you know any?" George asked.

"We may have spoke of them, but I would not know them," Mrs Withers replied.

Chris feeling that there was nothing else to ask. "Thank you anyway for calling in and telling us, should you remember any particular name she might have mentioned to you, you can always call in or even phone me, you can be assured we will appreciate it."

"I will," Mrs Withers promised. "I must get back to work now, but I don't know how I shall do it with poor Linda on my mind."

"Well that put the cat in with the pigeons," George remarked after Mrs Withers had left. "I suppose Mr Webb come to mind, Miss Marston did alibi him for Friday night."

"Perhaps we will never know," Chris replied. "It is hearsay anyway, I wish she could have told us a couple of names."

"So no progress there then," George remarked.

"A lot I would have thought," Chris replied with a smile. "At the moment we are looking for a reason and the connection between the two women murdered, If we believe Mrs Withers, and I personally cannot see why not, we no longer have to look for that connection. We assume that both women were killed by the same person, I feel that is true, but Miss Marston was killed because she was going to the police, that gives us the motive for her murder but not for Mrs Ewing, bits are coming together."

"Mr Webb still comes to mind," George argued. "I mean who else would she be close enough to be able to give him marching orders, she must have told him of what she thought after Cam had seen them Sunday, he could not let her talk to the police, so he killed her."

"It is a theory George," Chris agreed. "But why after a quarter century would he kill Mrs Ewing, she was an ex girl-friend for him, but I often ponder why the Ewing sisters gave us his name, after all they were not even born when Mr Webb split from their mother."

George shrugged. "Perhaps their father told the sisters about him, they obviously knew."

Chapter Thirteen

Cam strolled along the Vale Road looking at the house numbers, he was secretly pleased that Chris had allowed him to search the room, after all he was still a rookie, and rookies do not normally investigate on their own. He stopped outside number 49, the door was opened by Mrs Hanks, and Cam was welcomed with her toothless grin.

"What do you want?" she asked. "I know you young man don't I?" she asked.

"You ought to Mrs Hanks, we have said hello to each other many times while I was patrolling this area," Cam replied.

"Of course you are a policeman, why aren't you in uniform?" she asked, her mouth opening wider with her grin, allowing Cam see the full set of her toothless gums.

"I do not wear a uniform any more Mrs Hanks, I am a detective now," Cam replied as he waited to be asked inside.

"You have come about those children?" Mrs Hanks asked.

Cam had no idea what Mrs Hanks was talking about. "No, I am here to look at Mrs Ewing's room that you rent to her, are you having trouble with children?"

"Well you had better come in," Mrs Hanks said as her smile gone from her face. "I had a detective here this morning who said he would look into it," Mrs Hanks remarked as Cam followed her into her kitchen.

"That would have been Detective Sergeant House," Cam explained.

"He said he would look into it," Mrs Hanks repeated as she offered Cam a seat. "Would you like a cup of tea?"

Cam did not really want one, but wanted to keep Mrs Hanks sweet. "I would love one Mrs Hanks, milk no sugar."

Cam looked around the kitchen while Mrs Hanks had gone to the scullery to make the tea. "These children Mrs Hanks, they upset you?" Cam asked his voice raised a little so that Mrs Hanks could hear him through the open scullery door.

"When I go out, sometimes they follow me calling me hunch back, as though I am a freak of some kind, I cannot help my disfigurement," came the reply from the scullery.

"Do the children live in this street?" Cam asked in the same raised voice.

"No," Mrs Hanks replied carrying a tray into the kitchen, and proceeding to pour the tea. "I believe they come from the other streets around."

"So you would not know their names?" Cam asked.

Mrs Hanks shook her head as she placed a cup in front of Cam.

"Sergeant House will do as he promised I can assure you Mrs Hanks," Cam remarked. "It would be easier and quicker however if you could find out the name of just one of them."

Mrs Hanks sat down at the table, making a slurping noise as she sipped her tea.

"If I find out I will let the police know," she promised as she laid her cup down. "There is always four or five of them," she added. "I don't like going out."

"Well just find out one name, that boy would then be interviewed in front of his parents by the police, the boy would soon name the rest," Cam assured her.

"Your Sergeant searched the room this morning," Mrs Hanks remarked.

"In murder cases Mrs Hanks, we always double check everything, one can find what another might miss," Cam answered taking a sip of his tea. "Do you clean Mrs Ewing's room?" Cam asked.

"No, no, I am far too old to climb those stairs, I am over seventy you know," Mrs Hanks said with another toothless grin. "Doreen comes in several times a week, cleans her room, often washes her clothes, she is no bother."

"What about letters does she get any?" Cam asked.

Mrs Hanks shook her head. "Hardly, but then she did have one last week."

"What happened to it?" Cam asked interested.

"I put it on her bed, she has her own key, she comes and goes as she pleases, I might be out when she calls, I shall miss her rent money," Mrs Hanks replied.

"Can't you rent it out again?" Cam asked.

Mrs Hanks grinned. "I was thinking of having a man lodger, a house feels so much safer with a man in it, but then you know what people are like, they will think he is in my bed."

Cam finished his tea, he could not believe that people would think that way about Mrs Hanks. "I had better get on if you don't mind Mrs Hanks, now don't trouble yourself, just tell me the room, it will save your legs going up the stairs."

Mrs Hanks smiled as Cam stood up. "You are a nice young man, I have kept the room locked, the door will have a key in it."

Cam entered the room, and took a good look around, the flooring was lino covered with a wool rugs each side of the bed. Cam checked the corners of the lino, and found the lino was nailed down with small tacks all around the edges. He lifted the rugs, there was nothing underneath, Cam then started on the wardrobe, it was full of clothes, but he took each clothe out, after searching it laid it on the bed, until the wardrobe was empty. Taking a chair he looked at the top of the wardrobe finding the same result.

Satisfied that the wardrobe hid nothing, he put back the clothes and then closed the wardrobe doors. He looked at the furniture that had drawers, Cam followed the same procedure with the drawers as he had done with the wardrobe, even taking out the old newspapers that was lining the drawers, but disappointed he found nothing. His next job was to strip the bed, which he did, taking off the blankets then the sheets, he lifted the palliasse, which enabled him to look at the floor below the bed, there was nothing. Cam remade the bed, and sat on it, wondering, there was no photos around, the room was clean and tidy, but seemed unlived in. Giving up, Cam made for the door, and opening it, he gave a final look over the room, then he saw the pillows, he had missed them, they had a pillow slip on them. He crossed to the bed, taking a pillow, he took off the slip and shook it, but there was nothing there. He took the remaining one and did the same, which brought a smile to his face, as two envelopes fell out.

Unable to control himself, he picked up the larger envelope, inside the envelope he found a sheet of paper and money. He looked at the paper, it was a list of dates, by each date was written a sum of money, the list Cam could tell by the dates went back over a year. Cam counted the money which came to fifty six pounds, he replaced the list and money back into the envelope and placed it on the bed taking up the smaller envelope. There was just one small sheet inside the envelope, he took out the letter from the envelope. It was not addressed to anyone, Cam read the words.

"You will know who this letter is from, I shall be away when our next meeting is due, you will have to wait until seven pm at least, I will find you at the usual place."

There was no signature. Cam put the letter back into the envelope. He was pleased that he had found something, but disappointed with the outcome, in his mind, the envelopes told them nothing, only added extra problems to the case, however in his mind blackmail became a thought.

It was almost five when Cam entered the office and found Chris and George there, who looked up at him as he entered.

"I can see by your face that you found something," Chris said with a smile, seeing the satisfied look on Cam's face.

"Not much help I am afraid," Cam replied as he gave the two envelopes to Chris. "Found these."

"Where were they?" George asked.

"They were in the pillow slip of one of the pillows on the bed," Cam replied smugly.

"That is one place I did not look," George replied. "Good work."

"I nearly missed them, it was only when I had the bedroom door open to leave that I spotted the pillow cases," Cam admitted as he made his way to his desk.

"What has he found Chris?" George asked as he saw Chris looking at the envelopes contents.

"Money," Chris answered.

"There is fifty six pounds there," Cam explained. "Blackmail I thought."

"You could be right Cam," Chris replied, handing the letter and money to George.

"This note would have been interesting had it a signature, still who ever was paying money to Mrs Ewing might have written this note," Chris remarked as he passed the note to George.

"Do you think the note writer could have killed her?" Cam asked excitement in his voice.

"Again you could be right Cam, but we must not jump our guns," Chris replied his face serious. "What is your thought George?"

George who had looked at the envelope's contents passed them back to Chris. "If we find the note writer he will have need for some explanation, it is easy to agree with Cam, but with Mrs Ewing dead, who is going to confess should it turn out to be blackmailed."

"We have to wonder what Mrs Ewing could blackmail anyone for?" Chris added.

"Perhaps she had slept with a married man," Cam voiced, excitement still in his voice. "Threaten to tell his wife if he didn't pay up."

"The note could have been sent by a woman Cam, but we know it was posted in Winchester."

"We now have to get a sample of printing from all those involved," George pointed out. "Unless someone confess, that is the only way we are going to find out."

"Fifty six pounds, that is a lot of money," Cam remarked. "I would not thought she pays a lot to live, living with different men as she do."

"You did good work Cam," Chris praised him with a smile.

Chris looked at George. "We both had confidence in you Cam, George is right we have to get samples of printing from those involved, and without suspicion we have the perfect way by getting a statement from each of them, it might also be useful if we can find out who was away from Winchester last Friday afternoon."

Chapter Fourteen

*C*hris checked his pocket watch, it told him it was almost five, it had been a long day, but Chris was satisfied with the results of the day, he was getting a mental picture, but the motive still eluded him, although he was beginning to get thoughts as to what it could be.

"Where is your motorbike George?" he asked.

"Outside," George replied.

"I was thinking to call on April Marshall before seeing Mr Newman," Chris remarked.

"Any reason?" George asked.

"I would just like to know a bit more regarding Mrs Marshall's death, that is all," Chris replied.

"We will have time, do you want to go now?" George asked.

"Sooner the better," Chris replied with a smile. "I have finished my reports, and Cam is busy on his."

"Anything I can do?" Cam asked looking up from his writing.

"No you go home when you have finished, today you have been busy, tomorrow morning we start afresh," Chris replied getting up and going to the hat stand.

George brought his motorbike to a stop outside April Marshall house in Stockbridge road. Chris got off the motorbike pavilion seat and shuddered, although the trip from the station had not been fast, owing to the twisting and swerving that George had done passing the horse traffic without using to much throttle, Chris felt a little chilly.

"You get used to it Chris," George smiled as Chris knocked the door with a noticeable shiver.

April Marshall opened the door, her eyes showed she had been crying.

"You had better come in," April said without bothering to ask them why they were there or even greeting them.

Chris looked at George wondering. "We have come at a bad time?" Chris asked as they both followed April into the front room.

"Please seat where you can," April answered her voice low and quiet as she went to the mantel where she picked up a telegram and handed it to Chris. "This came a few hours ago," she said with a sob.

Having seated themselves, Chris took the telegram and read it, then passed it to George.

"I am so sorry Mrs Marshall, I can understand how you feel with us busting in during your grief, please forgive us, is there anything we can do?" Chris asked.

April had seated herself in an armchair, she dried her eyes and touched her nose with her handkerchief. "What can anyone do, no one can bring back my husband," she sobbed.

"Is there anyone we can inform?" George asked gently as he replaced the telegram on the mantel. "I have a motor-bike outside, I could go and inform your sisters."

April sniffed and shook her head. "They will be here within the next hour," April replied again sniffing. "Was there something you wanted from me?" she asked.

"Not really Mrs Marshall," Chris replied. "We were just passing, we wondered how you were, that is all."

"You are very kind Inspector," April replied knowing that he called to ask questions. "Answering question is beyond me today, perhaps tomorrow," she suggested with a sob in her voice.

"Please do not worry Mrs Marshall," Chris replied standing. "I am very sorry about the death of your husband, he was a hero giving his life for his country, is there anything we can do for you?"

"No Inspector, thank you, my sisters will be here shortly," April answered.

"Then we will leave you, again our apologise for interrupting your grief," Chris said gently.

Chris stood by as George mounted his motorbike.

"I was out of my depth in there George," Chris said as he prepared to get onto the motorbike pavilion seat. "I could not tell her about the death of Miss Marston, but I am sure her sisters will."

"This war is causing grief to thousands of people, mothers, fathers, sisters, brothers, wives," George remarked as he lowered his goggles. "Anyway," George said shaking the memory of his mates still out in France from his mind. "Mr Newman now," he said as he drove off from the curb.

George pulled up outside Mr Newman's house in St Cross, Chris got off the bike shivering, and knocked the door, which was on the side of the pavement closest to the road with no garden.

A man about forty with grey hair wearing glasses open the door, Chris noticed that he was well built about five foot, ten inches tall. "Is Mr Newman?" Chris asked.

"That is me," the man smiled looking at Chris then eyeing George standing by his motorbike. "What can I do for you?" he asked.

"I am Inspector Detective Hardie, and this is Detective Sergeant House," Chris replied half turning indicating George who was standing behind him. "We would like to ask you a few questions regarding Mrs Doreen Ewing, who we believe was staying with you."

Mr Newman stared from one to the other before answering. "She is not here," he replied. "But you might as well come in, I have just arrived myself."

"What is your line of work?" Chris asked as followed by George they entered the house, where Mr Newman took them to the kitchen.

"I am a thatcher," Mr Newman replied. "Find yourselves a chair, now how can I help you?"

Chris found himself a chair by the table, and noticed George doing the same. "I have reason to believe that Mrs Doreen Ewing was living at this address last week," Chris replied.

Mr Newman smiled. "She disappeared last Friday," he replied. "I left here early Friday morning, she was still in bed, when I came home she was not here, that is not unusual, but she did not return," Mr Newman shrugged his shoulders as though it did not matter.

"Were you not worried?" George asked.

"Not about Doreen," Mr Newman replied who had taken a chair around the table. "Who ever she stays with has the same trouble, she is here one day, gone the next day."

"So you know she stays with other men?" George remarked.

Mr Newman grinned. "Of course, it's a good thing really, a few days is alright, but you do not want her continuously, you might as well get married if that was the case."

"You are not married Mr Newman?" Chris asked.

"No, and I am not being the first," he replied still grinning.

"I am not sure what you mean Mr Newman," Chris replied.

"Let me explain," Mr Newman said still with a smile on his face. "During our school days, we were playing truant more times than we went to school, we were in a gang, we were best buddies just five of us, we made a pack never to get married, and share any women, girls in those days I might add," Mr Newman smiled. "Through the years we had many women, we all shared but of course we respected their wishes, some would share, others would not."

"We played truant because we had to work to get money, girl never went with you if you could not tempt them in some way," Mr Newman added. "The work we did just to earn enough money to tempt the girls."

"Really," Chris remarked. "And have you all stayed single?" he asked.

"The three of us are still single, two of our mates were killed during the Boer war."

"Who are the three of you are now still single?" George asked.

"Well there is Toby Woods, Roger Webb and myself," Mr Newman replied. "But Roger, I feel will be the first to marry, he has a soft spot for Linda, one of the woman we all shared in our time."

"Miss Linda Marston?" George asked.

"Yes that is right, Roger lodges with her now," Mr Newman added.

"We understood that Mr Webb was courting Mrs Ewing before she married?" Chris remarked.

"Not exactly," Mr Newman replied with a grin. "You could say we all broke up with Doreen when she started to court Mr Ewing, you see we never went with married women, we called them the untouchables, Doreen was Doreen Baker in those days."

"What about Mrs Marshall?" Chris asked. "Was she one of your women?"

"Brenda Silverstone she was back then, yes she was another like Doreen who was off our list when she got married, Doreen however left her husband a few years ago and came back on our list, although we did not have to go out looking for her, she would turn up unexpectedly on your door step," Mr Newman replied with a grin.

"What about Mrs Marshall?" George asked.

"Well she went off the list, she married, but some years ago her husband died, she came back on the list," Mr Newman explained. "Doreen and Brenda are two different kind of people, Doreen was happy just having her keep while she stayed with you, Brenda however was a bit cagey, when you went with her it was always at her house, no one must not saw you enter or leave the house, she also wanted paying."

"Mrs Marshall died as a result of an accident falling down the stairs," Chris remarked.

"So it is said," Mr Newman replied, his face blank.

"You have doubts Mr Newman?" Chris asked.

"Not really, but I saw her sister soon after, she was very upset, you see she could not understand how the carpet was torn at the top of the stairs, according to her sister, she herself had never seen at tare in her carpet."

"Really," Chris replied, "I had no idea she had a sister?"

"Yes they were very close, but they were totally different from each other, they really were as different as chalk and cheese, her sister Doris never drank, and certainly was not a loose woman."

"Would you know her address?" Chris asked wondering.

"I know she lives next to the Fox and Hounds in Upper High Street," Mr Newman replied. "I believe she is married, but I would not know the name."

"Miss Marston did she stay on the list?" Chris asked, very surprised at the information Mr Newman was giving them.

"In a way, especially if she had too much to drink, but she has slowed down during the last few years, I think she would also like to settle down," Mr Newman explained.

"Any other women?" George asked wondering if Mr Newman was just boasting.

"Through the years we had so many women, some would share, others would not, but we respected their wishes," Mr Newman replied.

"Well you have certainly been informant Mr Newman," Chris said wondering if he was disgusted or not.

"I know I am known as a talker," Mr Newman smiled. "Perhaps I have painted a bad picture of the gang, but remember we were all young healthy men, we wanted women, it was a part of our make up of being men," Mr Newman explained feeling a little embarrassed.

"You were out of Winchester last Friday afternoon Mr Newman?" George asked.

Mr Newman nodded his head. "I was finishing this bungalow at church lane in Easton, I did not get back until around eight that night."

"How do you get to work?" George asked.

"I have a horse and buggy, I stable the horse in the Bell Inn, almost next door."

"Then what did you do?" George asked.

Mr Newman thought for a while. "Let's see, I stabled the horse in the Bell Inn, then went to the White Horse for a pint, then came back to the Bell Inn for one before going home."

"As I said, Doreen was not here when I came home, and did not come back," Mr Newman replied. "Why are you so interested in last Friday?" he asked worriedly.

"Mrs Ewing was found dead, Saturday Morning Mr Newman," Chris replied.

Mr Newman looked at Chris, there was disbelief on his face, he gave a weak smile. "You are not serious Inspector?" he asked.

"I am afraid I am," Chris answered

"But how, why?" Mr Newman asked spreading his hands. "She was an attractive healthy woman, she never let on to me she was unwell," he said.

"She was murdered," Chris replied. "And as far as we know, you were the last person to see her."

"But that was about six o'clock on Friday morning when I set off for Easton, just a moment, you don't think I had anything to do with it do you?" Mr Newman asked.

"Just trying to get all the fact Mr Newman," Chris assured him. "Can you think of any reason why someone would kill her, did she have any enemies?"

"Poor Doreen," Mr Newman shook his head as he muttered. "Doreen was a good time girl, very attractive, was it a sex attack?"

"Not as far as we know Mr Newman," Chris answered. "She was killed with a blow to the head from an axe."

"Dear oh dear," muttered Mr Newman. "We have known each other since school days, and although we only saw each other for one reason, you do get attached to each other, you could say we were friends."

"Do you have an axe Mr Newman?" George asked. "We do have to eliminate people."

Mr Newman pointed to the back door that was in the kitchen. "You will find it just by the wall," he said as he watched George rise and open the door. "I use it very rarely," Mr Newman said looking at Chris. "I pick up twigs and logs at places I work and bring them home in my buggy."

"You have had that axe some time?" George remarked entering the kitchen, it's very old.

"It belonged to my parents," Mr Newman explained.

"When did you see Miss Marston last?" Chris asked.

Mr Newman shook his head. "Don't really know, I did see her with Roger one day a couple weeks ago, but with Doreen staying here I have not been to town, I have used the local pubs," he explained.

"Did you go to town Monday night Mr Newman?" Chris asked.

Mr Newman shook his head. "After a week with Doreen, a man needs his rest, I was not in the mood, I stayed local," he replied. "Who would want to kill Doreen?" he muttered again.

"I am afraid I have more bad news for you Mr Newman," Chris replied gently. "Miss Linda Marston was found dead last evening."

"Good God Inspector," Mr Newman responded. "You are certainly the bearer of bad news, how did she die, what about Roger, does he know?"

"Yes we informed Mr Webb early this morning after the body was found," Chris replied. "Miss Marston was murdered with an axe just like Mrs Ewing."

"Roger must be upset," Mr Newman muttered. "That means the three girls we met in our youth are all now dead, what a world," he added his voice full of sorrow.

Chris followed by George left the unhappy Mr Newman, by showing themselves out.

"Well one thing for sure George," Chris said as he sat on the back seat. "He did not write that note, no reason for him to write the letter and post it to where she rented a room while living with her."

"I was thinking about the same line," George admitted. "Another thing, would he have taken Mrs Ewing in if she was blackmailing him."

Chris did not comment. "Where are you dropping me off?" he asked as George started the motorbike.

"I will take you home Chris, I don't want Elizabeth getting too worried," he laughed as he drove off.

Chapter Fifteen

lizabeth was waiting at the door for Chris, she kissed him on the lips. "You look tired darling she said as she pulled away. "Let's go in, mother in the kitchen heating up your meal."

"It's been a long day," Chris smiled.

With each others arm around each others waist, Chris and Elizabeth entered the front room, where Ron who had been reading the newspaper, put it to one side and smiled as he looked at Chris over the top of his glasses.

"Just in time for a glass," he said lifting a bottle of beer that stood on the table.

"You look as if you could do with one," he said as he started to pour two glasses. "Olive will be a few moments warming your meal."

"I can certainly do with one," Chris replied smiling, as he disengaged himself from Elizabeth and sat at the table. "It's been a long day."

"You enjoy it darling," Elizabeth smiled. "I will see how mother is getting on," she said as she leaving the front room.

"Difficult case Chris?" Ron asked as they both lifted their glasses.

"Plenty of background, all involved have a connection, but not one that gives a reason for the murders, no motive at all."

"I am sure you will find one eventually Chris," Ron flattered as he took another drink.

"Do not seem likely at the moment," Chris replied. "Any war news?" Chris asked changing the subject.

"Casualties are just coming through regarding the Battle of the Somme that started last month on 1st July, it's terrible, it seems with the Commonwealth troops we have lost one million men, it seems incredible that so many can be killed in a battle," Ron replied.

"According to George my Sergeant," Chris answered. "It's trench warfare, when our men scrambled out of their trenches facing the enemy lines, they met a terrific fire from machine guns by the enemy, hundreds are killed without taking a step."

"I suppose the German side suffer the same," Ron added.

"Same for both sides according to George, just a waste of life, his opinion," Chris took a long drink from his beer glass.

Ron lifted his glass. "To those brave boys," he said.

Elizabeth entered followed by Olive with his meal. "Sorry to have kept you waiting Chris," Olive remarked placing the plate before him, I like to warm a meal up over a saucepan of boiling water, the oven would be quicker but I think it tends to dry the meal up a bit," she smiled.

"This is great Olive," Chris said with thanks. "I did not mind waiting, I enjoyed the glass I had with Ron."

"Give him a reason for a pint and he snaps it up," Olive remarked looking at her husband scornfully.

"Chris and Dad both like a drink mother," Elizabeth leapt to their defence.

"According to what dad was saying about the casualties we are suffering in this war, life is short, so enjoy it, I have no objection to Chris having a drink, and I am thankful he is not in this war."

"So am I," Olive remarked, her voice soft. "I remember the anxiety I suffered all the time your father was away in Africa, eat your dinner Chris while it is hot," Olive added as she turned away and left the room.

"She is upset now," Ron remarked as Elizabeth got up and followed her mother.

"She is very sentimental, feels very deeply for the boys out there, also for their relatives back in this Country."

"I am sorry Ron," Chris replied.

"It's not your fault Chris," Ron forced a smile. "Elizabeth will calm her, you'll see."

Chris finished his meal, then sat in the armchair opposite Ron, took out his pipe filled the bowl and lit it, puffing contentedly before Elizabeth and her mother appeared.

"Elizabeth is taking Chris home now," Olive said to her husband. "He looks tired."

Ron smiled. "I have to agree," he replied. "You had a hard day," Ron commented.

"All three of us have been busy today," Chris replied. "It has turned out to be a long day, to be honest I could do with an early night."

Chris laid in bed staring at the ceiling, he could hardly keep his eyes open, he felt the warmth of Elizabeth as she laid by his side with her arm over his stomach. The sound of an alarm woke him out of a deep restful sleep, he opened his eyes, he blinked and looked to Elizabeth who was resting her head on her bent arm looking at him with a grin on her face.

"What is the time?" Chris asked automatically without thinking. "I must have dozed off."

"You slept all night like a log, never even said good night to me," Elizabeth said pretending to sulk.

"Sorry darling," Chris replied turning towards her and kissing her. "I can't remember falling to sleep."

Elizabeth smiled. "While you wash and shave I will get the breakfast, do you feel refreshed?" she asked.

Chris nodded as he swung his legs out of bed. "Feel like a new man," he remarked.

"That's how I want you to feel when we go to bed," Elizabeth giggled as she also got out of bed. "Still I suppose I can put up with one night without a cuddle," she said her eyes smiling as she looked at Chris.

Elizabeth kissed Chris on the cheek as she left him outside the Police Station.

"Your sandwiches are in your pocket darling," she smiled. "Try not to over tire yourself today."

Chris looked at her, he saw her eyes were sparkling as she smiled.

"I love you Mrs Hardie," Chris smiled.

"I love you Mr Hardie," Elizabeth returned his smile as she left him.

Chris entered the office, George and Cam were already there at their desks, for once the weather was warm. Chris hung his trilby, he was not wearing an overcoat.

"Morning," he greeted them with a smile. "It looks like warm day today," he remarked as he sat at his desk.

"What have we got on today?" George asked.

Chris leaned back in his chair, he touched his moustache, and took his pipe and tobacco out of his pocket, and started to fill the pipe.

"Well we did a lot yesterday," Chris replied. "None of which gave us any leads to carry on."

"Have you got any ideas Cam?" Chris asked looking at him.

Cam thought for a while. "Perhaps I could get some handwriting from all those involved," he answered. "Might give us a clue as to who wrote that note."

"How are you going to do that?" George asked.

"I could call on them and ask to write their statement, I will tell them it will save them having to attend the station," Cam replied.

"OK Cam," Chris replied. "Remember the three men involved might be at work, but you could get from the Ewing sisters and perhaps Mr Ewing, however leave April Marshall, she has just lost her husband."

"Yes George was telling me," Cam replied.

"You will have to take pot luck with the men, might mean you will have to see them in the evening," Chris remarked. "Don't forget we want them to print their names as well when they sign, you can tell them that we want all statements signed and printed."

"Hope you haven't got a date to night?" George remarked with a smile.

Cam shook his head. "Not Tuesday nights, she is on duty."

"Why do you want the Ewings signature Chris?" George asked. "Do you suspect them?"

Chris shook his head. "Those girls have not told us everything they know, Mr Ewing seems clear, but don't forget, where his ex wife was found is just ten minutes from where he lives at Bar End, it's details like that, that one has to keep in mind."

Chris shifted in his chair and looked at the blackboard. "Let's take Mr Newman who we saw last night. Now last

Friday he could have taken Mrs Ewing's body to the Gardenia Road by his horse and buggy, he has no real alibi that he was working late, and the local landlords cannot remember him before his usual time which is after eight."

"You mean he killed her first, them dumped her at the Gardenia Road?" Cam asked.

"What I am saying Cam is that it is a possibility, however the note you found, do not fit in, why would he write such a note to someone who is living with him at the time, and if it turns out to be blackmail, would he allow the person blackmailing him to stay at his home?" Chris continued.

Chris knew that anything was possible. "Both Mr Woods and Mr Newman said Mrs Ewing had worn them out, and was glad in a way when she left."

"Perhaps they were boasting," Cam replied seriously.

Chris smiled. "These men are passed the age of forty Cam, I will admit that young boys and men might boast of their conquests, but not men of their age, anyway, they were both saying they were worn out."

Both George and Cam nodded their heads in agreement.

"Now," Chris said in between puffs of his pipe. "We have a situation here, where a group of young men and women, made a pact while they were at school, in this gang there were five males, two of which were killed for king and country, leaving three, Mr Webb, Mr Woods and Mr Newman, all three are still alive," Chris took another puff from his pipe.

"We know at least three women who were also a connected with this gang and sharing their pact, Mrs Marshall, Mrs Ewing and Miss Marston, all three are now dead, two we know were murdered," Chris commented.

"That sums it up," George remarked. "But no motive for the murders."

"Well the note Cam found at Mrs Hanks house, might be a start of one, should it turn out to be blackmail," Chris replied. "Now we know that recently Mrs Ewing had lived with Mr Woods and Mr Newman, we must consider what Cam said that her living with them might be a part of her blackmail."

"That leaves only Mr Webb," George remarked. "That she had not slept with of late, could it have been him that she was blackmailing?"

Chris shrugged. "Mr Webb has a lot of discrepancies in his answers to our questions, we will have to talk to him again, but are we assuming too much, could it be that Mr Ewing was giving his wife some money each week, perhaps not as blackmail but to help her, we know he idolised her and still do, also they are still married," Chris commented.

"But do we know that Mr Ewing was out of Winchester last Friday?" Cam asked. "That is what the note said."

Chris smiled. "That is another job for you Cam, while you are at the Ewings taking their statements, you try to find out."

"That is Cam settled for the day, what are we doing?" George asked.

"We are going to see this Doris, the sister of Mrs Marshall, she might be able to tell us something, she was close to her sister," Chris replied.

Chris and George found themselves looking to the side of the Fox and Hounds in Upper High Street. "This must be the house," Chris remarked. "Mr Newman did say next door to the pub, I'll knock, we will soon find out."

"A woman who Chris thought was in her forties answered the door, she was wearing a pinafore over her dress, and she pushed back strands of dark hair that had fallen over her face as she looked at them.

"What can I do for you?" she asked a little irritated.

"I am sorry to bother you," Chris spoke. "I am Detective Inspector Hardie, and my colleague Detective Sergeant House, we are looking for a woman named Doris, who was the sister of Mrs Brenda Marshall who once lived by the Red Deer in Stockbridge Road."

Pushing a few more strands of hair away from her face the woman smiled. "You are talking about my sister Mrs Marshall," she said.

"So you have finally realised, well you better come in, although you have caught me on my wash day, with my husband gone, I do other people's laundry to earn money," she remarked allowing them to enter. "Go into the front room, and take a seat," she offered closing the door behind them.

Chris took off his trilby as he entered, and soon found himself in a neat well furnished room, that looked out over the road. Chris and George found themselves a chair at the table.

"So you now know that my sister's accident was not an accident," Doris said clasping her hands in front of her resting on the table. "I wondered why it took you so long?"

Chris looked at George before answering. "I am afraid Mrs..?"

"Mrs King," Doris replied. "I am a widow, my husband was killed two years ago in France."

"I am sorry Mrs King," Chris replied. "We are here to ask you a few questions on another matter, I am sorry to hear about your husband, so many good man are being taken from us because of this war."

"It was two years ago Inspector, one learns to live with the grief," Mrs King replied. "But now I am in grief all over again, my nephew has just been killed," she said with a sniff.

"Mr Richard Marshall," George remarked. "We were told of his death by his wife April."

"Oh," Doris remarked. "Now I don't understand."

"Mrs April Marshall is a part of our investigation into her mother's death," George informed her.

"Oh yes, I did hear about that, I felt sorry for April who she has good morals, I had little to do with her mother, who I went to school with," Doris spoke with a sniff.

"I have called on April to comfort her about losing her husband, but her sisters were there to comfort her, we will both suffer in a way, we cannot hold a funeral and have no grave to visit," Doris commented.

"It must be heartbreaking Mrs King," Chris said with sincerity.

"Life goes on Inspector," Mrs King muttered softly with her head bowed. "But tell me, why are you here?" she asked looking up.

"Before we go to that Mrs King," Chris began.

"Please call me Doris Inspector," Mrs King interrupted.

"Very well Doris," Chris replied with a slight smile. "You told us that your sister's death was not an accident, what did you mean by that?"

"It is just a feeling I have always had," Doris replied. "Just an awful feeling."

"Were you not interviewed?" Chris asked.

"Oh yes I was, by a pleasant police sergeant, I also had to identify my sister, but I could not tell him anything," Doris replied.

"I have read all the reports, many statements, all seem to point to a tragic accident, no foul play suspected," Chris replied.

"Yes I know," Doris confirmed. "But I cannot help how I feel."

"Your sister got married about twenty six years ago I understand Doris," Chris continued. "Was it a love match?"

Doris smiled. "Hardly that Inspector, I loved my sister we were very close, she knew I hated her way of life, but how hard I tried, I could not changed her, she always said her way of life is not safe, violence can enter, that was why I was not surprised when I heard about the death of Mrs Doreen Ewing."

"Why did your sister marry Mr Marshall, was she in love with him?" Chris asked.

"No Inspector, she was not in love with him," Doris answered.

"So it was not a love match, why did she marry him then?" Chris asked.

Doris thought for a while before answering. "I have no wish to speak bad of my sister's memory Inspector, but I realise that the truth must come out, you obviously know that my sister was a loose woman, and unfortunately she became pregnant, she had to get married."

"So she married Mr Marshall, did he know she was pregnant?" George asked.

Doris shook her head. "My sister did not tell him."

"Could she not have married the real father?" George asked.

"As far as I know, the man she went with had a non marriage pact, what ever that means," Doris replied.

"We know all about the pact Doris," Chris replied. "It is your opinion then the father of your sister's child was one of the five men who made the pact."

"That is what I think," Doris replied.

"There are three alive," George remarked. "Do you suspect one of them?" he asked.

"No idea," Doris replied. "It could have been one of those that was killed in the Boer War."

"Your sister was lucky however," Chris remarked.

"You could say that, my sister was known for her ways, she was a loose woman having low morals, not many men would have taken her on, but Mr Marshall was not a man many girls would want to marry, my sister saw her chance with him, he was after all an accountant, had a good job and a house."

"But your sister never did name the man she thought to be the real father, it is said that most women know, even if they had been with other men," George remarked.

"As I said, we as sisters were very close, had few secrets from each other, but she never named a man although I do know he paid my sister maintenance until my nephew was sixteen years old."

"Well that gives us a clue Doris, your nephew I believe is twenty six?" Chris asked.

Doris nodded her head.

"The father paid maintenance up to when your nephew was sixteen?" Chris continued.

Doris nodded her head again.

"When your nephew was sixteen, the Boer War had been over at least five years, which means if the father had still been paying your sister, the father could not have been one of the two that were killed," Chris explained.

"Never thought of it," Doris admitted. "Never crossed my mind, yes, you are right, but which one, still with my nephew now killed what difference will it make."

"It could eventually fit in our investigations," Chris remarked.

"That is assuming that the father was one of the five, but my sister must have known other men," Doris replied.

"I agree," Chris answered. "But you did say the father was in the pact of non marriage."

For a moment silence prevailed allowing what had been said to sink in. "Now the reason why we are here Doris," Chris broke the silence. "How well do you know a Miss Linda Marston?" he asked.

"Another one of my sister's friend," Doris replied. "I know her, actually I like her, she is hard not to like, but like my sister she had the same low morals, but when I see her I do stop and have a chat."

"Miss Marston was found dead Monday," Chris informed Doris.

"God," Doris exclaimed. "What was wrong with her?" she asked.

"Health wise nothing, she was murdered just like Mrs Ewing," Chris answered.

Doris looking at Chris shook her head almost in disbelief.

"My sister always said that when a woman is loose, one time or another, she can expect violence, that is why she kept me away from that life, not that it was a life I wanted to be a part of," she added. "I am more sorry to learn that about Linda than I was about Doreen, what is the world coming to."

"Mr Webb is lodging with Miss Marston, or should I say was," George remarked.

"I know that," Doris replied. "But there was nothing going on, at least that was what Linda told me when I saw her in town about a month ago."

"Did she say anything else?" Chris asked hopefully.

"I took it she was about to settle down, she said she had almost given up her old way of life, she had met a man, a little older than she was, but if she could marry him she knew she would have a good life, which she said she now wanted," Doris explained. "I was really pleased for her, but in answer to your next question, she did not mention the man's name."

"Pity," Chris remarked disappointed.

"How was she killed?" Doris asked curiosity getting the better of her.

"The same way as Mrs Ewing," Chris explained. "Hit with an axe, a blow killed them both."

"What some wicked people we have in this world, our nice young men are being killed in a war, and we leave murderers roaming our streets," Doris commented.

"That is life I am afraid Doris," Chris remarked getting up. "I hope we have not put you behind too much with your washing but thank you for answering our questions."

"Do you think that there is a connection between their deaths and my sister's death?" Doris asked, making Chris and George sit again.

"At the moment I am afraid not," Chris replied. "But future facts might contradict that, you can be sure we will keep you in the picture."

"Just out of curiosity Doris, did your nephew know that he was illegitimate?" George asked.

Doris shook her head. "No, as far as I know, he was unaware of the fact, apart from myself I believe that only two other people knew, Doreen Ewing and Linda Marston, they were sworn to secrecy by my sister, it seems there was honour among whores as well as thrives," Doreen paused for a while before continuing.

"I hate to call my sister that, but one can't get away from the truth, however Richard never knew he was illegitimate, although he never really got on with the father he knew, and joined the army when he was eighteen."

"Really," Chris replied. "How did he come to know April Ewing, her father is very protective, especially where army boys are concern."

"I believe they met at a party while he was home on leave," Doris explained. "He joined the army a couple years before the war started, he wanted to go to Africa, but he never got his wish."

"Tell me about the wedding Doris," Chris asked. "I take it you were present?"

"Of course I was," Doris smiled. "Well Richard and April invited many of their friends, who I did not know, April's parents were there, so was Linda Marston."

"So April did invite her mother even though she had left the family?" George asked.

Doris shook her head with a smile. "My sister invited both Doreen and Linda, however inviting Doreen Ewing caused a little trouble, April was against it, Richard who had no idea about his mother and her friends he managed to talk her around, but April would not have her mother sitting at the top table."

"Mr Ewing?" Chris asked. "How did he react?"

"He seemed to accept it, got on well with Linda I believe, I remember seeing them talking over a drink together."

"I would suppose they knew each other before," Chris added.

"It would have been a hard job not to have known each other in a small town like this, everyone eventually know everyone in time, I felt sorry for him, he seemed to be a nice man, but unlike my sister who I know stayed loyal to her husband during their marriage, Doreen was completely different, she was unable to do so, she had to have other men, which eventually split the marriage."

Chris once again stood up. "We must really leave, and once again thank you for your help and honesty," he said.

"I can not see how, but I hope I have been a help," Doris remarked as she led the way to the front door which she opened. "Should I think of anything I will phone you at the station," Doris added as she saw them out.

"What did we get out of that," George asked as with Chris making his way back to the station.

"Rather a lot, I think," Chris answered as they passed under the Westgate. "A lot of which we already know was confirmed."

"But not a lot to help us going further," George remarked.

"I do have different thoughts on the case," Chris answered as they passed the Bank Elizabeth worked in, Chris looked at the Bank, knowing that seeing Elizabeth would be slim chance. "It seems to me that the mother and two other women who knew that Richard was illegitimate are dead, there's a thought," Chris added as they crossed the Jewry Street junction.

"Doris knew, she still with us," George replied.

"That is another worrying thought," Chris replied.

"I can not see how that fits in with the letter that Cam found about Mrs Ewing?" George queried.

"Nor can I George," Chris replied with a serious look on his face. "That is another worry, also it is strange, Mr Newman and Doris told us that Mrs Brenda Marshall was part of the same group, Mr Webb and Mr Woods denied knowing her, I wonder why?"

Cam was sitting at the table in the front room, both May and June Ewing were sitting opposite him.

"Father is out, he went to the doctor," June said.

"He is having trouble sleeping," May added.

"Has he any worry on his mind?" Cam asked.

"All these deaths I would think, father is a sensitive man," June replied.

"Who is his doctor?" Cam asked.

"Dr Green," May answered.

"Is that the one in St Cross?" Cam asked.

"That is him," May confirmed. "We are all under him, father pays sixpence each week."

"I know him," Cam said. "I met him a short time ago, he is very good."

"If he was not at the doctors he would have been out walking anyway," May added.

"He can't stay still, been active all his life," June explained.

"Do your father ever go away, outside of Winchester?" Cam asked.

Both sisters shook their heads. "Never known him to," May replied.

"He never takes an holiday," June added.

"Not even for a day, or part of a day?" Cam asked.

Again both sisters shook their heads. "He usually sleeps in the afternoon," June said.

"So he has not been out of Winchester in the last week or two?" Cam asked.

"We can swear to that," May replied.

"Is there a point to this question Sergeant?" June asked.

"Just checking all the facts we know, by the way," Cam continued wanting to change the subject. "I suppose you have seen your sister April, I was sorry to hear that her husband was killed in action."

"We saw her last evening," June replied. "She is very upset."

"Like we are, we all liked Richard," May added.

"Did you tell her about the death of Miss Marston?" Cam asked.

"Yes we did, that upset her even more," June replied.

"Lucky Richard's aunty Doris called in, they like each other," May said.

"April has had some bad lucks of late," Cam said sincerely. "What with her mother and her mother-in-law and now her husband."

"Father wants her to come and live here," June volunteered. "Richard's death was another shock to him, no wonder father can not sleep."

"It is the same with us," May remarked getting up from the table hearing the key in the front door. "Here is father, he is back early."

Mr Ewing entered the room, a slight smile appeared on his face as he saw Cam, he looked at his daughters.

"This is Detective Constable Streeter, father," June introduced as May placed a chair at the table for her father. "He works with Inspector Hardie, father."

Mr Ewing offered his hand which Cam took. "Have my daughter made you welcome Constable?" Mr Ewing asked as he sat.

"They have been most gracious Mr Ewing," Cam replied.

"You have news for me?" Mr Ewing asked.

"No Sir," Cam replied. "I have called to get you all to sign a statement of your interviews so far concerning this case, my Inspector thought it might save you coming to the station."

"Your Inspector is very thoughtful Constable," Mr Ewing replied as Cam gave him a foolscap sheet of typed paper. "I am allowed to read it first?" Mr Ewing asked.

"Certainly Sir, you and your daughters must sign and print your names."

Five minutes later, Cam put the signed document into his pocket.

"Tell me Constable, have you made any progress regarding my wife's murder?" Mr Ewing asked.

"We are still gathering facts Mr Ewing," Cam replied. "It is early days yet, but we have this extra murder on our hands, things are more complicated now."

"Do you think there is a connection between the two?" Mr Ewing asked. "My daughters told me about Miss Marston being killed, I can not see the connection apart from them knowing each other."

"We believe there to be," Cam replied. "They were both killed the same way, did you know Miss Marston?" Cam asked.

"Not really, I did know she and my wife had been friends since school, I did meet her at my daughter's April wedding," Mr Ewing replied.

"Our biggest problem is trying to find a motive for the crimes, we cannot find one," Cam explained. "Once we have, then we will soon clear the case up."

"I hope that will not be too long Constable, I will then be able to bury Doreen."

"Are you taking her funeral responsibility Sir?" Cam asked.

"There is no one else," Mr Ewing replied. "She is the mother of my daughters."

It was gone twelve when Cam left the Ewing family, he knew that Chris and George were interviewing Mrs Marshall's sister, and considered that they would not yet be back in the office. He still had Mr Webb, Mr Woods and Mr Newman's signatures to get, but knew that they would be night calls because finding them in during the day would be slim. He decided to call in the Heart and Hand for a dinner pint. He found the bar empty as he entered and went to the counter, a youngish man was wiping glasses.

"Morning Sir," smiled the man. "Don't normally get someone in so early, it is the situation of the pub, I would be full now if the pub was in town," he smiled.

"Not all of them," Cam disagreed. "Are you the landlord?" he asked.

"Have been for the last two years," smiled the landlord. "How can I help you?"

"A pint of bitter and a cheese sandwich would be ideal," Cam replied.

"That I can do," smiled the landlord who took a glass from under the counter and started pulling on a pump filling the glass. "There you are Sir, I will just get your sandwich," he said placing the pint before Cam.

Five minutes later having paid, Cam took a bite of the sandwich.

"Are you local?" the landlord asked as he continued to clean the glasses that had been left from the night before. "I have not seen you before."

"I am a policeman investigating the death of Mrs Ewing, just across the road," Cam replied.

558

"Are you," replied the landlord a look of surprise on his face. "I hope you find who done it, Frank was very upset about it, even though she had left him just after I came here."

"He came in here every night I believe?" Cam asked between bites of his sandwich.

"When I first took over here, Frank would be in here lunch times and nights, but since his daughter got married some months ago, he has not been in very much," the land-lord replied. "I think he must have a bit on the side," he winked.

"He is a retired man," Cam remarked. "A bit old for courting don't you think?" he asked.

"Frank is still an handsome man for his age, and as fit and strong as an ox, is there an age when men stop thinking of women?" the landlord asked with a smile.

"I guess not," Cam replied. "His wife was certainly a looker."

"Are you married?" the landlord asked.

Cam shook his head.

"Then beware, beautiful women do not always make the best wives, you feel much safer with a plain wife," the land-lord advised.

"I will keep that in mind landlord," Cam promised as he finished his sandwich and washed it down with a drink. "Mr Ewing never brought a woman in here then?" he asked.

The landlord shook his head. "No he used to come in about eight, and stay to closing time, now he comes in at the same time, but leaves after a pint, he do come in here lunch times however, after his walking I believe."

"Did you know Mrs Ewing?" Cam asked.

"I could be nasty if say who didn't," the landlord replied smiling. "Yes I knew her."

"Did she ever bring in a man when she called?" Cam asked.

The landlord shook his head again. "Not that I can remember, she had no need to which ever pub she went into, a woman of her looks would be eyed by all the men in the pub."

"I guess you are right," Cam said finishing his pint. "I had better get back to the station, thank you for the sandwich."

"Anytime," smiled the landlord as he watched Cam leave.

Cam entered the office, Chris and George who were at their desk looked at him then at each other, wondering how Cam had got on, Cam usually sprung a surprise on them.

"Did the morning go well?" Chris asked.

"Quite well, I have got statements signed by all the Ewing, I haven't seen anyone else yet, leaving them for tonight," Cam replied handing Chris the signed statements before he crossed to his own desk.

Chris took the statements laid them on his desk without looking at them. "Tell us about your visit them," Chris asked a smile playing on his face with expectations.

Cam related his visit to the Ewing and to the Heart and Hand, when he had finished, Chris smiled. "You have done well Cam, it was a good move going into the Heart and Hand, do you think he has a girlfriend?" Chris asked.

"Haven't given that much thought, the landlord I think was only joking," Cam replied.

"Anyway how did you two get on?" Cam asked.

George then told Cam of their morning's work, when he had finished Cam sat back in his chair thinking hard.

"Perhaps Mr Ewing was seeing Miss Marston?" Cam said.

"Could be," George answered. "But then he would be allowed to, you could say he was single."

"He is keeping it a secret if he is," Cam replied. "His daughters don't know about her, nor it seems do anyone else."

Chris thought on what was being said. "We know that Miss Marston works at Dowlings during the day, if Mr Ewing was having a relationship with Miss Marston, it must have been during the evening, the question in my mind is, would he go with Miss Marston, knowing she was just like his wife in morals?"

George shrugged. "It makes little difference any way, if he was having an affair with Miss Marston, I doubt it was really serious, it also takes him out of the picture for killing Miss Marston."

"Don't be to hasty George," Chris remarked. "Don't forget that Mrs Withers who worked with Miss Marston, she told us that Miss Marston believed she knew who killed Mrs Ewing, and was going to give him his marching orders and she was going to inform the police."

"You are saying that Mr Ewing killed his own wife?" George argued.

"Mr Ewing is still in the frame," Chris replied.

"So you think he killed his own wife and then Miss Marston?" Cam asked.

"No, I don't think Cam, what I am saying it is a possibility, however the timing is not good, you Cam saw Mr Webb and Miss Marston on Sunday last," Chris reminded him. "The very next day Miss Marston had seen her friend Mrs Withers and told her that she believed she knew who murdered Mrs Ewing and she was going to give him his marching orders, If Mr Ewing was the man who was getting his marching orders, how did Mr Ewing find out her opinion quick enough to kill her that same night in the church yard," Chris explained.

"Also," George interrupted. "We know Mr Ewing do not go out until eight at nights when his daughters get home from seeing their sister April, Miss Marston was killed around that time."

"What about the statements, I got them signed and print?" Cam he asked.

Chris took the statements and looked at the printing of their names, then compared the print with the note Cam had found. "I don't think they match," Chris replied after several minutes, then passing them to George. "At least he was not paying Mrs Ewing any money."

"I agree," George confirmed passing the statements to Cam, who also had to agree after studying them. "I still have the others to see tonight," Cam said passing the statements to Chris.

"This doctor Green who the Ewing family are under, is that the doctor you saw during the Suffolk Hotel Case?" Chris asked Cam.

"I asked them if the Doctor was at St Cross they said yes," Cam answered.

"It might be a good idea to go and see him, what you can find out about the Ewing family?" Chris said. "We are stuck at the moment, we might as well check everything."

"You have something in mind Chris?" George asked with a smile. "What is it?"

"Just a thought I had after leaving Doris, it's mixed at the moment, not sure what I am thinking," Chris answered.

"I am sure it is," George replied with the same smile knowing that until sure Chris would not divulge. "Anything for me?"

"Yes," Chris replied. "Go and see April Marshall, ask what question you like, such as about the death of Miss Marston, and perhaps about her wedding, but try to find out which doctor her husband had been under, we know he joined the army when he was eighteen, he would have been very lucky had he not the need for a doctor by that time."

"She will still be in shock over her husband's death," George remarked.

"We know her sisters were with her last night, also Doris, you will have to judge George," Chris answered.

Chris finished the reports he was on, he re-read them, then feeling satisfied, took a folder and placed the reports inside. He checked his watch and found to his surprise it was way passed six, he had missed Elizabeth. Chris decided that he would call and have a pint in the Rising Sun, he always thought best on his own with a pint in his hand, he stopped at the desk on his way out, Sergeant Dawkins was on duty.

"The beat bobby at Upper High Street, Sergeant," Chris said. "Would you ask him to keep an eye on number 6, which is next to the Fox and Hounds, I am a bit worried about the widow living there, I hope not, but she could be in a bit of trouble, perhaps he could knock and say hello to her."

"The one on is now going off duty, but I will pass your request on to the replacement, you want him to do anything else?" sergeant Dawkins asked.

"No," Chris shook his head. "As long as he makes sure she is alright, but I don't want her frightened, she has no idea she could be in danger."

"I will get Sergeant Bloom to keep an eye as well," sergeant Dawkins said. "He enjoys working for the CID," he added with a grin.

"Thank you Sergeant," Chris replied taking no notice of the sarcasm he expected. "I knew I could rely on you."

Alfie greeted him as he entered the Rising Sun.

"I have been worried about you, Chris," Alfie remarked. "Wondered if you were still with us."

Chris smiled at his morbid humour. "I have been busy," he replied. "However I can see you are well, your good lady is alright?" Chris asked.

"So, so," Alfie replied twisting his hand backwards and forewords in a half turn movement. "You know how women are, they are up one minute, down the next minute."

"I have not noticed that with Elizabeth," Chris replied.

"That is because you have only been married a few months, your honeymoon period is not over yet, but you will see, mark my words, anyway, bitter is it?" Alfie asked taking a pint glass from behind him.

Chris paid for his pint taking it with him to his usual seat. As he took a drink, his mind went back to Mrs Doris King, his mind wondered whether she was safe, after all it seems that everyone who knew that Richard her nephew was illegitimate was no longer alive except for her, however he hoped he had protected her as best he could, Chris deep in thought, kept sipping his pint, and was surprised when he found he was holding an empty glass, shaking his head he got up and went to the counter, Alfie was smiling at him.

"You must have been thirsty," Alfie remarked taking the glass to refill.

"Never realised I was drinking so fast," Chris replied. "I was deep in thought."

"Are you on Linda Marston's case?" Alfie asked as he pulled on the bitter pump.

"My office is the only CID department in this area," Chris replied. "All major crimes come to me, do you know her?"

Alfie put the filled glass in front of Chris. "Yes she do come in now and again, she was in here last Friday evening."

"Really," Chris said in a surprised tone,his understanding was that she was at the Fox Inn in Water Lane. "What time was that?"

"Oh it was just at opening time, she was waiting for Roger Webb," Alfie replied.

"Did Roger Webb turn up?" Chris asked as he paid for the pint.

"About twenty minutes or so later, while I was pulling his pint, I heard Linda ask why he was late, he replied that the people had not been in, they both left after he finished his drink, about around seven o'clock," Alfie answered taking the cost of the pint from Chris.

"That is very interesting," Chris replied. "Do you know much about them?" he asked.

Alfie shook his head. "No, not much, would come in about once a month, still what I have heard, it was not a nice way to go, still some men cannot control their desire, I hope you catch who done it."

"I can tell you one thing Alfie," Chris responded. "It was not a sex crime."

Alfie leaned on the counter. "Most blokes in here believes it was," Alfie remarked. "What other reason could there be?"

"That is what I have to find out," Chris replied having taken a drink of his pint.

"Anyway I must finish this pint and get home, Elizabeth will be worried."

Chapter Sixteen

Elizabeth kissed Chris on the cheek as she was about to leave him outside the police station. "It's Wednesday, I am only working a half day darling, I will do a little shopping and go home, will you be late tonight?" she asked.

"I will try not to be," Chris replied with a slight smile. "I will not stop for a pint tonight."

"You were restless in bed all through the night, I hope you can solve this case soon," Elizabeth remarked. "Anyway darling your sandwiches are in your pocket," she added as she once again planted a kiss on his cheek before leaving him.

Chris watched until she was out of sight before entering the station. Sergeant Dawkins looked at him with a smile on his face. "They are both in," he said referring to George and Cam. "They are very keen."

"That is why we are a successful team," Chris replied with a little sarcasm in his voice as he entered his office.

George and Cam smiled as he entered. "You look the way I feel," George remarked.

Chris smiled as he hung his trilby, and made his way to his desk.

"This damn case, could not get it out of my mind, couldn't sleep, I called in the Rising Sun for a pint on my way home last night, Alfie told me that Linda Marston was in the pub Friday night, and was joined by Roger Webb, who Linda Marston accused him of being late."

"The landlord of the Fox Inn in Water Lane swore to me that they were both in his pub Friday night," Cam remarked wondering.

"As I understand it Cam, both left the Rising Sun before seven that night, they must have gone straight to the Fox Inn," Chris stated. "Anyway Cam, how did you get on?"

"I got all the statements signed and printed, they are on your desk," Cam replied. "According to the Ewing sisters, Mr Ewing did not go outside Winchester Friday, and as far as they knew, he never left the town."

"So it comes down to the only man who was outside of Winchester last Friday was Mr Newman working at Easton," Chris remarked.

Chris studied the statements against the note that Can had found at Mrs Hanks's house. "I can not see any match with these signatures," Chris remarked as he gathered them up and passed them to George feeling a little disappointed.

"Yes but Mrs Ewing was staying with Mr Newman at the time, I think we can rule him out sending that note," George replied as he took the statements from Chris and started to study them.

Sergeant Bloom knocked and entered the office.

"Morning, Sergeant," Chris said looking up with a slight smile.

"Morning Sir," sergeant Bloom replied respectfully. "I just popped in to let you know that nothing out of the ordinary happened last night at Upper High Street, apart from the noise in the Fox and Hounds."

"Thank you Sergeant," Chris replied. "At least that is good news, but carry on for a few night, I don't want another murder at the moment."

With the departure of Sergeant Bloom, Chris found both George and Cam looking at him.

Chris smiled. "When I left for home last night, I asked for Mrs King's house to be watched, that is all," Chris explained.

"Any reason?" George asked.

"It was just a feeling George," Chris replied. "Three women are dead, all within the last six months, two we know were murdered, we know that they were all friends, but they all had another common link, they all knew that Richard Marshall was illegitimate, only one person is left that is Doris King who knows that Richard Marshall was illegitimate, plus I might add the real father," Chris explained.

"Do that make a difference?" Cam asked. "After all we all know now as well."

"I agree Cam," Chris replied. "I just wanted to protect Mrs King, just in case, that's all."

"Well I agree with you on these statements Chris," George changed the subject as he passed the papers to Cam. "Strange, I would have thought it would have been one of those we had in the frame."

"I would have thought so as well," Chris replied. "There must be someone we are missing, we know she must have known plenty of other men, perhaps who ever wrote this note, did it with his other hand, like a right handed person writing it with the left hand, that would alter the writing."

"Is that what you think?" George asked.

"At the moment I do not know what I am thinking," Chris replied. "Anyway you have both got calls to make."

George looked at Cam and smiled at each other, both getting up from their desk.

"I am off now to see Mrs April Marshall," George said.

"I am off to see Doctor Green," Cam added. "Hope I catch him in."

"It's early, he might be seeing his patients," Chris said looking at him. "Still you are in no rush."

Left alone Chris decided to go over each and every report that he had on the case, Inspector Noal always said, if you cannot go forward, go forward by starting at the beginning again.

George knocked on number 15 at Stockbridge Road, and April answered the door.

"Sergeant she said, her voice calm but without emotion. "Please come in, would you like a cup of tea, I have just made one?"

"That would be fine Mrs Marshall," George replied as he followed April into the front room after closing the front door behind him. "I am not here to intrude if you are not up to it," he said as he sat at the table where April was already pouring out the tea.

"I am a lot calmer Sergeant," April answered as she passed a cup of tea to George. "Please help yourself to milk and sugar," she offered. "My sisters and my husband's aunty has been to see me, my husband's aunty Doris has suffered the same as myself by losing her husband, I am glad she came to see me."

"Yes I have met Mrs Doris King," George replied. "She must be a comfort to you."

April sipped her tea, and replaced the cup before asking. "Have you news or is it questions?" she asked. "My sisters told me about Miss Marston, I could have done without that news."

"Life to many of us seems very unfair Mrs Marshall, you yourself have had a very tragic year, while there are many who have no worry or grief during that time," George spoke in the kindness voice. "Are you under a doctor Mrs Marshall?" George asked.

"Our own family doctor, a Dr Green at St Cross," April answered.

"That's a long way from the family home," George replied.

"There are no doctors at the bottom of the town, most are a mile or so away from where we live," April answered. "Still as a family we have always found Dr Green satisfactory."

"Would you be upset if I asked you a few questions about your wedding day?" George asked.

"Whatever you ask Sergeant, Richard will always be in the forefront of my thinking, I have to get used to it, Richard is gone, I am told I will begin to forget certain things about him, but I will never lose the memory of him," April answered, her eyes were moist with tears.

"Perhaps another time Mrs Marshall," George offered.

"No, no" April replied. "And please call me April, ask what you want."

"I was going to ask about your wedding," George replied.

A slight smile came to April's face as the memory of the day took over her mind.

"It was the happiest day of my life, I will always remember the look on Richard's face as I walked down the aisle, his eyes opened wide and his mouth dropped open," April said with a smile.

"He told me that no woman could be as beautiful, of course I knew he was saying only what he thought," April said with a sniff. "After all beauty is only in the eyes of the beholder, but to a woman who likes to look the best for her husband, it is a real compliment."

"I am sure it must be," George replied. "So the day went with a swing as they say, no upsets?"

April looked at George, the smile gone from her face. "The day went well, I was very happy, my father however spoiled it a bit for me, he left early, he came to me and hugged me, looked into my face and told me how proud he was, he had that smile on his face and look in his eyes that let you know he meant what he said, but I always imagined that I saw hurt and anger in them, I could not understand it, however he left just before the end, you see Richard and I did not have time for a honeymoon, he went to France three days later. We stayed at a Winchester Hotel for two days, I shall always treasure the memory of those two days, that was the last time I saw him," April said with tears in her eyes.

"I am so sorry April," George said with feeling. "I have upset you."

"No," April replied. "The happy memory makes me want to cry, I shall probably cry with the happy memory of it many times in the coming future."

"This anger or hurt that you thought you saw in your father's eyes, could there have been a reason for it, being proud of you and your sisters is beyond reproach, your father idolises all three of you."

"I know he does, and we feel the same towards him, I cannot explain why I imagine that look in his eyes," she muttered.

"Was he sitting with anyone can you remember just before he came to you?" George asked.

April shook her head. "I saw mother and Richard's mother with Miss Marston sitting at one table, father was sitting next to their table talking to one of Richard's army friends who we invited, I saw nothing wrong in that, I understood that father would never sit with those three, although earlier I had seen father taking to Linda, they seem to be getting on."

"You did not know Miss Marston well did you?" George asked before finishing his tea.

"I am afraid I might have mislead you at our earlier meeting, although I really did not know Mr Webb, I did know of him, and once I believe I met him, Linda I did know better, I believe that mother introduced her to us, I liked her, and I am very sorry that she has been killed," April replied.

"We called yesterday to tell you of Miss Marston's death, but after decided not to add to your grief, knowing full well your sisters would," George said with a smile.

"Yes, they were bursting to tell me the news, they are lovely girls," April remarked. "It do not happen often, but father told them they could stop the night with me on Monday, I am sure father would have told them to do the same had he known about Richard's death."

"All credit to you what I hear," George replied.

April bowed her head looking at her hands. "I like children, spent most of my youth looking after my sisters," she replied almost in a murmur. "I do regret not being pregnant, had I been I would have had a part of Richard with me."

George decided he could not carry on with his questions, it had to be distressing to April, he pushed the cup and saucer away from him as he rose. "Thank you for the tea April, it went down well, I will have to get along now, be sure we will keep you informed, but before I go, is there anything I can do for you get in touch with someone, what ever?"

"You are very kind Sergeant, but no," April replied.

"Will you be staying on here?" George asked as he made his way to the door.

"I have not made up my mind, father has told me that my room is ready for me should I want it."

"It might do you good to be with company for a while April," George said as he stood outside the door. "Even if it is only for a short time."

"My sisters told me that," April replied. "I am thinking about it," she smiled her goodbye.

Cam walked up the pathway to Dr Green surgery, it was a private house in St Cross Road. Cam had been there before on a previous case, he pushed open the front door, knowing that the doctor had his surgery on the right, Cam entered the first open door opposite. There were two women and one man in the waiting room, he looked at the receptionist who sat behind a kneehole desk, he crossed over to her.

The receptionist looked up and smiled. "Good morning," she said.

Cam introduced himself. "I would like a quick word with Dr Green if that is possible," Cam said as he looked at the young receptionist.

"I remember you Constable," she replied. "Are you able to wait, Dr Green is seeing a patient at the moment, and I have three waiting to see him."

"I'm in no rush," Cam replied. "I will read a magazine while I wait, thank you," he said as he turned to find a seat with the other patients.

Some forty minutes later Cam was shaking hands with Dr Green. "Sorry for making you wait Constable," Dr Green said apologetically.

"No Problem Sir," Cam replied respectfully.

"Then take a seat," Dr Green said as he indicated the chair. "What is it this time, another murder?" he asked.

"Two in fact," Cam replied, at the moment however my boss is interested in the health of the Ewing family that live at Bar End."

"Oh yes, I know about Mrs Ewing, I saw Mr Ewing yesterday," Dr Green replied. I don't as a rule speak about my patient's health to anyone but the family, can you tell me why your boss needs to know?"

"I have no idea," Cam replied honestly. "If you knew my boss you would understand, he checks everything in a murder case whether or not they have any bearing on a case," Cam replied with a smile.

"Yes, I remember the case you were on when I last saw you, you solved that one?" Dr Green asked.

"With your help I must say," Cam replied. "Every little bit of information fitted together in the end."

"I am glad I was able to help Constable," Dr Green remarked. "I did read about the cannibalism case a couple months ago."

"It is a case I would like to forget, but I can't," Cam replied. "I have never seen such sights as I saw in that room, and never want to again."

"Being a doctor, we see all sorts of wounds Constable, but I cannot imagine what you saw, still Constable, you want to know about the Ewing family," Dr Green sat up straight and clasped his hands in front of him. "As I told you I saw Mr Ewing yesterday, his blood pressure was way up, he worried me, he do not have a strong heart."

"He looks strong," Cam remarked.

"Looks can be deceptive Constable, Mr Ewing is not a well man," Dr Green remarked.

"As bad as that?" Cam murmured.

"I am afraid so, he has to rest, have no excitement or worry, or he will find himself in trouble."

"His daughters seem to look after him," Cam remarked. "I have seen them, they look after him as though he was a baby."

"Yes the two younger ones do I know, they have managed quite well since their step sister got married and since their mother left," Dr Green replied. "They must however make their father rest without any worry."

"You said step sister Doctor," Cam remarked. "Are you saying that April Ewing is not Mr Ewing's daughter?"

Doctor Green looked at Cam, wondering if he had said too much, there was no law against him giving out information, but he never liked giving it to any one outside the family.

"Let me put it this way Constable, I could not give Mr Ewing a blood transfusion taken from April Ewing, it would have been an incompatible blood transfusion, but I always had an idea Mr Ewing knew."

Chapter Seventeen

Chris sat silent as he heard from both George and Cam about their mornings interviews, with what he was being told, a picture was forming in his mind. He had an idea who killed Mrs Ewing and Miss Marston, and the outline of a motive for the murders was forming, but as yet he could not see any proof of what he thought.

"So Dr Green more or less told you that April was illegitimate," Chris said to Cam.

"That is what I thought," Cam replied.

"That will mean that both her and her husband were illegitimate," George remarked.

"I wonder if she knew?" Chris murmured. "How is she by the way George?"

"She seem to be holding it together," George replied. "I did get the impression that she thought the world of her husband, leaving her to go to France with only two days after honeymoon must have been hard on her."

"She has had a hard six months of it," Chris agreed as he picked up a lapel badge laying on his desk.

"I was searching my raincoat pocket last night, I found this lapel badge in the pocket, I picked it up when we found Mrs Ewing's body, it was pouring with rain so I put it in my pocket, and somehow forgot about it," Chris said with an embarrassing smile.

"Do you know what this lapel badge represent?" Chris asked passing the badge to George.

George examined the badge shaking his head. "No idea," he said passing it to Cam.

"Any idea Cam?" Chris asked.

"Looks like twelve spokes coming out of the hub of a wheel, carpenter perhaps," Cam remarked.

"Then off you go Cam, try to find out," Chris grinned. "Not much else we can do."

"Any ideas yet George?" Chris asked as Cam had left the office.

George shook his head. "If I did, I can not offer any proof, but Roger Webb still sticks in my mind, what about yourself?" George asked.

"Not quite sure George," Chris replied. "We have interviewed all the suspects as far as we can go, Mr Webb is a possibility, he has not been quite honest in answering our questions, nor has Toby Woods, there are several suspects, but we have absolutely no proof at all."

"What is your next step then Chris?" George asked.

"Unless the unexpected turns up, there is no where to go, I have studied all reports from the beginning, bits of what you and Cam have told me fits a little, so I am going to force it," Chris replied.

"Another one of your collective meetings," George smiled.

"What else can I do George?" Chris said with a shrug of his shoulders. "With all the information we have, we are unable to select one of those in the frame positively, and we still have no clear motive."

"So I have a job tonight," George asked.

"Have you a date with Rosemary?" Chris asked.

George shook his head. "No, not tonight," he answered.

"Let's see then, it's Wednesday now, give them a day to make arrangements, I will have Mr Ewing, Mr Newman, Mr Woods and Mr Webb in here Friday Morning around eleven, can you arrange that?" Chris asked.

"No problem," George replied. "A typist as well?"

"Yes a typist as well George, and make sure they know they can bring a solicitor should they wish, even though they are not being arrested."

"No excuses," George smiled.

"Definitely not, they will be brought here, should they not attend.

Chris and George left the station together, and found a smiling Elizabeth outside.

"So I am escorted home by my husband tonight," she smiled as she gave Chris a kiss on the cheek. "Hello George, how are you?" she asked.

"I am well thank you Elizabeth, just worked off my feet by your husband," he smiled.

"You both work too hard in that office," Elizabeth commented. "You both need a break, how is Rosemary?"

"Rosemary is fine," George answered.

"Well every thing is arranged for Saturday," Elizabeth replied. "It is lovely seeing you two getting on so well."

"We are both looking forward to it," George replied. "Let's hope we are not called out."

"If you are you won't go," Elizabeth smiled. "I'll not have my dinner party ruin by a call out."

"We will just have to keep our fingers crossed," Chris remarked. "You are OK for tonight George?"

"Nothing better to do," George replied. "I am off now for a spot of tea," George said taking his leave.

"You seem very happy tonight Elizabeth," Chris remarked as they walked arm in arm towards Magdalene Hill.

"I am happy," Elizabeth replied, clutching his arm. "I have been to the doctors this afternoon."

Chris stopped in his tracks as a shock ran through his system, he looked at his wife, a very worried look on his face. "What is wrong with you, do you feel ill?" he asked.

Elizabeth looked up at him, and saw the worrying look on his face, she smiled her eyes glistening. "Nothing wrong with me silly," Elizabeth scolded him. "I am pregnant, you have had your wicked way with me," she giggled.

Chris felt his mind go blank, he could not think or speak, he pulled Elizabeth to him and hugged her, and murmured thank you.

"Are you pleased darling?" Elizabeth asked as she pulled away from his hug.

"It's fantastic news, I am over the moon, my mind is a blank," he answered as they started to walk again. "Do your parents know?" Chris asked.

"How could they darling, I only found out for sure this afternoon, you are the first person I would tell anyway," Elizabeth remarked as she clutched tighter to his arm.

"They will be in for a shock when you tell them," Chris remarked.

"I will tell them while we are having our dinner," Elizabeth said with a smile of complete happiness on her face.

Chris felt in a stupor as they walked up the path to the front door, where Olive already had the door open.

"Hello dear," she said kissing Elizabeth on the cheek.

Olive looked at Chris. "Are you alright Chris?" she asked worriedly. "You look a bit vacant, are you alright?" she repeated herself.

"I am fine thank you Olive," Chris replied shaking himself. "A lot on my mind," he smiled as he kissed Olive on the cheek.

"Well dinner is ready," Olive smiled.

Ron looked at them as they entered the dining room. "Got away early tonight Chris," Ron remarked who was already seated at the table.

"Lucky me," Chris grinned as he also sat at the table next to Elizabeth. "George has some night work to do, he do not mind he is single living in lodgings, he likes to get out."

"If he marries Rosemary, that will change," Elizabeth remarked with a giggle as Olive started to bring in the meals from the scullery. "Do you think they will get married Chris?" she asked.

Chris shrugged. "For his part I would say yes, but I do not know about Rosemary, but she seems to like him, George is the only one she dates, and I am told by him that Mr and Mrs Morris throws out hints about Rosemary taking over the farm."

"Would George give up being a policeman to become a farmer?" Ron asked.

"I don't get that impression from George," Chris answered.

"Well eat up while it is hot," Olive said placing a meal in front of Chris. "It has not been heated up tonight."

"It looks fine, thank you Olive," Chris remarked as he picked up his knife and fork looking at Elizabeth as he did so.

They had almost finished the meal of shepherd's pie and vegetables, "Mum, Dad," Elizabeth suddenly said, unable to hold her news back any longer. "I want you both to be happy for Chris and myself, I am pregnant."

All eyes went to Olive as she dropped her knife and fork making a clatter as the utensils hit the plate. She looked at Elizabeth her eyes wide and astonished, and her mouth half open, then her face beamed with a smile. "Did you hear that Ron?" she said to her husband without looking at him. "My daughter is going to have a baby."

Ron who felt very happy with the news. "Your daughter, my grandson," he remarked. "He will just be old enough to take me for a pint in my old age."

"Don't count on that too much," Olive scolded him. "We could have a granddaughter."

"Then I will take her for a pint," Ron replied smiling and winking at Chris and Elizabeth.

"What do you think Chris?" Olive asked ignoring her husband's remarks. "Should Elizabeth continue work?"

"I will have to leave that up to her," Chris replied. "I know very little about having a baby, but I will learn."

"We will have to get a room ready for our grandchild," Olive smiled turning to Ron.

"Chris will make sure of that," Ron replied. "Now the child has become ours."

"I mean a room in this house, you never know if Chris and our daughter want a day on their own, our grandchild can stay with us, we must have a room ready," Olive said with a smile on her face. "Then there is the schooling."

Chris looked at Elizabeth who was smiling at the banter.

"Will you shut up Olive," Ron said smiling at his wife. "This is Elizabeth's baby, how far have you gone?" Ron asked looking at Elizabeth.

"The doctor said about ten weeks," Elizabeth answered placing her hand on top of Chris's hand that laid on the table. "The baby should be due around the end of March beginning of April next year."

"Then as long as you keep well, you can still work for a couple more months, it won't hurt you," Ron suggested.

"So you know all about having babies do you?" Olive interrupted. "Men should give birth, but should they, there would be no population, they could not put up with the morning sickness, the fatigue and pain women have to go through while carrying."

"The money I earn will help us even if it's only for a couple of months mum," Elizabeth remarked. "There will be baby clothes to buy."

Olive got up and went to Elizabeth where she hugged her. "Don't you worry love," she said. "You are a sensible girl, you will know when you must give up work, and Chris do not need to worry, we are here for you both in every way."

Ron got up and shook Chris by the hand. "Congratulations Chris, we always wanted a grandchild, someone to take the place of Elizabeth," he winked. "I am afraid your child will have two mothers," he smiled.

"It will be a lucky child having grandparents like you," Chris replied happy in his mind, expecting Olive to take charge where she was able.

"Mum and dad were very excited about having their first grandchild, they were overreacting I guess, you are not mad with them are you?" Elizabeth asked as she cuddled up beside him, her cheek pressed against the side of his chest in bed that night.

Chris who had been laying on his back, turned on his side his arm going around Elizabeth's waist. "Certainly not, I am very happy about it, I know that your parents will offer our child extra care and protection, they were delirious in their happiness you could tell that on their faces, anyway darling," Chris said with a smile. "We both know that Olive would take over when she can."

"Mum and Dad will treasure our child," Elizabeth remarked.

"If they adore our child the way they adore you, I shall be more than happy," Chris replied.

"You are so sweet," Elizabeth said as she pushed herself closer to Chris.

"You better not get too close," Chris said. "You know what could happen, and I am not sure whether it will be good for you, I have to be very careful from now on."

"Don't be silly darling, you can't hurt me, your love will help me, or so I am told, perhaps the last couple of months before delivery you will have to control your wicked way with me," Elizabeth giggled. "Perhaps a couple months after also, but I won't let you suffer," Elizabeth giggled again.

Chris accepted his usual kiss on the cheek from Elizabeth the next morning outside the Police Station. Chris looked at Elizabeth, her eyes were sparkling he could tell she was very happy, but Chris was worried.

"Am I going to worry over you?" he asked, there was a worried look on his face.

"Of course not darling," Elizabeth replied. "What do you want me to do?"

"Just follow what your parents told you, they know best, no lifting, no jumping, or falling, walk very carefully," Chris replied.

Elizabeth looked at Chris. "Darling I know you are worried, but please you must not put me in a cocoon, the doctor is pleased with me, I am healthy, of course I will not do anything that might hurt our baby."

Chris looked at her lovingly. "I know you will not, just take care that is all I ask."

Elizabeth planted another kiss of his cheek. "I am not telling anyone yet, not until I start to show," she said as she moved away. "I will see you outside tonight, if you are able."

"I expect I will be here tonight," Chris replied as she walked away. "Just go careful."

Chris watched until she was out of sight before he entered the station. George and Cam were already there sitting at their desk when he entered.

"You look very happy Chris," George said with a smile as Chris hung his trilby.

"Looks like a man who lost sixpence and found a shilling," Cam smiled as Chris sat behind his desk and took out his pipe and tobacco.

"Just left Elizabeth, and wondered what I have done to get such a woman," Chris replied. "Can't a man look happy sometimes?"

"I agree with you Chris, Elizabeth is a marvellous woman, what have you done to deserve her?" George teased.

"Your guess is as good as mine George," Chris replied lighting his pipe and taking a deep drag then blowing out a cloud of smoke. "I am double blessed, I have very good in-laws."

"I will agree with you there," George answered. "Anyway, I have arranged everything for tomorrow, I have seen all the people we want here, none seemed worried."

"One must be a little," Chris replied. "Because one of them is the murderer."

"I have no idea who may be the murderer," Cam stated a little embarrassed. "I have read all the reports, Mr Newman has transport, he could have taken Mrs Ewing's body to where she was found in his buggy."

"Plus the fact she was staying at his home," Chris remarked.

"Exactly," Cam replied. "He had the opportunity, but I can't think of a motive, unless he was being blackmailed by Mrs Ewing."

"I could make a reasonable case against him and Mr Webb," George commented. "I can not see it being Mr Woods or Mr Ewing, unless there are factors I do not know of."

"We all know what we have read and been told, however if any of you have any ideas, you should follow them up," Chris smiled as he put his pipe in the ashtray. "It will be quiet today, so I am going to do what I did yesterday, read all the reports through again."

Chapter Eighteen

$\mathcal{T}$hursday had proved to be a quiet day, while Chris left alone in the office studied over and over all the reports about the case for the second day. George and Cam went to clear up a couple miner cases that had been left unattended since Mrs Ewing's murder almost a week ago.

"You seem nervous darling?" Elizabeth said looking at her husband as she kissed him on the cheek outside the Police Station that morning.

"I suppose I am in a way, I will have all the suspects before me today, I am not so good at it as Inspector Noal was," Chris replied with a slight smile on his face.

"I do not believe that darling," Elizabeth replied. "But at least you had a good night sleep, you slept like a log," she smiled.

"I had been studying reports for the last two days, my mind was blank when I got home, then yesterday of course I kept thinking of our child," Chris said looking at Elizabeth with a smile. "It might have been better had your news came a day later, it was hard to concentrate on reports."

"You poor darling," Elizabeth murmured giving Chris another kiss on the cheek. "Did you tell George?" she asked.

Chris shook his head. "He asked me why I looked happy, but I did not tell him," Chris replied.

"Good, I will tell him and Rosemary tomorrow night at the dinner," she said. "I must go now darling, I hope all will go well with you today."

"Now do not forget, be careful what you do," Chris said as parting words.

Chris entered the station, and got a smile from Sergeant Dawkins. "I have put the extra chairs in your office," the sergeant told Chris.

"Thank you Sergeant, you have a cell empty?" Chris asked.

"All are empty," sergeant Dawkins replied.

Chris smiled to himself as he entered his office, his eyes fell on a row of four chairs in front of his desk. After greetings from George and Cam, Chris hung his trilby and went to his desk.

"This office is too small for interviews, perhaps one day we will have separate room for interviews to take place," Chris muttered.

"Normally interviews are carried out with just one suspect at the time Chris," George smiled.

"I know George," Chris replied. "And that is all you need if one suspect sticks out a mile, but we are never that lucky, Inspector Noal always said, if you have several suspects get them together, one will sometimes lose his cool, making the rest follow suit."

"It has worked since I have been with you Chris," George admitted. "I am keeping my fingers crossed for today."

"Me too," Cam butted in.

Chris smiled at Cam's excitement, then turned to George. "Typist ready George?"

"Yes she will be here by ten," George answered.

"Good, then I have time for a smoke," Chris said leaning back in his chair and taking his pipe and tobacco from his pocket.

"Are you both with the same opinion as to who the murderer could be?" Chris asked as he filled his pipe and lit it.

"I was thinking all night about who it could be?" George replied. "Although I have a couple who I suspect could be the murderer, I am still unable to get a motive."

George took a piece of paper and a pencil. "I will write the name down," he said as he wrote the name. "See if I am right after the meeting."

"Thank you George," Chris smiled. "You are sure I shall find out who the murderer is then?"

"I have no doubt Chris," George replied as he put the paper in his desk drawer.

Chris looked at Cam as he blew a cloud of smoke out. "What about you Cam?" he asked.

"I don't know if I will ever make a detective," Cam murmured. "I have a couple names I could guess who might be the murderer, but I have no real idea."

Around eleven o'clock Chris looked at the four men facing him, Mr Ewing near the door, next to him Mr Webb, then Mr Woods and finally Mr Newman.

"Gentlemen," Chris opened the meeting. "First of all I would like to introduce my colleagues Detective Sergeant House and Detective Constable Streeter sitting with the typist, the typist is here just to record this meeting, and I believe one way or another the murders of Mrs Ewing and Miss Marston concern you all."

"Do you know each other?" Chris asked.

"I know Roger," Mr Ewing remarked leaning forward so that he could see Mr Webb. "I have seen the other two, but do not know them socially," he continued looking at Mr Woods and Mr Newman.

"I know Roger and John," Mr Woods said. "But Mr Ewing I know him but as he said never met socially."

"That is the same with me," added Mr Newman.

"Well we all know each other now," Chris spoke with a smile. "Mr Ewing, I do not want to distress you, but I will have to mention your wife, not always in a good light."

Mr Ewing looked at Chris. "Why should it matter, I know what my wife was, as long as we find her killer, the stress will be worth it."

"Now before we start, I want to bring up the tragic death of Mrs Marshall who died it is said by accident some six months ago, I want to bring it up because I know of the school boys pact made by all of you except Mr Ewing. Mrs Marshall was a part of this pact before her marriage and after," Chris explained.

"You know about our pact?" Roger Webb asked with surprise in his voice.

"That must have been John?" Mr Woods butted in. "He could never keep a secret," he said looking at Mr Newman.

"I am sorry chaps, I did not think there was any harm in mentioning it, it was a long time ago," Mr Newman commented.

"Mr Newman did the right thing," Chris remarked. "You Mr Webb and you Mr Woods lied to us when you were asked if you knew Mrs Marshall."

"I did not think it was relevant," Mr Webb said throwing his hands out in front of him. "After all it was an accident that happened a long time ago."

"I felt more or less the same way," Mr Woods added.

"Answering a police questions with a lie is an offence," Chris replied. "We rely on the replies being honest, lies no matter how small can put us off and waste our time, still that is cleared up," Chris commented.

Chris looked at Mr Ewing. "Did you not know Mrs Marshall?"

"I knew her, having seen her around, she was so much younger than me, I really met her for the first time at my daughter's wedding, my daughter April married to her son," Mr Ewing answered.

"So that was the first time you met her, and you have never been to her house?" Chris asked.

"That is correct Inspector," Mr Ewing replied looking at Chris in the eye.

Chris looked at Mr Newman, Mr Webb and Mr Woods. "Now when you three made the pact never to get married and share any women, there were originally five of you, two we know died in the Boer War leaving just you three, did you not have a secret or usual place to meet, like an old shed, a tent or something similar?" Chris asked.

Toby Woods smiled. "Of course we did Inspector, it was way out of town, almost where Mrs Ewing was found dead. To the left of the bridge, there is an arch which takes you to the bottom of Catherine's Hill, just past that arch there is a clump of bushes, in the centre a clear space, that was our usual place, we often put a tent up there and stayed out for a couple of nights during our school holidays, you remember," Toby turned to his friends with a smile.

Chris smiled inwardly as he saw the three men smiled at each other with happy expressions on their faces.

"So let's get back to Mrs Ewing's murder," Chris suggested. "You Mr Newman, Mrs Ewing was staying with you at the time of her murder, according to you, you had left her at home early on the Friday morning, getting home late, the

reason for your lateness was that you had to finish a thatch-
ing roof job, you also told us that when you arrived home
she was gone, she did not return home that night, but you
were not worried, as her practice was to live with someone
for a time, then leave without explanation."

"That is right Inspector, that is the truth," Mr Newman
replied.

"But this is not the whole truth, is it Mr Newman?"
Chris asked.

"I do not know what you mean, she was gone when I got
home, and never returned," Mr Newman replied a little
angry.

"You did not get home late because of work, in fact you
have no alibi as to when you did arrive back home," Chris
remarked.

"Why would I need a alibi?" Mr Newman asked. "I am
a single man, I can come and go when I please, do I need
a alibi for every where I go?"

"Not as a rule Mr Newman," Chris replied. "But we are
dealing with murder, alibis do tend to help in any
investigation."

"Well had I known, I would have made sure of one," Mr
Newman replied, anger now showing in his voice. "A bloody
cheek I tell you."

"The local village policeman made a few enquiries, you
did not work at all Friday afternoon Mr Newman, where
were you?" Chris asked a serious look on his face.
"You must have been some where?"

"I failed to see if that is any of your business,"
Mr Newman said feeling furious.

"Very well Mr Newman," Chris continued. "Are you
able to tell us what time you did return home then?"

"I am not sure," Mr Newman replied waving his arms about. "Sometime around seven or eight I think."

"We are not sure whether Mrs Ewing was murdered where she was found or she had been brought there, the weather that night did a lot of damage when it came to clues," Chris continued. "Mr Newman we know that you put your horse and buggy to the stable about eight that night, you yourself were not seen before then, you could have met with Mrs Ewing at your usual place and left her there, even killed her there," Chris said.

"When you and your Sergeant called on me, I respected you, I have now changed my mind, if you think I killed Doreen, then prove it," Mr Newman scorned.

"I am sorry Mr Newman, I have not accused you of murder, just trying to get all the true facts together," Chris remarked. "Can you tell me, were you paying Mrs Ewing any money?"

"Only a few coppers for her to get herself a drink when she went out at night on her own," Mr Newman replied. "I was paying for her keep while she was staying at my home."

"She was not blackmailing you then?" Chris asked in a loud voice, which everybody could hear.

"Why the hell would she?" Mr Newman replied looking with alarm at his friends. "Had she been, she would never had stepped a foot inside my house."

Ignoring Mr Newman's anger, Chris turned straight to Mr Ewing. "Did you know of this usual meeting place they had Mr Ewing?"

"I know the area well, I know the place they are talking about, but did not know the significance of the place to them," Mr Ewing replied.

"Your wife never told you of the place, were you paying money to your wife Mr Ewing?" Chris asked both questions without stopping.

"No to both of your questions Inspector," Mr Ewing replied without adding more.

"Then what about you Mr Webb, were you paying any money to Mrs Ewing?"

Roger laughed. "Good God, no, I had finished with Doreen when she married Frank here, anyway what is all this about money?" he asked.

"We found where Mrs Ewing had rented a room, did none of you wonder how she changed her clothing while she was staying with you, she did not carry a suitcase did she?" Chris asked, his voice was firm.

"Never gave it a thought," Roger replied. "But don't forget she had not lived with me since she married Frank here, so I would not know."

"Did you not wonder Mr Newman and you Mr Woods?" Chris asked.

Both men shook their heads. "Like Roger, I never gave it a thought," Mr Woods replied.

"Like me," Mr Newman added.

"We found quite a large sum of money in her room, also a note telling her that who ever sent it would be late in turning up for their appointment," Chris said.

"At least I can not be charged with her murder, I do have an alibi don't I Inspector?" Mr Webb asked.

"Your alibi given to you by Miss Marston who is no longer with us, do prove that you were in the Fox Inn around seven that night, where were you before then Mr Webb?" Chris asked.

"Oh I was in the Rising Sun, I met Linda in there," Roger answered wondering.

"I wonder why you did not tell us that when you were being interviewed, however you were late in turning up at the Rising Sun, I believe," Chris smiled.

"My, my, you have been doing your home work," Roger replied sarcastically. "I was late because the person I had to meet did not turn up, I waited longer than I wanted to, it made me late to meet Linda," he added.

"Might I suggest that the person you were to meet was Mrs Ewing," Chris replied. "She was blackmailing you, this note that we found stopped her turning up at the usual time, she arrived for your meeting place about an hour after you left."

"Well I didn't write her that note," Roger almost shouted, then looked at his hands as he realised he had slipped up.

"What was she blackmailing you about Mr Webb?" Chris asked.

Roger hesitated. "I don't want to talk about it, it was not criminal, it was personal, that is all I am going to say, after all Doreen is now dead, so it makes very little difference."

"Very well Mr Webb," Chris said gently. "Your alibi do put you in the Fox Inn around seven that Friday night, but no one has been able to say whether you stopped or went out during the evening," Chris informed him. "Blackmail is a good motive for murder."

"Someone must have seen me, I did not leave the Fox Inn until closing time," Roger shouted. "You can't pin her murder on me."

"When I called on you and told you about Miss Marston's death," Chris paused. "You said to me, why would anyone want to kill her, at the time Mr Webb I had not told you how she had died, why would you say she was murdered?"

"I can't remember saying that, you had just woke me up, perhaps I said it," Roger tried to explain throwing his arms about. "Because of Mrs Ewing's death, I don't know just a slip of the tongue I suppose."

"Slip of the tongue often catches criminals Mr Webb," Chris replied. "You also told us that you were in the house when Miss Marston had left to go out, and you went to bed early."

"That is right, I did," Roger agreed.

"Then how did you meet Mr Woods outside the church in Parchment Street around eight thirty that night?" Chris asked.

Roger looked at Toby.

"Sorry Roger," Toby said. "When I was asked I just told the truth, I had no idea it might go against you."

"That is alright Toby, I did not lie intentionally, I just forgot, I had pop to Lewis's in the high street, they have a cigarette machine outside the shop, I had run out," Mr Webb said looking at Chris with a smirk on his face.

Chris looked at Mr Woods. "The question is Mr Woods, you were just a stone throw away from where Miss Linda Marston was found dead."

"I told you I had finished work late and popped into the Foresters for a pint on my way home," Mr Woods replied looking worried.

"You also told me that you did not know Mrs Marshall," Chris replied. "However, the landlord remembered you, you called in about seven thirty, you did not have a pint, you had a whisky, I am told you looked out of breath."

"So what, I had worked hard all day, I needed a stiff drink," Toby replied.

"I would want a stiff drink if I had just murdered someone," Chris replied.

"Come off it, I did not kill her, she hardly went with me, in fact I thought Roger was going to marry her," Toby said with a smile looking at Roger.

"Not a chance," Roger responded. "Anyway I think she had found another bloke, don't know who it was however."

"She knew who might have killed Mrs Ewing however," Chris informed him. "I have a witness who states that she was coming to the police with her belief."

"Oh I knew that," Roger butted in. "She told me, and I encouraged her to go to police," Roger said looking at Mr Ewing. "I told you Monday when I saw you, Frank," Roger said turning to Mr Ewing.

"You might have done, but I can't remember," Mr Ewing replied with a shrug.

Chris looked at Cam sitting at the back his chin resting on his hand taking everything in, then he looked over to George who smiled and winked at him, giving him support. Chris knew he was dragging the interview out, but he wanted and was getting the tiny details that would make the puzzle complete.

Chris allowed a short pause before continuing. "Mr Ewing," he said. "Your wife and Miss Marston were both invited to your daughter's April wedding by Mrs Marshall, the mother of your son-in-law."

"That is right," Mr Ewing agreed.

"You did not know them before apart from your wife?" Chris asked.

"That is also correct," Mr Ewing replied.

"You did make friends with Miss Marston however," Chris asked.

"Now how would you know that Inspector?" Mr Ewing asked his face colouring a shade.

"We have spoken to many people who attended the wedding Mr Ewing, we also know that you were sitting at a table near by where your wife, Mrs Marshall and Miss Marston were sitting and talking, it seems they were all a little intoxicated," Chris replied.

"In answer to your question, yes I have been out with Miss Marston one or two times, she is a likeable person, she did not seem to mind my age," Mr Ewing explained. "But it was purely friendship."

"I am quite sure it was Mr Ewing, but that did not stop you from murdering her did it?" Chris asked to the shock of the room.

Cam took his hand from his chin, but George grinned. Mr Webb, Mr Woods and Mr Newman all stared towards Mr Ewing who through the interview had sat quietly, answering questions when asked, but saying little.

"How did you come to that conclusion Inspector?" Mr Ewing asked taking no notice of the silence in the room. "You must have your reasons, though they are wrong."

"What did you hear Miss Marston, Mrs Marshall and your wife talking about at the wedding, drink loosens the tongue so they say," Chris said, his voice was firm and his words were loud and clear.

"Girls talk, no one can make sense out of that," Mr Ewing remarked.

"You did Mr Ewing, you found out that your future son-in-law was illegitimate," Chris said.

"There are many bastards around, what one can expect with all these army personnel hanging around, but that was not Richard's fault, one have to look to the mother," Mr Ewing remarked.

"Richard was born many years before the war started Mr Ewing, actually during the time these three men here had made the pact," Chris enlightened him.

"What are you actually saying Inspector?" Mr Ewing asked.

"Okay Mr Ewing," Chris answered. "I will tell you the full story, unfortunately at your daughter's wedding, loose tongue allowed you to hear that not only was your son-in-law illegitimate, but also who the father was, also you heard that the same man was the father of your daughter April."

"What are you talking about, I am the father of April, always have been," Mr Ewing shouted as he stood up. "Where do you get such ridicules ideas from?"

"Please Mr Ewing sit down and I will tell you," Chris said gently feeling a little sorry for him. "Because of what you heard the three women talking about, you came to realise that your daughter who you knew was not yours," Chris paused a moment before continued. "She was getting married to her step brother, they were actually step brother and sister."

"You are off your head," Mr Ewing replied with scorn. "Call yourself a detective you should be sacked."

"You are a kindly man Mr Ewing, adored by your daughters, had you not heard I believe you would have all lived very happy, but what you heard was unacceptable to you, it went against your faith, you took steps hoping that it would never be found out, and as far as you knew only three people knew the true facts."

"Are you saying I kill them all?" Mr Ewing asked. "I think you have gone too far, now all the people in this room know."

"The morning after we found your wife's body, I met you on the bridge at Gardenia Road, I accepted your story that you just wanted to see where she died, I said I wanted to have a look around, you followed me down the small embankment, but I did not go direct to the spot where she was found, but you did."

"Just luck I suppose," Mr Ewing shrugged.

"You were there looking for this lapel badge Mr Ewing," Chris answered picking the badge up and showing it to him.

"What badge is that?" Mr Ewing asked feeling a little frightened as he only glanced at the badge Chris was holding up.

"You are a carpenter by trade Mr Ewing?" Chris asked.

"I am, and that is not our badge," Mr Ewing answered.

"But you are also a wheelwright, and this is a wheelwright lapel badge, you were looking for this," Chris said. "What I am unable to understand why you left the axes?"

"You checked my axe, you were satisfied," Mr Ewing replied.

"We did not check your shed, you see Mr Ewing, these are special axes," Chris picked up the axes from below his feet and placed them on the desk for all to see.

"These are wheelwright axes, called by another name perhaps adze, you will see they have a curved blade used for hollowing out the fellies, as their action result in damage to the grain of the timber, and in consequence the wood is weakened, but it is my understanding that these axes are eventually thrown away, you must have these in your shed Mr Ewing?"

"There are plenty of wheelwrights axes around," Mr Ewing responded not answering the question.

"But none that is involved in murder Mr Ewing," Chris replied "I believe had you not come into contact with

Miss Marston you might just have go away with murder. After Constable Streeter called on her and Mr Webb last Sunday, Miss Marston was able to put two and two together. I do not know how, but it was perhaps your questions to her, I am sure you asked her a lot, going with her was just for you to get information. I believe you got your wife's address from Miss Marston, you were the one who sent her this note," Chris said holding up the note. "Please take a look at it Mr Ewing," Chris offered leaning over his desk and passing it to him.

"This is not my handwriting" Mr Ewing said throwing the note back on the desk.

"It is your left-handed writing Mr Ewing," Chris informed him. "You are by nature right-handed, but when one try to alter their writing, they still dot the Is and crosses the Ts in the same way, they do it automatically without thinking. When your wife got this letter she delayed her meeting with Mr Webb, she thought the note was from him, she could not have been familiar with his writing, Mr Webb got tired of waiting also he had Linda Marston to meet and he was late, eventually he left. When your wife came, she found you waiting for her, where you hit her over the head with an axe, a blow on the back of her head which killed her, you did the same to Miss Marston."

"So now I killed Miss Marston, forgetting I do not leave home before my two daughters arrive home, and that is around eight at night, I thought that Miss Marston was killed around seven to half past," Mr Ewing still defended himself.

"One can always add or deduct an hour Mr Ewing, guessing the time of death is not a complete science," Chris informed him. "However in your case, your daughters stayed with their older sister April during Monday night, you knew of Miss Marston's intentions to go to police that day, and told your daughters they could stay with April over night."

Mr Ewing bowed his head, he knew he had been caught, what ever he said, Chris had an answer.

"Had I known that Richard would be killed, I would never have done what I did, had Doreen married Mr Webb, it would never had happened, it's a wicket world where men can go around making women pregnant without taking the responsibility of their action, perhaps had their pact not been a non-marriage pact she would have been able to marry Mr Webb," Mr Ewing said with a sad expression on his face.

"I'm sorry Frank, I really am, I had no idea she was pregnant when she married you, we all thought she married you for the life you could give her," Mr Webb said in all sincerity.

Mr Ewing smiled. "You are a lucky man Mr Webb, you were going to be my last victim, I can tell you, you would have suffered as you have made me."

Roger got up took his chair to where Cam was sitting, he felt very nervous.

"Now Mr Ewing, you will be arrested on two accounts of murder, if that is how you want to leave it."

"Surely that is enough for you," Mr Ewing said having accepted his fate with a smile.

"I was thinking of Mrs Marshall," Chris replied. "I do have that feeling that she did not die with no one else in the house."

Mr Ewing smiled again. "You know Inspector, you are what we call a goer, you don't let up, but to satisfy your curiosity, I was in the house when she fell down the stairs, I did not push her, she did slip from the top of the stairs, I had chased her there because I threatened her if she did not tell me what I wanted to know."

"Thank you Mr Ewing, that is at least cleared up," Chris replied as he looked at George, who knew what was expected of him.

With the office cleared and Mr Ewing locked up, George sat at his desk and smiled at Chris, he took the slip of paper from his drawer and passed it to Chris. "This is the name of who I thought might be the murderer," he said.

Chris took the slip and read it. "Mr Ewing," he read with a smile on his face. "We work well together, and eventually come to the same conclusion," Chris said.

"Not me," Cam confessed. "I never gave Mr Ewing a thought."

"Early days for you yet Cam, you only have to put the small pieces together, you will get there," Chris comforted him.

"I must admit for the first half hour, I was sure I was wrong, but you came through for me in the end Chris," George smiled happily.

I had a good idea who it was before the meeting, but our job is to arrest and get a conviction, I do feel sorry for Mr Ewing and his daughters I have no idea how they will take it," Chris stood up rubbing his hand.

"I think we are all going across the road, we need a stiff drink," Chris grinned as he took his trilby and walked out of the station followed by George and Cam.

Sitting together at a table by the window in the Crown and Anchor, Chris, George and Cam sipped their whisky, they were able to look out over the Broadway, the Guildhall, Police Station and the Fire Station were in clear view.

Had it not been for Chris finding out about that lapel badge, I might not have consider Mr Ewing, I remembered it was June or May Ewing that told us their father was also a wheelwright," George remarked.

"It was the note that Cam found in Mrs Ewing rented room that convinced me, I spent hours studying the note and the signatures on the statements," Chris confessed. "Added to what Cam learned from Dr Green, I was convinced."

"You talk as though I solved the case Chris," Cam remarked with a grin on his face. "Yet I had no idea who the murderer was, I never thought it could be Mr Ewing."

"We solved the case as a team Cam," Chris replied taking a sip of his whisky. "We all make an input, both George and I know what you are best at," Chris added smiling at George.

"What do you think Mrs Ewing was blackmailing Mr Webb?" George asked.

Chris shrugged. "Not sure, but I would guess it was something to do with April, perhaps we will never know."

"Why would a mother do such a thing?" Cam asked.

Mrs Ewing was not a nice type Cam, yes she was very attractive, but she was not a good mother, we know that, because April was the mother of May and June during their childhood, on top of that Mrs Ewing had a lust for sex, she must have had numerous men in her life," Chris replied.

"I wonder where she got all that money?" Cam added. "Surely Mr Webb did not pay her that much, also consider she had the rent money to pay."

"I agree, Mr Webb would not be earning that kind of money," Chris smiled. "Mrs Ewing left her husband some two years ago, that is about one hundred weeks at least, the money she had, plus her rent would work out to about fifteen shillings a week, that is as much as a top skilled tradesman would get, she must have got it somewhere else as well as Mr Webb, I would guess that some men she went they paid her, perhaps even Mr Ewing gave her some, we know that he still loved her for all her faults."

"Strange case," George remarked. "What began twenty six years ago resulted in the resents deaths of three women," he said as he collected their glasses to go to the bar.

"Anyway, we now have to wait for the court case, in the meantime Cam, tomorrow night George and Rosemary are coming to our house to have dinner with Elizabeth and myself, we do not want a call out, you will be on duty," Chris said in a very calm voice.

"I will keep my fingers crossed," Cam grinned as George left for the bar.

THE END

Lightning Source UK Ltd.
Milton Keynes UK
UKOW02f0153050516

273590UK00001B/70/P